Also by Philip T. Nemec

The Chicago Syncopator:
A Bohemian Kid Tells About His Life in Jazz

by James Brody Watt (pen name)
Triumph in Kleptomadia

The
Shape
of
Crete

A Novel

PHILIP T. NEMEC

Chestnut Books Press
Leesburg, VA

© 2021 by Philip T. Nemec
All rights reserved.

Book cover and interior design by Monkey C Media
Copyedited by Stephanie Thompson
Author photo by Anne Lord

First Edition
Printed in the United States of America

ISBN: 978-1-7372468-0-0 (trade)
ISBN: 978-1-7372468-1-7 (ebook)

Library of Congress Control Number: 2021916483

To the memory of Costas Bourtsos

"There is no need to build a labyrinth when the entire universe is one."

—Luis Borges, *Labyrinths*

PROLOGUE

May 1941

With the German army pushing Greek and British forces from the mainland, and with "The Desert Fox," General Erwin Rommel, threatening Cairo and seizure of the Suez Canal, the Germans struck again on May 20, 1941, with a boldly conceived airborne landing on the Greek island of Crete. Placed strategically in the middle of the Mediterranean, the island had absorbed many invasions over thousands of years, but this was the first time that parachute troops were employed as an invasion force. Casualties among the *Fallschirmjaeger* were horrendous, so much so that the Germans never again attempted a similar airborne assault. Casualties among the British, Commonwealth, and Greek troops were staggering as well. In the end, the German airborne forces held on to key airfields, allowing German reinforcements to gradually build until the lesser trained Allied resistance bent, then cracked. Finally, with their backs to the sea, and under frequent *Luftwaffe* attack, the British performed a heroic evacuation by ship.

Some of the Brits never withdrew, but courageously stayed behind to struggle with the Cretan resistance. As their campaign progressed, lives among the belligerents entwined as they often do in war. One German officer, one Cretan resistance fighter, and one British officer by fate, by fog of war, by serendipity, spun together in a Gordian knot. They could not have seen how their lives would shape the future. Each was absorbed in stresses that only those who have experienced combat understand. Even if they had a crystal ball, they had no godly power to change outcomes. On an island like Crete, with its several thousand years of human history, mythologies and gods were created to explain the unexplainable. In this strange case, however, reality and mythology did, if not fuse together, live in tangent. The meaning of God's peace, human fulfillment, love, and the struggle to survive rattled around in an ancient amphora like bone dice in a game of chance.

CHAPTER ONE

May 2007

As Steffi Galabova waited for her flight from Sofia to Athens and rendezvous with the American, Jim Jana, she dug her nails into a hope that her past would not coil and strike back as it had before. An hour earlier, she had slammed the family's metal apartment door behind her, and the sound, like that of a prison cell door, had echoed down the cave-like corridor of that Communist-era apartment block. Her farewell had been helped neither by a fog-shrouded airport nor her mother shunning her embrace. She had longed to walk away, but walking out for the second time in the face of a mother's disapproval, even at thirty-five, was heavier baggage than she imagined.

Thanks be to God, she thought, that her sister had waited downstairs with her luggage stuffed with pens, paints, and brushes. For even though Katarina, with her tight, determined lips, had supported their mother by preaching, "It's impulsive and a gamble you can't afford," she had loyally cradled Steffi's hand all the way to the airport. Steffi agreed Jim was a gamble, and she understood about the casino always winning. How well she understood gambles!

After all, she had left before on a gamble and lost, but impulsive—no, this decision had been a long time coming.

When Steffi had pushed the button of the apartment block's creaking elevator, Katarina, her temperamental opposite, came to life in her thoughts, disagreeing with her on a tram, arguing with her at the dinner table, finding her art risible. "How can you and Mommy, the philosopher, be so cold and analytic," she had whined to Katarina long ago, "while Daddy, a scientist, was the gentle one?" Katarina had shrugged with a moue turn to her lips, "You only know Daddy as a little girl." Nevertheless, in times of crisis, Katarina was a loyal brick, and for all her slicing cuts and judgments, Katarina forgave and tried to forget. Steffi had clutched at that as the elevator jerked to a stop and its doors lurched open.

"*Feel* my art," she had begged. Her mother answered with comments like, "But please, you must invest in technique. Study Brueghel or one of the Flemish masters." She asked questions like, "Are you sure that is the way to mix oils?" She spoke of burnt sienna, cerulean blue, ultramarine, and viridian, but she never moved beyond pigment. She challenged Steffi about her "depiction of reality," and Steffi talked past her with, "What is reality, anyway?"

As boarding began, seeing her sister watching from behind the security barrier was fresh in her mind. The usual pushing and shoving in the security line had distracted her, but as she was about to enter the magnetometer, she turned and saw Katarina still watching—looking wistful if not melancholic. Steffi waved, and Katarina waved back, smiling enigmatically. What did it mean? For an instant, she had wanted to rush back and ask Katarina what her smile meant, but the line pressed against her hesitation. She strained to capture another glimpse of Katarina, but Katarina was lost in the chop of bobbing heads. Losing sight of her broke the bond with home like nothing else had, and ahead, the one with Jim was vapor. Steffi chose to stare straight ahead as the boarding line inched forward and disappeared into the jetway.

Crammed into a window seat and edgy with anxiety and a fear of flying, Steffi feebly tried meditation, but after beginning the same meditation five times, her mind was overrun by bad thoughts and bad memories. She fidgeted with her seat belt and plopped her handbag on the empty seat next to her, pulling out her brush. A flight attendant scolded her, ordering her to put the bag under the seat in front. Throwing her brush back in, she jammed the bag under the seat, mumbling unintelligibly. Not knowing what else to do, she rested her chin on her hand and stared out the window, willing the flight to be over before it began.

As the plane taxied, she asked herself, *how did I end up doing this?* She smirked, *It was mother. What an irony! She's opposed to Jim, and it was mother who made it happen—relentless—urging me to take the interpretation job for visiting American delegations. Always pushing languages—German, English, French. She blamed my artistic temperament, made me vulnerable to sweet talk—but the languages did it! Not my art.* Mother always brought up examples like the studio owner and collector she called a "snake."

She remembered arguing, "You can't evaluate him with a spectrometer! He's critiquing art! He thinks my work fits into his collection." She later admitted to herself that the only collection he was interested in was the notches he tallied on his belt representing women he'd seduced. "Seduction, that's all they want," she had said to her best friend, Liliana, and Liliana, oh my God, that was perhaps the grandest problem of all. What will Jim think? But how could she have told him before? Certainly not on a Skype call. In a tweet? With Liliana, as with so much about her history, she was like the pet sent to an uncle's farm that somehow finds its way back home.

Still, in the face of her mother's demands for proof supporting Jim's trustworthiness, what could she say? It had been over a year since she had seen Jim in person. Their correspondence had brought them closer on one level, but correspondence is undeniably theoretical. An email wasn't commitment. Commitments were something you made looking into someone's eyes; and yet, the collector's eyes, "that snake," were manifestly sincere. Her mother obsessed about gossip about her, which was a laugh compared to the scandal her mother had brought about during Zhivkov's Communist regime.

Steffi told Liliana and her sister about the trip, but to others she said she had taken a temporary job on Crete. It gnawed at her that she had lied to friends, but mother aside, she couldn't bear their judgments if things went badly. And worst of all—holding her breath as the plane rose and banked to the south—her mother had made her feel infantile instead of a woman who'd been kicked around enough to deserve better.

Etched in memory were the recriminations from the time when she had limped home, lacerated by the shards of a shattered relationship. Not long after the collapse of Communism in 1990, having barely turned eighteen, she ran off with a man. The end of Todor Zhivkov's 35-year regime and a few glasses of Champagne had mixed into a liberation cocktail. They traveled to France to paint because they could; then they married because they could. Paris was romance—why not marry? It was the rush, the rock songs, and the intoxication of freedom. Why not? This was the question everybody around them in the collapsed Warsaw Pact asked when choosing recklessness.

Instead of freedom, what she found in Paris was bondage. Her husband, Ludmil, who was 23, added opiates and philandering to his expression of freedom, and believed he had the freedom to smack Steffi whenever the mood suited him. For three years, she survived by the energy her painting infused in her. Fortunately, there were friends to lean on, painters most of them, who had also drifted from the old Communist east.

Finally, the abstract light of art could not overcome the darkness of reality. One evening, desperate, she found Ludmil in a Paris shithole of a hotel with a Moroccan or maybe Algerian waif, long lost from family and religion. Steffi howled when she saw the scene before her. Surely catching her philandering husband was part of the pain, but it was so much more. She felt as if she had entered hell itself. The room stunk of the stash they had been cooking, ejaculate, sweat, and neglect. One wall was smeared with feces.

From the soiled bed, the frail, dark-haired Moroccan stared at her with vacant, dreamy eyes. Only Steffi's hysteria had aroused her minimal attention. Her head was buried in Ludmil's crotch, and her hand loosely held his limp penis. Ludmil smirked but didn't move.

He wore a goatee, as he had said in sober days, "To remind us of Tovarish (comrade) Lenin." How clever it had seemed when she first heard him say it, and now how pathetic the goatee looked— more like a caricature of Satan.

"Shall I cook some for you? You need to chill."

She wanted to kill him, to drive a stake through his fluttering anemic heart. "Bastard, asshole!"

Somehow, Ludmil found the strength to leap from the bed. His bounding legs struck the Moroccan who flopped to the floor like a dropped rag doll. He slammed the door shut and pinned Steffi against it. "What, you don't like my French colonial slut?"

"I don't like you!" she shouted as loud as she could, spittle spraying his face.

His long, slender arm reached over and grabbed a syringe from the table. "This is good stuff. I don't like to share it, but I'm going to give you a little, just enough, okay?"

She pushed at him, but he was right back at her, locking her right arm in his. She pulled at his hair, but he seemed unaffected. Instead, with demonic concentration, he searched for a vein. She pulled and yanked. He elbowed her in the chin, and the salty taste of blood covered her tongue. "You'll get me arrested if you don't shut up. You have to mellow out like my girlfriend here." The Moroccan's eyes were half shut, her face pale as moonlight.

It was at that point that some rational sense found its way to the surface, and she slammed her left knee into his crotch. Ludmil collapsed. The syringe dropped and stuck in the wooden floor like a shot arrow.

She burst from the room and ran until she could run no more, her heartbeat throbbing in her temples. When she regained her wind, she ran to their apartment, gathered what money she could from her hiding place, found more money in one of Ludmil's pockets and, leaving the detritus of their broken life behind as well as years of paintings and sketches, she ran more. By running she earned her true manumission, finally ending up nearly a week later, half-starved, at her sister's flat in Sofia.

Divorce wasn't necessary. Not three months after her return to Sofia, police came to inform her that Ludmil had been found by the authorities, beaten to a pulp near an abandoned foundry on the outskirts of Lille, France. No other details were known. Nothing more was required by Steffi to imagine the circumstances and the scene. She refused to claim the body. Now, approaching two decades later, that angry gesture plagued her like an unhealed sore.

* * *

Jim Jana sat in the Athens International Airport waiting, filling vacant time with daydreams of Steffi Galabova. She stood naked before a dresser mirror; he sat on the bed behind her, propped up by two giant feather pillows. They stared at each other's reflections, and her smirk suggested she was aware of his arousal. Though he had never actually seen her naked, he imagined her so, with her small, curved rear and smooth skin. Her nearly black hair with its chestnut highlights spilled over her shoulders. Through an open window he heard the sea on Crete washing ashore, and a breeze fluttered the pale, gossamer curtains.

No, no, Jim thought, changing the fantasy. Instead, they sat facing each other, their legs wrapped together, their hands resting on each other's shoulders. Yes, that was better. The heat of her body was palpable. Concentrate on that. Okay, Jim thought, what comes next? She touches my cheek, soft hands on my gravelly beard. I hold the lobe of her left ear in my hand; the stud of her earring pinches my finger.

An announcement in Greek and English shattered his fantasy. His head throbbed from jet lag as he glanced at his watch. His butt was numb, and his stomach suffered from eating too much bread. The minutes crept, having slowly unwound to little more than an hour, but this hour seemed to last a year. His desire to see Steffi was the tumbler of Scotch denied a drinker.

As he waited, depressing thoughts about his history encroached, dragging him down like swimming with chains around his legs. As a military historian, Jim grasped how everyone is chained to a past. Still, that understanding didn't diminish his anxiety. When he said, "Everything about my relationship with Steffi is different," it was a Mae West that buoyed him among the whitecaps of his own doubts. Nevertheless, always leaching though the permeable soil of his life was another truth: History can be manipulated by anyone to justify anything.

The public reason Jim waited for his flight was to kick-start his new book on the German occupation of Crete during World War II. Were he not so jet-lagged and anxious about Steffi, Jim would have been intrigued to know the Athens airport was named after the revolutionary leader and founder of modern Greece, Eleftherios Venizelos, born on Crete near Chania, their flight's destination. Normally, esoteric historical facts and detail perked him up.

"This is neat; that's neat; if we could do that, it'd be neat. Isn't it neat the way the goddamned trenches are still there? Why always *neat*?" his wife, Jeannette, caviled as he dragged her across the Dardanelles to visit the World War I Gallipoli battlefield. She had wanted to spend the day shopping for decorative copper in Istanbul.

When Jeannette's illness had begun clarifying so much, or, perhaps better put, so little in their relationship, he admitted to himself that illness had rolled away the tarp that hid the truth. It uncovered how a loved one is not necessarily loved. Without a doubt, he discovered the frightening, guilty, and shameful truth that he did not love this woman nor ever had. He lived in abstraction and ideas, and she with milestones and sales numbers. For two years, while Jeannette battled cancer, he soldiered on out of a sense of duty camouflaged by playing the role of caring partner and suffering husband. "And eventually," he commented to a friend or two, "if you do that long enough, you're left with rot that no amount of scrubbing washes away." Trying to expunge it was like his boyhood memory of throwing a ball as far as he could out onto Lake Michigan, thinking it was gone forever, only to find it the next day a hundred yards down the beach.

Jeannette had legally changed her name from Ludmilla, declaring to her Polish mother, "I can't possibly move up with a name like Ludmilla." When her mother pleaded, "But it was your great-grandmother's name!" Jeannette merely shrugged. In the corporate world, she was a first-round shoo-in for the business development hall of fame. She knew how to prevail when others were sacked. Her winning streak was planned and scripted. In fact, Jeannette attempted to script and to manage everything. As part of her Chicago Polish lineage, the family was Catholic, Democratic, and pro-big labor, but she engineered keeping her blue-collar past secret. If she prayed for anything it was to be miraculously transformed into a "blue blood," with summers on Cape Cod. Jeannette wasn't keen to attend Mass at the geographically assigned parish, so they drove instead to her Emerald City of parishes in order to be surrounded by the "right people."

The first time they came out of that parish on a beautiful cool fall day, Jeannette's eyes glittered. "Did you see the shoes? There wasn't a pair of pumps under five hundred dollars!"

"You're telling me you just spent the last hour checking out shoes?"

She pointed a lecturing finger at Jim. "Shoes tell you more about a person than anything else. A lot of Christian Louboutin, and for the uneducated troglodytes like you, those are the heels with the red soles. They're classy!" Her voice was in rapture. "Goes with the Catholic Church, don't you think? You know, an ancient church, tradition-bound, College of Cardinals, and all that."

Jim had met Jeannette in Washington, D.C., after both of them were "established." Jim's work had brought him in and out of Washington over the years. After majoring in history at Michigan State, Jim was to be commissioned in the Marine Corps, but he convinced the Corps to delay commissioning a year so that he could earn a master's degree at the London School of Economics. With the encouragement of a professor there, he converted a paper he wrote on Civil War Union general Ambrose Burnside into a novel that earned respectable reviews, and a small nest egg he successfully invested during his three years as an infantry platoon commander. As a 25-year-old lieutenant, Jim saw a spark of action in Operation Urgent Fury, the 1983 Grenada invasion; thereafter, whenever he peered at yellowed photos of Marines from the long list of Caribbean incursions, Haiti, Tampico Bay, Dominican Republic, he experienced a wispy kind of melancholia that forever left him feeling less a part of history than a pawn of it.

After leaving the Marines, Jim earned a doctorate in history at the University of Virginia. A monograph he wrote on the impact of isolation on Special Forces units in Viet Nam was well received. A study he co-authored about the importance of discipline among World War II prisoners also attracted attention at the Pentagon and eventually led to a job offer. Another historical novel, set during the World War I battle of Gallipoli, which dove deeply into the psyches of both the Turks and ANZAC troops, was both a critical and financial success.

But Jeannette was the rock star and a force to be reckoned with at one of the big defense contractors. She poured over journals to glean the latest business trends and peppered her vocabulary with business catchphrases. Naturally, she was a "Six Sigma" Anaconda or whatever the highest order of that zero-defect business management technique was. Over a glass of wine after work, Jeannette would report stories of fantastic payouts and the rewards of going the extra mile to close a deal. The bombardment of it all shell-shocked Jim, and in his mind, he gradually began to believe she saw power, cash buyouts, virility, and attractiveness as synonyms.

Jeannette flirted with her shapely legs and short skirts, and Jim never could decide whether it was conscious or unconscious; but when she lifted her gams, it sent him flying and had more to do with him marrying her than he would dare admit. Her legs unnerved colleagues in meetings, who struggled to look away, fearful of lechery accusations. Jeannette had that year's look and turbocharged everything she had with the right makeup, the right hosiery, and the right jewelry. Still, if you stopped and studied her—put her under the microscope, as was Jim's scholarly habit—she really wasn't a knockout. Jeannette was what Jim labeled an "enhanced" blonde, and a bit anorexic, with a small supplemented bosom. She also had thin lips that communicated impatience. Several small scars from childhood chicken pox periodically sent her into a rage. "Why in the fuck did it take medical science so fucking long to come up with the chicken pox vaccine?"

Jim stared at his watch; hardly fifteen minutes had passed since he checked the arrival board the last time. He scraped his tongue over what felt like fuzz on his teeth and decided to brush them. He always carried a toothbrush in his carry-on. He remembered he'd packed a couple of antacid tablets and popped one of those as well, with a gulp of bottled water. Jim shouldered his carry-on and walked back into the terminal area. Though he didn't expect any surprises, the arrival/departure board indicated both the flight to Chania and the flight from Sofia were on time. He meandered over to another seat, attached the strap of his carry-on to his leg as a theft deterrent, and sat down, resting his head on the seat back, trying not to think of the bacteria breeding on it.

Closing his eyes and folding his hands prayerfully, he let his mind drift. The Jeannette compartment opened again, and the curtain went up on images in the hospital. At the time, she was forty-two and he forty-four. How long had they spoken about having children? Like some kind of merger negotiation that never quite reached wet signatures on a contract, they had balked too many times, sometimes for good reasons and sometimes for selfish ones. For a half-decade, discussions of family were pregnant only with possibilities.

Jeannette's first appointment with the oncologist had been a week after the 9/11 World Trade Center attacks. As her condition worsened, Jeannette decided to return to Chicago for treatment in order to be close to her mother, which Jim found both a relief and a painful comment on their relationship. "Never leave your post until properly relieved" was a general order he learned from the Marine Corps, and Jim obeyed, losing twenty pounds standing watch over Jeannette's final days. Despite the rocky soil of their time together, their roots had found ways to dig together and entwine, but sadly, most of all, choke.

While studying Jeannette on her hospital bed, he was struck with pathos, but more the unattached pathos one experiences looking at a painful magazine photo. How proud she had been of her high cheekbones. Once he'd caught her holding the cover of an *Elle* magazine to the mirror, comparing the model's cheeks to hers. What had been a sought-after commodity in life evinced a saturnine one in sickness. Without makeup, her flesh documented the consumption of her disease, absorbing instead of radiating light. He imagined he saw her again with that infernal brush and its powdery floral scent whisking away.

The nurse walked in, jiggled the IV lines, and reset the beeping heart monitor. She looked down at Jeannette and then at Jim, smiling at him faintly, "She's resting peacefully. Why don't you take a break? I'll call you if there are any changes."

"Maybe I'll just take a stroll down to the waiting room."

"Sure. The ball game's on. Watch an inning or two."

Jim nodded and padded out of the room and into the brightly lit corridor. He removed some coloring books from the seat closest to the TV and sat down, immediately resting his head on the palm of his left hand. The White Sox versus the Tigers. A blurry memory of sitting in the bleachers with his dad at Tiger Stadium formed and broke apart, a plume of smoke caught in a winter wind. Going to baseball games with his father substituted for intimacy, and hot dogs and peanuts as tokens of love.

Suddenly he sensed the presence of someone behind him. He turned to see a short, round, bald-headed man in a hospital gown and a pair of slippers liberated from a hotel on Oahu. He held a chrome stand for an IV bottle with a line that poked into his left wrist.

"Watchin' the game, huh? Who's winnin'?"

Not wanting to be rude, Jim said, "Don't know, just got here."

Jim heard the wheels of the IV stand drawing nearer. "Mind if I take a load off? Lying down in dat room. I'm bored outta my mind. Had to get outta there."

"Go ahead." But he wished he wouldn't.

Jim turned to look at the man, who had a common Chicago face, something Eastern European.

"I'll tell ya, this hospital stuff's for the birds," he announced more to the twenty empty seats in the room than to Jim. Not a minute passed and the man was on his feet again. "Hardly no sound. Mind if I turn it up?"

"There's a sign next to the TV. Says the sound's pre-set."

But the man fiddled with the remote anyway. "The sound don't go no higher. Must be broke." The man shrugged and put the remote back on the TV stand.

For a few minutes they watched the game. "Yes sirree, sir. Baseball, dat's my game."

Jim shrugged, and for a few seconds Jim forgot about Jeannette. Then, a splash of white. In a practiced, calm voice: "Ah, there you are, Mr. Jana. Wanted to update you."

The man's eyes squinted as he studied Jim bolting from his seat. "Hey, you take it easy, pal," his voice a half octave lower.

The nurse and Jim returned down the polished corridor. He heard his footsteps echoing. "Is there a problem?"

"The doctor would like to speak with you. We're having trouble getting a blood pressure." While he wasn't sure what she meant, he had a hunch Jeannette had died. He prepared his game face, knowing what was expected of him. To be sure, there was a knot in his stomach, but there was something else, something ugly he sought to bury like a murderer hiding a corpse, something akin to liberation.

More than two years had dripped away since Jim learned the euphemism "trouble getting a blood pressure" meant death. For one year after Jeannette's passing, late-night self-examination block-aded sleep. As an historian, his life's purpose centered on a mission to distill truth. Why couldn't he find the truth about why he had married Jeannette, or, for that matter, what he had ever wanted from marriage, or a woman? Or was it, he wondered with his clock radio relentlessly posting minutes of sleeplessness, that he didn't want to face the truth of who he was? He uncovered fragments about his past like pottery shards at an archaeological dig, but they only led him to speculation and theories. Like the ancient Minoan civiliza-tion on Crete he would soon visit, his artifacts teased but offered few certain explanations.

Jeannette, he derisively concluded, wanted a man who signed a non-compete clause. Love? That was tertiary. Marriage was about what it did to enhance the whole package. As she might say, "Just the way the right accessory makes the outfit." It was something that fit between business trips, social engagements, and having her nails done.

Groaning, Jim recalled the cocktail party with the high fliers from Jeannette's office. Wine had been served in numbered brown paper bags so that no one could know the estate or vintage. At the end of the evening, the game was for people to match the numbers with a wine list as a test of their palates. The person with the most correct answers would win a case of some snooty Cabernet Sauvignon, or as the folks at the party called it, "a Cab."

And so the conversation in Jim's group went, "Number two has some interesting blackberry overtones."

"And a nice finish," from a man whose considerable proboscis was jammed deep into a balloon glass.

From another man with shell-rimmed glasses, "I beg to differ. I find the finish a bit cloying. Too much fruit."

The conversation drifted to other topics like "exorbitant" tax bills. "You wouldn't believe what I pay in taxes on that pile of stucco."

"The whole damn economy is getting to be one big transfer payment to Uncle Sam. Pretty soon they'll make it illegal to earn a decent wage."

Somehow, the conversation drifted to him. "So, Jim, Jeannette tells me you're a historian."

"Well yes. I do historical novels, and I work from time to time as a consultant."

Mr. Proboscis pulled his nose from the glass. "You must be good at dates and names. That's what always killed me in history class. Night before the test, always trying to cram dates and names."

One of the others, a corporate attorney with a bow tie, spoke up, "My son wanted to major in history, but I said, how you gonna make a buck from that?"

"For me the draw is how good history uncovers truth," Jim said.

The corporate attorney chuckled, "And I spend all my day trying to keep the truth from leaking out!" They all roared with laughter.

"Hey, we trade hog bellies and cocoa, why not truth?" Between guffaws, "Let's propose it to the New York Stock Exchange. They're always angling for new products."

Just then Jeannette walked up, demonstrating mastery of the criss-cross walk of runway models. "What's so funny?" She took Jim's arm. "My hubby isn't boring you with curious facts from the past, is he?"

"*Au contraire!* I think he's helped us discover a new product to get us rich." Then they surrounded Jeannette and forgot about the truth.

"While you're here, can we talk about yesterday's deal you breathtakingly put together? We're anxious to pick up the crumbs."

From somewhere, interrupting his memory—was it on the airport's system or on someone's player or maybe in his head?—he heard Billie Holiday singing

"You Go To My Head."
You go to my head and you linger like a haunting refrain.
And I feel you spinning 'round in my brain
Like the bubbles in a glass of Champagne...

Whenever Steffi was around, this song played in his head. Over and over, sometimes for days after they parted, the lines played their slow haunting pace with Lady Day delivering her blues edge. Why he connected this cut with Steffi, he'd never been able to answer.

CHAPTER TWO

A t that moment they caught sight of each other. She saw him
standing akimbo in the middle of the concourse with people
streaming around him like water around a river snag, and he saw her
marching toward him with her typical martial gait. Time stopped.
Time accelerated. There was only the present. History and dreams of
the future extinguished themselves. Sound waves flattened beyond
even a dog's sensitivity.

In approaching Jim, it was as if she ran across the parted Nile.
On the other bank was hope, even if it wasn't a promised land. As
she marched through the parted mountains of water with the past
in hot pursuit, its sharpened bronze spears at the ready, she was
only aware of reaching Jim. Hope was always better than sadness
and cruelty. When Steffi had first recognized Jim in the crowd, her
apprehension faded. To see him again was to confirm that he was
not the ones and zeros of their electronic chatter, but a man whose
intense, fierce eyes, that so often betrayed his feelings, lived. Now,
those eyes bore into her with such longing her body involuntarily
tightened.

To Jim, the long swings of Steffi's arms, like a gymnast entering an arena, were part of the memory of seeing her for the first time. It was in the second year of Jeannette's illness. Jim had recently arrived in Sofia as part of an NGO delegation observing Bulgaria's NATO accession. Every evening from his hotel overlooking the Communist-era Tzum department store, he called his mother-in-law to check on Jeannette. As he watched the traffic merge from Boulevard Tsar Osvoboditel, he listened while Jeannette's mother prattled on in Polish-accented English.

"This Puerto Rican garage attendant in the hospital purple lot, oh my God, Jimmy! He don't make the change fast enough. He can't count, this kid. Everybody got backed up on the exit ramp for miles! I know I wrote it down Jimmy, but tell me again, what's your flight back to Chicago?" Her mother's blue collar and old country ways had always mortified Jeannette. It had never seemed enough that her mother loved her. Her mother was the soldier during the illness, visiting the hospital every day, leaving behind fresh flowers and changes of clean, crisply ironed bedclothes.

It had been in the park near the old American embassy that he first saw Steffi's march. Jim had strolled to the park to watch some of the local men play chess while he waited for colleagues to join for dinner. The old men, stinking of rakia, spit sunflower husks while they played. They competed fiercely, slamming their time clocks and banging the pieces on the board.

The spring evening was balmy, so he slung his coat over his shoulder as he watched the pawn storm in front of him collapse black's defense. The shoulders of the man playing black sagged, and Jim, ever the military historian, quipped to himself, "Must have been how German General Guderian looked when the Russian front collapsed." After checking his watch, he left the game and meandered to the meeting place on the backside of the Georgi Dimitrov tomb. From a distance, he detected his colleagues sitting at a park table.

It was then he also saw a woman, arms swinging like a sergeant major, walk up to his colleague, Bill Strong. As he approached, he noticed how she wore her hair in one of the strangest arrangements he had ever seen. Her dark brown tresses were swept in a semi-circle on top of her head and held there by hairpins she made no attempt to hide. What an odd bird, he thought. On that evening, contrary to what he later discovered of her nature, she wore a stern, almost mannish expression, accented by an absence of makeup. Her cheap-looking suit sagged and clung to the wrong places, and her shoes were scuffed and out of style. Nevertheless, even without makeup, her skin glowed, and as weirdly styled as her dark hair was, it sparkled in the dying sun. It crossed Jim's mind that perhaps her frumpiness was due to an attractive woman's wish to hide her beauty.

"The day is done," a colleague began. "Time for a cocktail and a hearty meal."

Somebody else cut in, "You mean cocktails."

Jim shook hands with his work mates. "Yo, Jim. That was a long one today, dude. Generals and their monotones!"

Bill Strong, sitting next to the young lady, turned to her and introduced Jim. "Jim, this is Steffi Galabova, polyglot extraordinaire, cultural anthropologist, Bulgarian historical encyclopedia, and den mother to this hopeless group of miscreants."

Jim smiled, "Bill always does challenge my vocabulary, but I think you have been praised, if I understood his gibberish correctly."

Before Steffi could answer, Bill cut in, "I forgot, Jim is a former knuckle-dragging Marine. Steffi, you will need to write down hard words on 3X5 cards for him."

For the first time Jim detected a hint of a smile, but he also noticed her flushed cheeks. "In any event, *zdravey*, nice to meet you, Steffi." Only then did her averted eyes chance looking at him long enough to shake hands. Her small hand fit comfortably in his, but her grip was surprisingly strong. He caught a glimpse of her nails— neatly manicured, cut short, and unpolished.

"*Mnogo blagodarya*, thank you very much. Nice to meet you, sir."

Bill cracked, "Oh you don't have to 'sir' him, Steffi, he's no general in civilian clothes or something. Jim's just an everyday civilian puke."

"It's true, Steffi. No need to use 'sir.' I'm just a backbencher, nothing but an academic. Please call me Jim."

"Okay, *chudesno* (great), then Jim it is."

His immediate impression was that her English conveyed no hint of a Bulgarian accent, but rather a slight British inflection, and he suspected she might have learned the language from an Englishman or in Britain.

A bantering about where they'd eat began. "I don't care where we eat as long as it's not the hotel. I'd rather eat an MRE. And no more pork, please," one of the men whined. "How about Restaurant Chiffon?"

"Too pricey," from someone else.

"Pizza then, the joint under the bridge near the Hilton."

All the while, Jim noticed Steffi staring at him. If not rude, it was obvious. When he glanced her way, she averted her eyes, but they were locked back on him as soon as his attention turned elsewhere. Apparently, she was unaware that her face had floated into the edge of his peripheral vision. The gaze wasn't flirtatious; rather, it seemed more akin to an entomologist studying a mounted insect with a magnifying glass.

"Then it's settled," Bill Strong smacked his hands together "To the pizza joint quick as summer lightning." Bill turned to Steffi. "Will you join us?"

She waved her hand no. On her ring finger she wore a narrow gold band with a blue stone. It wasn't a wedding band. "I have to be getting home."

Later that evening after pizza, salad, and a good Mavrud, a Bulgarian red wine, Jim returned to his room and decided he couldn't endure listening to his mother-in-law. As he changed into his pajamas, Steffi's image came back. "What an odd bird, what an odd bird," he repeated. "And *Steffi*, what the hell kind of Bulgarian name is that? No Bulgarians are named Steffi." Until he fell asleep, the memory of her lingered.

Now, as she came closer, he thought, how different she looks to me from that first time, except for that silly march of a walk. Had the sun brightened her face? And she wore the earrings he had sent her last Christmas, that he had found in a Virginia antique store near Petersburg. The delicate black drops wobbled seductively every time she moved her head. Her white cotton blouse barely masked the details of her bra. Now that she was so close, he saw that she had applied a barely visible layer of shadow to her eyes, and light pink lipstick.

Steffi's eyes widened as she approached, drawing Jim in as if her eyes were vortexes. The smile she wore was the same Bill Strong had commented on long before, "By the looks of Steffi's smile, I'd say she has a thing for you, Jim boy." At the time, Jim prevaricated, "Come on, she smiles like that at everybody," but he knew that smile opened him and made him vulnerable, flooding him with desire. At that time, his desire left him guilty, with Jeannette in Chicago having withered to a point that "further treatment offered no meaningful benefits." Any flirtation had seemed like dancing a jig on Jeannette's grave.

For a moment they stood there. Neither knew what to say. The tangible fact of finally seeing each other again overcame words. Jim clumsily stepped forward to wrap his arms around her, but when he leaned forward, his carry-on bag swung on his shoulder and landed between them. "That's awkward," and Steffi laughed. Instead, he took both of her warm hands in his. They pulsed with energy. Finally, Steffi pushed the bag out of the way, and they embraced. Jim whispered in Steffi's ear, "I think we have a flight to catch." If she said anything, Jim didn't hear it. He only felt her smooth cheek on his neck moving up and down in agreement. Slowly they moved apart, turned, and walked hand in hand to one of the far gates on the concourse where their flight to Chania boarded. For at least a few minutes, their minds were free and uninhibited.

Keeping his mind free had always been a challenge for Jim. All sorts of clutter and bothersome compulsions filled too many hours. He quadruple-checked locks, tied and re-tied his running shoes, and brushed his teeth too often. Typical of him, he explained his own imperfections and quirks by intellectualizing them into larger social and historical contexts. He wrote once, "In history as in biological systems, evolution is always a change but not always an improvement. More like a tree than a pyramid, evolution sprouts in multiple directions, but some branches never bear fruit. Others wither and fall away, leaving scars for the rest of the tree's life. History, and for that matter, societies and our personal lives reflect the same kind of development."

Quoting Thomas Merton while on his third beer with his buddy from East Lansing days, Rusty Pavlicek, Jim pontificated, "I don't see the road ahead of me, and I cannot know for certain where it will end." His performance unfolded on the stage of a Detroit neighborhood tap where men wore bowling shirts and slugged down "depth chargers," shots of Seagram's 7 dropped, glass and all, into draft beers. Jim concluded, "At what point do I gain the wisdom to understand where I've been, and by that time, it's too damn late. That was life with Jeannette. Didn't know the fucking road I was on."

With a sardonic, twisted smile Rusty answered, "What is this shit with the mental gyrations?" He shoved his beer mug aside, "Jeannette's dead, and you're still alive," he said, his green eyes bearing into Jim's. "Don't make it more complicated with your bullshit intellectualizing. You're feeling guilty, but you're always feeling guilty. And then the thermonuclear guilt option lands right on top of an asshole like you. Turns out Jeannette had a couple of million in insurance, so your guilt got cubed. Fuck that, man. Sometimes you get the bear, and sometimes the bear gets you. Buy a fucking Ferrari or something and get over it."

In a similar episode, about a week after arriving back in the States from Bulgaria, Jim met Dr. Marie-Claire Gordon at a local bakery for coffee. They often met for a friendly chat after teaching Wednesday seminars at the university where Jim was an adjunct professor. MC, as Jim called her, never sparked his sexual interest, and he believed the same was true with her.

MC sipped her latte through a stirring straw to keep the hot coffee from marring her dark brownish-red lipstick. "What are you doing with that weird lipstick?

"Well, I'll have you know my students love it. It makes me a woman of mystery."

"So, what's the mystery, figuring out if you're dead or alive?"

MC looked at him over the rim of her glasses, "More like, does the professor have an affinity for the punk generation? Perhaps dissatisfaction with society's norms? A gothic heroine rejecting modern advertising's happy message?" She sipped some coffee and without looking up queried in her bored-with-the-world jejune affectation, "So how was the journey to Moesia Inferior?" referring to the ancient Roman Province that contained a sizeable portion of modern Bulgaria.

"Great. Say, speaking of Moesia Inferior, you recall this woman Steffi I mentioned previously?"

"Ah, the young lady with the fascinating history you told me about with the Bulgarian father and German mother, or I should say, shouldn't I, a mother from the one-time fraternal socialist cousin to Bulgaria, East Germany." She smiled her brown smile. "Yes, you've mentioned the *fraulein* ad nauseam. And you've told me her story with enough repetition to convince me you're smitten."

She studied him for a moment. "His shifting eyes do reveal so much," and then she smirked and released an artificial bubbling laugh. "But the invisible chains of neurosis and guilt hold our young—excuse me—middle-aged hero to a hopeless position of denial."

"Am I going to get a word in edgewise?"

"But dear, can't you appreciate my mordant sense of humor? I'm so enjoying this. I have you on the run, and it is so delicious." She paused, "But in the end, I have no desire to torture you past a certain point. Pray continue." Placing her elbows on the table, MC rested her chin on her folded hands.

Jim leaned across the table. "I mean, in every poll, Bulgarians rank slightly ahead of Somalia in terms of how happy they are with their lives and countries. Her mother's family survived the fire-bombing of Dresden, and then the mother grows up with the Stasi secret police watching you take a crap. And yet, Steffi projects peacefulness, faith even. Every day's kind of a joy. I grow up in the land of the free and home of the brave, and I'm in turmoil. I can't figure it out."

"God, you Marines! Hopeless, but at the same time what would we do without you, so we must embrace your stupidity. Does it not occur to you that this young lady believes in something beyond the readily observable; it's an emotional connection. A loving cosmic force, if you will. You are a classic product of the secular modern world. You and most of your history and scientific colleagues slice and dice everything. You accept meliorism. You only accept what can be tested and verified, and you reject what you label irrational. And then you get depressed because surprise, surprise, nothing about humankind turns out much better after all your work. Two steps forward and two back. That's what humankind pretends is the great march forward."

Afraid that he might have told the story before, Jim refrained from recounting it now, but as MC spoke it played back in his mind. While he was preparing to return to the States because Jeannette's condition worsened daily, he received a call in his hotel room from her mother. The moment he pressed the receiver to his ear, he heard sobbing then angry bursts, "You do nothing. You don't help. You are a nightmare of a husband for my poor daughter. No wonder she doesn't get better. You secretly want her dead."

Shattered and insulted by the call, Jim sat on his bed staring at nothing and feeling so alone he might as well have been shrink-wrapped and packed away in a dark cabinet. Indignant at first, he tried to fight back mentally, but his conscience, more a parasite than a defender, burrowed through the shell of his defenses, until finally, exhausted, he conceded that his mother-in-law had struck the target's center ring. She had deciphered his heart through the smokescreen of his orchestrated performances. But she couldn't even dream of how frightened he had become to be in that room with Jeannette's sickness. How loathsome he viewed himself in the mirror, knowing that secretly he wanted the ugly, fetid sight of it over and the shackles of their loveless marriage broken. A few weeks later when Jeannette passed, and he staggered from the sterile smells and machine sounds of the hospital to breathe the fecund perfume of the forest across from the hospital, what overwhelmed him, beyond the fatigue, was the elation of being alive.

As the months passed after Jeannette's cremation, Jim understood nothing more of his life with Jeannette than he had before. He had stiffly, and by appearances to the outside world, gallantly processed through all the steps expected of him. Finally, as a last step, he fulfilled her written request to spread her ashes in the water among the San Juan Islands in Puget Sound. Standing along the rail near the stern of the car ferry with a layer of fleece and one of Gore-Tex to block the damp wind, he opened the box and watched the ashes burst free in a gray cloud. Jim remained unable to fathom her request. It seemed a contradiction of the Jeannette he thought he knew.

They had visited the islands on the recommendation of an old friend as a good place to escape the illness. The cobalt-colored water and deep green of the islands' trees were soothing, even Jeannette agreed to that, although she did so from behind the glass of the deck's waiting room. "Imagine that," she had said when they saw an eagle take flight. They had stayed in a rustic cabin in mid-March with a wood stove to keep warm. In his mind her every expression seemed to cry out, "How long must I endure this place?" They bickered over how much wood to put on the fire and whether to complain to the desk about the feeble hot water heater. Never once during the trip did either of them utter, "I love you."

CHAPTER THREE

Now they were on board another flight, his third of the day and her second. *Were they flights from something or to something?* crossed both of their minds. Because they had booked separately, their assigned seats were rows apart, which meant they spent the first few minutes negotiating seat trades. Steffi shifted easily with other passengers among English, German, and French. When they finally flopped down next to each other, they decompressed enough to exchange smiles. The vibration and whine of the twin turbo-prop engines overwhelmed conversation. Jim turned to the window for a moment to glance at the blur of the spinning prop blades. When the pilot released the brakes, Steffi's hand, with her ring with its blue stone, searched for Jim's.

When she did take his hand, Jim glanced at Steffi and smiled reassuringly, recalling how stressed she had been during a flight to the Black Sea port of Burgas as part of a delegation. She needed both his steadying help and Bill Strong's as they disembarked. It was during that trip that an intimacy first grew between them, through conversations during coffee breaks and while seated next to each other at conference dinner tables. For Steffi, their conversations were wind chimes that resonated in perfect A chords. They called it a friendship, which was a euphemism for self-protection. They tried to hide their growing closeness, but the glances they exchanged were on fire. One day they shared a taxi after work, and on the ride, their hands found each other. He wanted to climb out of the cab to be with her, but she stopped him. "It's not right."

There was that electric moment at a cocktail reception not long after when a small group huddled together talking shop. Steffi, translating, stood close to Jim with their backs to a wall. Jim lightly placed his arm around the small of her back, and Steffi answered by drawing closer and leaning into him. Of all the trysts and experiences in his life to that moment, her gentle yielding to his touch was the most erotic.

It was the night before he returned to the States that the bellman dropped off a postcard of the Rila Monastery, a tenth-century national treasure some seventy kilometers southwest of Sofia. On the back, Steffi had written in her even and circular cursive, "I visited Rila today, and in our tradition, I lit candles for you and your wife. Both of you are in my prayers. God's speed Jim and good-bye." It was the first moment Jim had considered the finality of their blossoming relationship. Then, to his surprise, at the airport the next morning at 5:30, she was there with her eyes tracking his every move. She believed she was hidden by the crowd and a pillar, but he detected her. He fought an impulse to rush up to her and promise to return some day, but then decided to pretend otherwise. Promises and expectations—he was so tired of trying to fulfill both. As the plane to Chania accelerated down the runway, Jim reflected. Had it really been nearly two years since he last left Steffi leaning behind that pillar at Sofia's airport?

The chop began as soon as they banked south. The sun shone brightly, and the Aegean sparkled cerulean blue, trimmed in aquamarine along the edges of the islands. The plane bucked, and the wings dipped. Each time it seemed to change the pitch of the props, causing them to groan. The pilot announced in uncertain English, partly muted by engine noise, "Ah…sure. Sorry…all the way to Kriti… from out of the Africa, Zephyr. Nothing to be done but endure."

In response, Steffi's head nestled on Jim's shoulder and her left arm wrapped around his right. With the rich fragrance of her hair and her body's warmth cradled next to him, her fear was his pleasure.

Only when the pilot began his approach to Chania did concern awaken in Jim. The pilot increased engine rpm, and Jim felt him muscling the plane, working to slip it onto the runway. But the cross-wind was daunting, and he guessed they couldn't line up. As if in answer to his thoughts, the throttles kicked in, and the pilot aborted the approach. When he circled and began to line up the plane again, Jim felt perspiration trickle from his armpits. He grimaced as they shot over a fishing boat and then the rocky coast. Then the wheels were down, and he watched the plane's shadow sprinting below. The plane took a nasty bounce and several passengers screamed, but they landed and then eased on to the taxiway. Once inside the small terminal, Jim fetched a cool bottle of mineral water for Steffi while she searched for the luggage.

Groggy but anxious to get on with things, they dragged their gear over to the car rental counter. The rental agent, a round-faced Cretan named Evangelos, showed them the Suzuki Jimmy 1.3 4x4 Jim had booked for a minimum of two months. Almost half of Jim's luggage, the heaviest part of it, contained research material. Steffi's portfolio and materials, while not as heavy, was, because of its odd sizes, even more challenging to pack in the small car.

Jim asked the agent in tortured Greek, "I will need into the mountain driving; will this auto be sufficiency?"

With a smart-ass grin, the rental agent switched to English. "No problem. It will get over anything here. Go where the goats go. Tough little cars these are. Enjoy!" he said with a flourish of his hand.

Even though the wind roared and the sky was hazy with dust, Steffi asked the rental agent, "Hey, Evangelos, how do we put down the top?"

A fine layer of sand already coated the car's hood. Evangelos cracked. "Shit sand from North Africa. Comes right over from shit Libya. But you want top down, we put top down."

Jim shrugged. "Okay, okay," and he helped Evangelos lower the top and secure it. Steffi jumped into the front seat, her hair blowing behind her, "Schon los!"

"Einverstanden." Jim slipped behind the wheel and cranked the car up. Toward the end of their time together in Bulgaria, they often spoke German. It was a neutral language choice. It had a way of subtly putting them on equal footing. Jim beeped the horn and waved to Evangelos as they pulled from the lot.

They would need to return to Chania several times, both for Steffi to draw Chania's elegant buildings that belonged to its time as a Venetian trading city, and for Jim's research. For now, they chose to push on, crawling through the city's winding streets, because the direct road from the airport to the east-west road was under construction. For a few minutes they were absorbed in the new smells and terrain. Jim was particularly conscious of how the area around Chania from Maleme to Souda Bay witnessed intense combat during the Nazi airborne landings in May of 1941. Both the Allied and German military cemeteries lie nearby.

Soon, they seemed to be caught in a labyrinth. No matter which way they turned, they ended up in the same spot. Exasperated and drained from jet lag, Jim pulled off the road beneath a rusted and dilapidated road sign. "We're not getting anywhere," he declared as other cars passed them, some irritatingly beeping their horns.

"Are you lost?"

"Does your comment mean you're not? If so, tell me how to get the hell out of here." He twiddled his thumbs, waiting for a reply. Steffi's question reminded him of Jeannette's authoritarian tone and her relentless maneuvering to dominate.

Jim's tone was the trigger. That's how it had started with Ludmil—the impatience, the sarcasm, the put-downs, like she was stupid. Ludmil's face flashed in her mind back when the goatee was first growing out and before the worst of the drugs. Always pushing, always grabbing. She promised herself she would never bend to that again. Steffi closed her eyes, afraid that if she opened them, Ludmil would be sitting next to her. She felt the wind whip her hair around her neck and face, and she imagined being choked and smothered.

"No, I don't know where we are. I thought you did. I guess we'll have to follow the signs now, won't we?"

That's just what Jeannette would have said, he thought. He tightened his grip on the steering wheel. He nodded toward the sign ahead that hung limply from a rusting metal pole. "You mean like that sign?"

Steffi shrugged, "Okay, why not? Start with that one." She folded her arms across her chest.

"All it says is Hania. Or am I missing something?"

She glanced at the Greek on the sign. "Yes. You are."

"Oh really? Looks like one word to me, Hania. All it tells me is that I don't wanna be in Hania." His voice raised above the wind and traffic.

"Well, in the first place, it's not Hania, it's Chania." Steffi was referring to the fact that the city's name in Greek is spelled with an X, which carries a guttural *ch* sound. "And don't yell at me."

Instantly, Jim realized that he was using an English transliterated pronunciation and was furious that Steffi had called attention to it. "What the hell's the matter with you? That was unnecessary. We're lost, tired, and stressed."

"You don't need to cuss at me."

"Hell is not cussing."

Finally, she turned to Jim, and her flaming eyes met his directly. "I'm not going to be pushed around, Jim."

"Nor am I."

"The point is I'm not sure anyone will understand us if we say Hania. Shouldn't we stick to the Greek pronunciation, assuming we will need to ask someone since you don't know how to find the road?"

"It is spelled H-A-N-I-A on this official map. See, it's on my map, authorized by the Greek government, and it is Hania. It's just a convention, for Christ's sake."

"It's English."

"Yeah, and your point? We've been out of the airport 20 minutes, and we're going to get bogged down in an argument about the pronunciation of," he pointed with his thumb over his shoulder, "that frickin' Venetian city behind us?"

"Sometimes Americans think they can impose their own rules."

"Are you joking?"

"You don't know what it's like to come from a poor country."

"Oh, poor me. Are we really going to start this whole thing off by arguing?"

"I'm not arguing, and you don't have to be rude."

"Rude?"

"Well, sarcastic, because I corrected your ridiculous American pronunciation."

A match ignited the tinder. His face twisted angrily, "Don't make this a war of nations." He had often announced to friends, "Relationships need teamwork, just like the Marines. That's Jeannette's problem, *numero uno*, never wants to work as a team."

With that, Steffi hopped out of the Suzuki and stood with her back to him, her arms folded in front of her and her hair whipping in the wind. She blared something in Bulgarian. Jim mumbled "Shit," and climbed out as well, walking around the car to her side. When she refused to make eye contact, he took hold of her elbows to point her at him, but she yanked her arms free. The words spit from her, "Don't ever grab me!"

What a cock-up this is turning out to be, Jim thought as the vitriol of Steffi's tone seeped into his gut. "This is what I get for letting hope raise its scurvy little head."

"What? Now you make comment about my looks?"

Just as a victim of an earthquake grabs hold of a support beam as the floor beneath him gives way, self-preservation wrestled his emotions under control. "Steffi, what are we doing?"

"Fighting."

"Why? Because we're lost?"

"Yes, probably, and scared. I'm scared."

"I guess maybe that's behind this. I put so much hope in this. Last great hope, or something like that. I guess it made it all the more fragile." Jim had to shout over the wind and traffic.

Steffi shouted back, "It's taken so long to get here, Jim. Not just the wait since I saw you last. No matter where I go, it's the same. Three years I was in Italy, you don't know about that, do you? To work on my painting. I saw this; I saw that. I went to Florence and saw that David and heard those tourists and their stupid jokes about his beautiful body, but always I felt so alone and so fucking cut off. And now it scares me this will end with me feeling the same way."

"You can't read what I've read or seen what I've seen of history and believe your or my stinking experiences have been unique. Life is tenuous on the best days. I'm, no, I was pissed, but something about you makes me want to believe what I've learned from history, about life, is a lie."

She broke into a playful smile. "This has gotten into a serious discussion damn fast for standing on the side of a busy road, Jim."

"Yeah, and the noisy road and diesel exhaust is making me dizzy."

"Let's try to keep it simple for now."

"Ah the KISS principle: keep it simple, stupid. I can do that."

"Okay so long as we agree it's Chania," giving the *ch* as much an exaggerated phlegmy guttural sound as she could muster.

"Don't want to insult the Cretans." Jim glanced at Steffi with a smile. "You know, some anthropologists believe Crete, or I guess I should say *Kriti*, was inhabited by Neanderthals 170,000 years ago."

"So we don't need to act like Neanderthals," Steffi cut in. "Is that what you are trying to say?"

"Precisely." Jim shook his head as they climbed back in the Suzuki.

When a passing car honked, and Jim shot it his middle finger, Steffi laughed and asked, "Do you want to make a comment about the driver's mother as well?"

"Nah, I'll let it go with that." Jim checked his blind spot and pulled out into traffic.

"Let's get out of here, Jim. I'm not sure the air in Chania," another guttural *ch*, "agrees with us." She touched his shoulder lightly. "I was cranky. Is that the right word?"

"Don't say any more. What you said is good enough. Right now, let's figure out how to get out of here."

Through trial and error, they finally reached the highway and turned east near Mourmies. Off to their right, the mountains, and especially the peak of Lefka Ori, remained snow-covered. Steffi gazed out to the mountains, but then she turned back to Jim, her dark eyes more glowing than sparkling, and shouted over the road noise, "Do you think the mountain wildflowers are still blooming? I so want to see them."

How precious her eyes seemed to him at that moment, and he reached out over the stick shift and clutched her hand. A million daydreams became possible. "Well, we'll find out."

Her eyes had occupied his mind since the day Steffi had taken him to a small museum in Sofia for an introduction to a sculptor whose work Jim admired. Looking at paintings while they waited for his arrival was among the first times they had ever been alone together. Their eyes turned from a painting of a Macedonian village and suddenly fell on one another. He wrote in his journal that night, "Her eyes are dark roses with tight whorls of petals."

For a while the road turned south, but the mountains stayed to their right. While Steffi's mind dwelled on wildflowers, Jim couldn't help but assess the terrain in terms of a battlefield. The plain they drove over was the logical area for the German airborne drop. Airfields were clustered in the area, and seizure of them would have been critical for bringing in reinforcements. At Vrises the road turned due east. After several kilometers, the sea became visible off to their left. The wind was not as remarkable, probably because they were on the leeward side of the mountains. Just past the port city of Rethymno they turned right on to a secondary road that led to the south of the island and their hotel near the village of Mirthios overlooking the Libyan Sea.

The decision to begin their adventure in the south had been Jim's. While the south had fewer of the ancient ruins both Steffi and Jim sought to visit and little access to records of the war, it was more secluded. Both of them shared an inclination to be in the world, but not of the world. The club scene fascinated neither of them. Their impulse was to exist apart from others. When Jim first suggested in an email they stay someplace quiet, Steffi wrote back, "I thought quiet was the whole point."

Very quickly they passed through the village of Armeni, where a Minoan cemetery had been unearthed. As exhausted as Jim was, the desire to stop to see it tugged at him. More than five hundred bodies had been buried there. The artifacts discovered in the tombs uncovered examples of Bronze Age pottery and weapons from the 13th and 12th centuries BC. Even the bones had been analyzed to determine how the Minoan diets favored carbohydrates over meat.

They had not driven far south when the wind picked up again, like it was trying to push them back to where they began. Before Koksare, they turned off on a still narrower road and began angling southwest, and at Kanevos they entered the Kotsifou Gorge. The wind howled, and the car shuddered; yet above the near-perpendicular stone walls of the gorge, not a cloud was in sight. Jim kept a death grip on the steering wheel, guessing the gusts at nearly 60 miles per hour.

The windswept, coarse grey rock walls, sometimes arching to the very edge of the narrow two-lane road, were fearsomely beautiful but their immensity left them feeling diminished. It did not take much imagination to believe they had entered a place where the Bronze Age Greek gods still played with the world—had the gentle west wind, Zephyrus, become enraged? Had Aeolus, the ruler of winds, frowned on them because they had not sacrificed even a single sheep in his name?

At Steffi's insistence, he steered the Suzuki into a gravel parking area on the left side of the road. Against the force of the wind, she shoved the door open, climbed out, then gingerly crept forward, guiding herself along the hood of the car. Jim followed, concerned for her safety, knowing a piece of flying debris possessed the kinetic energy to lop their heads off. Holding on to the grill for support, her hair flying perpendicular to her body, Steffi stepped out as far as she could while still keeping her left hand on the car hood. She stared down into the bottom of the gorge where a stream churned over boulders strewn along its course. Bunching her hair in her right hand, she turned to Jim and shook her head in an apparent gesture of disbelief. Her exuberance beat back the wind.

"Come on," he shouted, "Get back in the car. It's dangerous."

She nodded slightly and returned to her seat, never once taking a hand off of the car which seemed ready to roll over. As Jim backed up the 4x4, he glanced at the cliff wall. There, way above him, set incongruously on the cliff face and made of the same limestone, was an Orthodox chapel. He touched Steffi's arm and pointed. Her mouth dropped open in amazement as she craned her head and looked up at it. His mind registered how inviting Steffi's lips looked.

As they worked their way out of the gorge, the wind slackened. In the distance they caught glimpses of the sea between the rolling dry landscapes. At a T intersection, Jim downshifted to second gear, and they turned in the direction of Mirthios.

Off to the left below them, perhaps another few kilometers on, was the town and beach at Plakias. Steffi rested her head on the back of the seat, seemingly content to let Jim take her wherever. Only by a lucky glance did Jim notice the sign to their hotel. It required another downshift and hard brake to cut into the steep gravel driveway to the hotel too far above them to be visible from the road. The two-story hotel was a white, utilitarian poured-concrete building. Each room had a balcony facing the sea.

Once they climbed out of the car and stretched, they found themselves transfixed by the view of the coast below them. A distant rocky peninsula marked the east side of Plakias beach. From that point they could trace the crescent shape of the beach to the far end of the town at its western end. The contrast between the sea's shimmering azure blue and the dusty coarsely-hewn tan landscape with its scattering of shrubs and olive trees held their attention until, from behind them, they heard in English, "Hello, hello, welcome. What kind of salad are we speaking? Deutsch better, Français?" A rather squat and matronly-looking woman beckoned them to the side of the building.

Steffi and Jim waved back. "English is fine."

Under a grape arbor near the entrance to the office stood a table with a few old chairs of mixed heritage. "Sit, sit." The woman, with dyed raven-black hair in an uncertain arrangement, announced, "I'm making a Greek coffee. I'll bring you." She turned to go, but then hesitated and looked back. "You like coffee the Greek way. You like, right? You will take a coffee with me?"

Jim answered in Greek, "Yes, we like."

"You speak Greek! How beautiful! Just a minute; I'll have the coffee in just a minute." She giggled for no reason, then swatted her hand at the table. "Wait here." Then, almost as an afterthought, "Thank God the windstorm's mostly over. I am Maria Phindrikalis, by the way. This is the hotel of my husband and me, but he is a mariner and is at sea now."

The faded cotton dress, with a peculiar side-to-side waddle, disappeared into the office. For a couple of minutes they sat at the table with their eyes closed. They heard the woman inside mumbling, but beside that there was only the sound of the now gentle but steady breeze rustling the grape leaves of the arbor. The air held a dry earthy odor with a faint touch of thyme. Then the sharp scent of the boiling coffee floated in waves through the open door.

The woman shuffled back in her loose cloth slippers printed with bright red strawberries. "I hope you like sweet. I made it sweet. It's the best kind, the sweet is." She held a tray with three demitasse cups and a long handled *Briki* for coffee, scarred black from years of use. On the tray was also a plate decorated with tiny flowers and spread with a scattering of cookies. She carefully poured the thick black coffee. "There, so now, please take a cup." Steam spiraled from the delicate cups. "Have a cookie. Cookie, yes? With my German guests it's 'keks.'"

Steffi took her cup and a cookie and said, "You are so kind."

After they chatted for a while and sipped their coffee down to the muddy slurry, Jim signed the registration and handed over their passports. The woman exclaimed, "Oh, a *Bulgarka*. I didn't think you were English."

She looked right at Jim. "So why am I giving you a key to a room with two bedrooms? I don't see kids."

The bluntness surprised more than upset him. Steffi giggled. She took a second cookie and nibbled it nervously. The woman's stare remained fixed. Jim wanted to dismiss the question with something humorous. Was it a hint of smile on the corner of the woman's dry lips or merely the curl of life-long crabbiness? He tried in Greek, "You are correct. No kids now." His Greek was painfully slow. "I asked for two bedrooms. I'm thinking maybe—we are working fast—the kids they may come in future, yes?"

The woman shook her finger, "You are being very naughty," she answered in English.

Finally, they introduced each other by name and chatted for another thirty minutes. At one point, a man with muscled forearms and curly black slicked-back hair appeared. Jim guessed him to be in his thirties. In a sharp burst of Greek, he addressed Mrs. Phindri-kalis. "I need the car."

"For how long?"

He shrugged and frowned, "A couple of hours," offering no further explanation.

She reached into her dress pocket and handed him the keys. "Hey but I need it back by six, okay?"

"Yeah, yeah." He started to walk off.

"Yanni, please say hello to my guests." When he looked at them, he did so with an angry, taurine face. He offered a perfunctory wave and walked away.

Jim commented, "He doesn't seem very happy. Something serious?"

"Ah, my nephew—he's always like that. Angry at the world. He's big victim. Everybody else is the fault. What can you do? Every family has one."

Their conversation drifted back to more general topics. Steffi and Jim learned in detail how Mrs. Maria Phindrikalis operated the hotel while her husband was away. Jim thought the story was so timeless on Crete it could have been told three thousand years before. They learned a Swedish family and a couple from Athens were also at the hotel. She declared them all friendly. Then she whispered about a "charming" English gentleman who stayed by himself and marched out every morning to tramp over the hills. She shrugged and pointed to her head, suggesting he might be a little daft, but she also insisted he was warm-hearted and "knew everything about history!"

She egged on Steffi and Jim to leak their stories, but they only recounted bare-bones chunks. He was an historian working on a book and she a painter and linguist. They admitted having met in Sofia. Finally, after learning the location of the local grocery store and picking up an unsolicited tip for a good taverna, they broke free of Mrs. Phindrikalis and headed off to their suite of rooms at the opposite end of the hotel.

The other rooms opened onto the front of the hotel, but their room opened onto the side, as did the hotel office. A pergola was fixed to the wall above the door, and grape vines hung from it. A mottled splash of sunlight fell through the pergola and vines onto a table not dissimilar to the one they had just sat at. The sunlight on the table wavered as the breeze fluttered the grape leaves. Set off farther to the side of the pergola was an ancient plane tree with broad spreading branches making it as wide as it was tall.

Steffi immediately walked over to the tree and was dwarfed by its immensity. The misshapen trunk with its peeling bark was more than two meters across. As with everything, it seemed, Steffi had to touch it, gently probing the shaggy bark. As she did, she turned back to Jim. "Isn't it wonderful? Usually, in Bulgarian, we call it *chinar*, but sometimes *platan*. The *chinar*, it comes from ancient Persian."

Watching her framed by the wide trunk provided him immense pleasure. "Do you know the story of the plane tree on Crete?"

"No," she said with a tentative smile.

"Zeus is believed to have taken the form of a white bull, and to have abducted the princess Europa out of the Levant somewhere and brought her to Crete where, under a plane tree not far from here actually, they conceived three boys, all of whom became kings of Crete or what the Minoans might have called Kaftor or Keftie."

"You're serious?"

"Quite. We can visit the tree."

"It can't be living."

"The legend says it is like Buddha's fig tree, supposedly still living. Big things happen under trees."

"Let's call Crete Kaftor. Just between us."

"Why not?" He drew closer to the tree and Steffi. He thought there must be a spring running underground. Plane trees thrive on lots of water. Steffi returned her attention to the tree. Her hand brushed over the gray-brown bark. In places where the bark curled from the trunk, it was tinged in ochre.

"I shall paint it, Jim."

Watching her reminded him of a delegation excursion to Veliko Turnevo, a city in North Central Bulgaria which had been the capital of the second Bulgarian empire. Jim had felt out of sorts. As the tour guide droned on about the fine buildings in the city, Jim tuned out. The weather was overcast, fitting his mood. Jeannette's declining health weighed on him. He dreaded the upcoming heavy lunch hosted by city officials. He dreaded the forced smiles and midday drinking.

At one point the group was cut loose to scatter for an hour. Jim caught a glimpse of Steffi cutting behind a building and entering a path. On an impulse, he followed her down a steep series of inclines to the Yantra River. Just before he reached the river, he detected Steffi ahead of him, squatting along the riverbank with a stick in her hand, poking at something he couldn't see. Though he felt some guilt for his voyeurism, he chose to continue his clandestine surveillance. The way she squatted and played with the stick reminded him of watching his lone sister, Patty, play as a child. His sister had always been a fascinating mystery, just as this woman was. The family vacationed at a Michigan lake one summer, and after swimming his mother changed their wet clothes behind a pine tree near the shore. It was the first time he realized Patty was missing what he had between his legs. He had never thought of her being different before. Just then, Jim heard Steffi singing or humming. The delegation seemed to represent nothing but posturing, and here was this interpreter being what nobody else in the delegation could be—herself. Very quietly he turned around and returned to the city and its cacophony above.

Jim stood next to her now. She took his hand and put it on the plane tree's bark.

"Close your eyes." She moved his hand over the bark.

"Feels wonderful." He opened his eyes, and her face was close. "You smile too much."

"Don't be silly."

They embraced, and their cheeks touched softly together. Jim moved his lips along her cheek until he found her lips, and they kissed. It was a gentle, long kiss. As their tongues began to explore, Steffi's breathing became panting, explosively arousing Jim. Then Steffi suddenly broke away and nestled her head on top of his shoulder. "So light, your kiss," she whispered as her breathing calmed. Her warm exhales along the hair of his collar caused his neck to tingle.

A memory came back to Jim from years before while visiting the Gettysburg battlefield in winter. He spent the night at a B&B, and the next morning took a leisurely jog over the overcast and frozen landscape. Intermittent flakes of snow fell along the empty roads. As his body warmed, he turned onto a straight country lane that disappeared at the horizon, with a wooden fence running parallel to it. Up ahead and close to the fence stood several horses gathered together for warmth. As he came abreast of them, all but one of the horses scattered. A chestnut mare boldly walked up to the fence. Jim stopped and reached out to stroke the white blaze along her nose. She nestled her head next to him, and he wrapped his arm around her strong neck. Her exhales came in great, warm gushes that poured down inside his collar.

"Jim, we promised each other." The promise had removed pressure from Steffi in her efforts to justify the trip to Katarina, who didn't believe Jim was anything but an exploitative rich American with no other agenda than to play with Steffi.

"Right, we did, didn't we? And yes, I endorsed the idea, but a man can have a change of heart."

"Don't play word games."

"*Dann auf Deutsch?*"

"We don't need to do this conversation in German. You're being a little boy now."

He cringed, protesting, "I'm not a little boy." He pointed to his head. "You see these sprinkles of gray hair?" At that second a memory of his sister intruded. His little brother had been struck by a car while riding his bicycle and had broken his arm, wrist, and collarbone. Jim had cried, and his sister screamed, "Quit being a little boy!" Her coldness still shook him.

"Okay," Steffi smiled. "You're a big man." Both laughed.

"Well then, now that that is settled, I suppose I did say—what did I say? That I had a lot of baggage?"

"And that neither of us knew each other well enough."

"And it was all so confusing."

"And then, Jim, you suggested we should mix martinis and have a mature discussion about us before we did something rash."

"But that was mostly imitating old Hollywood movies."

"I know that. But then you said what I consider the main point of the conversation. 'Let's not put the cart before the horse.' And that's still valid. I want the fun of getting to know you without feeling like I'm, I'm, uh, *unter die lupe.*"

"It was a little like being under a microscope in Sofia for both of us, I might add."

Steffi twisted her head so that she looked directly at Jim, "I don't want to revisit Sofia. Let's unpack the car, and then we'll figure out sleeping arrangements."

"Oh, then that's that. I don't think the Minoans had this problem."

"It's that it is all so strange. Suddenly, I have you here. We are alone. I really never truly believed it would happen. At your core you always seemed to be self-sufficient and a loner." Steffi's eyebrows furrowed. "Did I say it the right way in English?"

"The way you say things is definitely part of my attraction to you."

Without probing further, they walked into their rooms which were arranged with a bathroom, a small open kitchen, a sleeping and sitting area and, in a loft above, another sleeping area with storage space. A scent of freshly cut cedar filled the rooms due to a ceiling of tongue-and-groove cedar planks. A double window in the kitchen area looked out onto the plane tree, and another double window over the downstairs bed looked out in the direction of the sea. The spartan furniture was of solid unpainted wood. The walls were painted white and the warped and split wood kitchen cabinets a midnight blue. A vase in the center of the dining table suggested, in its earthen tones and curves, something ancient. From the neck of the vase poked a sprig of flowered, wild thyme. The dark green leaves and stems, and perhaps a half dozen of the delicate four-petal lavender flowers with their long, paler stamen, created a powerful sense of color.

Jim stood behind Steffi and saw her shoulders rise and then fall in a long, relaxed exhale. "I like it," she declared without turning around. "You take the loft."

"Aye-aye, Captain. I'll start unpacking the car."

"And I'll take a walk down to the store to get provisions."

While Steffi was gone, Jim re-parked the car near their room. He separated their kit, dutifully carrying his gear up to the loft. Opening her portable easel, he set it next to the windows. Jim operated on autopilot now, as jet lag made his head ache and the adrenalin of arriving bled away. Steffi returned within a half an hour with two shopping nets filled with mineral water, wine, yogurt, grapes, cheese, bread, olives, coffee, juice, milk, and fig jam. A few beads of perspiration had formed along her hairline.

"Hast du alles selbst geschlept?" (Did you lug everything by yourself?)

"Klar," as she wiped off her forehead. "Let's have a snack. I think I'm hungry. How about you?"

They shared bread, feta, olives, and wine. The amber-colored wine was called Santa Helena and was not from Crete. The food awakened Jim's appetite, and he devoured the bread and fresh, sharp feta. As always, Steffi nibbled. Something other than bread nourished her power. As Jim popped one of the olives that resembled a shriveled grape into his mouth, Steffi's eyes bore into his eyes with the same clinical detachment as the first time they met. "Jim, take a shower and lie down. Sleep till you can't sleep anymore. I'll busy myself unpacking and maybe I'll read outside if the sunlight holds out."

The shower eased the aches and pains, and the slimy feel of the long trip washed down the drain with the soap's lather. With a towel around his waist, while Steffi fussed around downstairs, Jim went up to the loft. He yanked some clean cotton pajamas from one of his duffels, and carelessly threw the towel on the floor. Pulling on his pajamas seemed to take his last ounce of strength. As soon as did, he collapsed on the bed and was asleep within seconds.

CHAPTER FOUR

Steffi tiptoed up the open wooden staircase to the loft. Jim lay sprawled on the bed in his blue pajamas like a chalked outline of a homicide victim. Quietly, she bent down and grabbed the towel he had tossed aside. She held the towel to her face, smelling both soap and Jim, and then she folded it in half and hung it over her arm.

For a moment she stood with closed eyes, finally grasping that this leap had come to pass. For her, coming to Crete hopefully severed the harness that had bound her to her past. Having been under tension from the past for so long, her life now seemed to snap free, propelling her as if from a slingshot into uncharted territory. She liked the sensation, but she suspected changes come with costs. Did this mean Liliana was irrevocably left behind? Only Liliana had truly understood all Steffi's torments, offering affection instead of judgments and recrimination. She had used Liliana; she understood that now. Liliana had been a crutch, and now she must feel abandoned. Were the years of emotional treasure that only a friendship like that earns now be worthless currency? Only at the end did Steffi fathom that love, not friendship, had motivated Liliana. How could Jim ever understand? Steffi prayed that the friendship with Liliana could revalue that currency.

Even before Ludmil, Liliana and Steffi had stood together, marching from Alexander Nevsky Cathedral, protesting corruption and government incompetence. They had challenged the line of riot police, so close they smelled the tobacco on their breath. What good did it all do? The day she left Sofia, the corruption and other crimes remained the same. How furious her mother was when she gave up the scholarship to study engineering in Germany. "Your ticket out!" she had shouted and followed with a stinging slap. Out? Oh yes, she had wanted out. In the end, what a poor hand Ludmil had been to play.

Steffi opened her eyes, and Jim still lay in the same position. Carefully, she retraced her steps back down the stairs, grimacing every time a board creaked. Downstairs, she grabbed a book and a sketchpad and went outdoors. The late sun, even in the shade of the pergola, caused her to squint, but she wanted to study the true colors around her, so she resisted putting on the sunglasses hanging from a loop on her cargo shorts. Shadows had grown long. Already the hills off to the west were fringed in orange as the sun settled lower in the sky. She had an impulse to look at the sea, so she strolled over to the shallow stone wall that bordered the parking area. There she found a bench that offered a panoramic view of the water. She set aside the book and pad and sat down with her feet propped up on the wall. Some high cirrus clouds floated above, fringed in lavender and gold. Two ships rode the horizon. The coming evening turned the sea gray.

Jim had awakened something in her the first time she met him in the park by the old embassy. Was it really almost three years ago? That delegation of Americans had been a jolly lot, and she liked them all. They had treated her in a way no men had ever treated her before, more like a sister. She loved Katarina, but she had always wanted brothers. A couple of them had asked her out, but she had rebuffed them, just what her mother expected of her. She recalled her mother's instructions in Cairo to Katarina. *I was so little. How could I know what she meant?*

Her father, an agronomist, had been assigned to Cairo by Bulgaria's agricultural minister. Allegedly, Todor Shivkov, Bulgaria's strongman, had commanded the ministry to make Egypt's desert bloom. Wasn't Bulgaria the breadbasket for the Soviet Empire? Her daddy's passion was to demonstrate for the Egyptians how to do things the Zionists couldn't. Her daddy proudly showed her canned tomatoes from Bulgaria in the store. He whispered, "We give these to the Egyptians on credit."

She recalled the time the whole family had laughed when Daddy took Katarina and her to the big museum with the mummies. He made them hold his hands tightly. In front of the building stood horse carts for tourists. As they edged along, fearful of the crowds and traffic, one of the horses suddenly dropped its head and wiped its nose on Daddy's shirt, leaving wet snot all over his shoulder. Daddy didn't get mad. Such a peaceful man, content to read his technical books and maybe sip a glass of wine. Daddy had loved her so much. And in the museum, when she couldn't see properly, he lifted her up so she could peer at the exotic objects.

Mommy was serious that evening—she was always so intense. Even though it was mostly directed at her sister, who was five years older, Mommy's stern eyes turned to her, too. Mommy's eyebrows were knitted together, a sign to pay attention.

"It is your responsibility, Katarina." Had she said Katarina? Perhaps she didn't say Katarina. And was it in German or Bulgarian? Alone with the two of them, they most often spoke German. "If you let a man, they will not stop. It's a woman's responsibility. Two brains they have." She wanted to ask Daddy, too, but she didn't. She knew not to interrupt. Mommy would scold her. "You decide. If you let him decide, you will have a bad reputation." Katarina looked scared. But Katarina couldn't have been more than what—twelve? "This is the reality of life we face as women." What had brought that on? Katarina would never say.

Jim was different from the other guys in the group. From the first second she saw him, she knew he wasn't destined to play the brother role. When he wasn't looking, she watched him. "I can be sly about such things," she had told Katarina, who challenged her, unconvinced he hadn't seen her. What made him different? *A little older than the others, I think.* But he didn't belong. That's what it was; he didn't fit. *Just like me.* Not his smile, not his eyes, not the way he carried himself so upright, almost like a soldier. *When he looked at me, I had to turn my eyes away.* "That's a good thing?" Katarina had asked.

His eyes were strong, not scary, just strong—no, penetrating, like he saw inside me. I wanted to hide my face with my hands. She chuckled aloud. She remembered the monkey in the zoo, how he covered his face when she studied him. So, I looked at Jim when he talked to his colleagues, when I knew he couldn't see me while they chatted about dinner. These guys had so much money for things. Which restaurant? Oh my God! Nobody had money to talk like that except maybe the rich *mutri* (thugs).

She heard feet scraping on the gravel behind her. Was it Jim? Did he get up? Steffi turned to look behind her. Not Jim. In an instant she knew who it was—the eccentric old Englishman the woman had talked about, wearing a big floppy bush hat and carrying a long walking stick like a Bulgarian shepherd's staff. He was wiry and short, and under the brim of his hat she saw his ruddy complexion and wire-rimmed glasses. He had apparently come off the hill behind her and was walking with purposeful strides parallel to the shallow wall Steffi sat behind.

He halted a precise seven paces away. Carefully he unhinged his glasses and began wiping them with a large blue bandana. "The sweat clouds them up. Can't see a bloody thing." He jammed the bandana back into his front pocket. "For most of my life I didn't wear glasses. Can't get along without them now." He replaced the glasses and looked at Steffi. "Well, that's better. Hallo! And who might you be?"

She smiled, "I'm Steffi."

"And I answer to Robinson. Harold is my given name. Scottish in origin but most definitely British for generations."

"I am pleased to meet you. You were hiking, Mr. Robinson?"

"That too."

"And what else?"

"Well, I'm searching for something."

"And you haven't found it?"

"Indeed."

"Then I pray you find it."

"Thank you, Steffi. So do I, for it is important to me. You see, it is my past, or more accurately a person from my past, who left long ago and came here."

"And I'm here partly to leave my past behind."

Mr. Robinson chuckled, "Ah, I see. Well, I must admit I'm becoming rather obsessive in this search."

"Don't do that."

Robinson held up his hand. "Wait. Let me guess where you're from." He stroked his chin. "Please say 'The wildflowers on Crete are beautiful this year.'"

She repeated the line.

"Humpff. I should say, nothing Scandinavian about you. You're certainly not Portuguese or Spanish? Or are you?"

"No."

"No, of course not. I didn't think so." He looked up and mumbled half to himself, "Definitely not a Yank or other colonial." He raised a crooked index finger. "Could you humor an old man and say, 'The beach is curved'?"

He cocked his ear. "Ah yes. Let's discard the Romanians and French. And you did say not Portuguese? But you're dark, and so probably not Czech, though I have known many a dark Czech. And no Turk would be caught here." Robinson laughed at his own line. "Silly thought, that." He pulled at his ear. "Don't see many Macedonians and Serbs about. All right, here is my guess, dear lady Steffi. Are you ready?"

"I am."

"You're one of two. But the tone to your voice—and may I say your English is beautiful—has a touch of the Slavic to it. So, if I were to bet, and I am not a wagering man by nature, I would dismiss the Hungarian, not Slavic anyway, and declare you Bulgarian, but of Royal extraction, and the royal bit I borrowed from *My Fair Lady*, but it seems to fit."

"You're right. That's brilliant! Congratulations, Professor Higgins!"

"Oh, how very clever! Touché! Very good, Eliza."

"But really, Mr. Robinson, good guess!"

"Nonsense. Just a matter of deduction, my dear Watson."

"Thank you, Mr. Holmes."

"Ah, touché again." Robinson bowed theatrically. "I take it Steffi is not your family name."

"No, Galabova."

"Ah, Gabrovova."

With that Steffi doubled over in laughter.

Robinson smiled, "Seems I should be on stage. I've never fancied myself a stand-up comic, but then again. . ."

"Mr. Robinson, you see, my name is Galabova. It means dove, a bird. You said Gabrovova. Gabrovo is a town in Bulgaria known for stingy people. There are thousands of Gabrovo jokes. Books of them!"

Robinson chortled, "Oh that is good. I shall put that in my journal tonight." The hills to the west transformed into a deep indigo, and the glow around their edges had changed to fading embers. "Well, I must thank you, Miss *Galabova*, thank you for such a charming interlude at the end of this fine day, but I must be off. I hope we shall see each other again."

"I hope so."

"Gabrovo, a comic city. Good one, that. Good-bye." And off Robinson strode, making a military-style pivot to the entrance of his room halfway down the row of rooms.

Below, the lights in Plakias shone, and above her, a spray of stars sparkled. The hills had become silent blankets of darkness. She could just make out the horizon of sea and sky. The navigation lights of a ship held a course along the coast. As the evening inversion began, a calmness descended and brought with it mysterious fragrances.

Steffi looked down at her hands resting on her thighs. The blue stone on the ring her mother had given her caught some of the last vestiges of light. Her mother slipped the ring on her finger after Steffi had returned from the disaster in France. "Steffi, I've had this ring always with me, but I never wear it. It was your grandmother's, and your grandfather gave it to her for their first wedding anniversary. This ring survived the war with her, even the firestorm of Dresden.

She cherished it even after Grossvatti died. It's a survivor, Steffi. And now I want you to have it because you will survive all this too." It was, she thought, the finest thing her mother had ever said to her.

But who had been the grandfather she never met, who had presented this ring to her grandmother? She wanted to know where he bought it. What others had he looked at? It was singular, she thought. The blue was such a true color, and the stone was cut so nicely but simply. He must have been a sensitive man, a man not prone to overstatements. Was there something other than love he was trying to say with it?

Steffi recalled the time like it was ten minutes ago when Jim had come back to Bulgaria to wrap up his project. It was well after the death of his wife. Wasn't it in Banya? He had asked her about the ring while taking a walk after dinner. Both had drunk a little wine. A wooden bridge crossed a fast-moving stream that rushed from the Rila Mountains. They stopped on the bridge to look at the water. She set her hands on the bridge's wet wooden rail. She felt his presence as she never had before. He wore an aftershave or used a soap, the scent of which caught in the damp air of the bridge. As she inhaled the scent, it was as if she were breathing him in. Standing close to her, still talking about how he had noticed the ring when they first met, he reached over and stroked the ring with his long index finger. It slid over the stone and around the gold setting. It was as if electric current ran from his finger, conducted through the gold, and into her hand until it worked its way into every hidden part of her.

Night had fallen. Abruptly, she stood up, dizzy as her blood pressure adjusted. Gathering up her things, Steffi walked back to the room. After opening the door, she fumbled her way to a table lamp so she wouldn't disturb Jim by turning on the overhead. The indirect light softened the room. She wasn't tired yet. From the small refrigerator, she pulled out a handful of grapes and sat at the aged wooden table. As she popped grapes into her mouth, sensations and images from the past drifted in and out—the scorching heat of Cairo, the mossy woods in Bulgaria, Liliana's mother simmering *Yuntenitsa* with the scent of the tomatoes and other vegetables condensing into a paste. Liliana's mother sang haunting Bulgarian folk songs that at times resembled Celtic music and at others, Turkish. Steffi couldn't recall her mother ever singing songs.

She suddenly had an impulse to write to Jim, so she tore a sheet of paper from her sketchpad and, with one of her sketch pencils, wrote down random thoughts in her circular script.

CHAPTER FIVE

Jim woke suddenly, momentarily disoriented and fearing he had missed his flight. Sunlight reached up into the loft, too bright to be the evening before, but could he have slept the night through? His hand unsuccessfully searched the table next to him for his watch. Sitting up, he called, "Steffi? Steffi, are you down there?" but she didn't answer. He swung his legs out of bed and sat on the edge of the mattress a moment, rubbing his face. "Whew, what a sleep!" he whispered to himself. It was then he caught a glimpse of his metal watchband on a nearby chair. Standing up, he retrieved his Tag Heuer and, rather than searching for his reading glasses, squinted at the watch face.

"Eight!" He'd slept an uninterrupted twelve hours and couldn't recall ever having done that before. As was his habit, Jim made the bed with crisp hospital corners. He slipped on a pair of jeans and a t-shirt, found his still-tied running shoes, and wiggled into them. As he climbed down the stairs, still unsteady from deep sleep, he gripped the banister and scanned the room for Steffi. He called out again, "Steffi?" After a quick stop in the bathroom to brush his teeth and relieve himself, Jim noticed a piece of paper with Steffi's handwriting on the rough-hewn table. Fresh flowers had also been added to the earthen vase.

It was a letter to him, written on a sheet from her sketchpad and apparently written with the soft lead of a sketch pencil.

Dear Jim,

I didn't want the evening to end without writing you. I pray you sleep the night through and wake up rested. You missed a glorious sundown. And you missed the eccentric English gentleman our innkeeper spoke of.

The poem below is from Rainer Maria Rilke. I've been meaning to send it to you. Did you know Rilke was from Prague even though he wrote in German? Your grandpa's hometown, right? I like his poems very much. My mother read us his poems when my sister and I were old enough to understand a little. A volume of his poems was a treasured book of hers. I've translated it into English because I was in the mood. You might disagree with how I did it.

The smudged translation had many scratch-outs and erasures. She played with substitute words in the margin until she settled on her final choice by marking it with a tiny star. Unlike her usual flowing script, some words were jammed between other words in cramped, tight writing.

> *How ought I constrain my soul, so that*
> *It doesn't stir yours? How am I supposed to*
> *Elevate it above you and on to other objects?*
> *Ah, I would like to quarter it in some*
> *Lost place, dark, still, and unknown, so that*
> *Whenever your inner depth vibrates,*
> *It no longer resonates in me.*
> *Yet everything, that touches us, you and me,*
> *Lays hold of us together like a bow*
> *Which draws over two strings in a single voice*

For several minutes Jim stood over the translated poem. Would all the mornings with her be so rich? Jim was instantly suspicious of his exhilaration and sought to dampen his emotion, not wanting to believe in or hope for such an outcome. In childhood he had been wrapped tight by unspoken and spoken expectations—do well in school, keep out of trouble, then later serve the country, care for a dying wife. Though he scrambled to fulfill it all, the results disappointed. Nothing ever led to a universe he could believe in or wanted to belong to. Why would it be different with Steffi?

He opened the door and in the white morning light saw Steffi under the plane tree, sketching. Her hair was pulled back and held by a turquoise clip he recognized as the one he'd sent her from Arizona. It didn't match the ring from her grandfather, which had been his intent. All the saccharine tales of love somehow came alive, because he literally felt his heart skip a beat and the worrisome thoughts of before evaporate into the light.

Steffi must have heard him, because she turned around and smiled, but it was more than a smile; it was an expression of joy. Wasn't that what really drew him to her? Her joy. Isn't that what he wanted from her —to drink from where she drank, to know joy instead of doubt?

Steffi turned back to her sketch. "I'll be finished in a moment. We'll have coffee."

The coffee was strong but cut with rich boiled milk. They sat at the outside table and argued about how the taste of fig jam is hard to describe. "It's the seeds," he said as he bit into bread spread with fig jam.

"No, that's not a taste. It tastes beige," she said.

"Beige?"

Her laughter took flight into the hills behind them. "Yes, colors have taste."

"Dear, where's the chartreuse? I wanted to sprinkle some on my bread." He sipped his coffee. "Hints of magenta, don't you think?"

Giggling, "Stop it."

"But you're not serious?"

"But I am. I can taste colors. On my tongue," tapping the tip of her tongue with her index finger.

"Okay then," he folded his arms across his chest, "So how does beige taste?"

She waved her fingers over her mouth, "Flat, a little like cold well water."

Just then the Englishman crossed in front of them, decked out in field clothes, stout boots, rucksack, and a canteen hanging from a web belt. He apparently caught a glimpse of them in his peripheral vision and stopped his forceful strides just long enough to wave and say, "Good morning one and all."

Steffi waved back. "Good morning, Mr. Robinson. Still searching?"

"Ha! Yes, indeed. Still searching after all these years. And good morning to you too, Miss Steffi. Hello to you, lad. Off I go. Work to be done. So many questions, so few answers." Off he strode to what must have been a trailhead somewhere out of sight, hidden behind the plane tree limbs.

Jim stood and picked up the bread and metal espresso coffee pot from the table. "This 'lad' is going inside to change into his short trousers."

"Can I come too, young man?"

"Let's go to the beach. By the way, what was that about still searching?"

"Private joke."

"Flirting with older men?"

"You should know."

They packed a duffle with essentials and drove the kilometer and a half to Plakias beach. The day was warm, but when they dipped their feet in the cold water they agreed there would be no swimming today. A scattering of people shared the beach with them. Steady shallow waves lapped at the sand. An occasional wave reached far enough to wash over their feet with foam. "Whoa, bracing! Reminds me of dipping my feet in Lake Superior in the U.P. of Michigan."

Steffi cupped her hand over her brow and searched over the waves. "What do you think, Jim? Are the waves taking things away or bringing things back?"

"Well, other than a ball I found the next day after I threw it out into Lake Michigan, I haven't given it much thought."

"It seems to me the waves keep bringing what's been before back. Even the sound comes at you, not away from you."

Without saying anything else about the waves, they turned and walked east along the beach and away from town. "May I take your arm?"

"I was hoping you would." Jim instinctively looked down, searching the sand for shells. Steffi's arm slipped under his right shoulder and squeezed the top of his arm tight. In his mind he heard Billie Holiday again.

"For a young man, you have a pretty big muscle there," squeezing again. She pronounced muscle like Bulgarian, *mooskul.* The stretch of beach came to an end, so they climbed a narrow and sandy trail around some rocks. In a protected spot, a thick-spined weed grew with prickly leaves and a blossom on its crown. A bee hovered near the purple bloom. Steffi pulled his arm to stop and look. "In the name of the bee, and of the butterfly, and of the breeze—Amen!"

"Huh?"

"From your Emily Dickinson."

After the benediction they walked on in the same silence. The steeper grade forced deep breaths from them. Steffi stopped twice to run her hands over the coarse windswept stone outcroppings. The sea hissed as the waves broke and spewed up among the rocks below. Finally, the narrow trail opened onto another stretch of curved beach, smaller than Plakias.

Jim peered out over the horizon of the Libyan Sea, and his historian's mind saw Ancient Cyrenaica and Carthage. He saw Phoenician sailing ships plying their trade to the Adriatic, Tyrrhenian Sea, and beyond, carrying casks of oil, salted fish, pottery, and grain. He imagined the burned-out German tanks lying like tombs near Tobruk. And he knew his work would begin not far from here, at the Prevali Monastery where British and Commonwealth soldiers hid waiting to be extracted after the Germans crushed their defense. On moonless nights, the submarines crept close to shore, perhaps near where they stood now. Maybe Steffi was right—the same waves rolled into the beach then. Hearts must have rattled in the chests of those men as they made their escape, but then there were those intrepid few who stayed or came ashore to fight as partisans.

Steffi had a different vision as she scanned the horizon. Somewhere off to her left beyond the water was Alexandria, Egypt. She did not reflect on historical things: ruins hidden beneath the bay's water, or the loss of Alexander's library when the Muslims sacked the city. Nor did she give a thought to the lighthouse, the Great Pharos of Alexandria, one of the wonders of the ancient world that had stood more than a millennium until an earthquake broke its back. Instead, she recalled sitting outside an Alexandrian restaurant, close to the sea, with the same waves lapping at that shore. She was with her mother, father, and sister, eating fish grilled on charcoal braziers. Daddy drank beer from a bottle with a big red star on it, and when she asked if it was the Soviet star, he laughed. "No, sweetheart, it's just a picture they use for its brand."

Her mother's mood had been sour all day. Daddy had a smile that was at once sad and happy. "So what, we'll enjoy this meal! Tomorrow will take care of itself." Take care of what? Steffi had wondered.

"So tomorrow they stab you in the back!"

"The children, my dearest."

"They send you home, but they keep that rude fool Petrov?"

"I can't change what can't be changed."

"But Petrov isn't half the agronomist you are. *Verdammt mal! Diese Nomenklatura!*"

"Dear!" Daddy's face was severe, and Mommy stood up and left her plate with the good fish uneaten. Daddy said to keep eating, but who wanted to eat?

When they arrived back in Sofia they moved to a new apartment. Mommy seemed embarrassed by it, and Daddy was quiet. When Steffi asked Katarina what was going on, Katarina told her to shut up because she was too young to understand. Later they moved to a provincial town. Daddy said it was good to be in the country, and Mommy complained about "no culture." She kept talking about burdens and yokes. "You Bulgarians, always complaining about your yokes. The Ottoman yoke, the Fascist yoke, Zhivkov's yoke. You put it on all by yourselves, and then you help them adjust the harness!"

Daddy replied calmly, but his eyes were on fire, "A German is going to lecture me about yokes?"

Later he came to Steffi's room to say goodnight. He hugged her, told her how precious she was to him, and how he was a happy man because she lived.

It wasn't until the regime fell that they moved back to Sofia, and Steffi was old enough to comprehend the cost of what being out of favor had meant to the family. Daddy was near the end of his working life, but they wanted him back at the ministry and rewarded him with a respectable position. They did what they could to ameliorate the disgrace he had endured. But they couldn't take away the toll it had taken on his constitution. After all, no one had been more loyal. He had been a technocrat's technocrat. No one had done so much for the agricultural sector. But cold winters, bad health care, and confused politics followed, and Daddy withered. One day, the light in him simply winked out.

Eventually Mommy, reluctantly at first, and then in a torrent of emotion, told the story of his fall. "It was all my fault, Steffi," she had sobbed. "I ruined your father."

"*Nein!*"

"*Aber ya. Ich hab' ihn zerstoert.*"

"But how, Mommy? You took good care of him."

"I didn't want to bother you. First you were too young, but then so many problems with you and Ludmil. You had enough suffering. So why should I give you more?"

Finally, when Steffi held her to her bosom like a mother with child, Mommy, fighting for breaths between sobs, cried, "When I was a student so many years ago in Dresden, I wrote these poems critical of Ulbrecht, Honnecker, Ceaucescu, Zhivkov, Brezhnev, all of the clowns. They weren't meant to be published. I wrote them to show my friends how independent was my mind, a philosopher on the artistic vanguard! Somehow the drafts survived, typed copies spreading one copy at a time. A glacier that couldn't be stopped. And then they came to the attention of the authorities. They are very clever, these thugs. They've never read a book, but they suddenly become great literary critics. They took it out on Daddy. I suppose they were trying to show what a fool he was for marrying someone like me, an unreliable socialist."

"But they permitted the marriage. You told me so."

"They didn't know then. Some lazy bureaucrat missed the black spots on my socialist soul. At first, yes, fraternal socialist intermingling—the world one happy socialist family. But down deep they didn't like the German part. Couldn't get used to it. Blame the Germans for the war and for fascism. So proud of the Jews the Bulgarians saved, but they were in bed with the Nazis. They were lapping dogs for Ribbentrop. It's convenient to rewrite history, Steffi. In Serbia, Bulgarian soldiers loaded the trains to the death camps. They did plenty of the dirty work."

"It was the war. What choice?"

"You can't sit on the fence with evil, my dear. Ribbentrop had the Bulgarian King poisoned, you know. That's the price one pays when you try to have it both ways."

"And so for your poems and German birth, they destroyed Daddy?"

"Humans adapt to the circumstances they find themselves in. What was yesterday's fashion looks out of style this year. New rules. New morality. New rationalizations. New judgments."

"But the bombings in Dresden, the firestorm from the British bombs. The family was a victim of war, not a prosecutor of it."

"I have spared you, Steffi."

"Spared me what?"

"Grossvatti didn't die in the firestorm. Only Grossmutti. I know I've told you your grandparents died together. Another lie your mother has told. If there's a God, He will never forgive me. Better to simply have my rational universe without Him. I was an intellectual, so I decided to construct my own reality."

"Mommy, stop! There's nothing God won't forgive!" Tears welled as she saw the suffering of her mother.

"You see, Grossvatti died fighting for the Nazis. He died in the war. He was decorated for his fighting, but he was a good man. I swear. I know from your grandmother."

"But where, Mommy, where are his remains?"

"No one knows. Somewhere, nowhere. North Africa, maybe Russia. I never pursued finding out."

"Why not?"

"For what purpose? It wasn't fashionable to hunt for dead Nazis."

"Mommy!"

Mommy sighed, "It was a bridge too far—grandfather's memory was not to be rehabilitated. Like daughter like father—must be genetic. Seems he was quite a writer himself. As a German officer he allegedly wrote, I came to discover, the most painful diatribe about the superiority of National Socialism and what he called the syphilitic brain of Communist thought. His scorn for the people of the Balkans, in which he goes into great detail in his writing, was the *coup de grace*. All of this comes out at the time my poetry is revealed publicly. They called me some name, fascist or revisionist, irredentist, or revanchist. I don't even remember anymore. Branded is the point."

Steffi's head reeled; it all seemed fantastical. "But Mommy, how do you know he wrote this? Why didn't you make them prove it?"

"They could always prove what they wanted. Do whatever. Rewrite history. They made the truth they wanted, and these ignoramuses were proud of it. It was nothing for them to provide witnesses, documents, whatever they needed. They tell untruths until they become the truths. You were too young to see how these bastards operated. And Daddy and you girls paid a price—our family's happiness for my childishness."

"We paid no price. My childhood had its sadness, but it was happy too, like any normal life. I paid no special cost."

Her mother buried her face in her hands and shook her head, "No," her voice tentative and distorted behind her hands. "That's not all."

"What do you mean?"

A sob triggered a gasp, "I was so angry. Your father told me to leave it alone, but I wouldn't listen. I wrote to the great man himself—to Zhivkov." Her head rose, and her eyelids drooped over her reddened eyes. "I told him how unfair your father was treated. I told him how unjust his system, that his brand of socialism was a joke and travesty. A Potemkin village, I declared it."

"Brava, Mommy."

"Don't you see? That, they couldn't ignore."

"So you told the truth. I still don't see that Katarina and I suffered."

"Why do you think Katarina was denied university admission?"

Katarina's and Mommy's rage for her throwing away her scholarship to Heidelberg in order to marry Ludmil suddenly became painfully clear. "It can't be so!"

"You were young. You couldn't see what was going on. Now you wallow over your losses because of Ludmil."

"Is that what I've been doing, wallowing?"

Speechless for a moment, then, "What young man with a bright future wanted to be associated with this family? It wasn't until the wall came down that you lifted your head up from your studies long enough to be interested in a man, or you would have discovered the same. I provoked them, and when challenged, I didn't keep my mouth shut. I insulted them more."

"But now, surely, we can petition documents, find out the truth. Clear Grossvatti's name. I'll go to the authorities myself."

"What's the point? I thought maybe in Dresden there were letters or documents that could shed some light on all this, but with the firestorm everything was turned to ash, especially the truth, everything except the ring you have."

Steffi thought, *Poor Daddy and Grossvatti, a Nazi! Impossible.* She treasured a photo of him, and she couldn't reconcile the picture's kind face with her mother's story. None of her grandparents lived, and this single picture had always been a source of daydreams in which he came alive for her. She fantasized a loving voice, presents to her as a little girl, walks in nature where he explained things. She became determined to know the real man. Even if she couldn't actually speak with him, she wanted to understand him. She promised herself she would find the truth about him and all he had written, certain the communist accusations were fabricated trash. She tried searching records, but everything in Bulgaria was in chaos with records missing or ruined. Every request required a bribe. Finally, the search became almost as painful as the allegations. At some point Steffi decided to get on with life.

Jim and Steffi stopped and sat on a driftwood log, staring absently at the horizon of the wine-dark sea. Jim dug his feet into the taupe-colored sand. It was cool enough that Steffi welcomed Jim's arm around her nestling next to his chest. She trembled from the chill and the memory.

Closing her eyes, she asked, "What are your parents like?"

"My parents? Whatever made you ask that?"

"I don't know. It just came to me. There hasn't really been time to talk about them. They're alive, right?"

"Oh yes."

"And your grandparents?"

"On my mother's side, both died before I was born. On Dad's side, both died peacefully in nursing homes, if you can call anything about nursing homes peaceful. They were reasonably well taken care of, though. Grandma never had a shortage of chocolate, and Grandpa got his fix of Jack Daniels. But I remember the smell of that place. It was the institutional cooking smell more than anything."

"So where are your parents now?"

"In a smaller house than the one I grew up in, but not more than two miles from it. Close to my sister. She has the burden of taking care of them, mostly. She stayed around and raised a family back in Michigan. I'm the sibling who wandered off. I help when I can, but... I should do more than send checks." Jim pursed his lips, gathering his thoughts. "But my guess is they're pretty happy. No major health problems. Kind of typical of couples back there. Dad watches football on TV. Mom putters in the garden. They're content to be where they are. Dad was an engineer for GM, designed transmissions, I think. He was training to be a radioman on a bomber when the war ended, and went to Michigan State on the GI Bill. He has a good pension, health insurance. Last of a breed in America, I guess." He paused again, scooping sand with his toes. "They're snowbirds."

"Snowbirds?"

Jim laughed. "Yeah, folks who leave cold parts of the country for warm parts in the winter. After New Year's Day they pack up and go to Florida. Dad buys a new Chevy every three years. I guess he still gets a discount from GM. They have a place in Sarasota. Then in April or so, they come back. Don't know how much longer they can keep it up. My sister Patty says she worries about Dad behind the wheel. They're in their eighties."

"It seems so… different, like life on a different planet. But nice in a way." Steffi's voice was dreamy.

"It seems different to me too. Products of Pax America. Not that there weren't problems. Soviets testing hydrogen bombs, strikes at GM, the Berlin crisis, Castro, Viet Nam, racial violence, women in second place. But their life was apart from all that. In a bubble. They weren't about to poke a hole in it. Better to just float along. Nice pot roast in the oven. Eighteen holes of golf every other Saturday in the summer. I think it's what my sister wanted too, but you can't find it anymore. She and her husband are on a treadmill—two jobs, two kids, bills up their asses, no pension plan—praying somebody doesn't get laid off. I think maybe my dad helps them out financially, probably recycles my checks. But that's okay; my sister deserves it. I'm not there to help with Dad and Mom much. It's only fair. My sister's proud, and she won't take money from me."

"Who are we to judge? Your parents were born in that time and place. They adapted to what they were given. They made the most of it with the rules they had to play by," Steffi said, thinking of her family as she said it.

"Easily said, but I don't think that gets you off the hook."

He felt Steffi stiffen. "Really? I think we get swept along."

"Well, they certainly didn't rock the boat or cut a new trail, shock anybody with their artistic statements, commit political crimes, insult Stalin, or get accused a being a kulak." Every comment felt like a saber slash to her, cutting close to the bone. Jim brushed aside some of Steffi's hair that had blown in his face. He bent forward and kissed the top of her head. "But I guess you can only play the hand you're given. I was free of want growing up, plenty of food and heat. My father was distant, but he wasn't unkind. My mother made the best chocolate chip cookies. I don't know what she stood for. Looking back, I have to admit, they seemed afraid of Black people and change. It wasn't a storybook life, but I'm grateful for most of it.

I've always told them I love them, but as I get older, I wonder if it's really love. Seemed too superficial to be called love."

"Love, well—God's love? Love of a brother? A calling? One size doesn't fit all. It's what your heart tells you is true, dear."

"Did you call me 'dear'?"

"Yes. Was it wrong to?"

"No. Caught me off guard. Kind of tingled." For two years all they had shared were Skype calls, letters, and emails. Words like "dear," spoken with the breath of the speaker resting on your shoulder, supercharged the word.

"Are you finding any truth now?" She set her hand on his thigh, letting it move up his leg until her hand was half buried in the warmth beneath the hem of his hiking shorts.

"Oh yes. Some basic truths." He turned to her with his eyes closed, letting his lips find hers. As he turned, her hand unavoidably moved farther up his thigh until the tips of her fingers touched where he swelled within his underwear. Her kiss back, the sweetness of her mouth, the sound of waves, an ocean bird calling, his hardness, a breeze as delicate as her lips, her other hand exploring the hair on the back of his neck—it was a moment that can convince you that the world can be shaped any way you desire. Then, in a puff, the moment evaporated. A family ran down the beach, kicking a soccer ball among them, shrieking in unintelligible Greek. When the ball bounced off Jim's legs, all they could do was laugh.

They stood up and started walking back. Jim waved to the family to let them know they hadn't bothered them, even though they had. The man stopped and smiled, waving back, and bowing slightly. Steffi teased about their moment before, "Did I show you enough truth back there to put all the pieces together, Herodotus?"

"Wow, I'm honored, referring to me as the father of modern history. About what? My family? My book? About Crete?"

"A unified theory of it all," Steffi said in a teasing voice.

"Do I have enough of the pieces? I have a few grains of sand." Jim pointed over his shoulder with his thumb. "Steffi, just down this coast, I don't know, five kilometers? There is the Minoan port of Phaestos, more than 3,000 years old. Homer mentions Phaestos in the Iliad, for God's sake. I don't have a clue what Minoans were all about. Your Mr. Robinson was right. So many questions, so few answers. Nikos Kazantzakis died on Crete. They call him the hero of Modern Greek literature. Before he died he supposedly said, 'I fear nothing; I hope for nothing; I am free.' You've got to have a lot of pieces together to say that. I'm not there."

"I don't think you get how much truth I gave you with that kiss."

Jim glanced at Steffi. "Really?"

She frowned and changed the subject. "Let's stop in town and get something cool to drink, and then go back to the hotel and look at the sea from the bench outside and not say anything." Her accent changed "thing" to "ting."

CHAPTER SIX

Time passed. It took its twists and turns as it always does, through tunnels that often turned out to be labyrinths with the entrances and exits interchangeable. The difference was this time they traveled together. Their time on Crete was just as all time on Crete was. It took on a rhythm: coffee under the plane tree, sketching, writing, consulting maps. Their time together was like and not like the fantasies they had about the trip beforehand. It was in some ways better and occasionally worse. Over time, measured in days, secretly and in declarations to each other, they marveled over discoveries they made about the island and about each other. Each discovery chiseled away barnacles that exposed secrets they at times wished had remained hidden.

Faced with a choice, they chose as every generation for four thousand years on Crete had before them—warmth over cold, a full belly over an empty one, succor over rejection. Happiness drowns out demons. If only for a while, it intoxicates so that even the poison of life can be ignored. Happiness creates the illusion of elevating life from mortal to immortal.

Sometimes their conversations maundered over trivia. For an entire afternoon, all Steffi talked about was Gerhard Richter, the German painter who, like Steffi's mother, came from Dresden. Richter had apparently been a brief acquaintance of her mother's back in the DDR. Steffi praised his work one minute and declared it "crap" the next, proclaiming the millions his paintings fetched "utterly insane." They spoke of their motivations, his to discover and hers to interpret. They risked sharing dark parts with each other, to test whether their revelations would eviscerate or soothe. Steffi waited and agonized about the time when she would finally have to reveal everything.

On the seventh night Jim slept fitfully. Every time he woke, he was convinced he had slept hours while his watch proved it had been barely thirty minutes. At one point, he awoke startled from a dream about an electrical storm with driving rain, lightning, and thunder. As he opened his eyes, he was surprised to see the dark room lit by blue flashes of light, but he heard no thunder. Curious, he pulled away the thin summer blanket and sheet and padded over to the window. Seeing nothing distinct through the glass, he cranked open the casement and stuck out his head. The flashes came again, like flashes of artillery, he thought. They seemed to come from the south, over the sea's horizon, off the edge of the earth. Must be heat lightning or a storm a long, long way off, he thought as he checked his watch that showed 3:07 am. Completely awake, he had no desire to turn on a light to read. Instead, he sat on the chair in the loft blanketed by the darkness and staring off into the uncertain shadows and shapes that were sporadically illuminated by lightning.

Typical of him in times of sleeplessness, he relived moments of anxiety or anguish that skipped randomly over his life. He was a boy again, frightened to be in the doctor's office, the smell of the place as clear as if it had been an hour before. He remembered the nurse's kind smile as she let him pick a green sucker from a box after an inoculation. Then the memories shot ahead to his first love, Rebecca— whom he loved so much but simply stopped calling one day because of a quarrel the details of which were lost. The porter manning the desk of his officers' quarters begged him to call her back, saying she was hysterical, but he didn't. For years he never looked back nor felt remorse. And now, in the dark, he cringed with guilt.

He stood up hoping to cut off other memories from springing to life. In that moment he believed the antidote to wallowing in the past was to see Steffi. The contradiction of his life didn't escape him. He heard himself declaring to Jeannette, "I'm an historian with a mission to uncover the past." And now he wanted to run from his own history. Why couldn't he believe his old staff sergeant? "You can't do anything about yesterday today. You can't do anything about tomorrow today. You can only do something about today, today." History can't be escaped; yet some of it can't be faced in the light, so we do what dear Professor Campbell lectured. "We're all revisionists. We all rewrite and revise our histories every day, or we could never face tomorrow."

He carefully descended the wooden staircase, neither wanting to trip nor disturb Steffi. The occasional lightning flashes acted like a strobe. He lifted one of the chairs from around the table and set it quietly next to her bed. As stealthily as possible he sat down, his elbows on his knees and his chin resting in his hands. Under a coarse wool blanket, and in the eerie darkness broken only by lightning flashes, Steffi appeared spectral. The darkness smoothed the contours of her face so that it took on the quality of women painted by Botticelli, diaphanous, pale, and otherworldly. Her face floated on the white pillowcase. Jim wondered if his hand would pass through it if he touched her cheek.

Still, he knew from her electric kisses that more than a spirit lay there. He recalled one of his last times with her in Sofia. They had sat at a café table on the mezzanine of the remodeled Tzum. They'd sipped Amaretto and cappuccinos and carried on an animated conversation about the importance of doing something that reached beyond themselves. They argued back and forth. Emotions raged. Intense tears clouded their eyes. Then Steffi shot up out of her wicker chair, her eyes like obsidian. "My God, James, when you get like that I'd like to ravage you!"

The unexpected had dumbfounded him. Her persona had seemed demure and most of their conversations had been buttoned down and prim. Work had forced them to most often use emotionless diplomatic blabber. Jeannette's condition at the time had smothered the fire of life in him; but in that moment, Steffi had reignited something molten.

Another burst of lightning caused her eyes to wink open. She saw Jim sitting over her. "Hi."

"Did I scare you?" He moved his hands to his knees.

"No, but what are you doing?"

"In other words, weird, right? I couldn't sleep."

"I'm sorry." She pulled her arm from under the blanket and placed her hand on top of his. Her long slender fingers and soft palm radiated warmth from being under the blanket and close to her body. He detected the metal of her ring. She pushed herself up so that she rested her back against the bed's headboard. "What time is it?"

"After three."

"I'm a little thirsty. Would you get me some juice?"

"My pleasure." He found his way to the small refrigerator, and when he opened it, the light intruded the dark. *"Aprikosen Nektar oder Orangensaft?"*

"Aprikosen bitte."

He poured the apricot juice from the liter canister into a small glass and decided to pour one for himself.

She took the glass and sipped the tiniest amount. Then she tilted it again and sipped another imperceptible quantity. He thought to himself, people in America don't drink juice like that. They gulp it. It isn't precious enough or expensive enough to sip. Steffi savored it like a fine wine. "Mmm good, Jim. Cold and tasty." They clinked glasses and she drank a celebratory slug, but he doubted if it had been even an ounce.

She looked at him with a sidelong glance. The whites of her round, open eyes coupled to his in the dark. All women seemed pretty in the dark, Jim thought, but Steffi especially so. "What are you smiling at?"

Their hands found each other again and entwined. Jim shrugged and answered in a desultory tone. "Don't exactly know. Probably lots of things, I suppose."

"Give me one."

"Well, the plan worked out. We talked about it for nine months, the gestation time of a baby for God's sake. We're here."

"And are you happy about that?" She studied her glass and drank some more. He finished his juice and placed the empty glass on the floor. Another lightning flash followed.

"Uh huh. Yes. I'm happy about that." Her thumb caressed the knuckle of his thumb, slowly rubbing in circles. It was so deeply pleasurable that his chin involuntarily fell to his chest.

"At first, there were such long gaps between hearing from you. I thought you were walking out of my life without giving me a proper ending."

"I've done that before." Jim remembered Rebecca. "I was dreadful."

"Love 'em and leave 'em, huh? But that wasn't part of your plan with me?" He could see the faint ironic smile on her lips.

"No. I was stressed out about you judging me harshly for pursuing you so soon after my wife died. Like maybe you would find it—I don't know—crass? So I guess I did hold back."

"Almost a year." The tease was back in her voice.

"But not anymore. You don't feel me holding back now, do you, Steffi?"

"We'll see how this conversation goes." Her wide-open eyes blinked at him.

Jim raised his head from his chest and looked at Steffi. "How about you? Has anybody done that to you? Walked out on you?"

For a moment she stopped rubbing his thumb. "Of course with Ludmil, I technically walked out, but he had walked out emotionally long before. But there were a couple of boys. They seemed like nice chaps. They didn't exactly walk out on me, but they left me hanging, like one in Italy, but..." She couldn't finish. She remembered her mother's angry face when she poured out the pain, and she still heard her mother calling her a whore. She thanked God it was dark in the room and prayed the darkness hid her pain. "Would you lie next to me?"

"That's dangerous."

"Why?"

"I thought we wanted to know each other better before…"

"That's why I'm asking you to be next to me. Is it better if I say, will you sit next to me?"

Jim smiled and answered in a soft voice, almost a whisper, "Yes. I'll sit next to you."

"Here." She handed him her glass, and he set it next to his. So he could get in the bed, she slid over and raised the blanket, and he entered her bed's warmth. With his back against the bedstead, she cuddled up under his right arm much the way they had been on the beach. How small she felt in his arms. From a distance, she didn't look petite, but she was smaller than she seemed to the eye. Jim carefully pulled her long dark hair free in his right hand and played with it, combing his fingers through it. It seemed they stayed that way for a long time, not talking, but then again maybe it was only five minutes. There was a chill in the room that made him think dawn was not far off.

He pulled the hair away from the right side of her neck. In the faint light, he detected her pulse which left him longing to be one with it. Perhaps in response to that unspoken longing, Steffi draped her right arm over his torso, and with the tips of her fingers, stroked her hand along his ribs and then over his flat stomach. Slowly, she turned her head so that it faced his chest. Her warm moist breath penetrated his cotton t-shirt. She found a nipple and bit lightly. With her hair pulled back and her right ear exposed, he kissed her ear and then his tongue explored it. Finally, he blew into her ear ever so slightly. "Oooh," she moaned. Her breaths sharpened. "That's not fair."

She pulled at his t-shirt. He raised his arms while she yanked it over his head and tossed it on the floor. Steffi wore cotton men's pajamas. Slowly from top to bottom, Jim undid the buttons. With each button, Steffi's breathing intensified. He lowered his head and let his tongue dance over her firm breasts. In response, her body stiffened and back arched.

Between breaths, "James?"

"Mmm?"

"Take these off." She tugged at his pajamas. With some difficulty, he raised the bottom half of his body in order to free them of his erection and pushed them under the covers to the foot of the bed. When he settled back down, Steffi's hand explored him as if she were blind and saw by touch.

"Steffi, I guess you are getting to know me."

"So, this is you," she said in a husky voice. "I've been wondering. I didn't expect it to be so silky."

The pleasure was so intense all Jim could do was lie unmoving, not really listening. She held him in her hand and stroked the tip of it much in the way she had done with his knuckle. Finally, now driven frantically to be inside her, Jim yanked her pajama bottoms over the curve of her hips and freed them from her legs. The scent of her aroused him more. He reached between her legs. The inside of her thighs was moist. He pressed his hand against her, and she pressed back, moving rhythmically against him. His middle finger slid inside. Then he found the point of pleasure and gently caressed, and Steffi moaned.

For a few moments, they embraced, entwined as models for a Rodin sculpture, their embrace charged with unity and intimacy. They rolled together so that he was on top of her. Jim kicked the blanket free. Her legs spread wide, waiting to accept him. He glimpsed her face; her eyes were partially closed in narrow slits, her mouth full and open. He was nearly brought to tears by her beauty. She opened her eyes fully then. His deep, intense eyes, that had frightened her the first time they met, now seemed for her alone, sexual, and full of appetite. How she wanted that from a man.

Gingerly, not wanting to hurt, he pressed against her. She reached underneath and touched him with a couple of her fingers, guiding him to her. He raised his head up to look in her eyes. For several seconds they stayed that way, gazing at each other, as if they recognized that no other moment could equal this one.

Slowly, they moved together. With each stroke, her hands tightened against his back. She felt his warm temple next to her, and she smelled the rusty scent of his skin that now belonged to her. "Jim." She grabbed his small, muscular buttocks and pushed him in deeper. At some point they rolled over, and Steffi was on top. He was deep inside, and she leaned forward, pressing her clitoris against him. She began to slide back and forth. In each hand he cupped her breasts and caressed them. She screamed in pulsating pleasure as she came and collapsed against his chest.

Jim rolled her back over, ready to come himself. He shoved deeply inside and then almost out, and then once more, and he came in a deep orgasm that sparkled and surged into the far reaches of him. For several minutes they lay together spent. Their deep breaths returned to normal. He now lay on her right side. Barely touching each other's lips, they kissed.

"*Mir ist warm*," she said as their lips parted.

He smiled and stroked her damp forehead. "I'll open the window wider." He turned to his right and sat up enough to grip the crank of the double casement window directly above the bed. As he cranked it open, the cool pre-dawn air rushed into the room. Jim peeked outside. Already the sky overhead showed a hint of gray.

"Oh, the air feels lovely." She reached down and grabbed the crumpled sheet at the end of the bed and covered them with it. Cradling each other, they both instantly fell into a deep, dreamless sleep.

CHAPTER SEVEN

They awoke simultaneously. "Bright," Steffi said to no one in particular. Naked, Steffi climbed over and then straddled Jim in order to look outside. "What a nice day." One of Steffi's breasts was dangling over his face. He tweaked it with his index finger. "Hey," she jumped back to her side of the bed and covered her chest with her arms. "I'm being attacked."

"They all say that." He buried his face in her neck and blew raspberries.

"Ahhh. Don't, Jim," she giggled. "I'll scream."

"Whatever will the neighbors think? What if Mr. Robinson hears?"

"He'll come to protect my virtue."

"Okay, I won't do it anymore." He paused a moment, "Maybe just one more time," and he pressed his lips to her neck.

Her body stiffened, and she giggled louder. "Act your age! You probably have eraser fights with all the other geek professors."

Jim sat astride her. "Where did you learn those terms?"

Steffi was flat on her back, looking up at Jim. "Movies. You know they have movies in Bulgaria, and Internet, just like all the first world countries."

"You're a smart aleck, you know that?"

She ignored him. "So, what's on for today? I'm bored."

"You are a smart aleck." Thinking of her fear of flying, "I thought we would go flying."

"I thought that was what we were doing."

"Haha. Come on. I'll rent a little plane."

"Oh, a joke. So funny. I'm not going up in any planes for a while, boob."

"I told you, not boob, bub. A boob is this thing," touching her breast. "Of course sometimes we call total morons boobs, like this guy I used to work with, McAllister."

"Be serious now *Herr Doktor*, Jim." She giggled again, "What's up, Doc?"

"I'm supposed to be serious, and you're acting like the Bulgarian Bugs Bunny."

"Shall we go to that monastery?"

"Prevali? Yes, let's do that. I do really need to get there. It definitely is a part of the book."

"Jim? Do you remember the postcard I sent you from Rila Monastery?"

"Of course, I remember the card, and how could I ever forget Rila? I remember walking along the empty rows of the monks' cells, very haunting. I remember the stones, the gate, the smell of the paraffin candles, the incredible ceiling of the church."

"Did you cry?"

Jim took a deep breath and exhaled slowly. "I guess I did. I felt something there that I'd never felt in a church. You have to understand, the Eastern Church is very alien to me. At first, I thought the strangeness accounted for it. It was palpable. Don't know what word to use, holy, maybe."

"I feel that when I'm there, too. Like the spirit of God is right there. It feels forever."

"That's an interesting way to put it. I haven't thought about Rila lately." For a moment, Jim stared off into nowhere. He recalled the dark quiet of the church; the only sounds were murmuring whispers and shuffling feet. The olfactory memory of the pungent incense reawakened. "It was as if some mystical blanket covered me, and tears did come."

* * *

They took a leisurely and roundabout drive to Prevali, pausing in the mountain village of Spili because, according to Jim, the Germans were "quite active here during the occupation." Jim jammed the Suzuki into a space between a pair of Spili's buildings. Before stopping for coffee, they climbed parts of Mount Vorizi, that sits on the edge of the village. The grade was lung-sucking, but the higher they climbed, the more the mountain beckoned. Scents of rosemary, sage, and oregano arose everywhere. A lizard dashed out in front of them, and Steffi yelped. She frenetically snapped photos of borage and malva in bloom, and she demanded Jim hold the star-shaped blue borage flowers in his hand while she shot picture after picture. Then she created another frame with Jim holding a hairy malva stem between his fingers. "Your hand and the flowers are so beautiful. I must paint them."

At one point, Steffi was on her hands and knees studying a rosemary plant bushing out from under a lichen-covered chunk of limestone. "Isn't that contrast beautiful, Jim? The pale gray-green of the lichen, and the mottled gray of the rock, and then this rosemary plant with its pretty green leaves like pine needles, and the nice lavender flowers." She yanked some of the leaves off the plant and crushed them in her hands, then held them to her nose inhaling the herb's power.

"Ancient Greek legend has it that when Aphrodite emerged from the sea, she had rosemary strung all over her body."

"Aprhrodite—goddess of love and beauty."

"And pleasure and procreation."

Steffi gave him a sidelong glance. "Procreation? Do you expect me to believe that? You just pulled that out of your shoe."

"Hat. Like a magician. And Miss Galabova, doves are sacred to her."

"But I want to know if doves are sacred to you?"

"Just one."

"We should get going. It's becoming warm, no?" They stood up and slowly walked and sometimes crawled down the steep mountainside. At some point as they descended, their feet were no longer touching the earth. Instead, they walked unsteadily on a carpet of wild thyme. With each step, as their weight crushed the plants, the oil of the plants sent its vapor into the heavy, warm air. The scent was so powerful that it overwhelmed their senses. For several minutes it was the only thing. The scent of the sea, the coppery aroma of their sweat, the dry soil, all were gone, replaced by thyme.

After a quick coffee, they continued along the road, finally arriving at the steep incline that brought them down to the Prevali Monastery, which sat behind a curved lagoon with a beach surrounded by a glade of palms. The beach itself was cut in half by the Megole Patamos River washing into the sea.

When they entered the restored part of the monastery, the sun shone high overhead, casting almost no shadows. The coming summer's heat baked the walls. They strolled around the buildings for a while and finally entered the museum and took a few seconds to adjust to the darkened room. Jim enjoyed Steffi telling him about the painting techniques used on the collection of icons with their stylized forms and gold paint. She could date them by their styles alone. They next moved to view some ecclesiastical garments behind glass. Jim, not wanting to dampen Steffi's enthusiasm, thought to himself, *Anchored in tradition or gagged by it?*

"Aren't they beautiful, Jim?" She took his arm. "The designs are so complex."

"I'd never give them a second glance unless you called my attention to them."

"I wonder how long this monastery has been open."

"That I can answer. The original goes back to Byzantine times, maybe the 10th or 11th century."

"The buildings are that old?"

"Well, I think the original was destroyed. And if I recall from my reading, Prevali refers to a Venetian Lord Prevali. So that suggests it really got underway in the late 1500s, when Venice controlled the island."

They started a slow walk along the display of chalices and stopped. "So this is like post-modernist stuff next to the Minoans."

"True, but quite a history. It wasn't just during the Nazi occupation that the monks resisted. Every time Crete rose up, the monks were in the middle of it."

"I should say!" They turned around to see Mr. Robinson, hands folded behind his back and feet spread precisely 24 inches apart in a modified parade rest. "In 1770 Abbot Efrain participates in a revolution and is condemned to death but later pardoned. In 1821 Abbot Melchissedoh hoists the Greek flag over the monastery and the Turks reward the gesture by burning the bloody place down. In the 1866 through 1869 revolt, Abbot Papavassiliou apparently either didn't read his history or chose to ignore it, and gets entangled in the mess. The Turk, Resit Pasha, not to be outdone by his predecessors, torches the lower monastery."

"Mr. Robinson, how nice to see you."

"My dear Miss Steffi." He took her hand and kissed it.

Jim held out his hand, "Let me introduce myself, I'm Jim."

"Sir James. I am delighted," and he grasped Jim's hand firmly. "And under what lucky star do you reside that allows you to accompany Bulgarian royalty?" Up close, Jim noticed Mr. Robinson's eyes were ice blue. Though the skin around his eyes had deep crow's feet, and bags sagged under them, the skin of his face was otherwise smooth, taut, and weathered brown. A neatly trimmed pencil-thin white moustache adorned his upper lip. His nose was prominent and appeared to have been beaten about over the years. Several large liver spots were sprinkled over the back of the right hand that held Jim's. Today's costume, Jim thought, made him look like a Boy Scout from the 1920s. He wore brown leather walking shoes, thick ribbed knee socks, khaki shorts, and a shirt of similar color with at least ten pockets. A bush hat with a drawstring sat comfortably on his head. Jim imagined him carrying a giant butterfly net and restrained a chuckle at the thought.

Mr. Robinson raised a finger. "Have you seen the cross?"

Steffi shook her head no. Jim answered, "What cross would that be?"

"Why the great silver cross of the monastery—a legend in itself. Magical and holy powers ascribed to it." With that, Mr. Robinson turned on his heels and started to walk out, but then checked behind him to see if Steffi and Jim followed, "Well, come along then. You do want to see it, don't you?"

Steffi and Jim smiled at one another. "Lead on, Mr. Robinson."

"It's in the church, you see." And with that, he was off, setting a torrid pace with Jim and Steffi scampering to catch up. Mr. Robinson pulled the heavy church door as if it were made of plywood. "The story's really quite remarkable."

He led them to the elaborately carved silver cross that appeared to be a meter or so tall. Mr. Robinson smoothed his already neat moustache. "Well there you have it. Carried into battle more times than you could imagine. The Cretans carried it the way British regiments carry bagpipes." He raised his eyebrows, signaling either amazement or skepticism. "It's also supposed to somehow or another cure eye diseases."

Steffi asked, "Is that what you meant by magical powers?"

"A lot more than that, my dear." He lowered his voice in a conspiratorial way. "Tradition has it that a Genoese sailor early in the 19th century recovered it on a battlefield and took it on board his ship as war booty. When the ship reached the Rock at Limni, suddenly the Genoese's ship was becalmed." Mr. Robinson inserted a pause for dramatic effect. "Only when the sailor returned the cross to the monastery was the ship able to get underway again."

"Amazing!"

"And Steffi, that's not all, as a Brighton huckster might call out. In World War II, 1941 to be precise, the damn Jerries removed it from the monastery with the intention of sending it to Berlin. Well, the engines on the aeroplane wouldn't turn over, so they switched the cross to a different plane, and the same thing happened, the engines wouldn't start. Must have had some profound effect on the heathen bastards because they returned the cross to the monastery and never touched it again for the rest of the war."

Jim moved as close as he could to the cross and carefully studied every detail of it. As he backed up he bumped into Steffi. They reached for each other's hand. Jim turned toward Mr. Robinson. "Thanks for telling us."

Steffi's mind drifted and repeated, "Thanks for telling us"—us—that means together. It had only been fair to give him time alone after Jeannette, but she needed him back then, and it angered her. And she was angry at herself too because she knew how disastrous it was to need a man so much that fear of losing him makes you do regrettable things.

The conversation between Jim and Mr. Robinson continued. "So, yes, that sounds wonderful. The taverna above the village. Restored building? Wonderful. Right, Steffi? To have dinner with Mr. Robinson?"

Back in the present. "Yes, yes. That would be lovely."

"Well then how about 7:30, a little early by Greek standards, but I'm not as spry as I once was, you know."

When they opened the door to their room, Steffi grabbed Jim around the neck and leapt up, wrapping her legs around his waist and squeezing as hard as she could. As they stumbled toward the bed, kissing along the way, Jim navigated with one eye, a Cyclops getting his bearings from glimpses around Steffi's ear. They collapsed on the bed and were consumed by unbridled lust. There were no discussions of the relationship, no cautions or admonitions. Each wanted the other with the same reckless drive. And when it was over, they felt more like they had been wrestling than making love. For several long minutes they lay on their backs staring at the cedar plank ceiling, each physically sated.

The sound of Steffi's breathing led Jim to roll on his side and study her. She was slack-jawed and in deep sleep. She purred like a cat asleep on a sunny windowsill. For a moment, though it was warm, he considered covering her with a blanket because she awoke in him a desire to nurture. He dug his arm under a pillow and drifted off by watching Steffi. At some point as he slept, wild and absurd dreams raged.

"Jim! Jim! Wake up! Is it a nightmare?"

Jim rubbed his eyes with his left hand. "You wouldn't believe it. I was a fight referee that started with me being an emcee of a television quiz show. The contestants were the Roman Catholic Pope versus the patriarch of the Eastern Orthodox Church, and Pope of the Coptic church."

"*Nein, das is ganz Absurd!*" Steffi sat up with her arms wrapped around her legs. "But a referee? Why, did they really fight?"

"Are you kidding? One of them launched his staff across the stage like it was a Spartan javelin. Can't figure out what triggered it— maybe talking about Rila and Prevali. What do you think?"

"I think you've got some kind of religious phobia."

Shaking his head, Jim said "Oh, the smart aleck again." Changing to a serious tone, "Maybe the dream was a symbolic portrayal of what religions have done to one another over the millennia, including on this island, especially after Mr. Robinson's recitation."

"And maybe you're wrong, Herodotus."

Jim checked his watch, "Oh man, it's past six; we should get up."

Steffi smiled but pulled Jim's arm back as he tried to rise. "Just for the record, I'm not ignorant of what horrible things have been done by religions, Herodotus, but humans and their fallen natures made it happen. It bothers me that people use what's been done in the name of religion as an excuse for not believing in God."

"Then why does God let it happen? Why give us such fucked-up natures?"

"I don't know," she shrugged, then she stroked Jim's cheek. "You want to take a quick shower? Maybe the answer will come to me while you're in there."

Jim suspected she held a piece of truth that she couldn't or wasn't prepared to explain. He shelved the topic for now. "You go first. I'm going to go for a quick jog."

CHAPTER EIGHT

The *taverna* was perched on a hill overlooking the sea and on the edge of a village. Traces of an ancient Dorian wall ran along the village's periphery. Most of the old stone houses had been restored. A potter occupied one, and a metal smith another. A few buildings seemed to be second homes for absentee landlords. The owners had installed modern windows, and the outside walls had been tuck-pointed and cleaned. To reach the *taverna* required a climb of a few flights of stone stairs off the single village lane. A limestone wall, in a sweeping half-circle, outlined the outside dining area. Its floor was paved in flagstones of various colors. The tables were covered in peach-colored linen tablecloths, and the ladder-backed chairs were strung in straw colored wicker. Like many places on the island, the tables were shaded by grape trellises made of rough-hewn planks.

Mr. Robinson was already seated along the edge of the wall and energetically waved them over. After kissing Steffi on both cheeks, he grabbed Jim's hand, pumping it vigorously. "So very pleased you could dine with me. Very pleased indeed."

"Our pleasure, Mr. Robinson," Jim replied. Before sitting, they admired the view of the island's southern coast visible for several miles in either direction. At this elevation and distance, the sea seemed a calm mountain lake, and a container ship off on the misty horizon appeared frozen in amber.

"Oh, Mr. Robinson, how truly marvelous!" Steffi said.

"Harold will do."

"But somehow in my culture that doesn't seem right."

"Well, as you wish, Steffi, I answer to both."

"Yassou," a waiter arrived wearing a white cotton dress shirt with sleeves rolled up to his elbows. His forearms were muscular and bristled with coarse black hair. Jim thought he had a street punk hardness about him. While his smile was practiced, his eyes were challenging, and Jim couldn't help but think he'd give you that smile while he jammed a blade in your belly. It dawned on Jim that he'd seen him before, when they checked in. The guy who looked like a pissed-off bull.

"Yanni, right?"

"Right," he said, without making eye contact.

Mr. Robinson answered in Greek. "Ah, so you've met. In case you don't recall their names, let me introduce you to Miss Steffi and Mr. James." Mr. Robinson's friendly demeanor relaxed Jim, but he tensed up again when he caught the hard, sexual look Yanni directed at Steffi. "Please bring a pitcher of good red wine and a bottle or two of mineral water; but first let's start with a glass each of your best retsina."

"You got it, boss." Yanni's tone reminded Jim of "shitbird" privates in the Marines who called you "Sir," but their tone pushed the border of disrespect.

Steffi's foot found Jim. She wrapped her leg around his, arousing the teenage brain between his legs. At the same time, his adult brain indulged in studying this woman who sat across from him, viewing her as a perplexing knot of creative intellect and strength that wonderfully co-existed with the delicacy of hand-painted porcelain.

The retsina arrived along with some crusty bread and a plate of taramosalata. They clinked glasses and sipped the chilled retsina with its hint of pine resin. The pink fish roe salad was decorated with a single black olive in the middle. Each of them forked some onto a piece of the yeasty bread with its sesame-sprinkled crust. Steffi declared the taste divine.

Mr. Robinson began, "So now we are neighbors and acquainted with our innkeeper, Mrs. Phindrikalis."

"Yes. We like her very much, actually. And her first name is again?"

"Given name is Maria, and her sailor husband is Elias whom I have met but once. As I mentioned—or did I?—Yanni, our waiter, is part of her family, a nephew to be precise. Curious chap, Yanni. Eternally seems dissatisfied and disgruntled, always carrying on about his life in Athens and how good it was. Why didn't he stay, you might ask? There are rumors he had to get out of Dodge, as your Westerns say."

Jim interjected, "I noticed his attitude."

Mr. Robinson smiled, "Not a stereotypical Cretan, I should say. Morose and a bit choleric, one of those chaps who believes the world has done them in, twists the world into conspiracies and unresolved grievances, but I've learned to get along with him. I've learned it's safer to leave an angry snake alone. And Maria, or I should properly say Mrs. Phindrikalis, is one of a kind. Marvelous lady. Do anything for you."

Steffi spooned taramosalata on bread. "I liked her immediately and wish she was my aunt."

"And she found you fetching, my dear. I have that from an impeccable source." Steffi colored in response.

Jim sipped retsina. "She is a native Cretan?"

"I should say, yes. Big ties to Prevali, lad. Her father was an Orthodox priest and fought in the German resistance. 'The Lion of the South,' they called him. Children learn in school of his heroics."

Latching on to Robinson's British speech patterns, Jim replied, "You don't say? I'd love to talk with her about that some time."

"I'm sure she'd agree, if you bribe her with some good sweets that is."

They all laughed, and Jim continued, "And so, Mr. Robinson, I must admit I'm curious. We see you heading off."

"In full kit no doubt." He jammed bread with taramosalata in his mouth. "I take it my wanderings are becoming quite the talk," he said with a muffled voice.

"As former military, I couldn't help but notice your—what we call it—military bearing. Do we share a similar background?"

Mr. Robinson chuckled following a sip of wine, his blue eyes glancing everywhere but then connecting back to Jim and Steffi, "I suppose there are things that are beyond hiding, drilled into you, are they not? Indeed, Jim, Royal Artillery, Army of the Rhine. Fought only theoretical wars in West Germany, preparing for the big show with the Warsaw Pact during the Cold War. And you?"

"I was a Marine Corps officer, a reasonably calm few years as well. But that experience is years behind me. I've softened into a military historian."

"Ah, that explains your interest in Mrs. Phindrikalis's father. I say, the Marines. I fancy myself a bit of an historian myself."

"From your comments at the monastery, I gathered you had more than a passing interest in history. We see you striding off every day. You do it to stay fit, or you're a naturalist? We both admire your energy."

Steffi cut in, "Mr. Robinson has already told me that he is searching for something."

"Crete, splendid place, unique on the planet." Mr. Robinson gave an exaggerated wink. "But I confess I am looking for something quite special. Worth its weight in gold to me."

Yanni cleared the empty taramosalata plate and nodded to arriving guests nearby.

Jim leaned forward. "You're looking for contentment? Buried treasure? Your past?"

Mr. Robinson seemed to muse, then answered, "I suppose a bit of all that."

"So there's a nugget of gold hidden somewhere?" Jim teased. Yanni was back.

"Gold? Oh, something much more valuable," was Robinson's retort.

Yanni took the opportunity to interrupt and take their order. When he leaned on the table, Steffi noticed his body odor, not so much foul as reminiscent of Ludmil. She concealed a shudder. Mr. Robinson ordered green salad, broad beans, fried calamari, mountain greens sauteed in lemon and olive oil, and grilled smelt. As if apologizing, he turned to Steffi and Jim and added, "Don't worry, they'll bring potatoes and rice." Then, as an afterthought, he called out to Yanni in English, "And some of that marvelous grilled homemade sausage."

"We'll explode!" Steffi smiled, and forced Yanni's scent out of her mind.

Mr. Robinson leaned across the table with a half-smile, "I have to admit that I have a weakness for sweets too. They have a wonderful *galaktaboureko* here. With a Greek coffee, it's—"

"Divine." Steffi finished his sentence.

"Precisely. I see you practice idioms," looking over the top of his glass as he prepared to sip retsina.

"It's a hobby." She twirled her half-empty glass around.

"But you were saying?" Jim reached under the table and caressed Steffi's knee. She started, not realizing for a second who had touched her, and returned Jim a twisted, scolding grin.

"Ah, ever the pragmatic historian, impatient to gather data. Well, where to start?" Mr. Robinson took a deep breath. "Journeying to Crete has been a passion, but that sounds too much like entertainment." He paused in reflection. "The reasons? Perhaps I'd best start at the beginning. You see, when I was a young lad, I had an older brother, Ian. Strapping big fellow, chiseled features, ruddy complexioned. Why, he was practically a god to me. Followed him everywhere like a puppy. In my earliest memories I remember him on the rugby pitch. A marvel to watch. At the dinner table he could give me a wink, and I knew just what he meant. Taught me to be intellectually curious. Took the time to show me things which my father—but that's another story. He taught me why airplanes fly, lessons on human decency, how to saw a piece of wood. Ian—always ready with a smile. When he went off to Oxford I cried for a week."

Yanni was back with a sweating crockery pitcher of red wine. "Food coming," Yanni flicked his hand, "in moment."

Steffi poured wine into fruit juice glasses and passed the bread around. For a while they sat silently, sipping the bold wine and waiting for Mr. Robinson to continue. Finally, he frowned and said, "Well then, the Nazis invaded Poland, and that changed everything."

Another pause followed as Mr. Robinson gathered strength. Clearing his throat and folding his hands on the table, he continued, "Well, the war was on and of course Ian volunteered straight off. Surprised no one in the family."

Steffi's asked, "How old were you?"

"When he went off to war, five or six, I suppose."

Yanni returned balancing plates on his left arm. "Is hot, *heiss*, *kaito*." He placed each plate down with a snap. The table was covered with a cornucopic feast of warm, fragrant food.

Steffi looked up at Yanni. "How do you balance it all?"

Yanni shrugged. His hands turned up to signify he had no idea.

Mr. Robinson's arm swept over the plates of food, "As they say in your American Westerns, Jim, dig in." He chortled at his own joke.

Intrigued by the story, Jim encouraged Mr. Robinson, "The war, your brother leaving, must have set you adrift…"

"Yes, yes, of course, Jim." Mr. Robinson popped a ring of calamari in his mouth. "Scrumptious. You must try it while it's hot. Shall I squeeze some lemon on it?"

"Let me help you," Steffi offered, and she squeezed two quarters of a lemon over the sizzling fried squid. The sharp lemon fragrance rose in the evening air.

Mr. Robinson closed his eyes and looked down at the table. His voice softened, "Ian died in the war. Someplace here on Crete. He would have been 90 this month."

"I'm so sorry." Steffi wiped her hands on her napkin. "My grandfather, he died in the war too, but I don't know where."

Jim cut in, "Whoa, Steffi! I didn't know."

"It's so sad, war."

"The older I become the less I understand nor can tolerate human savagery." Mr. Robinson reached for the plate of grilled sausage with its distinct aroma of thyme.

Jim stopped cutting his food. "I've had people say because I'm a military historian, 'You must love war,' but that's not it. It's that it is this incredible distillation of human experience. It brings out the worst evil and some of humankind's greatest impulses. But it's always a horror in the end. Why we do it? I at least try to shed some light on it. As a 22-year-old, I wanted the experience, wanted to prove my manhood, and now I'm glad I missed war. Oh, I got near the edge in Grenada, but when I landed it was essentially over."

Steffi looked up from her plate. "My grandfather," she said, seeming to be confirming dates in her mind, "Yes, he would have been one hundred this month, so we have a little bit in common."

"In the Bulgarian army?"

"The German army. My mother's side of the family is German."

Just then, in the fading evening light out over the crest of the hill, level with their line of sight to seaward, a hawk soared then dove at its prey, somewhere near the bottom of the hill. "Oooh," Jim's eyes widened. "This portends great things. A sign from the ancient gods."

"Ah, Jim, you've read your Homer."

"This sighting would have inspired confidence and bravery on the battlefield of Troy."

Steffi smirked, "Come on, gentlemen. How do you say it, you're going over the top. Too much retsina."

They were all picking food from the serving platters but both Robinson and Jim couldn't help but think. "Over the top." That was the World War I term for climbing out of your trench and attacking the enemy. Mr. Robinson had speared a grilled smelt with his fork, which he now pointed in Steffi's direction. "If ever there were a place where such signs could be true, then certainly Crete is it."

"Wasn't even the Cyclops supposed to have been in a cave here somewhere?"

"Most think Sicily, chap. Perhaps you're thinking of Daedalus and the Minotaur and all that." Glancing up to see if they were bothering to listen, Mr. Robinson continued, "Daedalus, quite the inventor. He's the one who made the wings for his son, Icarus. Lovely scheme until the lad flew too close to the sun, and the bloody wax wings melted. Warning to us all in the modern age. Inventions are lovely until they destroy you."

"But I forget the connection to the Minotaur." Jim looked up over his cup of wine.

"Ah yes. The Minotaur was a fearsome creature, half bull and half man, lived in a labyrinth, designed and built by none other than our mad scientist inventor, Daedalus. Some say in the palace at Knossos, others in a cave some other place on Crete. Myth has it Daedalus damn near couldn't figure out how to get out of his own labyrinth when it was completed." Mr. Robinson paused long enough to consume another smelt, some greens, and a swig of wine. "No one who entered the labyrinth ever escaped the savagery of the Minotaur, nor could they find a way out. To make a rather complex story short—the damn Greeks could spin quite a yarn, couldn't they?" Mr. Robinson chortled.

"Didn't Daedalus kill the Minotaur? I seem to remember from school."

"So here's what happened. Young Prince Theseus arrives from Athens a prisoner, or I should say as war reparation paid to King Minos. Well, wouldn't you know it, Minos's daughter, Ariadne, falls in love with Theseus. So dear daddy responds by sending Theseus into the labyrinth to be devoured by the Minotaur. Daedalus has warm paternal feelings for Ariadne and provides her with silk thread and instructions for how Theseus can find his way out. The trick was counterintuitive. He was to run the thread from the entrance of the labyrinth, always straight and always down. Theseus takes Ariadne with him into the labyrinth and promises that if they can get out alive they will elope. Our lad Theseus, armed with a sword, cunning, and good intelligence, fights the Minotaur in a titanic brawl, slays him, and escapes the labyrinth with Ariadne." Mr. Robinson took a long breath. "Afterward, the whole bloody thing gets bollixed. Seems Theseus took a blow to the head by the Minotaur because he clearly loses all common sense. Shows heroes bugger things up too. What happens after becomes a tragedy beyond my patience to recount at this lovely meal. You'll have to read that on your own."

"Did people actually believe this?" Steffi asked as she cut a piece of sausage.

"Oh indeed they did. Bulls were very important to the early Cretans. I'm sure you'll see how the pottery and frescoes depict dancing or acrobatics with bulls. The creature is far-fetched, but the bull connection is intriguing. The whole thing probably had some link to religious rituals."

Jim scooped some of the broad beans on to his plate. "I seem to recall the German Army using a cave here to store ammunition which some believed to be the labyrinth, but then they blew the whole damn thing up toward the end of the war."

"Curious." Mr. Robinson stroked his chin. "The labyrinth even plays out in modern literature. Lawrence Durrell did a bang-up job in his novel, *In the Labyrinth,* about tourists on Crete being trapped in a labyrinth."

"Sometimes it feels like we're all in a labyrinth. Don't you feel that way at times, Mr. Robinson?"

"Sometimes I do, indeed, but then at my age, one must shut up about such things or others will declare you daft."

For a while they ate in silence. The olive oil, lemon, and salt sharpened the taste of the greens. The feta cheese on the salad was fresh. The outdoor air made it all taste better.

Jim mused, "Everything crisscrosses here. I understand the Philistines of biblical fame may have originated here."

Mr. Robinson chewed for a while then swept his hand in the direction of the coast. "I told you of the Genoese sailor who stole the cross from Prevali and how his ship was becalmed until he returned it. At the same point along the coast, just out of sight over there," he said, pointing to the coast east of them, "in 61 AD St. Paul came ashore in a hurricane. Then, dear friends, I offer Homer in book three of *The Odyssey.* King Menelaus goes aground on the island near Phaestos at least 1,100 years earlier."

Steffi perked up, "I recall Saint Paul in Corinth, Phillippi, and Thessaloniki."

"Quite definitely dashed about here as well."

Jim, nibbling some greens, added, "And we'll visit the ancient city of Phaestos soon. Do you recall me mentioning Phaestos when I was talking about the British subs landing here during the war?"

"In fact—" a smelt Mr. Robinson speared split in half and he mumbled, "Bloody hell." Chewing one half at a time he finally finished his thought, "Paul baptized Titus not far from here."

Meanwhile, Yanni was in the kitchen communicating with his own muse. Into an empty can that had once stored olives, Yanni added three fresh slips of paper with cryptic notes on each.

Nik, an acquaintance of Yanni's—Yanni had no friends—took a drag on a cigarette and asked him, "What are you doing with that can?"

"None of your business."

"What do you think, you're 007, man of mystery? Knowing you, you're probably up to no good." He leaned against the wall and flicked his cigarette butt out the window. "Were you like this in Athens too?"

Yanni looked up with a downward curl to his lips. "Give me one of those cigarettes." Nik threw him the pack. "One thing I learned in Athens, be patient and keep your mouth shut. And that means you. But I'll tell you this much, every time I put something in here—" he pointed at the can—"it's pure gold. It means I'm one step closer. I'm tired of everyone screwing me. This time I'm going to get what I deserve."

"You're a weird fucking animal, you know? Writing things down and putting that shit in a can." Nik turned to leave.

"By the way, Nik, fuck you." Yanni knew in his heart he could never use Nik in his scheme.

The cook, also named Maria, came in wiping her hands with a towel. "Hey, everybody's looking for you—customers, Yanni."

"Fuck them."

"Boss says get up there."

"When I finish my cigarette." The cook flipped her hand as she stormed out, and Yanni asked himself why he worked with such assholes. She'd complain to the boss. So what? It's what he expected from her. The only reason he could figure out why people acted like that was jealousy. "That's what happened in Athens. They were jealous, and they set me up to take the fall. Not catching me in that trick again. So now I got a record hung around my neck, and the Hellenic Police framed me, fucking threatened to hang me out to dry. What other choice did I have but to come back to this shithole, something I swore I'd never do." As Yanni took the last drag on his cigarette, he thought about the Mercedes he'd buy when this was all done.

Outside, the dinner continued. Yanni appeared out of nowhere and cleared some of the plates. "But, Mr. Robinson," Steffi's brow was knit with concern, "We were speaking of your brother earlier. You know he was here? In my case I have often wondered where Grossvatti died. My mother claims his remains never came home."

"Ghastly war. Especially if he had been on the Eastern front, and the odds are he was. Many bodies never made it back and sometimes the families back home had died in the bombing and there was no one to take custody even if the body did return." Mr. Robinson's tone turned dreamy once more. "Ah, Ian. Yes, yes. Fine lad. You see," Mr. Robinson cleared his throat. His voice had grown thick. "It's true. Ian apparently died here on Crete. Unlike the mystery of your grandfather, I know some fragments. He was with the 2nd Battalion of the Black Watch. A young subaltern in May of 1941 when the Germans unleashed their airborne landings."

Jim cut in, "Operation Merkur. Began 20 May, to be precise. That's what I'm here to write about."

"You don't say?"

"Merkur—Mercury," Steffi translated.

Jim cut a piece of calamari. "What a message that airborne landing was. It was the first time airborne troops had ever been used in a strategic role. The Germans took appalling losses and never tried another major parachute landing after it."

"Still, the bastards took the island by the first of June." Mr. Robinson suddenly looked up. "It didn't occur to me until just now, but it is a grim anniversary of sorts. Three days ago to the day was the 69-year anniversary of the campaign."

"Let's drink to that being over." They clinked glasses and took a swallow of wine. "What have you learned so far about Ian?"

"Well, Jim, Ian was in the thick of it. I know that from unit histories. He retreated with the other lads. Most were evacuated from the island along this coast much farther to the east, but Ian either refused to be evacuated or there hadn't been space aboard the ships. Either way, he went off into the mountains, was cared for by the locals, and eventually fought with the partisans in the organized resistance. He was one of the liaison leaders, which hardly surprised me to discover. He had some Greek, you see, mostly the ancient variety, but that wouldn't have stopped Ian. Derring-do. That was my brother."

Steffi topped off the juice glasses with red wine. She picked at her salad while Mr. Robinson continued, "The partisans had good cover and concealment, and the people were on their side, something that would have helped you Yanks in Viet Nam."

Jim looked up from his plate. "And both your government and mine in Afghanistan and Iraq. The people, not some of the people, need to be with you. I understand that in '41, women and children resisted the landing with farm tools, and the men used ancient muskets."

"That's the tradition, and it has more than a grain of truth to it. But there were collaborators too, I'm sad to say."

"It's part of the psychology of being occupied."

Steffi's corvine eyes looked up. "I imagine it was something like the Stockholm Syndrome with hostages. They start to identify with their captors."

"I fear it's so, Steffi. But getting better food and money played its part. The war was tough on the average Cretan, and people became desperate. They did things they would have never dreamed of doing. I've always had a soft spot for the young girls. When you're sixteen or seventeen the occupation must have felt like a lifetime. You grow fond of some German lad and the next thing you know, you're being hanged as a traitor when the fortunes of war turn." Mr. Robinson cut a piece of potato, and after poking it in his mouth chewed slowly, his eyes drifting off in the growing darkness.

The sun had set, but the three of them hadn't noticed. Yanni lit a candle on their table and lingered nearby, annoying Jim. Yanni appeared nonchalant in a staged way. "Shifty-eyed creep," Jim mumbled to himself.

"So Ian hid and moved mostly at night. The island is littered with caves, especially as you ascend into the White Mountains. Plenty of places to stay out of the weather, hide a radio, and spot Jerry if he's coming your way." Mr. Robinson rubbed his brow, then brushed his white moustache with his thumb. "Eventually, you see, his luck ran out, poor bloke. Apparently got cornered somewhere up there." Mr. Robinson pointed to the mountains they knew in the darkness were north of them. "But I don't know precisely where, so I'm here searching. Ian's body, like your grandfather's, never came home. I have some descriptions of where he was, but they fit so many places. Somehow, I trust I'll recognize it when I see it. I'm looking for artifacts of any kind that could offer a clue."

"So you are searching only for the place?"

"You are a clever lass." His fork suspended in mid-air.

Steffi caught Jim's wink and smile. She read his smile that said, "Oh, lass, is it?" She had teased him about Robinson calling him "lad." Robinson was so kindly. It didn't bother her, but then she thought, maybe it should.

"I don't think I'll know or ever understand all the reasons I'm searching. I suppose if I could find his remains, I'd like to bring Ian back. Don't mean to deaden our conversation, no pun intended, but it would give me satisfaction to know we were buried in the family plot together. The search—well, he deserves it. What are brothers for?"

Yanni dropped off a basket of fresh bread. "More drink?"

"No, thank you, Yanni," Mr. Robinson replied. Many more of the restaurant's tables were occupied now. The crowd appeared to be a mix of foreign tourists and Greeks. Now, out in the direction of the sea, navigation lights from several ships were visible. A light, warm breeze arose.

After a few glasses of wine, the breeze became a soporific for Steffi. She felt as though she were floating. Steffi called Yanni over. Yanni's expression brightened, and Jim watched him scanning the front of Steffi's top. She tried in Greek, "Yanni, can I be having coffee Greek?"

Yanni laughed, "Okay, why not."

Mr. Robinson added, "And you might as well bring it for all of us. And bring the *galaktaboureko* too."

Steffi protested, "So much."

"You'll regret it if you don't try it." Mr. Robinson's eyes twinkled. "Poor lass, are we putting you to sleep with our incessant academic chatter?"

She wanted to say, "I'm a thirty-six-year-old woman," but Robinson was so harmless. She knew about men who meant harm. Waving her hand, she said, "Oh no, but the breeze and the wine, so dark at night here. So peaceful."

"It is, isn't it?"

Jim added, "It's hard to imagine how many wars have touched this island. If history is any indication, it's probably a temporary peace." He caught himself. "Okay, so stop with the negative vibes." Jim turned to Mr. Robinson, "It's my intention to search some of these caves too. It's such an important part of the resistance. If I could be of help in your search?"

"That's generous of you, Jim. It does get lonely at times. The companionship would be a pleasure. Steffi, are you a hiker?"

"I am, and I want to help too. It will somehow let me feel I am searching for my grandfather."

Jim, not wanting to violate the Englishman's sense of privacy, added, "Of course we don't want to impose. This is so personal. It's not our place to—"

"Nonsense, Jim. The weeks of searching have not been without their frustrations. I've learned the value of companionship."

Steffi's dark eyes appeared molten in the evening. Unlike many women, she did little to shape her eyebrows. Somehow their thickness imparted sincerity, especially when she furrowed her brow as she did now. "It must be difficult. I mean, after all, not knowing what happened."

"I suppose it is quite un-British of me to admit, but I'm an old man now, so I don't mind revealing a bit of emotion now and then." He raised his hand before Steffi could respond. "It's true, Steffi. My dear departed Anne knew this as well. We were devoted to each other, and my family was hardly disagreeable. But what I learned about human love—the rock-solid foundation of it, well, that came from Ian. It would do my heart well if I could touch where he'd been at the end."

Yanni reappeared with the coffee and galaktaboureko. Mr. Robinson recognized that the mood had grown somber, so as Yanni served the coffee and sweets Robinson brightened and began a lighter story with a broad smile on his face. "And then, of course, there's the matter of the missing several hundred gold sovereigns which would fetch a tidy sum if we found them."

"Gold?"

Yanni placed the pastry in front of Mr. Robinson. "Oh Yanni, tell the cook she's outdone herself this time. My, it looks perfect."

Yanni flicked his wrist. "She made big complaint. She disappointed. Not very good. But I will tell her and then maybe she stop complaining for two minutes."

They all chuckled. "Yes." Mr. Robinson turned back to Jim and Steffi. "The British sent clothes, food, guns, radios, and yes, gold to help the resistance. Some of it, well let's say, there is a tradition of sheep thievery around these parts."

"Casualty of war," said Jim.

"Hah, right you are. The cost of doing business. I suspect some of it is tucked away to this day in one of these caves."

Yanni cleared the dinner dishes and carried the load back to the kitchen. He told the cook he needed a break, and she glared back. Yanni walked outside and worked his way to the base of the wall beneath where the conversation continued.

"Do you really think there is this gold?" Steffi's fork sank through the honey-soaked filo dough and into the firm semolina custard.

"You know the effect gold has on people. Most of the stories are rubbish and exaggerated, no doubt, a myth just like the Daedalus story. I'm sure some was unaccounted for, as Jim would say, a casualty of war. Whoever stole it or borrowed it has spent it all by now. I actually found one coin in a cave. Do keep that hush-hush. I declared it my talisman. I'll turn it in when my search is successful."

Jim examined the muddy grounds on the bottom of his coffee cup. "They say you can predict the future from these grounds."

"Good luck doing that."

Jim probed the grounds with the tip of his index finger, commenting absently. "If war's a distillation of the human experience, then Crete's a microcosm of that."

"I say, that perked me up. Microcosm of?"

"The best and the worst of humans. Who knows about the gold? No doubt some went for a good purpose and some for bad. We spend tax money to eradicate poppy production in Afghanistan, and then we turn around and buy heroin on our streets for billions of dollars. That's collaboration of a sort. Why are there always collaborators? People driven by self-interest. Sometimes pretending to be for one thing but secretly working at cross-purposes. Still others sacrifice beyond what one would consider normal human endurance for a higher purpose."

Jim continued, "I recall the story of one eighteen-year-old Cretan boy caught by the Germans. He and another were about to be executed by a firing squad. I don't recall the circumstances precisely, but there was a sudden opportunity to escape. One did, but this boy remained. Those around encouraged him to escape. 'Run,' they told him, 'Save yourself!' But he stayed there calmly waiting for the firing squad to return from chasing the other. He refused to leave because he knew there would be reprisals against his family if he got away. The firing squad did, indeed, return and shot him instantly in a fit of bloodlust and anger. As the soldiers neared, he called to those around him, 'I am eighteen years old and sentenced to death! The firing squad will be here in a minute. Long live Greece! Long live Crete!' Just a simple peasant boy. By God, you have to reach outside yourself to do that!"

"Damned courageous." Mr. Robinson tapped the table for emphasis.

"It was, Mr. Robinson, but there's always a story on the other side, and that's the part that makes us all a little uneasy. As you commented earlier, I imagine many of those German young men were charming. There's a picture I've seen of a column of German soldiers moving along a pathway on Crete. Their helmets are off. Without those distinctive German coal scuttle helmets, they could pass for kids in my own Marine platoon. I can see how they could have been appealing to a young and lonely girl. I'm sure those soldiers, especially from the *Gebirgsjaeger* (mountain troops), could tell charming stories of mountain life in Germany or Austria, probably not unlike the life the girls here knew."

"Then there is the fascination of every adolescent for what one can't have."

"Oh, this galaktaboureko is good. I have a weakness for custards and puddings." Steffi cut in, really wanting the topic to change.

Jim wiped his mouth with the linen napkin. "And don't forget the judgment of right and wrong is often defined by the winner. It becomes their story, and besides, we are forever re-writing history to suit ourselves. It's like the old Soviet joke about rewriting history—one citizen says to another, 'The trouble is, you never know what will happen yesterday.'"

"Right you are, James. It seems like humans keep going through cycles of darkness and light and history that repeats itself. And what is historical truth in the end?"

Frustration began to stir in Steffi. *Historians*, she thought, *bah*. They are missing the truth in front of their eyes.

Mr. Robinson stretched in his chair, and the wicker back creaked. "Always more questions than answers. Human life is like a Matryoshka doll." Robinson demonstrated by holding an imaginary doll and pulling apart its smaller and smaller pieces. "There's always one more hidden part."

Mr. Robinson and Jim had been so enmeshed in their alcohol-induced conversation that they had become oblivious of everything around, including Steffi. When she spoke with pent-up emotion, it startled both of them. "If you don't mind, I'll make my presence known." She paused and gave each of them a fiery glance. "I don't feel I'm trapped in history repeating itself. Oh no, Mr. Robinson, that is not what I experience. I trust in prayer and an open heart. It leads me out of darkness, not into it. We choose darkness. We're called into light."

CHAPTER NINE

M̲r. Robinson's journal entry for the evening read, *A delightful repast with a charming Bulgarian young lady and engaging American man who thankfully do not seem to look at me as some shriveled, useless, and eccentric old Brit. I'm grateful for their interest in Ian. Anne, you would like them, especially Steffi with her lively eyes and sharp wit—just like you—hard as flint beneath the surface. They seem to care, and that is refreshing. James understands as only an historian can about what went on here during the occupation. Steffi's responses are more emotional but no less meaningful.*

Both of them seem to be searching for something too. I have learned Steffi's grandfather also died in the war, details unknown other than he served in the German Army. It has left a hole in her. Perhaps that is the connection to explain why we hit it off. This young lady, Steffi, marches to the beat of a different drummer. She appears moved by deep and mysterious spiritual currents. Even in her moments of silence, her emotions scream from her eyes. Jim, several years older than Steffi, fit and with a ruddy complexion, appears to grasp the connections between things on a very deep level, but at the same time, he does seem to tread on uncertain ground emotionally. Like many other achieving men I have known, he may see himself as a failure. He needs a crucible experience of sorts where he comes out on top, and I suspect a successful relationship with a woman is the right prescription.

In thinking over the dinner conversation, Steffi chafed at how Harold and Jim viewed the world. Her experiences had spun her differently. She recalled how, not so many years before, she had peered into a bottomless pit of darkness. There had been days—weeks—when suicide called, a siren from below. There was that terrifying time when she woke to Ludmil, high from drugs, choking her on their dilapidated couch, and still, that had been only one episode in her fall. What followed Ludmil were broken relationships, no job, no heat, the long bout of bronchitis, and then self-doubt about her artistic talent. All of it had sapped her spirit. There had been the married government official, an educated man in a nice suit. She still heard the steel door of the cheap apartment slam when he walked out. Then, one day, bewildered, despondent, having hit bottom, light poured through her bedroom window as if the sun shone right outside. At first she shuttered the window, but the light couldn't be ignored, so she opened the shutters and let the light bathe her. She told no one of the experience, but she believed it had been God.

Jim, on the other hand, had been enthused by the evening. Meeting Mr. Robinson had been fortuitous. Already his book was becoming a more personal exploration of Crete's partisan movement than he had anticipated. Maybe it should become a novel? Ian, with Mr. Robinson's permission, of course, would be the central character.

During the next few days Jim and Steffi drove every day to Chania and returned to the hotel in the evening. The trips were primarily for Jim's research, though the museum and Venetian-style buildings attracted Steffi as well. The buildings had long been favorites of artists working on Crete, and Steffi wanted to try her hand drawing and painting them. She brought sketchpads, charcoal, and colored pencils.

One morning, driving past a stand of tamarisk trees on the road to Chania, Steffi's mind dwelt on the conversation at the taverna and how it raised questions about her own life. Why had her mother wanted to keep Grossvatti a family secret? Why had mother made father's problems a secret, and hid the truth about her poems and letter to Zhivkov? Then it shocked her to realize she was acting the same with Jim. She had hidden her personal secret and was afraid to expose it. She had justified the deception because she believed he needed to hear it at the right time. But that was just another layer of deceiving herself. Down deep, she knew how secrets peek around corners, appear like ghosts, but end up popping out of hiding no matter how you try to bury and control them. They rot when you try to hide them and then float to the surface, buoyed by their own putrid gas.

* * *

While Steffi daydreamed as they drove past the tamarisk trees, Mrs. Phindrikalis sat under the pergola outside the hotel office with her nephews Apostolos and Yanni. Yanni lounged cockeyed in the chair with one leg slung over the armrest, his mahogany wingtip dangling in midair. Mrs. Phindrikalis scolded, "Don't ruin this for Apostolos."

"Ruin what?"

"This is good work for Apostolos what he's doing for Mr. Robinson—finding these caves. Makes some good money."

Yanni twisted the right side of his mouth up and snorted, "Good money? Good for nothing. But I still don't see what I'm ruining."

For his part, Apostolos sat primly in his chair, sipping a glass of juice his aunt had poured. The conversation made him feel uncomfortable. Mother had always respected her sister, and Aunty had always been good to him. He could still hear mother implore, "You listen to Aunty when I'm gone." After all, Aunty was a successful businesswoman, and Yanni sounded disrespectful, and Yanni had grabbed two of the cookies already. He eyed the one that sat alone on the plate. It seemed to grow bigger the more he watched it. His hand sweated with the desire to snatch it, but it was not part of his nature to reach out and grab things. Life as a shepherd tamed impulsivity.

"Why do you want to go along on these walks? It makes no sense. What do you know about the countryside? And besides, why should Mr. Robinson pay one Euro more?"

"The old man doesn't know what he wants. What's the difference if I go, anyway? Look, I don't need a couple more Euros. I'm trying to protect Apostolos from being taken advantage of. Maybe I don't know the countryside, Aunty, but I know people."

"Oh sure, the big man from Athens. Mr. Robinson is like the kind of people you know?"

"Oh, I get it. I got framed in Athens for something I didn't do, so all the people I know are low life? But this old Brit. He's not here to take advantage? How do you know that? If I'm with Apostolos, I can keep an eye on things."

Maria Phindrikalis peered suspiciously at Yanni, then burst out laughing. Her laughing set Yanni back, and he protested angrily, "Now wait!"

"No, you wait! Don't take me for a fool. You! Keep an eye on things?" she chuckled. "I don't know what's going on here, Yanni, but you leave Apostolos and Mr. Robinson alone. I want this to work out for Apostolos, and I want Mr. Robinson to be happy."

"Aunty, I'm trying to start over here, but this family never gives me a chance. So tell me, you're not curious about why Robinson wants Apostolos to find caves?"

"To find out about his brother."

It was Yanni's turn to laugh. "And you believe that? The war's been over for what? More than sixty years? There's something else, and I can smell it."

Mrs. Phidrikalis's sudden sharp tone upset Yanni's composure. "I don't know all the details of what happened in Athens, and I really don't want to know, but I can guess. I will tell you this. You have a second chance coming back home, and no matter what you say, the family's been willing to take a chance…"

Yanni squirmed in his seat and tried to interrupt.

Mrs. Phindrikalis put up her hand. "Wait! The taverna, this hotel, the taxi service uncle Odysseus has, his wife's shop—stupid nonsense will hurt business, and none of us will put up with it."

"No, you wait!" Yanni pointed his finger, and Apostolos sat up shocked by the rudeness. "Everyone in this family does nothing but pick on me. And it's because you're jealous. You know I have a future, and the likes of you and Uncle Odysseus put me down."

"You talk like a little boy."

"And you talk like you are my mother."

Apostolos couldn't help it. He liked Yanni. Yanni didn't feel like family; he did things differently. He seemed free. But Apostolos liked Aunty, too.

"I tell you, Mr. Robinson is a good man…"

"These rich tourists come here and think they own our land. I don't want them soiling Kriti."

"Saint Yanni."

"Shut up."

"And don't put ideas in Apostolos's head," she said, as if Apostolos was out of earshot.

With that, Apostolos's head perked up just like that of his sheepdog, Argos. He heard steps approaching on the gravel.

Mr. Robinson appeared from around the corner. "Ah, there you are, Apostolos. Shall we be off?"

Apostolos only understood, "Apostolos," but he knew it was time to go, so he stood up and smiled. He said in English, "Go."

"Mr. Robinson," Mrs. Phindrikalis asked, "Shall you take a coffee?"

"*Tempus fugit!* Time flies. Have to be off, my dear lady. Perhaps some other time."

"Are Jim and Steffi going with you?"

"Not this time. They're gallivanting around Chania, I believe. They were with me yesterday afternoon after they returned from Chania and will join tomorrow. It was good to have them along." Mr. Robinson adjusted his wide-brimmed bush hat.

* * *

Chania, the second largest city on Crete, had been the location of the German headquarters toward the end of the occupation. The environs around the city, Souda Bay and the airfield at Maleme, were virtually at the *Schwerpunkt* of the Axis's attack in '41. Jim viewed Chania as the beginning of his story. He carried letters of introduction to a couple of Greek scholars who had promised to speak with him, and he hoped they could help arrange interviews with residents who remembered the occupation.

To avoid the heat of midday, Jim and Steffi rendezvoused in a taverna, sipping a beer and eating a modest lunch. Steffi showed Jim some of the pastels she had done of the harbor. Her ability to communicate texture never ceased to amaze Jim. After their lunch and before returning to work, they strolled through the market. Steffi wanted to work in the late afternoon light, and Jim used any excuse to delay a return to the tedious drudgery of combing through war records.

Jim marveled watching Steffi at the market. On one level, her life floated above the world on an ethereal plane, but while shopping she was all practical grit: pulling, stretching, weighing, and scrutinizing every detail. She checked prices three and four times, and then left, only to walk a few stalls away and return for another examination. Many of the men stall owners tried to connect to Steffi with their practiced sales pitches. "My customers love these. I can't keep them in stock. The price is still off-season price. I'll give you two for extra ten percent off." They brought out variations from under the counter, and yet Steffi remained unmoved. The women stall owners locked on to Steffi's mindset, letting her feel they were part of her world. They quietly placed alternatives in front of her, and just as quietly removed them when Steffi's attention turned elsewhere.

He was intrigued by how this Bulgarian woman moved in ways identical to women from America to Japan. Some unspoken behavior code must be communicated, then learned around the globe, and he wondered if men behaved similarly? Why, for instance, at every counter did Steffi lift her right heel and pivot on the ball of her foot as she combed through the merchandise, so that her ankle turned and her right knee folded into her left? He had seen women, but never men, do this everywhere. He thought how women invest a fortune in accentuating their breasts, painting their faces, and squeezing into tight-fitting clothes, and all the while this visual cue—a pretty turn of the ankle, the collapse of a leg—was every bit as powerful.

He wondered how he appeared to women. He jammed his hands in his pockets like other men everywhere. What else are you going to do with your hands? Okay, he thought, but when I fold my arms across my chest and spread my legs in a swashbuckling pose, does it do to Steffi what her turn of an ankle does to me?

Steffi caught him staring at her and peeked through strands of her long hair that had fallen over her cheek. "You want something, sailor?"

All Jim could do was smile. "Okay, you got me."

She walked up to him, taking his arm. "Let's go over to the leather store."

"I thought we'd already gone there?"

"No, that was a different one."

Steffi eyed a bag and sandals. A saleswoman was using a long-hooked rod to bring down samples hanging along the rafters. Jim came up behind Steffi and whispered in her ear. "Why don't you get them? They'd be a gift from me."

"Jim, that makes me feel like a kept woman or something."

He wasn't sure whether to be pissed off or understanding. Defensiveness crept into his tone. "How could you think you're a kept woman?"

"Well, who's paying for the hotel?"

He had no comeback. Then the true and demoralizing answer whacked Jim over the head. Jeannette's life insurance actually paid for the hotel. Talk about dancing on somebody's grave! "Okay, okay," he said, placating. "But if you care for someone, you want to make them happy."

She turned to Jim and smiled, "I don't want to be some desperate woman on the edge of middle age from a poor country, a gold miner."

"Gold digger."

"Whatever."

"But if you get the sandals, it will make me very happy."

That stopped Steffi for a moment. Apparently, the saleswoman overheard at least some of the conversation. "Let him buy them. I can't get a Euro from my man. If he asked me to go out shopping I think I would faint." They all laughed.

Jim said in a teasing tone, "And I have another reason for the request."

"You? And what's that?" Steffi eyes were still examining the sandals.

Very quietly in her ear, he said, "You are wearing the ugliest sandals I have ever seen. They should be burned."

"Really? They are old." They looked down at the old gray suede orthopedic sandals.

"And ugly. Use them when you want to take out the trash."

The saleswoman sensed a thawing and spread before Steffi various sandal and bag combinations, all the while extolling the virtues of her products.

"Well… you're sure they're okay?" Steffi sounded like a bashful child in a candy shop.

"Yes. Madame, wrap them up, and I expect a discount for helping close the sale." In fact, the woman wrapped them up in record time and the transaction was completed before Steffi could object.

"You're sure they're okay, Jim?" she asked again as they walked into the sunlight and away from the shade of the stalls. "But I wonder if I should have gotten another style?"

"The ones you picked are great. Don't have buyer's remorse."

"Buyer's remorse? What's this buyer's remorse?"

"I'll explain later, let's just go." Jim pulled Steffi along by the elbow. They wandered for a while, finally ending up in the Kastelli area of the city. "You know, Steffi, even Herodotus mentioned Chania. It's in his *Histories* back in something like 500 BC. He called it Cydonia."

"Shhh. Don't lecture. Let me feel the place." She held Jim's arm and rested her head on his shoulder. "If you want to lecture, visit Mr. Robinson." His shirt was damp from perspiration, and his skin smelled tangy and coppery, but not unpleasant. Soon they entered an area of ancient damp, moss-covered stones and the scent of spoils from an archeological dig. It was there they separated, leaving Steffi to sketch and Jim to wander off to inspect the remnants of a Venetian dry dock. They agreed to meet at the car no later than six.

CHAPTER TEN

Steffi and Jim also indulged in experiencing what they could of Crete's Bronze Age Minoan civilization. After systematically visiting the ruins at Kato Zakros in the east of the island, Knossos near Heraklion, and the nearby ruins of Phaestos and Ayia Triada, they began to feel it come alive again. The more they walked the ruins and touched the stone blocks, just as the archaeologist, Arthur Evans, had who had unearthed Knossos in 1900, the more they speculated about where the Minoans came from and why they disappeared. Was Ayia Triada a summer palace, a series of temples, or a place to distribute food? Had the Minoans made love and not war, like Hippies in the '60s thought?

Over lunch along the beach below Kato Zakros they argued about things Minoan with their cheeks full of food and after long draughts of cold beer. They marveled how no one until the 1950s had deciphered the 3,000-year-old Linear B tablets in the Minoan language found at Knossos. Steffi passed a Cretan guidebook across the table with a color plate of one of the clay tablets with its peculiar etched writing. "Look at this, Jim! It's so otherworldly but so beautiful. Was it some kind of early Greek?"

"I don't think so. Predates written Greek by several hundred years. If I'm not mistaken, written Greek emerged from Phoenician. This stuff is dated to something like 1500 BC."

"I wager Mr. Robinson knows."

"No doubt." Jim studied the plate. "It is unique, isn't it?"

"Reminds me a little of Egyptian hieroglyphics."

"But different. It has pictures, but I understand it has some of the qualities of Japanese—written in syllables, and yet has grammatical endings like German. No wonder it took so long to figure out. And then they found some similar tablets in Mycenaean ruins on the Greek mainland."

Steffi had her beer glass halfway to her mouth and looked coquettishly over the rim. "Is this what they call flirting and dating in America?"

"Pre-dating."

"Carbon dating if you ask me. You can get unromantic."

"You started this." Jim sat back in his chair and jammed his hands in his pockets. He called the waiter over and said in Greek, "One more Mythos, please."

The frosty green bottle arrived a minute later, and the waiter filled their glasses from it. Jim asked, "Why so silent? It makes the mood grave."

"Grave, I get it."

"Shall we bury the whole conversation?"

"Oh yuk, what a silly academic kind of pun," but she was smiling nonetheless.

For a while they were silent, enjoying sitting in shade along the beach, with the peaceful Mediterranean in front of them, sharing a happy buzz from their beer. Finally, Steffi spoke up. "Okay. I knew one of us would crack. Academic or not, I've got to ask. How does it all end?"

"Well, you get on a plane to Sofia."

The olive Steffi threw bounced off Jim's forehead. "The Minoans!"

"Ow! Act more civilized, will ya? The ending's a mystery too. One possible theory is the volcano that erupted and formed the caldera on the island of Santorini—you can still see it, one hundred kilometers or so north of Crete—must have darkened the sky. Maybe the island was swept by devastating tsunamis that, if not crushing Minoan dominance on the island, hobbled it until others could pick away at the carrion. Some say a gigantic earthquake collapsed the whole thing. Endings are never pretty." Jim mused. "A volcano, earthquake, Doric invasion, pestilence."

"The natural stuff doesn't bother me, but the brutality of humans. Human evil that can multiply like a virus."

"I would think the Roman conquest in 67 BC must have been even nastier than the Nazis."

"Enough, Jim," Steffi pleaded. "Let's see some beauty. We must get to the museum in Iraklion. I badly want to see the Minoan sculpture. The pictures I've seen of the sculpture—they made the human form so gentle."

"Iraklion? Lots of fat German tourists on crowded beaches wearing Speedos."

"Stop it," but Steffi was giggling. "They come to our Black Sea beaches too. I want to see the sculpture, not beer bellies in Speedos. Come on, please?"

"Let's do it soon. You know me. Great fan of the Bronze Age maritime powers."

"Oh please. Speaking of bronze," she said, wanting badly to change the subject, "just how bronze you're looking. You look nice, Jim. The sun's not good for you, I guess, but you look great. I'm proud to be with you. Do you think people can see we're attached?"

"Yes, duh." With that, they left the table and walked hand-in-hand down the beach before they returned to the car.

They also invested time with Mr. Robinson, searching for caves where Ian might have hidden. Many of the mountain caves were hidden from easy observation. They discussed how some had mythological connections and one was alleged to be the birthplace of Zeus. Mr. Robinson managed navigating to some, but Apostolos often guided them. Mrs. Phindrikalis recommended her nephew, Apostolos, because as a shepherd, he knew the terrain and trails through his routine of moving his flock to better pasturage.

The sheep were often penned while Apostolos trekked with them. His sheepdog, Argos, free from the daily grind, joined them as well. At first, Apostolos reacted jealously of Steffi because Argos, adoring Steffi's fawning attention, ignored him; but after a few days hiking and sampling the delicious snacks she brought for both him and Argos, Apostolos came to accept that a friend of Argos was his friend too. Had he a tail, Apostolos would have wagged it when Steffi approached, and he described the beauty of the mountains he knew so well to her first, rather to Mr. Robinson, who paid him. Mr. Robinson remarked that Apostolos was visibly saddened on the days when Jim and Steffi didn't hike.

Back in the room, Apostolos became a topic of conversation more than once. Jim and Steffi agreed that, now and then, Apostolos became inexplicably unsettled and distracted, always looking behind him, but they agreed the moods passed quickly enough. What did he see that they didn't?

Steffi commented after Jim dismissed Apostolos as a "weird duck," "He reminds me of boys I've met in Bulgaria's Rodope Mountains. They're good boys, close to nature, and their emotions, well, they're pure and primitive, but I don't mean that in a bad way. They are like the mountains they live in. I believe something's bothering Apostolos that doesn't fit in his world, something apart from Mr. Robinson and us. But weird? No, I don't find him weird."

* * *

A few days later, with Jim needing to return to Chania for the day, Steffi struggled to pull herself out of bed for the commute to Chania but then decided to remain behind to paint. They had hiked with Mr. Robinson after finishing in Chania the day before. The city heat had wilted them, and the hike finished them off. They never uncovered the cave they searched for, and came back to the hotel in near-darkness, feeling defeated. "Better luck next time" is what they all agreed on. Mr. Robinson was drawn and wan after the trek. As soon as Jim closed the door behind him, Steffi rolled over and fell back to sleep. Not until Jim entered the main road to Chania did he notice a sheet of paper sticking out of the glove box. Curiosity grabbed hold, and he pulled the car onto the gravel shoulder where he yanked the paper free.

He unfolded it and read, "Darling (very Hollywood, no?). This is to replace not having the energy to cook you a feta omelette, ha, ha. See, I was already scheming to stay in bed this morning. My apologies for the deception. After you are asleep, I will take this out to the jeep. Yes, it is another Rainer Maria Rilke poem. Have a good day of work; I already miss you. Your Steffi."

> *Along the sun-drenched roadside is the great*
> *Hollow tree stump which for generations*
> *Has been a trough, refilled*
> *By an inch or two of rain—I quench*
> *My thirst: taking the water's crystal coolness*
> *Into my whole self through my wrists.*
> *Drinking would be too powerful, too clarifying*
> *But choosing this measure of restraint*
> *Still fills my whole consciousness with shining water.*
> *Just as if you were to come to me now, I could be sated*
> *By letting my hand rest lightly, for a moment,*
> *Lightly, upon your shoulder.*

After reading the poem once, Jim folded the sheet back up and returned it to his portfolio. As he prepared to drive on, he was conscious again of a black dream that had awakened him before dawn. The Rilke poem was unable to bleach away the memory of the nightmare in which he wandered lost in a labyrinth while Steffi mournfully called out to him.

In Chania, he imagined the ways he might act were he living under occupation. To be conquered by anything, fascists, Stalinists, or booze, left you powerless. Without communicating that emotion, he knew his book would turn out empty. Research filled in details, but walking the ground, smelling the air, and hearing the rhythm of the language around him breathed life into the manuscript. As he peered out the window of the Technical University's library, he imagined looking up at the parachutes opening and floating down, the rifles and machine guns around him barking, and grasping how drastically his life was about to change.

As an afterthought, he photocopied German and Allied casualty lists. He had no idea what, if any, role they might play, but collecting the data gave him confidence that he was leaving no stone unturned. He jammed them in his portfolio behind the poem and broke the speed limit on his drive back.

When Jim arrived in the room, he noticed a sheet from a sketchpad propped against the vase on the ancient split and warped table. "Jim: I'm at Plakias beach for a swim. Join me if you can. Steffi."

As he set the note down, he caught a glimpse of the easel in the corner of the room. Set on the easel and bathed in the afternoon light was a new painting, almost a meter and a half on each side. The strength of the painting's colors grabbed him, and so distracted him that he bumped into a chair as he approached it. It resembled nothing of Steffi's previous work. Her pastels and charcoals had always impressed him—the way plants grew before your eyes and how arms and legs seemed to move—but this was a singular departure.

The canvas, an abstract in oil, was divided by four separate colors formed in rough oblique and obtuse triangular slices from the top to the bottom. The longest line segment of each triangle ran horizontally. Each color distilled Crete: the sky, the earth, the vegetation, the sea. The painting required no other details because everything was held captive in the colors: time, warmth, fecundity, birth, death. It was as if she had distilled Crete. He dragged a chair to within a few feet of the easel and straddled it, resting his arms on its back. For a long time, he stared at it, then finally declared, "You've done it this time, Steffi."

"Steffi," he said to himself. He stood up suddenly, longing to see and hold her. He quickly changed into his bathing suit, rushed to the car, and took off for Plakias. Once at the nearly vacant beach, he scanned the shore. Gentle waves broke, hissing and scraping over the coarse gravel beach where he expected to see her. Instead, he saw her emerge from the water directly in front of him. In typical fashion, her arms swung like a British sergeant major's. Steffi, a little nearsighted, hadn't spotted him yet.

Steffi wore a simple midnight blue one-piece suit. Her dark hair hung limply, soaked with seawater. She had muscular calves that he knew made her self-conscious, but the rest of her body was slender. Under the wet bathing suit, her firm, small breasts drew him. Her demeanor spoke of a self-effacing and humble character, which mysteriously made her more seductive. As she turned to look east toward town, the beautiful line of her long neck riveted him.

Just then, she recognized Jim and waved. She picked up a towel, having arrived at where she had set her things, and began to dry off. When Jim reached her, he said, "Give me that," and he took the towel from her and used it to vigorously rub her hair. He gently wiped each breast, and Steffi's soaked body leaned into him. The lobes of her ears were chilly and salty. Jim buried his nose in her hair and breathed in the broad back of the sea.

"Did you miss me?" She stared off somewhere across his shoulder.

"Every second." Jim's wet shirt cooled against his skin as the water evaporated.

She used Jim's shoulder to steady herself as she put on her new sandals. "Let's go back to the room. I bought some red wine. The lady at the store said it was a good one—from Corinth, I believe she said."

They gathered up her things and walked to the car. She slid onto the seat, putting a towel down first, and teased as he closed the door, "Was it a hard day at the office, dear?"

Back in the room, shadows crept across the floor and onto the painting, giving it a gray, monochromatic quality. Her back was to him as she faced the easel. He couldn't tell if she was studying her painting or something else. He offered, "Later, we have to discuss your incredible painting. Let's get you out of those wet things." From behind her, he moved the shoulder straps down and pulled the suit free of her breasts.

Steffi grabbed the suit by the sides and wiggled until it plopped to the floor. His swelling erection hardened. When she turned around and faced him, he noticed for the first time an asymmetry between her smaller left and larger right breast. "Ach so, I have detected a difference in the size." He cupped each gently in a hand. "Where are my calipers?"

"So now you know even that about me." She looked down sheepishly.

"It's nothing. It makes me joyful."

"What? How could their different size make you joyful? It has tormented me since puberty."

"Because it's another secret about you that I've learned."

The comment reminded her of a bigger secret. She deflected the thought with, "You better keep this a secret between us, or I'll take those poultry shears in the drawer and cut off your you-know-what."

They embraced and kissed. Jim tasted the brine from her swim. "Do you want to shower? Are you itchy from the salt?"

"Later. I like the feel of the salt. Lets me know I belong to the sea." Slowly, she undid the buttons of his damp cotton shirt.

Jim let his trunks drop next to her bathing suit. Steffi pressed against him. "Uh-oh."

She turned toward the kitchenette. "Why don't you lie down, Jim? I think I want to make the mood sexier and more romantic."

Jim settled on the bed naked. "Is that possible?" He noticed that his tan line was becoming sharper. Looking over at Steffi, he noticed how her legs and arms had become a deep honey brown, and he could trace where the straps of her bathing suit had been. While she assembled various candles and distributed them around the room, Jim commented, "I think we have to go to that nude beach to even out our tans. What do you think?"

Steffi stopped a moment and looked over at him. Her deep, dark eyes, glowed. "You are so full of ideas."

"Well, I don't think it's healthy to have too much of a contrast, do you? I don't want to look like a barber pole."

"Don't be silly. You don't look like a barber pole. And the one pole I do see isn't striped." Steffi turned off the one electric light. Candlelight caused the painting's colors to flicker.

"The painting is so otherworldly as I look at it from the bed."

Steffi approached the bed ghostlike in the flickering candlelight. She ignored Jim's comment about the painting and slid on top of him. The sensation of her warm body drowned him in arousal. She whispered in his ear, "I've wanted you inside me all day."

* * *

They wrapped each other in their arms and closed their eyes, though neither of them slept; rather, they luxuriated in the pleasure of intimacy. Sometime later they agreed they were hungry. Jim climbed out of bed to uncork the red wine Steffi had bought while Steffi pulled an earthenware dish from the oven. "While you were gone, I made a *Gyuvech*, a Bulgarian dish. I baked it while I was painting. It's still a little warm."

Jim peeked at the darkened, oven-browned crust. "Looks wonderful. I see potatoes and eggplant."

"And onions and green beans, and some tomato. Let's have some of the crusty bread I bought too."

They hardly spoke while they ate at the old table. Neither ate much. "Don't you like it, Jim? You don't seem to be eating much."

"I do. I promise; it's really good!"

She smiled and forked a single baked green bean into her mouth. "And the wine?"

"A wise purchase."

Her hand reached over to him. "I feel wonderful."

They left the dishes. Steffi put the remains of the Gyuvech in the refrigerator, and they crawled back into bed. For a while, Jim rubbed Steffi's shoulder, which she said ached from holding the paintbrushes so long. He kneaded her neck muscles, and they loosened to his touch. Jim studied every square inch of her back. A couple of small moles marked her left shoulder blade. Otherwise, her skin was smooth, with traces of sea salt clinging to the downy hair in the small of her tanned back. The muscles running along her spine were like taut rope. At the base of her back, just below the tan line, was a small red blemish. Steffi's arms were folded under her head, stretching her shoulders and revealing the bands of the muscles along her ribs.

"Jim?"

He knew now that she never looked directly at him when she asked difficult questions. His head rested next to hers. "Mmm?"

"What drew you to me?"

But damn, the question wasn't easy. The truth of the matter was, he wasn't entirely sure, so he skirted the issue with humor. "Lots of things."

"Name three."

"The way you wear your hat. The way you sip your tea. The way you sing off-key. The memory of all that."

"I know the song," she said in a bored drawl. "Why, really? Don't joke."

"So we're going to be serious..." He stretched his legs, and his mind raced to find the true answer which then popped in his head. "It was that you didn't belong."

"Huh?"

"Going back to the bedrock beginning of geologic time, I've never felt like I belonged, and I sensed you felt the same way, like we were members in a special weird club. The other stuff, the incredible physical attraction I felt for you, your mannerisms, your goofy hairstyle when we met, I don't know, all that stuff. That part is mysterious, and the answer to it is buried deeper than I can uncover now."

"But you are self-confident, like you have a plan."

"But that's different. Yeah, I know how to take charge, get things done, get across the goal line. Inside, that's something else. But you, you seemed okay with yourself, and that was so appealing."

"So strange the faces we have to the outside. You never know the suffering or even the happiness going on around you."

"And the hidden secrets."

That caught her off-guard. Jim noticed the pause. The tone of her answer seemed to braid together whimsy and despair. "So many joys and so many empty places." She thought of her grandfather. And there was Liliana. She was everything in those years: survival, nourishment, counseling... And the secrets.

"We find what we need to survive, I suppose."

The secret was leaking from its compartment, so she sought to change the subject. She beamed effervescently. "Anyway, the past is over."

"But history never goes away. The truth of the past will keep knocking at the door."

She dared not reply. Within a few moments, as the sun set, they both fell into deep sleep.

CHAPTER ELEVEN

As Steffi and Jim were uncovering the truth of each other like paleontologists chipping fossils from rock, Maria Phindrikalis brooded at her kitchen table. Viewed by all as happy, peaceful, and lovable for her charm as well as her benign eccentricities, she was besieged by dark thoughts. She had not heard from her husband, Elias, in nearly two months. His usual pay deposit was late. She wasn't desperate for the money. The hotel kept her above water, but not in a decade had Elias been late with a deposit. The last time was when an engine room accident jetted scalding steam on his back which, she found out later, left him howling in pain for days.

Maria knew she was not the first wife of a Greek trader or sailor to sit at a table anxious and depressed. Wasn't Homer's Odyssey framed around Penelope waiting for twenty years for the return of her Odysseus? Sailing the "broad back of the sea" had always carried risks. Elias had previously been on a crew sailing the trade routes in the pirate-infested waters off Somalia, and merchant ships were often not tranquil islands. Owners cheated, and crew members at times turned violent. She laughed and said how Elias's ample stomach and age were her best guarantees of a loyal husband, but she also knew how desperate her sex could be. A sailor with a good income was better than working a bar. Offspring of Greek sailors dotted the world, and no port was without a Greek married to an ex-bargirl. The sea could steal a man's memory and history.

Maria brooded alone, confiding in no one because her role was to play the strong one. People sought her out for advice. She was, after all, the daughter of the "Lion of the South." As she sat there, she felt the weight of trying to live up to her father's legacy. She knew, no matter what, she would be judged through the prism of a hero. As Maria sat there crossing herself, not touching her plate of cookies that had previously served loyally as self-medication in lonely times, she prayed for a sign that Elias was okay. She wished she had the guts to take drugs if only to escape for an hour.

* * *

Harold Robinson stood alone in his room folding his newly washed field kit. The room's silence oppressed him. As an attempted antidote, he imagined himself at his cottage in the Cotswolds, listening to the birds whose songs had always thrilled Anne. Utterly catching this retired Major of the Royal Artillery by surprise, Harold suddenly burst into tears. He instinctively looked about him, confirming no one had seen his "emotional outburst." "Unmanly," he choked in a hoarse whisper. To be sure, Harold missed the company of Anne, as he had every day. He admitted that staying at a holiday hotel brought on a touch of melancholia, what with laughing toddlers dashing about and lovers like Steffi and Jim seeming to float above the earth. They brought back memories of past joys never to be had again.

Harold leaned on the table with his fists and stared blankly at the stack of folded khaki. Slowly, the answer surfaced like water trickling through a web of cracks in a stone cellar wall. *I'm bloody mortified!* What was the point of this fiasco? His second season of searching had achieved nothing but converting local curiosity to derision. *They must think of me as a mad hatter!* Even in old age, judgment stung. Did the whole thing matter anymore?

So often on the telly he listened to people, especially Yanks, peppering their language with psycho-therapeutic terms like "closure." "We have to have closure. Our bloody house burned down, and we need closure." *I haven't found Ian, so is that what it means? I have no closure? Well, I have news for them and me. One can't tidy up life. Life's messy from birth to death.* For the first time Harold entertained abandoning the search and leaving "this damnable island." He knew pain had gone on so long here that memory of his would have the impact of a single drop of rain on Crete's parched soil.

* * *

Yanni's room, festooned with posters of Sylvester Stallone movies and tucked in the corner of a cheap building with a common toilet and shower, was eternally hidden in shadow; and yet, a fierce, ominous energy, like the charged and roiling clouds of a summer thunderstorm, lived inside. While Yanni lay on his bed, knowing he had to leave soon for the taverna, a job he hated, he stewed about the losing cards his life had been dealt. This theme was his personal creation, his obsession, and his protector; otherwise, he had to face the withering, naked truth of his decrepit choices.

As a child, Yanni learned to hatch fantasies and conspiracies to deflect truth and defend his crippled ego. Truth he played with as personal modeling clay. While in prison, the reward for living in Athens as a grifter, fantasy became his one successful survival tool. Having been conditioned as the compliant pawn of every prison gang that slapped him around until he accepted risks for no guaranteed return, he would lay on his bunk, much the way he was now, escaping into fantasies. He most often fancied being a lithe martial arts killer that only fools challenged. He imagined a burly gang member attacking him, but before the man's tattooed arms could touch him, Yanni crushed his windpipe with a single punch. Instead of allowing the guards to shame him, he imagined setting fire to their guard room and blocking their exit.

Somewhere in the course of his sentence, he became a "Sect of the Revolutionaries" wannabe. He learned their political patois. He sneered when he denigrated "rich tourists." He declared to the prison yard, "Greeks have become the 'whipped dogs' of foreigners, begging for food scraps thrown their way." His new idiom conflated "foreigner" and "exploiter," and then exploiter became "capitalist exploiter," and capitalist exploiter became a "target for elimination." The idiom seduced him, and he wanted nothing more than to be a part of this group. His skin tingled when he heard them pledge, "We will cut the faces of those who oppose us."

Nevertheless, no matter how he swore his allegiance, the group would not have him. When he was finally released, despite his rejection, he nurtured a single dream for the future: to prove his worthiness to the Sect of the Revolutionaries. If not by the Sect, Yanni's allegiance was taken seriously by the Hellenic Police, the national police of Greece. They swept him off the streets of Athens and roughed him up, swearing that if he didn't work for them, they would "kick his ass" back to prison with the story that he had snitched on the Sect of the Revolutionaries, a prison death sentence.

The thought made him bawl like a little boy. Running back to the family in Crete was the best of bad alternatives. He'd let things cool down, get the Hellenic Police off his back, and work on a way to prove his loyalty to the Sect. "Foreigners," he sneered, they had raped this island of its majesty. After the headlines he planned to make, the Sect would welcome him.

* * *

When Jim awakened the next morning, Steffi's warmth was absent. He glanced toward the table but didn't see a note. No coffee brewed, and no fresh crumbs were on the bread board. He pulled on his jeans, slipped into his boat shoes, and set out to find her. As soon as he opened the door he spied her sitting, with her back to him, beneath the long curving branches of the plane tree. She sobbed, and her shoulders convulsed.

The first thing crossing Jim's mind was that he had done or said something terribly wrong. Had he blabbed some other woman's name in his sleep? Had he unintentionally delivered one of his famous off-handed zingers? Had he missed a cue? That had always been the problem with Jeannette. She forever accused him of not "picking up on things." Had he ignored something Steffi said? "Men don't get prompters in real life," Rusty Pavlicek declared once in a beer-induced funk.

As he approached her, Jim at first felt confident that he could explain any misstep, but then he grew anxious. Histrionics were not typical of Steffi. Something must be horribly wrong. Perhaps a call from home? From her sister? My God, maybe Steffi's pregnant? But that thought isn't bad news, even at my age. Could our child be inside her? They should have Champagne, not tears. *No, you don't drink when you're pregnant, fool. But the crying, she must think I'll be upset.* Carefully, he reached out and touched her shoulder. The lines from the Rilke poem came back:

I could be satisfied
To let my hand rest lightly, for a moment,
Lightly, upon your shoulder

"Steffi? Is something wrong?"

Her head cocked in his direction. Her nose and eyes were red-rimmed, and her gentle, happy mouth was stretched agonizingly, like the death masks he had seen in Mathew Brady's daguerreotypes of Civil War fallen. "Oh Jim, there's so much brokenness in my life you don't know about."

"You've endured so much crap, Steffi."

For a moment, her voice failed her. So much history—so much self-loathing—so much shame. Steffi had blotted it all up and trapped it inside her. Unconsciously, she measured herself through the prism of how she believed others viewed her. Though she would deny it, Bulgaria's brand of Communism and the corrupt regimes that followed had imprinted biased values and stereotypes on her mind. Through those lenses, she viewed herself as shameful. She had convinced herself that Jim would also find her shameful when she revealed the truth. For all that, however, she needed to unburden herself with a confession. Not unlike a drowning woman reaching out for something to grab in order to pull herself to the surface, Steffi's confession was a flailing attempt to free herself from the past. Finally, her voice managed, "I've done things I'm sure you can't accept. I should have told you before, even before we came here, what I've kept hidden."

As she spoke, a queasy gut announced fear of his whole plan unraveling. In a flash, his past despair came back. *Why can't I get control of anything? Every gamble, a loss. History repeats itself, professor. Déjà vu all over again.* Without bothering to hear another word, he pictured putting Steffi on a plane back to Bulgaria and paying Mrs. Phindrikalis the final bill without a cup of her coffee and a cookie. His cottony mouth caused his words to slur drunkenly. "Can it be all that bad?"

Steffi buried her face in her hands, the blue stone of her grandmother's ring appearing cold as ice. Not knowing what else to do, Jim sat down on the bench next to her. "Come on, Steffi. We can fix this." But in his heart he prepared for disaster and was already assembling the same defensive wall he had so often employed. *Get it over with. Nothing lasts.*

She responded in a voice muffled by her hands, "After you do something, you can't take it back, and it's there forever for people to judge. You can't rewrite it."

"If that's the problem, people rewrite the past every day. We talked about that the other night. Don't worry about that." With a cold edge that shocked Steffi and surprised himself, he asked, "What's this all about anyway?"

Her hands opened, and her drooping eyes looked up, "Jim, do you believe that something a woman might do that makes sense to a woman might not make sense to you?"

"Mostly, I think that's bullshit, but okay, theoretically, so?"

She shook her head and closed her eyes. "This is hopeless."

"Don't do that!" he said sharply.

She winced in response, but she soldiered on. "After Ludmil…"

"Yes, after Ludmil, what?"

"I didn't want a man to touch me."

"Of course, that makes perfect sense."

"I saw Ludmil's face every time a man came close." Steffi drew a deep breath and wiped tears away with her fingers. She stared blankly at the trunk of the plane tree. "When you fall, Jim, there's no bottom… There's no bottom to falling. When you fall, you think you are unworthy of everything—respect, love, fairness. So with men what you feel is empty. I was empty, Jim, as empty as how the saddest prostitute must feel."

"Steffi, could you just tell me the key factual pieces here?"

After this stone, slung at her from Jim's hastily constructed citadel, she gulped as if swallowing her emotion in order to gather her courage, and then charged on, her steadfast voice revealing a determination to finally say it all. "For a long time, when I couldn't look at a man, I hid all my feelings from mother and my sister too. Even the smell of a man revolted me. Surely, I thought, something was wrong with me."

Seeing himself in heroic terms for sitting quietly while Steffi finished what he regarded as her litany of woes, he built the walls of his fortress still higher so that Steffi disappeared from sight. Only her voice remained.

"I could never trust them. I believed men only wanted to use me."

"Do you think I'm using you? That I'm trying to do that with you? Have I given you reason not to trust me?"

She waved her hand to dismiss his comment but didn't answer. Instead, she pressed on. "I ended up hating myself. Everything in my life was worthless. Maybe I was no better than Ludmil. Maybe I was worse. When this starts, Jim, you go down like a corkscrew." She used a finger to demonstrate something corkscrewing down.

Jim scratched his ear. "Wow." In the back of his mind he thought, she's going to prove she's a head case.

"So thanks be to God I had some girlfriends I could talk to. It's not so unusual what I went through, Jim. You may not think so. But I find so many of my friends…they went through similar things."

"Evil men—men from Mars—I suppose we're all nothing more than a contained mass of rapists."

"I didn't say this." Her head turned to him.

"Thank God for feminine sensibilities or civilization would have died off long ago. It's the glue—"

She cut him off. "Stop it! You're being dreadful! This is not what I'm talking about."

"Okay, okay. But I have had unpleasant experiences too. Lots of peoples' histories…"

"This is about *my* history. It's my history I'm trying to talk to you about. Not the Minoans, and not Jeannette—me, Steffi." But the fact was, her history and Jim's as well as the Minoans' and Jeannette's had intersected and entwined already more than either could grasp. She poked herself, now enflamed, "The person you just made love to, or did you only fuck me?"

He winced. "Steffi!"

For a minute they sat in stunned silence. Jim's posturing included keeping his eyes averted, but he caught a glimpse of her trembling hand, and it made him feel guilty for his coarseness, but he fought that back by shouting to himself, *Guilt making, the card they all play.* She took another deep breath as if to steel herself. "I must tell you even though I'm certain now how you will react."

"And what does your crystal ball say?"

"That you will run from me and reject me. Just please, try not to be cruel."

"Okay, okay." But his emotions grew hotter. "But we won't know unless you say it, right?"

"I've been carrying this burden I hide from you."

"So unhide it." He thought, maybe it was divine payback for the way he had treated his first love.

"Do you remember my friend, Liliana? I introduced you to her. She worked for the state theater in set design, and writes wonderful short stories. And Jim, I've known her since we were little children in school, and we come from the same village, and we both always loved nature."

"Long, straight blond hair, combat boots?"

"I don't know what you mean, combat boots. Liliana and I marched in the protests together in front of the National Assembly to stop Communism. We protested the stupid governments that came after Communism. We celebrated the freedom. All my life I could always tell her anything. Without her I never could have survived the pain and guilt of Ludmil. She nourished me, Jim, when no one else cared. When all these other men just pretended they cared but wanted me for a toy." She mumbled something incomprehensible in Bulgarian and then switched back to English. "One night, we were back in the village at her parent's dom (house). They were gone someplace."

Dark thoughts rose in Jim, and he stiffened in response. "Wait, do I have the right person? Liliana, with the stud in her nose, purple streak in her hair?"

"She was always big counterculture."

"Counter-matter."

Steffi chose not to swallow the bait and forged on with tightly closed eyes. "Jim, I arrived at Liliana's, shaking. I, I was desperate. I wanted to rip my heart from my body. I hated myself; blamed myself; I wished I had never been born. Love was absent from me and only cold dark things haunted me. I expected a charon to take me. Charon, yes? Is this the right word?"

"I guess."

"But Liliana, she soothed me. She comforted me like God was speaking through her. She made it seem like all was not lost. She was the only person... who..." She couldn't continue for several seconds, then she uttered with finality, "We touched. We had sex between women."

Jim froze. "What?"

"Off and on for maybe, I don't know, couple of weeks maybe, we did this."

"You got to be shitting me!" His reaction was less a judgment than a reawakening of the humiliation he felt with Jeannette.

"At the time, Jim, she was the only person I felt close to. We let each other touch because... like, it was trust. It helped me, Jim. I know it is difficult to understand, but it helped me. I know it sounds crazy to you."

"So, you're telling me sex with Liliana somehow untangled the mess. Well, brava to her. We obviously haven't reached that exalted level. So that's my competition?"

Steffi shook her head. "I knew you wouldn't understand. This is exactly what I expected. But I couldn't hide this secret. Why can't you understand, Jim?" she pleaded. "I came to understand. Liliana only wanted to share tenderness. Touching her was not my nature. For some women, they deny who they are and pretend. They shouldn't do that, but for me, it was something else. Not love or that I want women over men. It saved me from drowning. Then we stopped before all of it could end in hurt and regret. I survived because of Liliana, and I will always be her friend. I would die for her. The physical part—it was not the same as I feel for men—definitely not what I feel with you."

Steffi sensed Jim ignored her explanation. "I saw you two once, remember? Near Alexander Nevsky cathedral, walking down the street with her in her goddamned combat boots, the two of you holding hands."

Now her voice contained a note of insult. "Jim, that was in Sofia, not America. Women friends and sisters hold hands when they are together."

"Or lovers."

"It's our culture to hold hands. It's beautiful."

"At the time, that's what I thought, but all the time you and Ms. Punkrock were getting it on in the back room."

"How dare you cheapen Liliana and what I've shared with you! I hate having secrets—not telling you—it made me feel guilty. I was so confused when it happened, so I went to a priest. And he told me I was trapped in sin. That convinced me God could never love me. That I could never be forgiven. With the Communists, there were laws to say I made a crime. I was afraid to tell you, but I thought, because I showed you understanding about Jeannette, maybe you had the heart to forgive. But no, in the end, you act just like the priest and other Bulgarian men with their fast cars and small brains. Why are you so cruel, Jim?"

"Because this hurts. Because I've been tricked." Jim stood up, abruptly. "Because it might have been useful to know you were bi-sexual or lesbian or whatever the hell you are before we invested in this trip."

"You think this is an investment like buying stock?"

"Of course the hell not. Emotional investment! You're not the only one taking a risk in this relationship, you know. Doesn't it occur to you that I've had some rough times too, that I need to count on somebody? I need to lean on somebody too, but I didn't have sex with my best friend because of it."

"Women know tenderness differently. It wasn't about sex; it was about caring. Maybe to you it seems inside out. And Jim, I can't say it doesn't confuse me, but at the time, it was what, like a life preserver. My life was so," Steffi searched for the right English word, "Shattered. Believe me, I didn't want to hide this. I've been so happy with you. I want you to know everything about me." She sobbed again, and between sobs cried out, "I told myself God couldn't love someone like me. My mother showed no love. I remember I looked at the picture of my Grossvatti in the mountains, and I believed he could have comforted me, but he was gone. Liliana was there."

"Any port in a storm."

Her voice turned sharp, "What an ugly thing to say! In the end, I knew you couldn't accept me. You want life your way. You ordered me to accept your life."

"I never ordered you to do anything."

"Take it or leave it. Is that the American idiom I should use? Jim, big hero—Steffi should feel lucky. Ah, I get it, Jim decides every-thing—thumbs up or thumbs down for Steffi, yes, maybe no. He cares for me, he doesn't. I wait on a shelf, a poor girl from a poor country." With that she stood and ran up the trail Mr. Robinson often used.

Jim smacked his hands together and bawled, "Come back here!" but she kept going, and he didn't chase after her.

CHAPTER TWELVE

For a while, Jim stood there with his hands on his hips, holding his ground. His jaw jutted out defiantly, a boxer challenging an opponent. Then he turned on his heels and stormed back into the room, slamming the door behind him. He paced back and forth, a caged panther, screaming obscenities. At one point in his circuit of the room, he picked a pillow off the bed and whipped it at the wall. For some unreasoned reason, he compulsively repeated the German words toben (rage) and austoben (blow off steam).

His head cleared, the rage replaced by iciness. Grabbing his large North Face duffel, he began packing clothes. "I'm outta here! Never should have done this," he announced to himself. He didn't bother to fold the clothes. Instead, he stuffed them with his fist as deep into the duffel as he could, pressing and squeezing the clothes until the air was out. After several minutes of frenzy and with the duffel half full, his energy ebbed. His legs ached like he had run a ten-kilometer race. In the corner of the room, he spied the stack of books and notebooks for his manuscript. "How am I going to get this crap packed up?"

Finally, he collapsed in a chair at the old worn table. Folding his hands on the tabletop like a little schoolboy, he stared at the split and bleached sections of wood. He stared at one dark crease with an intensity that crossed his eyes, and the dark fissure in the wood appeared as double. As in a hypnotic trance, his thoughts attached themselves to the table. He speculated about the history of the table. How many homes had it served? By the looks of it, the table was old even when the Nazis occupied the island. Where had the tree grown that the forester felled? Certainly, it was born from a mature hardwood tree that must have stood even in the days of the Ottoman occupation. He envisioned a man sanding the wood planks spread across two sawhorses. How many family quarrels raged around it? Maybe a child was born on it, or a wound dressed on it. Was that the reason the surface was bleached, to remove bloodstains?

Slowly his meditation on the table tranquilized him and released his rage, only to be replaced by the even more painful feelings of betrayal and humiliation. Instead of his relationship with Steffi reaffirming his worth as a man, the whole episode left him feeling enfeebled and craven. He had longed for order and found cacophony instead. *I carried this attraction, this hope for so long, and somehow managed to bank the fire until I thought the time was right. I went along with her idea—let's start from the beginning. All built on a lie. She ruined everything I had planned.*

He folded his arms on the table and rested his head on them, closing his eyes, deciding one moment to finish packing and the next not, one second wanting to throw Steffi's things outside and the next second not caring. In the impenetrable darkness before his eyes, no answers came; flickers and shadows crossed his blindness from time to time, but otherwise, he felt wrapped and lost in darkness, the single thing at that moment he was grateful for.

Mysteriously, a memory from childhood arose, illuminating the darkness. He saw himself standing at the living room window crying. His father was pulling the Chevrolet station wagon out of the driveway. His mother was in the front seat touching up her makeup, and his brother and sister were jumping around in the back, laughing. Jim could almost hear his father's reprimand. "Now settle down you two. If you want a hot dog at the stadium, you'll settle down." They were off to see the Detroit Tigers play the Cleveland Indians, but he couldn't go. He had stepped on his sister Patty's doll and broken its arm. He said it was an accident, but it wasn't. That's what made Dad angry. "Jimmy, be a man! Admit what you did was wrong!" But he didn't admit it. Why should he? Patty picked on him all the time.

Grandma was in the den watching TV. She was there just to watch him. He heard the TV, but the words were indistinguishable. His grandmother laughed at something, but he didn't care. Father said he had been bad and couldn't go to the game, but his father had promised the trip to him originally. Nobody loved him, and he wished he could run away or live in a boys' home with other boys who had fathers who didn't love them. Grandma didn't really like him either; she only pretended to be nice. What he should do is pack his suitcase. No one would even notice if he left. Maybe after a week someone would ask, "Anybody seen Jimmy?" By then he would be in Chicago enjoying himself, eating ice cream and working at Comiskey Park as the bat boy for the White Sox. And his father would see him on TV. All the ball players would like him and pay attention to him. He knew all their bats, and Dad hated the White Sox.

Then other memories, or were they dreams, tumbled from somewhere. Some of the images Jim recognized in half-conscious awareness. Others led him into a sleep that more closely resembled something induced by a hallucinogen. Dissociative images propelled him on an unintended journey which he at first fought but then surrendered to.

As all this played out in Jim's mind, Steffi climbed the trail, stumbling along without proper shoes. She slammed her toe against a rock. "Ah! Stupid sandals," she shouted in Bulgarian. Finally, with her lungs aching from her ascent and her toe swelling, she collapsed on a patch of dry ankle-high grass. For a few moments, she leaned back on her hands and recovered her breath. She then undid the straps of her sandals and pulled them off, placing them neatly beside her. Steffi studied her swollen big toe. When she tried to massage it, the pain stopped her. The first signs of a bruise were forming under the toenail, and she thought, "Great, now I'll probably lose a toenail because of cruel Jim."

A fresh surge of tears welled up. She pulled her knees to her chest and wrapped her arms around her legs, letting her head drop to her knees. The convulsive sobs were gone, replaced by a steady stream of hot tears. Off to her right, from under her arm, she peered down into the grass through the foggy lenses of her tear-filled eyes. A beetle of some sort negotiated the stiff blades of grass. For a moment, its struggles distracted her. *Where is the poor thing going? Where am I going?*

She raised her head up and looked around, not paying any particular attention to her surroundings. Not a thought about painting, purpose, or plans for tomorrow came to mind. She felt betrayed, humiliated, and cheated of happiness. Ludmil, the priest, the other men, Jim—they were all the same. "Smothered," she shouted. Not even an ember let alone a bush burned. No one or thing reached out to rescue her. She cried out to God in Bulgarian, "Why now do you abandon me?" God did not answer. Not even a bird called.

Automatically, in desperation, she recited one of her daily prayers. She had read that the poet and painter, William Blake, had said the same one every day: *"Dear God, fill me with your spirit of forgiveness and love. Annihilate the selfhood in me. Be thou all my life."* But she didn't feel selfish; she felt empty. She couldn't forgive herself, so how could she forgive others? One side of her brain felt shame, and the other side saw it as beautiful. Why couldn't she be more like Liliana? Liliana was at peace with it. "Steffi," she had said, "it just happened. You needed someone. You needed something other than words. Now you can step back from it because it's behind you. It doesn't change who we are. In fact, we're better for it." When Liliana had seen that Steffi remained uncertain, she added, knowing Steffi's beliefs, "And if there is a loving God, no God could be angry. What we did was not selfish, hurtful, or hateful. Sometimes touching is the only thing that can fill emptiness in this world."

But she also raged with indignation because Jim had judged her and Liliana wrongly. On one level she wished she had lived with the secret. On another level, she asked, what was the purpose of not telling him? She knew she couldn't have lived with hiding it anymore. A direct crystalline answer occurred to her. "I had to tell him, and that's good enough." With that, Steffi collapsed back on the grass, emotionally and physically spent, her toe throbbing. Like Jim, she didn't immediately fall asleep, but her mind skipped through time, trance-like.

She remembered after Cairo when the authorities banished the family to the countryside for reasons she didn't understand at the time. Mommy offered at the time, "Poor Daddy, the way he's been treated."

"Why, Mommy?"

"Cruel things they did, but your father's not a fighter, Steffi. I have to accept that; you girls have to accept that." Mommy sighed in resignation.

Steffi had wanted to surprise her father to make him laugh. She knew he was sitting in a chair in the living room reading something about plants. Her idea was to sneak below the window in front of where he sat and then suddenly surprise him by bursting up like a giant, snarling, jungle cat, scratching at the window with her pretend claws.

Skulking around the side of their tiny house, she crawled the last few meters until she found herself just below the corner of the window. Furtively, she peeked inside from the bottom corner to be sure Daddy was still in his chair, reading. It had been her intention to sneak just a glimpse. When she saw him, however, she couldn't help but stare. She treasured this man who had showered her with affection. Now, the way he looked, alone in the room with his own thoughts, evoked a conscious awareness of pathos for the first time in her life.

The thirty-five-year-old Steffi asked herself, why did mother always tell him to fight back? "Don't accept this! You don't deserve to be treated this way." But when she had seen the lines on his drawn face, somehow, she had grasped how much strength it took to always smile for her and her sister. It must have taken all his strength. What strength was left to fight? Hadn't her mother seen it? Her poor Daddy, sitting in the chair with his shoulders slouched so low it was as if an invisible giant had pushed him down in his seat. Even his eyelids had sagged. Mother, the great analytic mind, had been wrong as usual.

Her childhood memory came back. He was the strongest man in the world. He spun her like a windmill until she was too dizzy to stand. Mommy cautioned, "Be careful, you'll upset the girls' tummies." When the little girl Steffi saw him sitting there, she wanted to carry him and bounce him up and down on her knee to make him laugh and not look so sad.

She carried that memory as a weight in her life's rucksack. Back then, she had promised herself to ask Daddy to explain. She imagined comforting him. Never once did his love slacken. Over time, even after they moved back to Sofia, she hesitated to ask, knowing how painful it was. "But how do I take away his pain if I don't know what he's feeling?" Her single answer to that question was, "Just love him. Show him love," but then he was gone. The memory of him lying in bed, having passed away during the night, was agonizing; but most agonizing was his expression in death, the same sad expression she had seen while spying on him as a little girl.

Steffi had come to believe Jim, like Daddy, loved her without condition. As she lay on the ground, absently staring at the sky, she realized she had told Jim about Liliana because she trusted him as she would her father, and that, she decided, was naïve. Now Jim was gone and his love with him. All the men in her life were gone. Grossvatti was only a picture. Jim walked away from her without trying to understand. And Ludmil… She forced her straying thoughts to stop. She listened carefully to the mountain, but still no sound came. She folded her arm over her eyes and directed all her energy to listening to the mountain, and somehow, that led her into a deep dreamless sleep.

* * *

The better part of two hours passed before Jim emerged from his stupor, sparked by pain in his deadened arm that had been cramped under his head all that time. Still half asleep, he massaged his arm until it slowly tingled back to life. The emptiness and silence of the room frightened him. For a moment, Jim entertained the notion that he suffered from Cotard's Syndrome, because he seriously wondered whether he was dead. Impulsively, he called out, "Steffi?" Though wobbly, he stood up and staggered to the door. As he opened it, he called out again, "Steffi!" Seeing the empty bench brought back the full force of the scene under the plane tree.

"Fuck it," Jim announced, "I'll go to the beach then I'm getting outta here," but he did little more than strut around in circles pretending to look for his beach clothes. "Liliana, I was suspicious all along. Always giving me the evil eye! Ooh, big counter-culture tootsie from some podunk village. And then Steffi thinking I'm going to understand that." His voice was lathered with indignation, but he couldn't sustain his rage, with his energy spent, so it fizzled like turning off the heat beneath a whistling kettle. Other feelings came back, inchoate and vaporous; he fought defining those, for fear of what they might reveal, pushing them back down like a sour belch. *I wasn't wrong*, he protested. *She's the one. How would she have reacted if I had bleated, "Please try to understand Steffi, every once in a while I like to do it with goats"?* Even as he said it, he cringed at his childishness.

Nothing Steffi said had been flippant. The memory of her sobs struck like cannonballs against his defensive wall. "No!" he countered, "She's the one." *One what? My cock's not enough for her?* Even as the thought escaped his mind, he chuckled, picturing himself as an enraged, quacking gander or a peacock in a feather display. "Damn." He finally voiced the word that truly explained his anger. "Humiliation."

He plopped down at the table again, staring at nothing in particular. It was then that he noticed Steffi's sketchpads on the left edge of the table. He reached over and grabbed the first pad on top of the stack and began absently leafing through it. No matter what they struggled with, he couldn't deny her phenomenal talent. The pad contained mostly fragments of things drawn in pencil: a twig, a leaf, a shell, the old and charred stovetop espresso maker. He recognized his ear on one page and his hiking boots on another.

At one point, he reached a page that stopped him cold. It was a portrait of him he had known nothing about. It was drawn from his left front with his head down, apparently in thought. He suspected Steffi had done it while he concentrated on his book. The portrait wasn't merely a likeness, but something much more. Every line and shade of her pencil revealed truth. It was as if this woman had opened his cranium and removed and then exposed to light all his thoughts hidden in the dark labyrinth of neurons. In one sketch she said more about him than he ever uncovered in his endless musings. He didn't know what to do with the sketch: burn it, frame it, deny it, embrace it. He whispered, "My God, this woman really sees me."

He turned the pages more carefully, stopping to absorb the power of Steffi's work. Between two pages he found a letter written on pale blue stationery. The letter, in Steffi's curving cursive, was written in German and addressed to her mother. Jim could hear her voice as he read:

Mother, you have been through so much with me. I struggle so much with you. Ah, you can be so scientific and rigid! It can drive me crazy. Your emotions remain a mystery to me; and yet, I want you to know, I'm grateful for you. I have accused you of many things, but in the end, what do they matter? Let's try to love each other. What else should count between a daughter and mother?

To be honest, I had hoped you would bless this trip to be with Jim. Since you didn't, out of anger, I have not written until now. I have decided to tell you how I am doing. I can tell you I am happy, and your predictions of doom were wrong! I know you were only trying to protect me. Ludmil and Italy and all the rest scarred both of us. You know I sometimes find it is easier to draw my feelings or use the words of others to explain myself, so I have enclosed a poem by Sappho. I have told you about her, haven't I? She lived in ancient Greece and had a mother she loved, too, named Cleis. This poem is what I have to give you from Crete.

It's no use
Mother dear I
Can't finish
Weaving
You may
Blame Aphrodite
Soft as she is
She has almost
Killed me with
Love for that boy

So now there you have it. My love of Jim and the conviction (Here Jim found two lines scratched out beyond his ability to decipher them.) *And I understand how this girl feels sitting at that distaff so long ago that..."*

Jim slid the unfinished letter back in the sketchpad and closed it, putting it back on the stack with the others. Tears of frustration, guilt, and pathos burned. This poem, a relic of ancient history, by a poetess whose work survived only in fragments, left him with awareness of how much had been blocked by the opaque stone of his selfish wall. What emerged after reading the letter was a granite-solid realization of how precious this woman, Steffi, had become and how empty life had been before her. To be sure, Steffi's revelation still dizzied him, but at the same time, and perhaps for the first time ever, nothing blurred a conviction that he could choose how to react. It was the closest he had ever experienced to an unseen hand reaching down and opening his eyes. He could choose to remain angry and chase a hologram of idealizations as temporary salve for his wounds and emptiness, or he could choose to accept life as imperfect. Without question, the letter for him was exculpatory evidence that Steffi's love of him was pure of heart and light-years ahead of his own confused emotions. She offered him more than life had ever offered him before.

* * *

Steffi awoke, measurably calmer, but the ugliness remained in her conscious thoughts. It was a sailor's calmness once a tempest has passed, who sees in the now gentle swells the storm's dross washing along the hull as reminders of the horror just experienced. Sleep had rewarded her with renewed certainty that she had been right to tell Jim. What had happened with Liliana had happened. Nothing could change that. A monk had told her that God forgives and then forgets. She knew it was up to Jim to either understand or not and to forgive or not. She wished to not be pilloried by him, but that was not hers to decide. By some mysterious process during their parallel comas, Steffi arrived at much the same conclusion as Jim. She could choose how to react. Between what she told Jim and how he reacted was a gap she must fill, either with beauty or ugliness. She nodded in acceptance of this choice. For a moment, she scanned the horizon of this island that had seduced her in so short a time. A fragment of another Sappho poem came back:

And their feet move
Rhythmically, as tender
Feet of Cretan girls
Danced once around an
Altar of love, crushing
a circle in the soft
smooth flowering grass

Was it on this spot? She smoothed the grass with her hands. Already her body had left an imprint in the blades growing in the dry Cretan air just as dancing feet might. Life will go on, she thought.

Just then Mr. Robinson appeared, coming down the trail. Spotting Steffi he declared, "Hallo! Fancy meeting you here."

"Hello back to you, Mr. Robinson."

He paused in front of her, leaning with his hands on the hilt of his walking stick. "Whatever are you doing up here, my dear? Is Jim with you?" Two dark sweat stains darkened his khaki shirt.

Putting on as brave a face as possible, she said, "Oh Mr. Robinson, don't worry about me."

"But I do, my dear, I must. It's an imperative of family Robinson to worry about ladies. I suppose I drove poor Anne crazy—always worrying."

"I'm fine. I wanted to have some time of solitude in these high areas. I see you've been wandering. Find anything?" She hoped the remnants of her tears gave nothing away.

Mr. Robinson brightened. "I've spotted a couple of caves that have true possibilities. I don't wish to be too optimistic. It's been so discouraging up until now. I sent Apostolos home and told him we'll resume after the weekend. I need the break."

"These new places, are they where you believe Ian was?"

"Yes, or I should think. That's the jackpot anyway."

"To find something will be so enriching for you."

"Indeed. Now stop this New Age meditation nonsense and walk down with me." He sensed something was wrong. "This is a charming piece of real estate, but there are some scoundrels about. There are sheep rustlers, you know."

"I'll be fine, really."

Mr. Robinson twisted his head to show hesitation. "As you wish, dear, but I'm not sanguine about leaving. I shall give that Jim of yours a piece of my mind, letting you wander off like that."

Steffi braved a smile. "Not to worry. I'll come along soon."

"You promise."

"I promise."

"Modern girls, so damn headstrong."

Among the shrubs farther up the trail, hidden but in hearing distance, crouched Yanni. What he heard brightened him—"Jackpot, rich." He knew those terms from American TV. He saw this opportunity as redemption, earning the riches he deserved and the acceptance from the Sect he craved. It was perfect. *This Britisher will lead me to the gold, and then I will make an example of these rich tourists. Everyone on the island has heard of this gold. There were kilos and kilos of it left over from the war. It's been sitting under the noses of these dumb peasants all these years.*

Yanni listened carefully. Who was it he was talking to? A woman's quiet voice. Yanni peeked from around the bush. From the back, he recognized her, the girl with the American. They dined with the old Britisher. She had ordered coffee in bad Greek.

Mr. Robinson walked off. Yanni crept closer for a better look. Her hair was nice the way it picked up the sun. He wished he could see her ass, but the damn grass blocked it. She's the kind that can get you stiff. Where's the Yank? Maybe she wants some company? Sure, why not with a real Greek man.

He made a plan. He would crawl over to the trail and start walking down, and be surprised to see this woman like the old man had; but as he moved on the slope, his foot slid and a rock tumbled and banged into another one, making a sound like two colliding billiard balls.

Steffi turned her head in the direction of the sound. Instinctively she called out in Bulgarian, *"Koi e tam?"* Then in English, "Who's there?"

"Please to excuse. Is someone there?"

Steffi spotted Yanni on the trail, but the sound had come from farther off to the left behind her. Wary, she replied, "Yes."

He stood in front of her and wiped off his brow. "Whew, it's getting hot today. I'm just now out looking for herbs, you knowing, for taverna." He smiled unctuously.

"You're Yanni, right?" She thought it best to identify him by name.

"Yes, Miss." His head cocked from side to side in a Balkan gesture of agreement Steffi recognized from Bulgaria.

"You know Mr. Robinson is quite close by," she said in halting Greek. "Did you see him?"

Switching to halting English, "Mr. Robinson, the British gentleman? No, not see. He here, just now?"

"Yes. I'm surprised you didn't see him."

"Well, I'm all time looking at the ground for the herb."

Steffi thought that sounded credible. Maybe that's why she heard the sound behind her. He was back behind her looking for herbs. "Were you behind here," she pointed behind her, "Looking for herbs?"

"Where?"

"Back here." She pointed again behind her.

"Me, no," and Yanni smiled. He came closer, still smiling. Yanni had enormous, muscular forearms, covered in thick black hair. Steffi noticed them when Yanni had set the plates of food on the table.

"Don't you have a bag or something for your herbs?"

"Please?"

"Bag, sack, backpack or something to carry, to carry the herbs."

"Oh," Yanni looked sheepish, "Not today," prevaricating. "Today I'm out to hunt where the herbs are. When I find, I come back." Yanni pointed to the ground near where Steffi sat. "Do you mind if I sit down for a moment? Hot day, no? Whew, tired." He made a show of wiping his brow with a white handkerchief.

Before Steffi could answer, Yanni sat on the grass. "Ah yes. Soft ground. Feels good."

"Well, Yanni, it is late." Steffi pointed to where a wristwatch would be. "I must return. My boyfriend Jim will get worried."

"So what, wait a minute. Keep me little bit company."

Mr. Robinson ran into Jim a couple of hundred meters from the trailhead behind the plane tree. Jim was now frantic to find Steffi. "James, there you are. Are you aware that Steffi is wandering alone through these hills? I know it's the twenty-first century, but I don't approve."

"You saw Steffi on the trail?"

"Indeed. Fifteen minutes farther on at my pace."

"That's a help. I was beginning to worry. Was she okay?"

"As well you should worry. Actually, she appeared distraught to me."

"Thank you, Mr. Robinson."

"Shall I accompany you?"

"No need," but Jim was already moving up the trail, leaving Mr. Robinson standing there, about to raise his finger to make another point. Jim set a blistering Marine Corps pace. As each stride dug into the steep incline, he was reminded of the infamous Hill Trail he had suffered over during Marine officer training at Quantico.

Enough banal conversation passed between them that Steffi decided it had been enough, but before she could stand up, Yanni pointed to her toe, which had become noticeably black and blue and swollen. "What has happened here?" Yanni reached out and gently touched her toe, then gently grasped it between his thumb and forefinger. Steffi was afraid to pull back because it throbbed as it was. Pulling it free was bound to hurt more. "Such a pretty toe now made so sad." She couldn't believe it, but Yanni bent over and kissed her toe.

"Yuk!" while not the most politic riposte, it accurately expressed her revulsion. She yanked her foot free and stood up. "Yanni, really!" Steffi decided against strapping her sandals on, to keep Yanni from detecting her quivering hands.

Yanni leaned back on his elbow and peered into her eyes. "I can't help myself in the midst of a woman such as you. I am man; you are woman. We all have feelings, no?"

"Yes, and they're not very nice right now. I'm leaving. Go take a cold shower!" Realizing he probably didn't understand a word of her rapid-fire English, Steffi limped around Yanni, giving him a wide berth.

Yanni sprang up, catlike, and blocked her way. "When I saw you in the restaurant, I thought to myself, this woman is a goddess."

"Yanni," Steffi pleaded, "Don't end this badly. If I have somehow given you an impression that I'm interested in you, I'm sorry." The old patterns with Ludmil formed in her mind. Her mouth grew cottony.

Recognizing some rising fear, Yanni's voice softened, "You are a little kitten to be gentle with. I am the very sorry. My feelings must being more held back," and then he said in Greek, "Please accept my apology."

"Accepted." Steffi leaned on her sore foot, but her injured toe sent a bolt of pain through her leg, and it buckled. Yanni was there in an instant, holding her arm by the elbow and lifting her up. The power of his arm frightened her as she realized he could pick her up with one hand like a sack of potatoes. What if they struggled? The drugs had weakened Ludmil, and she could fight him to a draw; but this man was immensely powerful. Steffi's body trembled. She stifled a scream by commanding her emotions to obey. "I'm okay. Thank you, but I'm okay."

Yanni swung around so that his left arm wrapped around her waist and his right gripped her elbow. Her hair brushed his neck. "Please, let me help you."

Yanni's body odor was cloying. Strands of her hair caught in the bristle of his beard. "Yanni, please, I'm okay," but when she twisted to break free, he held her fast.

"I will walk with you. You are hurt." As they tentatively walked forward, Yanni's left leg was between her two legs, and she imagined— no, knew—that his left leg was pressing against her rear. She glanced down and saw his mahogany wingtip, so absurdly incongruous on this mountain trail.

"That's it, Yanni, stop! I don't want your help." She twisted again, and when she did, her right leg brushed against him. Had she imagined it? Was he hard?

Down the trail, Jim heard Steffi's voice. Though the words were not clear, her voice sounded stressed. He pushed even harder. His breaths became deep, sucking drafts of air like a bellows.

Yanni's breaths came in short gasps. Steffi twisted and dropped. The move surprised Yanni, and Steffi broke free. Before Steffi could get up, Yanni was by her side. "Please, you are hurt." Seeing her beneath him awakened a deep animal lust. Just as he was reaching down to yank her to him, Jim appeared.

"Ah, your American friend," Yanni declared with his best waiter smile. "Come, the girl is hurt."

Jim uttered no sound, but his expression was fierce. When Jim reached them, his most primitive emotions were aroused. From the climb, his chest heaved as he sucked air. He managed, "What happened here?"

"Well, sir, I am thinking she hurt her toe."

Jim cut Yanni a dismissive look then turned to Steffi, "What happened?"

She could not hold Jim's look, and her eyes trailed off to the side. "I stubbed my toe, and Yanni here was kind enough to offer help." She wanted no violence. Jim was fit and strong, but he was 50, and his two forearms together didn't match one of Yanni's. Other things went through her mind. *Maybe Yanni has a knife?* She knew men like

Yanni in Bulgaria. They could be very dangerous—the kind who stab you when your back is turned. She resolved to defuse the situation.

"But when I heard your voice… " Jim's breathing was returning to normal.

"As I started to walk, I couldn't stand well. It scared me. Yanni offered to help."

Jim turned back to Yanni. His voice was flat, not fully convinced. "So how was it Yanni was here in the first place?"

"I was collecting the herb and came upon the lady."

"It's true, Jim."

"Well, then." Jim doubted he had the whole truth. "Thank you for your offer of help."

Yanni smiled, "It was my pleasure, sir." His voice was supplicating as he treated Jim as the alpha male for now. He all but rolled over on his back.

"Where are your shoes?" Jim asked.

Steffi pointed to the grassy spot. "I took them off when I was sitting over there."

"You were going back without your sandals on?"

"I'll be getting it for the lady," Ever the good waiter, Yanni rushed over and picked up the leather sandals, delivering them to Steffi with a faint bow.

"That makes no sense."

"My foot was sore. I didn't want them on. Can we go?"

Jim looked deep into Steffi's eyes. He wasn't convinced, but decided the best thing to do was leave. "All right. Let's get going then." Steffi stepped off but immediately struggled.

Yanni commented, "You see, sir. Hurt. This I saw too. Tsk, tsk. Cold water soak."

"Thank you, Yanni, yes." Steffi hadn't the courage to look at him.

"Please come to the taverna, it will be good to see you."

Steffi feared this was a personal invitation.

Seeing her slowly limp for another several paces, Jim ordered, "Don't argue! Hop on my back." She did as she was told, holding Jim around the neck and wrapping her legs around his waist. Steffi thought, maybe Yanni will see where her affection lay. Instead, what

Yanni thought about was how much he wanted her legs wrapped around him.

Yanni stayed back. "I will just now seek some more herbs." He waved to them, but neither noticed. He cursed at them in the Cretan dialect.

Jim held on to her legs for support, and they headed back down the trail. Jim mumbled, "If I find out he did something to you, I'll slice his damn balls off."

CHAPTER THIRTEEN

In the room the weight of their silence continued, and the walls seemed to compress them like a vice. Steffi fidgeted and Jim sat on the edge of the bed with his hands folded. Steffi marched like a wind-up toy, back and forth, albeit with a limp. Her spring finally wound down, and she stopped barely an inch from the wall. Finally, Jim, unsettled over their earlier scene and furious about the encounter with Yanni, burst the silence. "So, on a scale of one to ten, how do you rank me and how do you rank Liliana?" He regretted the tactically stupid remark the second he uttered it.

Without turning around, she spit out her words in sharp cadence. "What a juvenile thing to say!"

Jim tried a different tack. "Well, you could apologize or ask for forgiveness."

"For what, exactly?"

"Well, to begin with, for being untrustworthy, and for humiliating me, and—"

Steffi spun around. "*Schau* (look)—I already told you how badly I feel about not telling you this earlier."

"That gets you off the hook?"

"What was I supposed to do, put it all in an email?" Jim wasn't sure how to respond, and Steffi continued, "And I should ask you for forgiveness? I don't go to Jim for forgiveness. Forgiveness is between God and me. Besides, I don't know if what I did was wrong, or it was the best thing. I'm not trying to trick myself or make up a story to sound good. But it's over, the past. *Fertig* (finished)." But in saying this, she knew the past lived on.

Jim didn't know why he had restarted everything. *How knuckle-headed*, he thought, and changed the subject. "What happened up there?"

Steffi turned around again and faced the wall. She responded to Jim's softer tone, her voice nearly a whisper. "I don't know, who cares?"

"I saw your face up there. The pain. Did he try something? Sexually, I mean."

"I don't know… My toe hurt—probably it was on his mind. You know men, don't you?"

"A little bit."

A single bristle from a paintbrush was embedded in the wall in front of her like a fly in amber. "It didn't start that way. Things were confused." She hesitated, then continued, addressing the wall and wishing not to face Jim's eyes. "I'm sure I misread him. I don't want to talk about it now on top of everything else." How could she explain the disgust, the revulsion, when he didn't even have the sensitivity to understand about Liliana.

"Did you say something that maybe he took the wrong way?"

Steffi's anger flashed. "Sure. I propositioned him. So now I'm not just a pervert, I'm a whore?"

Jim winced. "I didn't mean it that way. It's just that Yanni's English isn't good, and your Greek isn't much better. A misunderstanding, I mean. It's—it's just when I saw you. My instinct. I wanted to smash him when I saw him, Steffi. You don't know how close I was to—I don't know. Him touching you. You have to be careful of men like that."

She turned ever so slightly and gave him a sidelong glance. "Oh, now Herodotus gives lecture on men. You know all about that, huh? I know nothing."

"You're right. I don't know a damn thing." It was Jim's turn to face away.

Steffi scrutinized his back and tried to interpret his meaning. She might as well have used an ouija board. For his part, Jim fought against the exhaustion that comes from being alive on the planet a half century. The lines of Sappho's poem entwined with a jumble of other thoughts. When Steffi ventured, "I don't think you understand what you've come to mean to me," Jim almost blurted out that he had read the letter to her mother.

Instead, he stood and walked to the kitchen area. Steffi watched him cautiously. From under the sink he pulled out the large galvanized washtub. He turned on the warm water tap and heard the flash heater ignite. After adjusting the temperature, he began pouring pots of warm water into the tub. When it was half filled, he carried it to the aged table and set it on the floor near a table leg with its artifacts of blue paint. Some water sloshed over the tub's edge, darkening the stone floor. Then he disappeared into the bathroom and returned with a towel and soap.

"Steffi?" he said as he carried them to the table.

Steffi had slumped down and sat on the floor, crossed-legged. "What?"

"It's like we're running through a labyrinth without a clue how to get out."

"That's about the first thing you've said today I agree with. What went on under the plane tree this morning—" but she ran out of words. Then she cleared her throat, but her voice croaked nonetheless. "I feel—empty."

Jim paused a minute then asked, "Steffi, could you please come over here?"

"Why?"

"Please, no words. Just come here."

To obey made no sense in her present state, but some deep faith in Jim made her relent.

Jim tapped the seat of one of the chairs. "Here, please sit down."

"Sit?"

"Yes." When she acquiesced, Jim settled down on his knees. Without looking up at her, he reached out and lifted her legs. At first, Steffi resisted, but then she let him gently set her feet in the warm water. "Your feet are filthy, and that big toe looks like hell."

"I hadn't noticed."

Jim lathered his hands with scented olive oil soap they had bought in Chania. The aroma filled the room.

"What is that, Jim?" Her vexation was dissolving in the warm water.

"The nard-scented soap."

Her shoulders loosened. "It's a peaceful smell. I remember when we bought it you lectured me about how Achilles used nard to perfume the body of his friend, and I told you about it in the Bible. But you shouldn't waste it, it's so expensive."

"Shh. Let me be." She accepted the gift without further complaint. He lifted her left foot by the instep and began to wash it. From time to time, he cupped his hand and dipped it in the water, then poured the water scented from the nard over her foot. Next he lifted her right foot and did the same. He carefully washed around her bruised toe. "I don't think you're going to lose your toenail."

"Really?"

"It doesn't look that bad to me. I suppose Yanni was right about one thing—you should put ice on this, or at least soak it in cold water to keep the swelling down, but the warm water feels good, right?"

"Very."

"Let your feet soak." Jim stood up. "Would you like some tea? I'm in the mood for a cup of sweet tea."

"Tea? Okay."

"I remember my mother coming home on those cold winter days in Michigan. If her feet got wet, she would soak them in a pan like this one. And she would complain about how the neighbors weren't shoveling the snow on their sidewalks. I used to do my homework at the kitchen table, and she would speak to me like I was grown up. I liked that. And she always brewed a pot of tea. Whenever I hear a kettle whistling, I think of her. She would offer me tea, and if I put enough sugar in it, I enjoyed it, and she would sit there and ramble on about the neighbors, the supermarket, her bridge group. And then, at some point she'd say, 'Jimmy, can't laze around all day. You finish your homework; I've got to get dinner ready.' In all my years living in that house, I never remember dinner being late."

Without waiting for Steffi to reply, Jim walked over to the sink, filled the kettle, and set it to boil. He reached into the cupboard for two cups. With his back to Steffi he asked, "Where's the tea?"

"In the cabinet on the right side above the sink."

For a moment Steffi watched Jim busy himself, then she closed her eyes in an effort to block the physical and emotional pain of the day. Some minutes passed until the sound of the whistling kettle compelled her to open her eyes.

"It'll be ready in a jiffy." Jim poured hot water into ceramic cups with the strings of tea bags hanging over the sides. He added some wild honey to each cup.

"Jiffy?"

He turned his head toward Steffi and smiled, "Oh, idiom. Sorry. Weird little idiom, isn't it. Means it will be ready in two shakes of a lamb's tail. My mother used to say that, too."

"So it means fast?" As he walked over, he picked up a teaspoon.

"Right, fast." He brought the steaming cups to the table and set them down.

"Don't worry about using idioms. I like them. My mother never said things like that or had dinner ready on time. She was always talking about Nietzsche or Marx or the dialectic. She wanted to make everything fit a structure. A lot can be buried by being that way. Definitely overbearing at times, but Daddy was patient with her. 'You Germans,' he used to say. 'Always have to show off, especially in front of us peasant Bulgarians.' If anyone asked them, if they answered honestly, they probably would have said that if they could have done it over again, they wouldn't have married. But they were stuck on an island together, so to speak."

Jim lifted his cup from the table. "It probably never occurred to my parents to imagine being married to anyone else. I don't think they looked at their life together as an island—maybe a life raft, floating around other life rafts."

As he handed the cup to Steffi, he almost pointed out that they were on an island, but he caught himself. "Be careful; it's hot. I put some of that wild honey in."

Steffi held the cup in two hands and blew on the steaming tea. She stirred it with the teaspoon Jim had placed between them. She tried to sip the tea, but the spoon was in the way, so after wringing the tea bag out on it, she returned it to the table. She sipped tentatively, "Hot, but good; the right amount of sweet. The honey's so good on Crete."

Jim fetched the kettle. "I'm going to pour the rest of the hot water in the tub. Slide your feet over a little so I don't splash you with it. It's still near boiling, I imagine." Jim carefully poured the remaining water. "Too hot?"

"I wouldn't want more." She leaned back in the chair and wiggled her toes in the water. "Luxurious." She took a whiff of air. "The nard's nice. Not sweet."

"Old."

"Old, that's right, ancient rooms, dried flowers, old split pine boards, stones hot in the sun. I want to paint the smell." She set her cup on the table.

Jim placed the kettle next to her cup, figuring it was cool enough now to not leave a mark. "It's been a rough day."

Steffi cast her eyes down, her long lashes making dark crescents above her cheeks.

He pulled one of the other chairs over and sat. Quietly he asked, "Do we need to do something about Yanni?"

Keeping her eyes hidden, "No."

"You're sure?"

"Yes. It's okay."

"Do we need to do something about us?" Again, softly.

"Yes."

Jim exhaled and scratched his head nervously. "Before I raced up the mountain, after I stopped being hysterical, I thought about everything." He was tempted to tell her about the letter.

In a cold voice designed to disguise her vulnerability, she said, "I already heard your opinion on everything. I saw the judgment in your eyes. I'm a weirdo pervert."

"I don't think you are."

For just a second, she looked up, but just as quickly cast her eyes down again. Her hair hung along her cheeks. The matted ends tempted Jim to reach out and untangle the strands, but he restrained himself.

"My reaction—male pride—I mean, what was I going to tell the guys?"

She could tell by his tone he was teasing, and if she looked up he'd have that sweet but ironic smile she had come to love. She teased back, "Men!" Then she pleaded, "But Jim, it wasn't about choosing women over men."

"Shhh. I don't really completely understand, but I understand enough."

"Enough to want me?" Her thick eyebrows were curled sincerely.

"Steffi, there's a squad's worth of other women out there I've known intimately. I can't say the memory of them has left me with anything positive. Something good and positive came out of what happened with Liliana. How can I be critical? I do know, after all the miserable experiences you've had with men, you gave yourself to me. I find that humbling." After a pause, "You know what I think is the most important dividing point of my life?"

"When Jeannette died?"

"No, when I met you."

Folding her hands on her lap like a prim schoolgirl, she glanced up and tried to hold Jim's gaze. Jim leaned forward with his head only inches from Steffi's. "In my life pre-Steffi, I allowed myself to be led by narcissists. I compromised to adjust to other people's values even when those values would make Genghis Khan shudder. Thinking something wrong with me, I tried to adapt to cold people, people without empathy, misanthropes, people who admit nothing, deny everything, and make counter-accusations—people without the maturity to be honest about their own fragile selves. I had affairs with wounded sparrows with their busted wings, forever victims. Then to top it off, I married someone I understood no better after she died than the day I met her." He paused, wishing not to lecture, but also wishing to say it all out loud. "What's worse, I didn't know myself, and I called that life. Decades of it. And then you came along, and I've come to realize that what I have with you is a different path. You unlocked something."

Steffi looked up now and frowned. "Jim?"

"No, Steffi, let me continue, please." Jim collected his thoughts and then took her hands. "A lot has come to me in the last handful of hours—a whole burst dam of it. I can't pretend to know what you were going through after Ludmil. You must have craved intimacy. Any human would have. To have a warm, comforting soul next to you, something that cut through the cruelty and chill of it—someone whose touch you could trust." Jim squeezed her hands, "Knowing that your mother was probably clinical when you needed feelings and then your sister returned to Germany for study. Liliana was there, and for all the wild emotions I feel about it that include anger, I'm glad she was." Jim adjusted in his seat but still firmly held her hands, "My reaction was impulsive. Who am I to judge? I realized sitting here alone that I'm not prepared to throw away all that you are to me."

"You came to all this while I climbed the mountain?"

"Your care and affection for me has transformed me." Steffi avoided his eyes once again. "Listen, Steffi. What are the choices for me? To be offended by your honesty? By the courage to bare your soul? By the risk you took to be with me on this island? And then I should reject how you have opened my eyes allowing me to see so many things differently?"

Steffi's voice cracked, but no intelligible words came out.

"Should I dry your feet?"

"No, I can do it."

"Let me." He used the towel to gently dry each foot. The rough cotton made her feet tingle as he rubbed. Without looking up he commented, "I'm old enough to understand that we all have hidden parts, locked away from even those closest to us. I think we need those things. Little strongboxes kept in storage. Good historians understand that. We see it in the people we research. I'm honored you opened up one of those boxes to me in spite of me acting like a child before. It's nothing for you to regret."

Slinging the towel over his left shoulder, Jim hoisted the tub carefully to keep from spilling the sloshing dirty water and returned to the sink, pouring the water down the drain. He leaned against the counter, out of energy. He didn't hear Steffi come up behind him. Her arms wrapped around his ribs below his chest, and he felt her cheek resting against the top of his back. For a moment he hesitated to move, not wishing to disturb the moment.

Neither of them stirred for a long time. Jim peered vacantly out the window above the sink at the plane tree that appeared so unmoving it was hard to believe it lived. Blades of sunlight cut through the branches. A most remarkable sensation came over him, as if he were suddenly vaporous and everything around him was too, one thing melding into the other. There were no lines, just shadows, one shading into the other.

He twisted around so that now Steffi's head rested on his chest, but her arms still held him tightly with her hands clasped together. Jim's arms wrapped around her, and his head dropped to the top of hers, breathing in the scent of her hair. He still leaned against the counter's edge, which dug into the small of his back. Finally, after a moment, or perhaps it had been a half-hour, Jim gently cradled Steffi's soft cheeks in his hands. He turned her head so that she met his eyes. At first Steffi fought the intensity of them; but slowly, in small doses, her eyes steadied on his until she saw nothing else.

Jim spoke softly but clearly. "Steffi, I love you."

Steffi felt as though she had stepped under the lintel of a great door and passed from one room to another, a room so different that it seemed the rooms could not have been attached to the same structure. Yet, her rational side doubted the change. "In spite of what I told you, you love me?"

"I can't promise there won't be a time when somehow this thing with Liliana flares up. Maybe I'll have a moment of self-doubt, that's kind of me anyway, but I can promise you, no matter about Liliana or anything else, above it all, I love you."

"I feel it, Jim. Now, really, I know you do. Do you feel what's in me right now?"

"Love?"

"More."

"How can there be more?"

Steffi's eyes glistened with emotion. "You remember the Greek word *Erota*?"

"Love, right?"

"But something more, like we have become the same bubble."

That night they lay together, entwined as one. Their feelings were such that they found no expression in sex. Neither was hungry or thirsty. Few words passed between them. Instead, they listened to the night's silence and felt the occasional breeze spill over their naked bodies like a rippling bolt of silk. Their eyes opened at the same moment to witness a meteor streak across the firmament, framed by the window, disappearing someplace south over the Sahara. Once, in a stiff breeze, the plane tree soughed.

In half-sleep, Steffi mumbled, "Erota. This is Erota."

Through the entire night they stayed that way, sometimes sleeping, sometimes awake. The waning gibbous moon rose, its cool, ethereal light touching them just as it had touched this ancient island uncounted times, casting its shadows and pewter light over Bronze Age Phaestos, on the Dorian throne sitting nonsensically by a road within earshot of the surf, and over the triremes, xebecs, and tartanes anchored or bumping at their moorings in the ticking history of Chania's harbor. Jim was startled by the final stillness of the inversion that arrives before the beginning of morning nautical twilight. Then, in an instant, and dramatically, the shining doors of dawn opened.

CHAPTER FOURTEEN

The pain and torture of the day before had cut too deeply for a total cure, but at least the wound had clotted and begun to scab, accelerated by mutual tenderness and forgiveness. The day promised to be warm and sunny, and Steffi and Jim accepted that sometimes small things are enough. In the following days, like aftershocks of an earthquake, memories of the pain sent tremors through them. As time passed, the tremors slackened, and trust fortified the foundation of their relationship. The solitary work of painting and writing ranked in second place behind experiencing the island together. In exploration during subsequent days, both the joyous experiences and the disquieting ones bonded them.

Yanni became an unhealthy miasma that the sea breezes on the island seemed unable to purge. Steffi hid the worst bits of what happened on the mountain, causing her to despair because once more she hid truth from Jim. She rationalized her half-admissions to Jim's questions as justified to protect him from violence. For Jim's part, he could suppress but not void his anger and suspicions of Yanni. Anger left untreated, however, is a malignancy that burrows silently and deeply. Yanni's periodic appearances around the hotel and in town put them on edge.

One time they saw Yanni with Mr. Robinson at a beachside café. Later they learned from him that Yanni "ran into me and insisted on treating me to coffee so he could thank me for employing his cousin, Apostolos." As an afterthought he commented, "The chap does ask a lot of questions, but," in contradiction to Jim and Steffi's cautions, "I do believe he was trying to do the proper thing. Saw less defensiveness over our coffee. Give him time—these provincial types are often slow to warm up."

Many of their following days involved trekking over the trails with Mr. Robinson, who forever apologized for the hot and sweaty work. Jim insisted the effort brought to life what he was writing. From those caves tucked away in the rugged terrain, no doubt freezing and bleak in winter, Jim tasted a hint of life in the resistance. He imagined runners delivering reports of atrocities. Fragments of news from off the island in the early years were dismal: Leningrad under siege, Cairo threatened, shipping sunk by U-boats. All the war material they received arrived on the island from risky clandestine landings by night or parachute drops that often missed their targets and landed in German hands. Precious radio batteries ended up dunked in sea water. Still, centimeter by centimeter, they fought the invaders back until, by the end of the war, the Germans held nothing of Crete but a tenuous perimeter around Chania. Another invader had come and gone.

The repetition of the trio's searches, the pattern of departing early in the morning and often returning with the setting sun, took on the quality of a Gregorian chant, hopeful but melancholic. The cost of the war was never far from their minds. None of them, not Jim the historian, Steffi the artist, or Mr. Robinson with love for his brother could answer the whys they asked every day. They couldn't reconcile the natural beauty around them with the cruelty of the war and the countless previous wars on this island. They trekked on in the faith that finding traces of Ian would somehow offer peace.

Jim observed a change in Apostolos as they searched. "Something distracts him. Makes him concerned," he said to Steffi. "Maybe I'm missing something. I mean, we didn't have mountains and shepherds around Detroit. Plenty of wolves there and in Washington, but not many shepherds, at least not the kind that tended sheep."

Steffi seemed lost in a different time, "I remember one man up in Bulgaria's Rodope mountains who had been a shepherd and then became a Muslim Imam. He was holy, Jim."

On another early morning, armed with the encouragement and recommendation of Mrs. Phindrikalis, Steffi and Jim hiked the Samaria Gorge, which runs eighteen kilometers through rough country from the White Mountains to the south coast. Jim was intrigued by the gorge because the resistance had used it for a bivouac and as a protected route to the coast. The heat of the day ground them down even though the narrow, high stone walls of the gorge protected them from the worst of the sun. Steffi's water bottles ran dry with six kilometers to go. Jim worried about Steffi, who appeared flushed and disoriented. It reminded him of a hike he had led his platoon on years ago, in the middle of which two Marines collapsed from heat exhaustion.

At the end, with Steffi barely ambulatory, they arrived at Ayia Rumeli, where they dove into the surf, shaking from the chill and laughing in relief. Still dripping, they sat in a taverna pouring glass after glass of cool and bubbly mineral water from liter bottles, and enjoying a couple of icy bottles of beer that instantly made them tipsy. From there they boarded a ferry back to a town with a bus stop. As the ferry pitched over the gentle swells, they drifted asleep from the cradling movement and rigorous exercise.

A constant regimen of hiking, swimming, and lean Cretan cuisine cranked their fitness levels up a notch. Jim did pull-ups from one of the low-hanging branches of the plane tree, and Steffi often practiced yoga below it. They grew wiry, and their skin seemed enriched by the island. Physical energy surged in them. Secretly, Jim asked himself whether it was truly unreasonable to have a child with Steffi at 50. Little did he know that Steffi was asking similar questions about her 36-year-old body.

One evening they huddled at the aged table with candles and an oil lamp providing shadowy light. When the lamp smoked, Jim trimmed the wick. They sipped some rough local wine that tasted vaguely like sherry. On a small sketchpad Steffi doodled, drafting lines that captured the feminine curve of the lamp's glass chimney. Their chat wandered aimlessly over every imaginable topic. They laughed about heavy-handed politicians in Bulgaria; they worried over the melting polar ice cap; Jim explained the differences between Memphis and Carolina barbeque; they spoke of their common Slovak heritage and why autumn was and wasn't their favorite season.

As Jim scratched away some peeling skin he said, "You know, Steffi, we only have a couple more days left in this room. It came to me suddenly today. I asked Mrs. Phindrikalis earlier, and she confirmed it."

"Really? I had no idea. It doesn't seem possible. Do we have to go?"

"Well, she does have another reservation. Remember, our original plan was to move to another part of the island after our stay here."

"I do, but still we've grown together here. These recent weeks have felt like the best of my life."

"But Maria had an idea that I wanted to ask you about. Remember how we chatted with her about living on the island and about what people grew, and the differences in growing seasons from back in the States and Bulgaria?"

"Yes, over a coffee and sweets under the plane tree." Steffi smiled, "Mrs. Phindrikalis does like her sweets."

Jim returned the smile. "She does, indeed. Anyway, she mentioned that not far from here she has a plot of land with a mostly restored stone house. It's been her intention to finish fixing it up so she could rent it for the season. She claims it has a patch of good soil next to it, good water, and the land gets plenty of sun. She even claimed there's a little spring somewhere in the back of the house with a plane tree. She knows how much you like the one outside. She warned that it's not as grand as this one. . ."

"Yes."

"Yes what? I haven't asked you anything."

"You were going to ask whether we should rent it. The answer is yes."

"She likes us, so the price is ridiculously cheap."

"Oh Jim, let's do it!"

"Thank God for electronic banking."

Steffi blinked, "Okay. This island has seen prayers to Aphrodite, Zeus, to the conversion of infidels, safety in storms, and victory. Why not electronic banking?"

"Ah, no wonder I love you, Steffi. Shall I count the ways?"

"Give me the short list."

"The way you wear your hat. The way you sip your tea. The memory of all that."

"That again! What's that from, Keats?"

"George and Ira Gershwin."

"Knowing you, darling, it figures."

* * *

Early the next day they drove up the hill behind the hotel with Mrs. Phindrikalis. The cottage sat a few hundred meters behind the hotel and on the north side of a clearing and was embowered by a stand of cypress trees. As Mrs. Phindrikalis described, a plane tree about half the size of the one next to their room grew next to a rocky and largely dried out streambed behind the house. To the front, the hills rolled toward the sea; between two hills covered in olive groves was a funnel-shaped glimpse of the Libyan Sea. To the left and front of the house was the garden, measuring about ten meters square. Jim figured it hadn't been tended for a couple of years. A primitive shade made from branches and decaying palm fronds, apparently designed to protect plants from direct sun, covered part of the garden. When they walked over the garden, a gecko shot out and startled them. With hand tools and a few bushels of sheep and goat dung, Jim reasoned, they could restore the soil. Mrs. Phindrikalis offered them tools she kept in a shed.

"We'll compost, Steffi."

"We will? Well now, I'm glad that's settled."

The cottage entrance required Jim to duck as he entered. If Steffi stood upright, the lintel lightly scraped her head. One large window on either side of the door had been covered by freshly made wooden shutters, painted a Hellenic blue. The heavy gray stone walls of the house delivered a sense of being an archeological relic. Some of the stones on the north side were covered in sage-colored lichen. One small glass window peeked out the west side of the house, and on the south side stood a rusted metal table and chairs Steffi promised to scrape and repaint. All in all, the cottage was smaller than their hotel rooms.

The inside confirmed what Maria Phindrikalis had described. Thankfully, it had a modern flush toilet connected to a holding tank. A small shower stall filled a corner of the room, but there was no flash heater or tank for hot water. The sink required using a hand-pump, but the water that splashed out was fresh and cold without a trace of brine. A portable two-burner stove sat on a simple stone countertop and was connected to an empty LP gas tank. A small refrigerator sat unplugged in the corner. Mrs. Phindrikalis promised to have everything, including hot water, ship-shape by the next day, which turned out to be five days. Whoever had begun the overhaul of this cottage had apparently done the work on the hotel as well. It contained many of the same characteristics, with a cedar ceiling and stone floor. A smaller round table of a similar vintage to the one in their hotel room sat in the corner. The double bed appeared hand-made from pine and was stained a light color.

In the best bargaining tradition of the Greek traders who scoured the world, she offered, "Now I was thinking I would ask the new tenants if they would rather stay here than your room."

"No, no, no, don't you dare," from Steffi. "Jim, tell Mrs. Phindrikalis we'll have this or nothing."

Mrs. Phindrikalis couldn't stifle her laugh. She had known the deal was sewn up the minute she watched Steffi touching everything in the cottage and the way Jim stroked his chin walking the garden. "So, let's go down to the hotel and have a nice coffee and some keks my niece brought me; and you both can tell me what you'll grow." She was already waddling to the car, thinking how the rent would come in handy. *And they're going to help fix it up, and I didn't think I'd rent it until next season.* Over her shoulder she said, "I've got some broad bean seeds, and I know where you can buy a tomato plant or two and maybe some eggplant even so late in the season."

The next day they plunged into their project of preparing the garden. The helves on the shovel, hoe and pick were weathered. All the metal parts were coated in rust, so Jim sharpened and oiled the blades and sanded the helves. Mrs. Phindrikalis also contributed a pitted old metal watering can. At a store in town, they found seeds for a green that appeared on the package to be similar to chard, as well as various herb seeds. Warned by the shopkeeper about laboring in the ferocious sun, they bought cheap wide-brimmed straw hats.

Curious about what they planned, the shopkeeper's wife joined the discussion. "It's so late to plant, but if you tend the plants with care and water twice a day, well, you'll still harvest some tasty things." In combinations of Greek, English, and exaggerated hand and arm gestures, reminding Steffi of an improvisational acting class, they puzzled out some of the challenges. The wife convinced Jim to buy a bag of what he figured was bone meal to help enrich the soil. She demonstrated how to shade some of the most delicate plants from the sun. She found some sprouted onion sets in the back and threw them in their shopping bag for free.

They cut or dug up the most tenacious weeds and grasses and gathered them together. After they dried in the sun, Steffi and Jim carefully burned them and spread the ashes to add nutrients. After the first day, their hands reddened from the rough work. As they turned the soil and worked in goat manure, which was available on every hill on Crete, the metal blades of the tools sparkled in the sunlight. Blisters formed between their thumbs and forefingers. They had reached the point where the soil was chopped finely enough to level it with a rake, and as Jim worked the rake back and forth, Steffi picked out fragments of weeds and roots that the rake pulled free.

When he looked up from his work, Steffi was grinning at him. She wore a bright red headband under her straw hat and a blue long-sleeved work shirt to protect her arms from the sun. The tail of the shirt was pulled from her shorts, and the collar was turned up. It was smeared with dirt and stained with sweat. She wore her old gray sandals.

"Those sandals are so ugly."

"I know that. You already told me."

Jim asked, "What are you grinning at?"

"What was that Marine term you taught me? I like the slice of your sail or something."

"I like the cut of your jib."

"*Na ja.* I like the cut of your jib."

"You're cute, you know that?" Jim walked over to her and held her in his arms. "You smell like a man."

"So does my manly scent turn you on?" He held her tightly. Steffi chuckled. "Oh, yes, well I guess it does."

"Let's stay off the sexual orientation thing, touchy subject, don't you think?" His tone was teasing as he walked Steffi backwards to the cottage door that was already ajar. Once inside, he began unbuttoning her work shirt. "This has got to come off." After throwing it on the floor, he asked, "Why aren't you wearing a bra?"

"It's too hot for a bra." She fiddled with his fly. "How am I supposed to get this open over this hump?"

"Let me help." Jim adjusted things to assist Steffi's task.

She yanked the shorts to the floor. "And why aren't you wearing underwear?"

"I'm too hot for them."

Naked, they backed up to the bed. "Wait right here." Jim ran back and slammed the door shut and locked it. His erect penis bounced around like a piece of lead pipe.

Steffi giggled, "You crazy Neanderthal. I should take a picture and send it back to your university."

Jim hunched over and walked apelike back to the bed, snorting all the way.

"Ooh, that sounds disgusting."

"It's my mating call."

"Yuch." They pressed together and dropped back onto the bed.

Against the white sheets, their tanned bodies stood out, hers more honey brown and his more bronze. Steffi rhythmically thrust her pelvis against him. Though his body rested on top, to Steffi, it felt like something other than weight, more strength and vigor. She explored every sinew and muscle of his back with her hands. The sheer power she discovered drove her to open her legs and invite

Jim inside. He slipped so easily inside her that for a moment she was uncertain he was there until he moved his hardness against her softness. Jim pushed against every spot of feeling in her. He seemed to be able to somehow pull straight up so that it rippled along her clitoris, sending paroxysms of pleasure through her.

She squeezed his rock-hard buttocks as he drove inside her. When it seemed he was close, he paused to massage her breast with his tongue. Steffi's eyes closed in pleasure. Suddenly, she felt him withdraw, and he sat up, resting on his folded legs. She felt him lift her by the small of her back and set the back of her thighs on top of his. Her eyes remained closed. It was all dreamlike. It was then she felt his finger probe her vulva and find her. In an instant he found the spot, but his touch was too light, so she grabbed his finger, urging him to rub harder. She pressed her body against his finger until she exploded in orgasm.

Jim entered her again. The spasms of pleasure continued as he thrust. She felt his orgasm and grabbed him to hold him inside. She selfishly wanted every cell of him deep in her. He sighed into her ear. Their heavy breaths rose and fell like sea swells. Slowly, very slowly, their senses returned to the world. They heard a bird on the roof; a faint sound of an engine reached them, probably from the beach road. The scrape of Jim's beard over the sheets suddenly seemed intrusively loud. Only after they agreed a shower was in their best interests did they rise and cram themselves together into the tiny shower stall.

CHAPTER FIFTEEN

Mrs. Phindrikalis was under pressure to prepare their old room for the next occupants, so they had agreed the night before that Steffi would go to the room first thing to finish packing. She had already made one trip to the room to retrieve her easel. It was set up in the corner of the cottage, with the wooden case for her oils lying next to it. Jim rubbed his cheek, confirming that a shave was in order. No evidence of breakfast was strewn about, so he assumed Steffi ate something down at the room to let him sleep longer. Jim had learned that Steffi was scrupulous about eating breakfast, not that she ate a lot: coffee with milk, a piece of bread and jam, perhaps some fruit and a couple of spoons of yogurt was typical.

On the table Jim noticed another letter from Steffi. Her letters had become one of the joys of Crete. A stack of three pages waited for him on the table. On the top was a small sketch of the plane tree from their hotel room. It required no annotation. It had become special to both of them. Below the sketch she'd written, "I tried translating another Rilke poem for you, but I gave up. Not enough time! How can we be so busy doing nothing? It is another love poem, *Liebling*. I guess you can figure out where my mind is. Anyway, I have left you the part I worked on. Until later, Your Steffi."

Rings lag schon die Nacht so barmherzig und mild,
All around the night lay reposed so kindhearted and mild
des Tages Getön war verklungen:
The clamor of the day had faded away
wir gingen selbander durchs weite Gefild
We went the two of us through distant fields
und hielten uns selig umschlungen.
And held each other in blissful embrace
Da war es durchs Herze so jauchzend und wild
There through hearts so exultant and wild...

Just as he read the last of the unfinished draft the door opened, and Steffi dragged in her suitcase in one hand and a bundle of sketchpads under her arm. Jim rushed over and took the case from her, setting it next to the wardrobe.

"You're making me feel guilty."

"Don't be. There's still plenty to do."

"We'll go down together on the next trip," Jim suggested.

Steffi opened the small refrigerator door and pulled out a liter carton of orange juice. She poured some in a glass and took a tiny sip. "I saw you reading my letter when I came in."

"Uh-huh. I love your letters. Good start on the poem."

"It's a lovely poem, Jim, and it reminds me of us. I found it on a German website and had put it in a file before I left Sofia. The site had put it together with this incredible Van Gogh painting I'd never seen before."

Jim poured some juice in a glass for himself. "Van Gogh, huh?"

"You need to shave, by the way." She reached out and tickled his beard.

"I know." He slugged the juice down. "What was the painting?"

"In German it was *Landschaft mit Spaziergaengern untern Halbmond.* But it's not a half moon—it's crescent."

"Landscape with couple strolling under a crescent moon then."

"Sounds right." She needed to touch the man she loved, and she stroked Jim's upper back. "Jim?"

"What?"

"I want to see this painting with you someday."

"Sure. Where is it? Holland?"

"São Paulo."

"São Paulo? Well, that's not so easy."

"I know, I know. Just promise me. I want to see it so badly."

"Okay then, I promise. Now what else can I get you? Do you want a pony?"

"Don't be a wise guy. This painting is special. It's us. This couple is walking in moonlight among these trees, like maybe olive trees. It reminds me of Crete."

"I promise."

"Hurray! You're easy… you shave, and then we'll get going."

Steffi busied herself moving her things around and unpacking her suitcase. As Jim was scraping off his beard, Steffi called out, "Jim, as I was cleaning up, I noticed those lists."

"The casualty lists from Chania?"

"Is that what they were? Casualty lists from the war?"

Jim mumbled something as he struggled with his razor.

Steffi came to the door of the bathroom with her arms folded across her chest. "From all the sides?"

Jim splashed his face with water. Steffi pulled the white towel off the bar and handed it to him.

"Thanks." He turned around, wiping his face. "Why are you asking? You didn't seem interested in them before."

"Well, I saw something, Jim. Can I show you right away?"

"Sure. Let me get dressed, and we'll take off." Jim dressed quickly and grabbed a piece of bread as they rushed out the door.

Steffi led the way into the room and right over to the lists which were now spread on the venerable table. "Look here, Jim." She leafed through the papers. "Which are these?"

"Let me see." Jim looked over Steffi's left shoulder and rested his hand on her right shoulder. "Those are the Germans for sure. You could tell by the names, right?"

"I thought so, but I wanted to be sure. See this one?"

"Let's see. Gerd Rohrbach. A major."

"What is this code next to the names?" Steffi's slender finger pointed to a number and letter in the Greek alphabet at the end of the name.

"They mean various things—killed in action, wounded, missing and presumed dead. Let me check." Jim turned to the first page that explained the index of terms. "Yeah, that's right, I thought that's what it meant."

"*Gott im Himmel!* Don't be obscure."

"I had to be sure. It means missing in action and presumed dead. Body not recovered due to action in territory under control of the Allies or the resistance. Why this sudden interest, anyway?"

Steffi's hands were on her hips, a sure sign to Jim that she was in no mood to be fiddled with. "Because Jim, grandfather's name was Gerhard Rossbach."

"But there's a big difference between that and Gerd Rohrbach."

"But grandfather was a major. That's one of the few things I know about him in the war."

"Do you recall what unit he was with?" Jim walked over to search through some other research material piled in the corner of the room.

"Unit?"

"Sure. Generally, a number or special name, like the Gross Deutschland Division or 12SS Panzer. Something like that. Sometimes the units suggested the location where they were from."

"Grandfather was from Austria."

"Austria? I thought the family came from the east near Leipzig or Dresden."

Steffi pulled out a chair and sat down. "It's confusing. With the end of the war and the Iron Curtain, it's all mixed up. I think my grandfather's family was originally Austrian from the Steirmark. He was an engineer though, and moved to Dresden after the Anschluss, where he met Grandmother, and her family also lived in Leipzig."

"So your grandparents worked pretty fast. The Anschluss was '38, and if your grandfather was deployed in the war, your grandmother must have gotten pregnant about then."

"Mommy was born in '40."

"I didn't realize she was a war baby. That means she never really knew her father. You know, that could explain a lot about how your mother treated you. Not to be too Freudian here." He thought aloud. "If he was from the Steirmark, he's from the mountains. Did he know the mountains?"

"He was a climber. A technically good one from what I understand. Remember, the picture I have of Grossvatti—he was climbing in that one. There are carabiners hanging from his belt and a climbing rope over his shoulder."

"It's reasonable with those skills that he might have gone back to Austria to serve in a unit from there." Jim's tone shifted, and he suddenly seemed more intent. "Well the 5th Gebergs (Mountain) Division fought here. First, they fought in the Balkans, and then they brought them in here. Started landing them as soon as the airborne troops secured the airfield at Maleme. Crack unit. Well trained by a tough if not brutal commander, a guy by the name of Ringe. And if I'm not mistaken, he was from the Steirmark area. I'd have to check, but I think the division was constituted in Linz, Austria in 1940."

"Do you think Grandfather was here?" She hesitated and then asked tentatively, "And died here?"

Jim's face softened. "I don't know, Steffi. It's kind of a stretch. Hearing Mr. Robinson's story can influence—"

"But it's not total fantasy that I'm thinking this?"

"The names are quite different despite the same rank. There were zillions of majors. Just on the basis of probability, it's not likely your grandfather died here. Most of the casualties were on the eastern front. This was a sideshow. It's really hard to confirm these things."

"Jim, I have a feeling. Intuition."

"Okay. I'm not blowing you off. I'm taking this seriously. Just that the odds are so totally against this. Hey," Jim snapped his fingers. "I have an idea. We can take a trip to the German Cemetery on Hill 107 near Maleme. I actually need to go there anyway. I think there's a monument with the names of something like 300 soldiers whose bodies were never recovered."

"Could we go right away? Where is this Maleme?"

"Not far from Chania actually, near the airport where we landed."

Jim paced a little, and Steffi's mind drifted back to the conversation when Mr. Robinson spoke of his brother Ian. She thought at the time how wonderful it would be to find out something about Grossvatti. When they went on their hikes with Mr. Robinson, she fantasized searching for Grossvatti the same way. Now the thought that Grossvatti could have been here, no matter the probability, left her in a frenzy to discover the truth.

Jim suddenly stopped pacing and held his chin with his left hand, "Aha, I just thought of another investigative angle."

In spite of her agitation, Steffi couldn't help but chuckle. "What do you think you are, Sherlock Holmes?"

Jim ignored her remark. "I think I have somebody to call."

Steffi wouldn't give up. "Do you pace around the room like that and hold your chin when you lecture?"

Ignoring her again, Jim returned to his research material. "It's right here; I'm sure it is." Jim pulled a business card from a notebook and waved it at Steffi. "This guy knows about such stuff." Jim unholstered his cell phone and poked the number. "*Yassou*, Xenophon, this is Jim Jana… no, you flatter me." With that Jim stepped outside. Through the window, she watched him pace back and forth under the plane tree.

Steffi kept her hands balled together. She heard Jim laugh. He opened the door. "Yes. Yes. Next time in Chania, we'll drink a Metaxa. Why not? Thank you for your help. Yes, yes."

Steffi could hear Xenophon's loud bass voice. She was ready to explode. She sidled over to within several inches of Jim and stared right in his eyes, mouthing, "Hurry up!"

Jim grinned and laughed out loud, holding up his left palm to urge Steffi's patience. Finally, after another excruciating minute, Jim disconnected the call.

"Well?"

"Xenophon checked some lists he has. Very strange, very strange indeed."

"What is, Sherlock?" she asked with a caustic edge.

"Seems there's a name on his list of Gunter Rossbach, but not a Gerd Rohrbach, and it matches the Maleme cemetery stone."

"*Mein Gott*, this is a torment!"

"And so unlike German accountability. Different casualty lists? I'd never expect their admin to make such mistakes. But in war things get screwed up."

"Come out with it." Then she spluttered some obvious invectives in Bulgarian.

"According to Xenophon, this Gunter Rossbach was listed with the 95th Mountain Regiment. That was part of the 5th Mountain Division I told you about. I know part of the 95th got into a dust-up trying to relieve some besieged paratroopers in Kastelli Kissamou."

Steffi's hands were on her hips again. "So what are you trying to say?"

"Just trying to put things in context, Steffi. The 95th was a catch-all unit. Artillery, reconnaissance, engineers."

"Grossvatti was an engineer!"

"That might or might not be significant. Combat engineering isn't necessarily the same thing as you think."

Steffi picked at her fingernails. She looked at them and then at the simple ring with the blue stone that had been given to her grandmother by Grossvatti. "Look at me! My hand is shaking. This is *recht absurd*."

Jim was too distracted to pay attention to her comment. "I have one or two books from Germany on the campaign. Let me see what they say about the action of the 95th at Kastelli Kissamou. But let's calm down. Whatever the connection or lack of it, it's going to take time. First thing, we have to vacate this room, so let's finish moving."

CHAPTER SIXTEEN

Sitting under the pergola next to her office, Mrs. Phindrikalis was sipping an after-dinner retsina with Jim and Steffi when Mr. Robinson showed up. "Hallo!" Mr. Robinson's exuberant wave was surely visible from the next distant hill.

Mrs. Phindrikalis beamed, "I am offering to you a retsina. Come, please join us."

"What, no keks?"

Mrs. Phindrikalis dismissed Mr. Robinson's comment with a swipe of her hand. "We're having good talk."

"I wouldn't miss this postprandial for all the tea in China."

Mrs. Phindrikalis, with her peculiar side-to-side waddle, disappeared into the office, declaring, "I'm getting drinking cup."

When she returned, Jim poured the amber, heavy-bodied retsina into a juice glass. The unique bouquet of it filled the still air around the table.

Mr. Robinson raised his glass, "Well now, shall we have a toast?"

"To the memory of Steffi's grandfather," Jim began, "and we'll explain later."

Looking affectionately at Steffi, Mr. Robinson added, "To those who paint Crete's colors."

"Hear, hear!" from all as they sipped their retsina.

Mr. Robinson turned to Mrs. Phindrikalis. "Shall we tell her, Maria?"

A "why not" shrug from Mrs. Phindrikalis. "We can talk of other things later."

Mr. Robinson hungrily rubbed his hands together. "I want to reveal a little secret plot Maria and I have hatched between my forays into the mountains, and while you two have been tending your garden these many days."

"And what's that?" Jim watched Steffi in his peripheral vision. That grin! So welcoming. No wonder Mr. Robinson and Mrs. Phindrikalis took to her. Damn charismatic.

"Well, you see, we must confess our crime. We broke into your room before you moved everything and took that abstract painting, a few sketches, and one of your luscious pastels to an acquaintance who owns a gallery in Iriklion. We returned them before you could discover it. Please don't be upset with our deception. You see, if I might summarize, he wants to show your work. Yes indeed, right, Mrs. Phindrikalis? He wants to show your work, and he thinks he can fetch a handsome price for it, too."

All Steffi could muster was, "You know, I thought some things had been moved in the room. But nothing was missing, so I didn't worry. But are you sure? My work he wants to show?" Between her charged emotions over finding a possible link to her grandfather and this good fortune, her brain felt scrambled.

"Oh yes, indeed. Right, Maria? He wants to do it right away during high tourist season."

She waved her hand as if to dismiss Mr. Robinson's comment, "Faster than right away."

The impact finally caught hold, and Steffi burst upright from her chair.

"My, no apoplexy my dear. These balmy evenings can sap one's energy." Steffi responded by giving Mr. Robinson and Mrs. Phindrikalis warm hugs. Mr. Robinson added, "We all admire your work. Others should as well and make them pay for it, I say."

Steffi sat back down, wiping her eyes, unsure of what to say, "I don't believe anyone would want to actually pay for my work, but both of your thoughtfulness—it's, it's so kind. You both wonderful friends."

Jim cut in. "And timely."

"Timely? How so?" Mr. Robinson's eyebrows arched as he stroked his thin moustache.

"We may have discovered something which I suspect will interest you, Mr. Robinson. We hoped to run into you this evening to tell you. We may have a whole new slant on your search, and its history seems to have entwined us all. You might recall that Steffi's grandfather—" Jim paused, then said, "Why don't you tell it, Steffi."

"Okay." She took a moment to gather her thoughts because her emotions were boiling over. "As you know, my grandfather, whose name was Gerhard Rossbach, fought as an officer with the Germans in the war. His body, like so many others, never returned home, and I never knew where he served. My parents didn't talk about it, and when I heard about your hunt for Ian's past—" she made eye contact with Harold Robinson—"it left me longing to find out about grandfather. Then the weirdest coincidence happened. I was leafing through casualty lists of Jim's, and I discovered, what was the term you used, Jim, ambiguous, I think, an entry of a major with the 5th Geberg Division by the name of Gerd Rohrbach who was listed as missing and presumed dead. At first I was excited but skeptical, dismissing it as a coincidence of a similar sounding name with the same rank. The unit was essentially an Austrian division, and you see, Grandfather was Austrian. Since then, we've scoured several places, but the information keeps contradicting itself. When we checked against another list of fallen where no bodies were recovered, we found a Gunter Rossbach but no Gerd Rohrbach. Was this Rossbach a relative of my grandfather or my grandfather? Is it the same as the Rohrbach mentioned on the other casualty list? So now I'm on edge. I want so much to find out the answer." Steffi wiped her eyes, "I believe Grandfather was only in his mid-thirties in the war."

Robinson's head nodded, "About right for a major. Curious, the German administrators rarely confused such things."

"Same thing I said," Jim added.

Mr. Robinson raised his head like a hound catching a whiff of his quarry. After fingering his moustache, he said, "It seems the Fates are going to have a bit of sport with us, aren't they? And Maria, I told them a wee bit about your father."

Mrs. Phindrikalis held her cheeks. "This war holds us still, no? My poor mother was burned badly, and a little brother died in it somehow. So first Ian and now maybe your grandfather. You know my father, they called him The Lion of the South, fought here with the partisans. To the day he died, he cried for the loss of his son. I think he blamed himself. He was Orthodox priest and also great patriot and hero. Every schoolchild knows of his courage and his great holiness. Little boys are still taught to imitate his character. Even songs in Crete dialect are sung about him. I was born after the war and have no memories of that time. I know only the stories." Mrs. Phindrikalis shook her head solemnly. "Crazy. War tears us all apart," she made a gesture of ripping cloth, "and brings us together."

"What a strange and incredible set of events! Life is ever more mysterious than we think. Six degrees of separation among us, or is it seven? Whatever."

Mrs. Phindrikalis waddled inside and returned with a black-and-white photograph of a black-bearded man wearing two crossed bandoliers of ammunition and carrying a German Mauser. "You know my father die only four years ago." The picture was passed around. "Big solemn mass at the monastery."

"We are all traveling under the light of the same star, it seems," Steffi commented while looking at the picture.

"Mmm. Of course," but Mr. Robinson sounded distracted. His mind was on the hunt. "I believe there are a couple of pragmatic avenues of investigation I can follow. You know, dear, there were Germans snatched by the resistance throughout the occupation. Of course, the most famous example is that jolly capture Patrick Leigh Fermor and his lads made of that imperious snot, General Kneip." A restrained guffaw followed.

Jim cut in, "They took him right out of his staff car, ran his ass to a landing site, and then took him off the island on a submarine or destroyer, I forget which."

"Took him to Cairo, you see."

"But what does that have to do with Grossvatti?"

Jim continued, "What Mr. Robinson's trying to say is, in the confusion of battle, especially early on, it's not impossible to think that your granddaddy was captured by the resistance for his intelligence value. Maybe he was sent on to Cairo as well, assuming he was, in fact, here."

"Well, whatever the answer, I want to know. Even if some other poor man died, and it's not Grossvatti, then I want to do it for that man's memory. Precious lives, all of them. But for me, and maybe mother, to know about Grossvatti would mean so much."

"If he was sent on, Steffi, I can find that out. But I must warn you from my experiences in my search for Ian, one does often become lost in mazes, and such searches can also uncover troubling revelations. Not everything is heartwarming. You must be prepared for that."

"Whatever the consequences, I want to know. I've always wanted to know this man, the truth of him." And yet Steffi only addressed the myth of him. "You see, he was my fantasy friend and confidant who always understood me and helped me in all the tough times. I trust knowing about him will help me understand my mother too."

Mr. Robinson swallowed his emotions, thinking it best not to reveal how Steffi had won his heart. He imagined just then what having a daughter could be like. "There's a network of us old rascals out there. The British may have lost their empire, but we're still a curious lot and love our research. I'm confident I can discover whether a Gerhard Rossbach was taken to Egypt. And if he wasn't, I have found tidbits of information about captured Germans and yes, dead soldiers throughout my wanderings that might help."

"Oh, Mr. Robinson, you can't imagine how I would welcome any news."

"I do, my dear, I do. I wouldn't be wandering these hills and mountains if I didn't."

Jim interjected, "I've emailed some contacts to see if I can query the division records."

"Well done. No matter how old I get, James, the work of fate never ceases to amaze me. That on such an issue our lives could twist together. How many other hotels besides that of kind Mrs. Phindrikalis," Mr. Robinson bowed in her direction, "could we have chosen and never once encountered each other? You, Steffi, sitting on that bench looking out over the water with evening coming on. Do you remember that evening when we first spoke?"

"Of course." Steffi's smile was back.

"It brings a smile to me too. Pure serendipity. I could not have dreamed we would have a common search. 'And so it goes.' Who was the bloke who wrote that? One of you Yanks." Mr. Robinson continued, "And of all things, Jim here—writing a book on the occupation. We were on the same sheet of music from the beginning, merely different instrumental parts? Such things set life ablaze!"

"You can't make such things up!" Jim said, smiling.

Mr. Robinson continued, "But, as I'm sure Jim understands as a former Marine, we have to prioritize, and the priority right now is to make Steffi a famous artist. We're all wanted in Iraklion for the opening of a show of her work. Then we'll resume the search. Your Grossvatti would want nothing less."

* * *

That night Steffi and Jim lay awake. Never since they had been on Crete had night seemed so quiet and dark. It was as if they were encased in a giant opaque and impenetrable cloud. Turning on a light served only to make the darkness powerful, its luminescence unable to overcome the night. They spoke in hushed tones, not wanting to disturb the awesome darkness. Fear from a deep forgotten past before Cretans had harnessed fire rattled their bones.

Jim said, "The whole thing makes no sense."

Steffi whispered, "What doesn't?"

"The 'Fates,' Mr. Robinson called them. I call them the probabilities. I'll tell you one thing—we should have played the lottery this week. You had your Ludmil, and I should tell you, my Jeannette's actual name was Ludmilla—too much coincidence—my book on the German occupation, our decision to come here to explore our feelings—your granddad might have been here, for Chrissakes—Mr. Robinson's Ian—even Mrs. Phindrikalis's father is wrapped up in this! Other guests check in and check out of Maria's hotel, but our lives don't get entangled with theirs. We give them casual waves. Like that Swedish family with what… eight kids?"

"Three."

"Seemed like eight."

She whispered, not wanting to disturb the silence. "For me, life just became a grand symphony."

"I don't see a maestro—some invisible hand or a grand puppet master pulling strings." In the darkness Jim couldn't see Steffi; he only knew she was there by the puff of her sweet-scented breath on his cheek.

"No invisible hand, no *Strappenzieher* (puppet master). Whoever it is who whispers in my ear and fills me with love and hope and never manipulates me."

"You always say that. 'Whispering in my ear.' Is that what really happens?"

"Not exactly; it's the closest I can come."

"A sense, a knowing?"

"Maybe that." She paused. They listened to the utter darkness. "Did you hear something?"

"Nothing, nothing but silence. You know, the world feels foreboding and empty right now. This would be a perfect time for some divine statement or a burning bush."

"Now you are being like a child, sufmurchick."

"Sophomoric."

He detected the fingers of her hand on his belly. "Typical boy. You interpret the world with mysterious explanations like in a comic book. You want a big angel with wings to tell you how to save the world from some death-ray. Then, when that doesn't fit, you become the scientist and put everything on a timeline and measure it."

"So the timeline goes—God makes his personal *Spielraum*—let's call the playroom Earth. The globe cools. Slugs grow into fish. Some slither on land and turn into T-Rex. Next thing you know the Minoans come along, and then the Nazis invade. Now we're here."

"Oh, sometimes you piss me off. Typical of someone who's closed his heart. The world is more beautiful and mysterious than your cynicism. We have been given this moment and all the other moments in life, and we can choose to do something with them. Good or bad. Beautiful or ugly. All of us doing that makes the world we know. Something gave us that freedom. And I believe it was a great act of love."

Jim whispered too, in deference to the darkness. "I'm an historian; I look for the truth. Scientists do, too. To make the world more understandable, to get over our rotten natures, to cure our ills."

"Sometimes. Scientists making nerve gas is probably a bad choice. I laugh when I hear about these groups back in Bulgaria obsessing about the end of the world and how to prevent it. Of course the world is going to end. So what? It changes nothing for me. What I can do is decide how I will respond in this moment."

"Then why bother about Granddad?"

"Because he was part of my flesh, and I am connected to him. But to finally know a little of him will help me understand me. I don't hate history, Jim. I love you, and you are Mr. History. Learning the truth does set us free, right?" Before Jim could answer, Steffi added, "Isn't that really why you are an historian?"

"I've said that, and what you've said, Steffi," Jim said in a languid voice, "is a beautiful construct."

"I'm not creating a new philosophy—Marxism or Capitalism or whatever, or following the empty promises of self-serving politicians—these are the puppet masters."

"And when the volcano erupted on Santorini and people were choking here, why do I get the feeling no one was waiting for a whisper."

"Bad things happen, and bad things will happen to me and to you. So my hope for the future should be based on human inventions and technology? That will stop the bad stuff? Is that what history has taught you? It would be funny if it weren't so sad. The world is the way it is. It's up to you to give it meaning or value or not, and it depends whether you can believe something without touching it. Technology changes but human nature doesn't. No final answer will come from humans."

* * *

It wasn't until dawn that fear of the night passed, and they settled into a short but deep few hours of sleep. They awoke almost simultaneously. Jim stepped outside, stretched, and then did pull-ups from a pipe he had affixed between two of the cypress trees. Steffi strolled over to the young plane tree and sat on a rock, meditating on her belief that God was in all things. By doing so, all creation humbled her.

After a while, they inspected the garden, noticing many of the seeds had germinated, but the sun had tortured some of the transplanted vegetables into shriveled and brown stubs. A couple of the tomato plants, and one of the cucumbers, did well under the shade of the sunscreen. Cup by cup they watered in the early morning and evening as if the plants were hospital patients on IV drips. An agreeable sound of hoes cultivating the soil filled the bright morning as they worked. Jim was drawn to Steffi's soft voice singing a song he remembered from primary school. It was a universal song from the Middle Ages about planting and harvesting. She sang it in Bulgarian; the words were about sowing seeds in the spring and gathering the crop to the sound of birds sweetly singing.

Steffi stopped in the middle of the chorus and asked, "Jim, did your family have a garden when you grew up?"

"No. Well, Dad grew tomatoes."

"Just tomatoes?"

"He said there was nothing like a home-grown tomato. Being an engineer, he was compulsive about them. He kept a log of the fertilizer he used and which hybrids produced the best."

"Sounds like my father a little bit."

Jim stopped hoeing and leaned on the tool. "There was a ritual about those damned tomatoes. At some point in the summer, probably early August, he'd call out to us kids to report to the backyard. 'Jimmy' he'd say, 'bring the salt.' We had this tin shaker about the size of a coffee cup that was dented on the side and had a handle like a cup. By the time we reached him he was almost through selecting tomatoes for us and himself and then he washed them off with cold water from the garden hose. 'I don't ever want you to forget the taste of a Jana home-grown tomato. So here's what we're going to do.' We each held the tomato, warm from the sun and bulging from ripeness. Cold water beaded up on the skin. 'On the count of three, we each take a bite, but one bite only. When you've swallowed, raise your hand.' The tomato exploded in your mouth and the sweet juice squirted everywhere. Then, on Dad's instruction, we passed the shaker around and sprinkled salt on the spot where we had just taken a bite. With the next bite, the taste exploded more. We all complained about the ritual, but I've never forgotten the taste of a Jana home-grown tomato. Dad was making memories for us."

"That's a lovely story."

"Did you raise tomatoes?"

"You remember the tomatoes in Bulgaria, don't you?"

"They were wonderful. It must have been the soil."

"Well, Daddy could have told you. He could talk for hours about the soil. He always carried a little shovel with him, and he'd dig out scoops of earth and show it to me in his hand, like it was gold dust, and then tell me things about it. I thought he was the smartest man in the world." She smiled at Jim. "He tried to teach the Egyptians to grow tomatoes like in Bulgaria, but I guess it didn't work out."

"You can take a horse to water, but you can't make him drink."

"There's a saying in Bulgarian just like that."

They went back to work, but Jim guessed Steffi wanted to talk more. "Is there something on your mind?"

She continued hoeing. "Yes, but I've been afraid to raise it."

Without looking up, because he didn't want to meet her eyes, "Well, I understand after what we put ourselves through over Liliana. There's still trust to be rebuilt…"

She dropped the hoe and squinted at him, not sure if she wanted to say something about Liliana. A couple of long seconds passed. "Except to go to São Paulo, I want to stay here with you, Jim."

"Okay."

"Okay?"

"Yes. Okay. There might be some issue about visas."

"Besides that kind of thing."

"I'm in no hurry to leave. I don't see us shaking hands and you heading off to Sofia and me to Washington."

"And there's another thing."

"Uh oh."

He watched her take a deep breath in preparation. "Have you ever thought about having a baby with me?"

He had kneeled down to pick a weed, appearing at first blush to ignore her. When he rose, he felt light-headed and steadied himself with his hoe. "Yes, I've thought about it."

"And what did you think?"

"That I'm 50."

"And I'm 36. That's not what I asked you." Her gaze bore into him.

Jim cast his eyes down. "I think about it all the time. It won't leave me alone. I'm afraid because of my age. At the same time, I can't get it out of mind."

"It won't leave me alone either. So?"

"So, uh… in the time we were apart. If I think about it and try to recall as honestly as I can what I was thinking, even as I was afraid and confused about whether we should see each other and come here, in the background, the longing to have a child with you was there. It's never left me, not even for a moment. Does that answer your question?"

CHAPTER SEVENTEEN

They showered and went back outside. No words passed between them. In that moment everything on Crete was blissful. No war, no invasion, no occupation, no tsunamis—everything seemed eternal—the rocks, the plane tree, their love.

Just then Mr. Robinson appeared. "Hello." He was still a few yards from them. "I know we are meeting tomorrow for our pilgrimage to the art gallery, but I simply couldn't wait longer. Thought I would pop up here. I hope the time's not inconvenient, but I am the purveyor of news."

Steffi smiled, "You are always welcome, Mr. Robinson."

"I like to deliver information promptly, face to face if at all possible."

Jim led them to a large boulder in the dry streambed beneath the plane tree. "Have a seat."

Settling on to the curved limestone boulder, Mr. Robinson said, "Ah, I see I conform rather nicely to its shape. You know, as one grows old, one doesn't have quite the cushion of former times."

Jim and Steffi shared a nearby rock. Jim inquired, miming Mr. Robinson's prolix style, "So you come bearing news?"

"First. The gallery lorry was here and spirited away all the work you selected. They mentioned having begun a proper public relations campaign. Truly, Steffi dear, I'm enthused. Can't wait to see how they display it all. The variety is remarkable, and you are even more prolific than I had imagined."

"I surprised myself. The work has gone so quickly here. At times I guess I've kept a manic pace, but it hasn't seemed so. It's been effortless, as if someone or something else has been guiding my hand."

"Truly remarkable." Mr. Robinson spanked his thighs. "Now, for the second agenda item. Don't wish to brag, but as expected, my network has promptly reported back." Mr. Robinson betrayed a hint of a smile. "I have learned that a Rossbach was never taken to Cairo from Crete. There is nothing to suggest he was a prisoner of the British there or elsewhere in the North African theatre, but…" Mr. Robinson's voice assumed more gravitas, "Now brace yourselves. The communications records reveal a wireless transmission from Crete reporting that the British in the resistance held a wounded German officer by the name of," and he paused for dramatic effect, "Rossbach." He leaned back and with a self-satisfied smile, crossed his arms.

Jim couldn't resist thinking, what a fascinating story for the book, but then a glance at Steffi dissolved his selfishness. As was her habit in tense situations, she balled her fists until her knuckles turned white.

Mr. Robinson filled the gap of silence and shock. "The lads found nothing else. They're thorough, you see, so there's nothing more to come."

Steffi's face relaxed. She spoke softly but firmly. "No one ever spoke fondly of Grossvatti. He was the fascist, after all. Was there a dirtier word to a Communist? It's not like my mother could have a picture of him hanging on the wall in his *Wehrmacht* uniform. I saw black and white pictures of him from before the war with my grandmother smiling in front of an apartment house somewhere, probably Dresden, and another, a group photo of some Alpine hiking club. He was pointed out to me. 'Das ist Grossvatti,' but then that picture and the others of him were put away. He was spoken of like the subject of a school text. 'The Hottentots inhabit Africa. Eskimos live in igloos.' Grossvatti came from the faraway Austria. Mother claims he wasn't keen on Dresden. When I asked questions about him, the answer was always, 'It was so long ago, who can remember?' If pressed, my mother would use the excuse, 'I was born while he was at war. I know nothing more about him than you do.'"

Steffi folded her hands on her lap, and then absently began rotating her blue stone ring around her finger. The tone of her voice grew languid and detached. "I suppose, what was Mother to do even if she did know more? She was already labeled 'the German.' She probably didn't want me blabbering on at school about him. But I didn't forget him, and I used to pull the box out and look at the pictures of him. My mother became upset with my sadness and took the pictures away, but I saw where she hid them. One day I plundered the box and swiped the one of him on the mountain in climbing kit; and I kept it hidden away in my things."

She looked over at Jim, "Is swiped the right word?"

"Sure, it works."

She turned to no one in particular, "Sometimes, when life went horribly, I would talk to the mountain picture of him. It gave me a certain peace. I was on the mountain with him as surely as when we climb here. I fantasized that he brought tasty things to eat that we shared in the meadow in that picture. I even gave him a voice, an announcer on the German radio station mother listened to. And now to think he was really here! I knew it; I could feel it in my heart."

Jim's hand rested on her back as Mr. Robinson spoke up, "Steffi, promise me, you won't torment yourself if we find nothing more. We believe he was here and so was Ian. Sometimes we have to be grateful for mere shadows."

"Oh, I am grateful, Mr. Robinson. So grateful."

Mr. Robinson hid his emotion by speaking in a gruff military tone. "We have a lot to do tomorrow, Steffi, as we launch your fame as a painter. No doubt your granddad would be proud."

"Do you think?"

"I know it. I can only imagine how I would feel as a granddad. It would provide me the most immense feeling of hope and give my life meaning." Even as he said those words the pain of loss of not being a grandfather stabbed him. Mr. Robinson sought to change the topic. "So when do you think we should shove off?"

Jim checked his watch and parroted Robinson's tone. "Tomorrow about this time?"

"Jolly good. I'll report our departure plans to Mrs. Phindrikalis."

* * *

The Suzuki's usually peppy engine groaned in protest during the 70-kilometer drive to Iraklion with Jim, Steffi, Mrs. Phindrikalis, and Mr. Robinson packed inside. Mr. Robinson hummed the opening bars to Mozart's 25th Symphony over and over again, and Mrs. Phindrikalis incessantly used a large manila envelope as a fan. Jim's glance in the rearview mirror framed Steffi's pensive expression as she clutched the portfolio of her latest work.

Steffi used the excuse of road noise for her silence, but her mind twisted into a knot of conflicted thoughts. *Who wants to buy my work anyway? I never sold enough to pay even half of my grocery bill. Why has no one told me Grossvatti was here? Had mother really not known? I'll never forgive her if she has kept it a secret. Maybe that's why she was against me coming here? I want to get out of this car. And do what? Sit there. Yes, sit there until the end of time like the rest of the crumbling ruins. Oh, how I hate myself when I'm like this! And what am I doing with this man? When will the shine turn to tarnish?*

She stared at the back of Jim's head. *Can he feel the dagger digging in? I can see it in there, twisting. When we arrived, his salt and pepper hair had been cut short, military style. Now it's grown over his collar. I like it this way. It's thick and soft and not prickly anymore.* She hoped he wouldn't cut it short again. *Maybe he's too old. That's what Katarina said. She judges everything harshly. God, sometimes I hate her. And she hates Americans, and she's probably right. They come to Sofia so confident. Confident of what? Their big refrigerators? Their dental hygiene? Their nasal voices?*

She was mad at herself for making Jim the object of her funk, but it felt good to use him because she could. Is that what love is?

He said something to Mrs. Phindrikalis. She caught a glimpse of his sincere smile. In the beginning that was what attracted her, his sincere smile and the way he listened. *He wanted to know what I thought. When he spoke, people on the team listened. And he was just a— what did he call himself—a 'back bencher.' The other boys he worked with were nice. Good to me like cocky brothers. But people trusted Jim. I trust him. That's lovely.* She chuckled to herself. *It makes me want to have sex with him. Is that silly? There are lots of reasons to want to have sex, why shouldn't trust be one of them? But he has a cute ass, too.*

Chatter among Jim, Mr. Robinson, and Mrs. Phindrikalis brought her out of her daydreams. They were crawling into the center of Iraklion. Mr. Robinson and Mrs. Phindrikalis seemed to be giving Jim contradictory directions to the gallery. Jim had promised a stop at the museum. Finally, she spotted the Minoan statuary. She thought of the picture she had seen in the National Library in Sofia of the amphora made from translucent amber rock crystal. She had dreamed about seeing it for so long. She wanted to see that 3,500-year-old vase as much as she wanted to sell her pictures. It was the most beautiful thing she had ever seen in a picture.

As they parked, Mrs. Phindrikalis twisted around in her seat. "See the front? See the sign there?"

Steffi bent down in order to see the gallery's window. It said in Greek and English: *Special Exhibit – the works of Steffi Galabova – The Dove.* It made her blush. Her impulse was to stay in the car.

The gallery owner came out to the street, smiling under a great black dragoon moustache. "Welcome, welcome," he said, looking at Steffi with his broad smile, "I am Constantinos. Welcome to my gallery. Please, please, come inside, and we'll take a coffee." Once inside, they all stood transfixed. Steffi's abstraction was centered on the white wall in front of them. A sign hung from the bottom of the frame: *SOLD, Title: Crete Distilled – 900 Euro.*

"Who bought it?" Jim asked, pained that he would no longer be able to look at it. It had come to represent so much of their time on Crete.

"A very nice Dutch couple bought it within an hour of my hanging it."

Jim smiled at Steffi. "You'll be competing with Gerhard Richter next."

Steffi mumbled, "Maybe then Mommy would think I'm a serious artist."

The gallery owner swept his arm in the direction of another, smaller blank wall. "Every pastel I hung there is gone, 150 Euro each." Everyone clapped. "And a watercolor from over there and some of the pen-and-ink sketches." The gallery owner made a sign with his hands like an explosion. "Gone, pouf!" He smiled. "I put signs around that you, the Dove, would be here today, so I think maybe a big crowd comes."

Like a business, Steffi thought to herself. *I had never done them as a business.* But she knew what Jim would say: "Let the market set a price for such beauty." He had said that over dinner. Somehow that seemed wrong, but still, that someone valued her work intoxicated her.

People from all over Europe stopped by the gallery. Having seen the signs that Steffi would be there, two of the people who had bought pastels earlier came back to have her sign the backs. One of the many oils she had done of the plane tree sold for 300 Euro. They raved about the way she captured the texture of the bark. An American couple bought the oil of Jim's hand holding the star-shaped blue borage flowers Steffi had photographed on their excursion to Prevali. They said they knew exactly where they'd hang it in their San Francisco townhouse. For Steffi the time rushed by, spinning her with the velocity of an amusement park carousel. At some point, she felt Jim's hand on her lower back. Constantinos brought out a light lunch, but Steffi was so distracted that she ate only when Mrs. Phindrikalis forced her.

One woman became enthralled with a watercolor Steffi had painted of wild thyme, and bought it on the spot, paying 200 Euro. The woman, of matronly appearance with a sunburned face, and gesticulating with an arm of rattling bracelets, commented in a Nordic accent, "Suddenly, the color! The color! It's, it's too perfect. The thyme grew alive before my eyes!"

A German couple spent nearly an hour discussing Steffi's work with her and asked how she ended up painting on Crete. At that moment Mrs. Phindrikalis and Mr. Robinson returned. Mrs. Phindrikalis needed to sit for a while, so Mr. Robinson treated her to a sweet at a nearby café. When they realized how late it had become, they decided to spend the night in a local pension. Since they hadn't visited the museum yet, they resolved to be at the doors when it opened the next morning. Constantinos warned that the museum closed for fully two hours at midday, so being there when the doors opened was best. He arranged three rooms at a pension run by one of his cousins, and Mrs. Phindrikalis cajoled a nephew into watching her hotel until she returned the next afternoon.

The next morning broke cooler than the preceding days, and a breeze cleared the stuffiness from the streets. Their immersion into the museum elevated Steffi to a creative high. She virtually exploded into each gallery room, giving every display her full concentration. At each object, she uttered one excited cry after another. She moved her hands in front of a glass display box to recreate the shape she saw inside. At one point she squeezed Jim's arm. "I am so happy."

Jim, on the other hand, was overwhelmed by museums and tended to skip past objects. Steffi herded and focused him. Watching Steffi's physical reactions to the colors of the frescoes and painted objects entertained him more than the displays. At one point she stopped and asked him to concentrate on a baby toy rattle. At first glance, it was an unremarkable piece, vaguely brown and simplistically designed. It was, however, by its universal and timeless nature, an incredible bridge to the past. The same loving impulse to encourage a baby's play was apparently as powerful with the Minoans as with moderns.

Once again, as happened over and over on Crete, the weight of history churned and spun him like water rushing through a cold underground labyrinth of chasms, finally emptying from a mountain into a sunlit rushing stream. Was it even possible, he thought to himself, that the potter who had fired the vase that brought Steffi to her knees so she could see it from below have even fantasized that 3,500 years later someone could be so moved by his work? The cinnabar-colored vase had delicate white lilies adorning its side, and Steffi declared them "Perfect!" Was there a battle, a politician, a monarch, an invention that could claim having elicited such intense emotion over three and a half millennia later?

With that thought, the theme of his book came into sharper focus. Crete's constant cycle of invasion and occupation, whether by the Dorians, Romans, Venetians, Turks, and most recently Germans, was ultimately tawdry and loathsome—driven by brutishness and a lust for power. None had the redeeming power of what moved Steffi this day. One piece of pottery, fired for no other purpose than to store olive oil, remained in its enduring beauty more significant than any of those conquering wars. For whatever tactical brilliance the German airborne landing represented, Jim thought its meaning would be lost on those living three millennia hence. Many historians had told the military history of Crete in World War II, and several books discussed the resistance, but the real story was how this invasion, at the end of the day, was like all the others, a moral wasteland—another step back, with Gerhard and Ian serving as the story's protagonists.

"What are you writing in the pocket notebook of yours, darling?" Steffi peeked over Jim's shoulder.

"The true theme of my book came to me. I have it now, the story I want to tell."

"When we get back to the cottage and after I ravage you, making love until I can't move, will you share it with me?"

"I like your plan."

"I think we should go. Mrs. Phindrikalis needs to get back, but she suggested we go tonight to the taverna where her nephew Yanni works, so we can celebrate."

Jim raised an eyebrow, "You okay with that? I saw him the other day chatting with Mrs. Phindrikalis. I was about to sock him just because."

"You saw him?"

"With Apostolos."

"The shepherd boy."

"The same. I don't like the way Yanni keeps getting connected to our lives."

"Jim, let's not make too big a deal of this. Balkan men are like this. Let's agree to let it go. I know I'll be starved, and the food's so good. I'll be all right. I promise."

"You haven't eaten much. You need something more than I can fix you. But I'll tell you, if that creep looks at you wrong, he'll get a knuckle sandwich for dinner."

* * *

What they hadn't realized as they drove along the coastal road to Iraklion was that Yanni passed them in a bus traveling the opposite direction. He had been to Iraklion on his day off to meet a man named Stephanos, whom he knew from Athens. Over a Metaxa or two in an Iraklion bar, Yanni and Stephanos reminisced about the life they experienced together, working Athens streets, hawking cheap t-shirts, and luring tourists into restaurants for a kickback. On the side, they duped any sap they could find with endless schemes. They chuckled over the naivete of their marks and of a couple of quick escapes. They roared about the time they shilled for a pro who sold counterfeit ancient Greek coins.

For different reasons, both ended up doing time, their sentences overlapping by a year. Prison case-hardened their hearts. Their stories about prison had to do with more sobering things. He was already violent, but prison turned Stephanos into what Yanni called a "tough, wild fuck," someone who could take a beating and thrill in doling one out. While Yanni's efforts to impress "The Sect of the Revolutionaries" resulted in smirks, they sought out Stephanos.

Yanni needed Apostolos to help lead him to the gold. Without him, he'd have to follow the old man every day, and that made no sense. Soon enough he'd be discovered, like he nearly was when he ran into that "Bulgarian bitch." What did he learn in Athens? Chicks could ruin everything, *but she's got a sweet ass,* he recalled, *and I think she wants me to give it to her. She's the one that pressed against me. They all want it. But I can wait. After I have plenty of cash, the women will beat my door down. Stephanos, on the other hand, I need him to make this plan work.* Stephanos was made of the right stuff.

Yanni was buying whatever Stephanos wanted to drink. "What the fuck! I couldn't believe you were in Crete. How the hell did you end up here?"

Stephanos had a little ponytail you didn't make fun of if you wanted to keep a blade out of your belly. "After I got out, I worked with this crew doing cigarette deals out of Cyprus. Things were getting a little warm. Problems with the competition, so I decided to come here for a while, if you know what I mean?" Little could Yanni appreciate, nor care, that the deal Stephanos spoke of was a variation of a deal a distant relative of Yanni's 110 generations before had done with a crew of Phoenicians.

"You still in touch with the Sect?"

"Too dangerous right now. The Hellenic Police are all over it, and they got snitches everywhere. Why you asking?"

Yanni tensed, wondering if Stephanos had somehow heard about the police approaching him. Maybe Stephanos was testing him. As casually as he could, Yanni explained, "Well, I'm into something here. Kinda tripped over it. These yokels here don't have the brains to see something right before their eyes. It's got the potential for a big payoff and a way to show these rich tourist assholes who runs Greece."

"So you're thinking that there could be something the Sect can use?"

"If this goes down like I'm thinking, it'd be perfect for them." Just to tantalize Stephanos, Yanni said, "Might need their help fencing old gold coins." Yanni reviewed what he knew about the rumors of gold the British left behind after the war and the searches Mr. Robinson conducted. He developed the story the way conspiracy theorists spin their yarns, with sincerity, vague and seemingly verifiable facts, alleged access to secret information, and thinly veiled accusations of cover-ups. He finished by saying, "A pile of gold stolen from the Greek people, and a rich American, a Brit, and a bitch go down on national TV."

"That'd get some attention." Stephanos's right eyelid twitched.

Yanni outlined the plan. And the best, he told Stephanos with the confidence of a practiced huckster, was that he had used his thick-skulled cousin, Apostolos, to figure out what the foreigners were up to. Apostolos was doing all the legwork, and the old man and the other two were none the wiser. Stephanos and he just need to come in at the end to collect the prize.

After their fourth Metaxa, a flushed Stephanos shook Yanni's hand. "I've been sitting around long enough. Life here is starting to get interesting." Stephanos sneered, his empty, sallow eyes turning on Yanni. "Let's get rich. My round to buy."

* * *

Once back at the cottage, Steffi made good on her promise. They made love until they begged each other to stop. Physically drained, their bodies called out for sustenance. "I want lamb, Jim, and eggplant and squid with lots of lemon squirted over it and a big salad with feta."

"And two hard-boiled eggs."

She offered a twisted expression.

"It's from a Marx Brothers movie. *A Night at the Opera*. It's a great scene. Someday we'll watch it together."

"I want to see it, Jim. But right now, I want to eat! You know, there's so much I don't know about you, the movies you like, and your life in America. Simple things, like what did your grammar school look like? I wonder if your friends are weird? I checked on the Internet about what your students think of you."

"You can do that? Really? What did they think?"

"Something between drooling pervert and hunk."

"Damn."

"Will you grow impatient with me with all these questions? I want to understand you and your America."

He hugged Steffi. "America and me—I don't understand either. America's a contradiction. Everything you say about it is simultaneously true and false. Like, I doubt five percent of the population has even seen *A Night at the Opera*. There's a patina of sameness, the strip malls and chain restaurants, but hiding underneath is this pot of, I don't know what, something teeming. Oh hell, that isn't right either."

Jim continued, "Where I grew up, nobody wanted to look too closely at anything. My house was maybe five miles from people living in poverty, but it wasn't in front of my face growing up, so it wasn't there. No one wanted to destroy the dream. When I was ten, I worried about my Little League team; you worried about the great dialectic."

"Maybe Bulgaria is too small. For a Bulgarian it seems you know everybody, and if you don't know someone, and you tell them the village your family comes from, then they already have comments to make. No place to hide."

"My neighborhood was block after block of houses on quarter-acre lots along streets it was easy to get lost on because they all looked alike. The houses were separate little anonymous compounds. All the parents wanted yards for their kids to play in, but we never did. Engineer Dad built a swing set, but I doubt I played more than two hours on it during my whole childhood."

"In the country, the village, we had a pear tree and raspberries."

"That must have been nice. Still, one thing I remember about Bulgaria is how gritty it all felt. Garbage burning, gasoline fumes, grease; urine in the underpasses. Nothing sterile about the place. Life in the raw. Definitely not like the Detroit suburb I grew up in."

"How do you think it was here, back when people called it Kaftor? When I think of those narrow streets in the ruins of Phaestos, they remind me a little of my village in Bulgaria where my father was sent to work."

"People are the same, but life must have been more tenuous."

"Then definitely more like Bulgaria."

"Life is always about doing the best for your family, succeeding with the hand you're dealt, trying to have meaningful relationships. Desperation and elation, anger and joy, must have been felt here too, along with jealousy, forgiveness, revenge…"

"And regrets."

"No doubt. Now we're sounding like Edith Piaf." As Steffi wiggled into her panties, Jim ran his hand lightly over the curve of her bottom, viewing her more as sculpture than a sexual object.

"Jim, I was thinking of our conversation the other night. It's frightening to think—Do you really believe only technology has changed? After all these centuries and not people?"

Jim sat on the edge of the bed and hugged half-naked Steffi from behind. She responded by collapsing on to his lap. He talked into her back. "Technology changes a sense of time and distance, but we're the same creatures. In the Odyssey, the Bible, the people are the same—driven by the same things, same hang-ups, same neurotic bullshit. They love and hate with the same passion. Maybe on Kaftor a couple argued over who broke the oil pot instead of who lost the TV remote, but I bet the basic conflicts would fit to any modern soap opera. Human history goes through seasons like cold winters and warm winters—radicalism then reactionism—liberalism and fundamentalism."

"You'd be called a revisionist Trotskyite in the good old days in my part of the world." Steffi patted Jim's hands, and he released his hug. She stood up and put on her bra with her back to him. A sweetness wafted from her. Even the way she arched her back when she clasped her bra owned a sensuality that attracted him beyond his understanding. She still possessed the freshness of a young woman despite all she and her country had been through.

Steffi's head popped out of her white short-sleeved top. She pulled her hair free of the narrow collar. As she adjusted the tight top that flattered her breasts, she fluffed out her hair. Then she stretched an elastic band between her fingers and tied her hair in a ponytail. Her broad smile locked on to Jim's. Only in small crows' feet was there a hint of her real age. For a moment everything seemed to stop, the rotation of the earth, the march of history, the death of their cells, and all the cycles Jim had prattled on about.

"What kind of nectar did the Greek gods drink for immortality?"

"Ambrosia, Galabova. The story goes that doves first brought it to the gods on Mount Olympus."

"Doves, huh?" In her mind she imagined the doves painted on icons. "I think we should get some ambrosia."

* * *

Steffi had felt fine until they climbed the stone stairs of the outdoor restaurant and noticed Yanni sitting on the wall along the edge of the dining area. A desire to run and to snub him hung in balance. Her jaw clenched. Alone, she suffered thoughts of him which she hid from Jim. The encounter with Yanni replayed over and over in her mind. Her intuition convinced her Yanni had been spying on her out of sight and had been following Mr. Robinson for some reason. Animal stares from men were as much a part of life in Sofia as potholes on the roads, so why did this man's stares bother her so? She blamed herself. She had made herself vulnerable by falling; that was the ingredient that sparked it. The strength of those forearms, the scrape of his beard, the razor-sharp smell of him—had she felt him hard against her, or had her imagination run away? The thought of it was a bite of rotten meat.

It was a little after 7:30, still early by Greek standards, so few patrons were dining. Shadows were long and night not far off. A mellow change of pressure was in the air, a first warning that summer's end was closer than its beginning. The air smelled of grilling lamb and rich *Arnaki Sto Fourno*. When Yanni saw them, he rushed over to greet them. In a wink, juice glasses appeared and a chilled bottle of retsina followed. Yanni did not so much as glance at Steffi, which relieved her. Jim interpreted it as Yanni's guilt. From the moment they sat down, Jim kept on eye on Yanni, but his own suspicions angered him. He wanted to relax and enjoy the evening, not be distracted by this clown.

Mr. Robinson and Mrs. Phindrikalis blabbed with Yanni about the success in Iraklion, so Yanni turned to Steffi and shouted, "Brava!" He played the part of the attentive waiter at a friendly taverna. As if to prove it, he returned with ouzo and more glasses. As he set the glasses down, he commented, "So, the lady has had a success and is now rich. Please everyone take an ouzo to celebrate on the house." Beneath his calmness, Yanni's mind raced in overdrive. His primitive radar detected Jim's scrutiny and Steffi's anxiety. Still, he stole a glance at Steffi every chance he had. Her suntanned arms and sun-highlighted hair drove him to distraction. He fancied that she smiled at him. Back in the kitchen he repeated like a mantra, "Yanni, you have more important shit to do with these people than to fuck one of them."

Jim thought, *Damn, I wish they hadn't told Yanni that Steffi had made money with her paintings. Rich! Oh great. He comes near that cottage I'll kill him. Like a dog in heat, that guy.* But Yanni wasn't interested in the couple thousand Euros he had heard Mrs. Phindrikalis brag about. He wanted the British gold, and he'd let the old man lead him to it.

The mood turned giddy after the ouzo. Yanni brought out saganaki, soaking the fried cheese fritters in Metaxa, then igniting them in a ball of blue flame that scorched leaves of the overhanging grape vine. He doused the fire with lemon juice, and everyone in the restaurant shouted in unison, "Ooopah!" Jim lost count of the glasses of retsina he had drunk, but noticed the bottle was nearly empty. He was sure Mr. Robinson and Mrs. Phindrikalis were each at least a glass ahead of him. He watched Steffi devour a salad with a big slice of feta on top. Lamb arrived, followed by a bowl of steaming spinach rice. Not long after, the singing began.

As if on cue, a bouzouki musician and his partner with a good tenor voice and an accordion showed up to play *rebetiko*. A bottle of a pale red, almost blush wine arrived and seemed to evaporate at the uncorking. Whatever other sounds there were that night, they were drowned out by loud, raucous singing in Greek and imitations of Greek.

The inevitable occurred when a table of guests on the other side of the restaurant stood up and began a traditional Zeibekiko. Steffi joined, laughing; the line-dance step was similar to a Bulgarian Horo folk dance. Mrs. Phindrikalis flicked her jiggling arm at Jim and said in English, "Go on. What you waiting for?"

"What the hell," he said, and joined in. Mr. Robinson was not far behind. Most of the people were so tipsy and laughing so hard, the line's discipline broke down, but that deterred no one.

At one point, Jim took a break and sat down. The woman who had danced on his right wore a scent that reminded him of Jeannette. The memory of the scent connected him to the past the way linking arms connected the dancers.

They had been out with corporate acquaintances. Jim had long since given up trying to mix in. He was an inconvenient appendage. Jeannette was in the corner with a man who was vaguely familiar. Was it at the Christmas party he had seen him? They turned away, and he passed something to her. What the hell? After a trip to the ladies' room, Jeannette dragged Jim out to the dance floor. God, he loathed dancing in such places; it made him self-conscious. "I don't gyrate well." But Jeannette didn't care. She put on a spectacle as she pulsed and thrust to the beat. Three songs and "cool interruptions" from the DJ later, Jim decided it was pointless and sat down.

When Jim returned to the table, one of the other women from the office was grinning with dazzling red lipstick. "Pooped out, Jim? Jeannette's still going strong!" The man from the corner was now dancing with Jeannette.

"Time to take a break. Out of juice."

"No time for that. It's Saturday." She shouted over the music. Jim barely heard her, reading her lips to help him understand. "That's why God invented ecstasy."

It wasn't until the next day while he was waxing the car that Jim realized the woman might have meant the drug Ecstasy. He marched back into the house to confront Jeannette and to ask about the man in the corner. When he saw her in deep sleep on the couch, with the newspaper over her chest, he chickened out.

Jim discovered that the man was Lance Nixon, VP of marketing, and that he had been with Jeannette on business twice in Tucson. Could that be the reason for Jeannette's sudden interest in tennis and tennis fashion? Lance was the company's complete country club whiz kid—a scratch golfer with a dynamite tennis serve. Jim told MC of his suspicions, but she dismissed them. "You're projecting."

"Projecting what?"

"Your own insecurities. I once tried to attract a young man with tennis fashion and my backhand. It was only when I looked in the mirror I realized, who am I kidding? But women do it. Get all gussied up to snare a new attraction. Just saying, in the jungle the mama lion hunts. I read that somewhere—*Popular Mechanics* or *People*."

"Well, that gives me confidence."

When she saw Jim's unsettled expression she laughed. "You could hire a private eye."

"Oh please!"

"Whatever you say." She smiled in her self-satisfied way. "But now I'm off to a meeting to discuss moving departmental offices. Western civilization rests in the balance. Who gets the interior office? The wooden four-drawer filing cabinet? The back-friendly desk chair? The 1814 Vienna Peace Conference was hardly less daunting."

Jim sipped wine, leaned back in his chair, and took pleasure in watching Steffi dance. A child's joy radiated from her. Jim exhaled and then took a deep breath of the evening air. A rush of life filled him.

At that moment, a more sober-minded Mr. Robinson stood and tapped his grease-covered knife on one of the juice glasses. All he got was a dull thud. "Damnation," he shouted. "Yanni, bring out the fine crystal, I have an announcement to make." The words slurred from him. Yanni seemed at a loss. "Alas, Yanni, does that vacant expression signal there is no crystal? Very well." He shouted above the din. "Ladies and gentlemen, I have an important announcement to make." The dance line collapsed on itself, and the last strum of the bouzouki escaped into the night.

A stentorian Mr. Robinson bellowed, "Admittedly, my reputation for persci—persicspac—perspcipacity—perscipaciousness, precedes me so I shall not refute the point. Rather, I shall forthwith get to the purpose of my interruption." Jim folded his arms across his chest with Yanni seated nearby on the retaining wall. Mrs. Phindrikalis waved her hands over her flushed and sweat-dampened cheeks.

"Since I have been on this fair island over the months, I have lost count of the number of ways the Fates, the fine points of history and time, the personal histories of my two good friends Jim and

Steffi—" he pointed to them, "Please do take a bow," Jim nodded, Steffi curtsied, "have come together in magical ways. You are no doubt aware of Steffi's recent successes with her art." Mr. Robinson led applause, although most of the listeners probably didn't understand a word.

"But excuse me, dear Steffi, for while the success is amazing, I must say it is mere trivia next to what we shall embark upon. I wish to announce the purpose of my campaign here in Crete is reaching its conclusion." With that he withdrew a gold coin from his pocket and raised it drunkenly over his head. Yanni's eyes bulged. "This is my talisman, a British gold sovereign I have found recently, which portends the personal treasure of my long search has finally come to fruition." He bowed, and more applause followed. "I have withheld until now, a great discovery. Soon, I am confident, in the company of Steffi and Jim, I will revisit the cave or caves where my dear brother passed time and, who knows, perhaps Steffi's grandfather too." Then looking at Mrs. Phindrikalis, "And for all I bloody well know, Mrs. Phindrika, Phindrinkalis's father as well. So now I must make haste, for this bag of bones seeks rest in preparation for his exertion on the morrow. Goodnight one and all!"

Mr. Robinson took a few staggering steps toward the exit, stopped, and rose his arm and once again declared, in a voice Jim found vaguely like the Wizard of Oz's speech before ascending in his balloon, "As the British government sent many a gold sovereign to Crete to help its loyal allies, so they sent some of its finest men. So tomorrow will be a time of reuniting lost memories, and we will be richer for it." With a flourish of the arm, Mr. Robinson continued on to the exit, accompanied by thunderous applause. Jim and Steffi hurried behind Mr. Robinson to escort him back to the hotel. "Oh, why did you do that, Harold," Jim mumbled.

CHAPTER EIGHTEEN

Both Steffi and Jim assumed Mr. Robinson's comments about the search finally reaching success were alcohol-induced. Mr. Robinson had previously shown them the gold coin he had found. Whatever motivation they had for hitting the trails the next morning was blunted by headaches and upset stomachs. Steffi stayed in bed until mid-afternoon that first day and asked to suffer alone, so Jim took a book and sat at a café. He squandered most of the time daydreaming about money, about what his children might look like, adventure vacations, and fantasies of critical acclaim for the new book.

When Jim checked in on Mr. Robinson, Robinson blamed the "bloody lamb intestine dish" for his "rebellious stomach." As soon as Jim was out of sight, however, Mr. Robinson, thumping headache and all, quietly set off with Apostolos to return to an area in the mountains he had triangulated based on intuition, Apostolos's knowledge, two seasons of trial and error, and a startling bombshell of new information his "rat line" had uncovered in researching Major Rossbach. Robinson now had copies of messages of transmissions by Ian recorded by Cairo that provided convincing reference points of his last hiding place on Crete. Those messages also identified the capture location of Major Rossbach. Both of the locations were in the same area of operations. The fact that Ian sent them suggested that Rossbach might very well have been held by Ian's partisan fighting group.

Mr. Robinson was irritated with himself as he foggily recollected his "braggadocio" and "bacchanalian performance" at the taverna. "Nothing sabotages success faster than declaring victory too early," he mewled while sipping a pick-me-up cup of tea. He felt guilty about being secretive, but he wanted to confirm it all before creating false hope for Steffi.

* * *

While Mr. Robinson declared himself "fit as a fiddle" on day two, Jim and Steffi agreed with Mr. Robinson to cancel that day's hike as well. A fine misting rain fell that presaged November rather than early September. Harold Robinson again secretly set out, this time alone, wearing a Gore-Tex anorak. Steffi and Jim played chess. Droplets of rain dotted the windows and fogged their view. Steffi recalled how her father had taught her and her sister to play chess. "Learning chess is part of being Bulgarian," she commented absently. Jim shared his memory of the chess players in Sofia on the day he first met her.

The foul weather, the click-clacking of the wooden chess pieces, their melded concentration, and the tea they sipped created a cozy atmosphere. The temperature was mild compared to Crete's normally blazing summer days, so Steffi wore a lavender cotton sweater and Jim a plain gray sweatshirt. "Did you play chess when you grew up, Jim?"

"No, we watched TV."

"Sometimes it's nice to have a TV switched on in the evening, especially when you're alone."

"Well, for my part, what I got out of TV was having about a million ad jingles pounded into my head. I can still recite them. Can you imagine if I had memorized passages from Shakespeare instead? I'd probably have invented cold fusion by now."

"We had some American TV shows. *Shogun* was a big hit, dubbed in Bulgarian, of course."

"Really? Right out of the '70s. Wow! That's wild. I watched *Gunsmoke* dubbed in German once. Very weird."

"But my father always preferred chess."

"Did you ever beat him?"

Steffi grinned. "Never. Even after we were sent to the country, Daddy always managed to find people at his skill level. He was very good. Looking back, I'm sure it was an outlet for his frustrations. In fact, he became regional champion, and of course my mother appreciated the logic of the game."

Their conversation drifted in a desultory way. For a break, Steffi spent some time painting, and Jim sat behind her and watched. At one point he asked, "So why do you do it, the painting and drawing, I mean?"

"I like to make something that wasn't there before." She turned around to meet Jim's eyes, "But actually, I mostly haven't figured it out. I only know I must."

"Well, it's clear other people like what you do."

"I've been thinking about that. I have to admit I like people wanting to see it. It's what I have to give. We have to try to do things greater than ourselves, don't you think?"

As night came on, they retired to bed and slept soundly, confident for one night in the steadiness and immutable quality of their lives.

The next day broke clear and warm. Summer returned, but the shorter days and the rain the day before gave fair warning of its demise. Steffi found the longer, darker mornings left her skittish with a sense of foreboding. Inside the cottage, she worked on a painting with darker colors and more shadow, with a perspective that seemed to peer down a long tunnel. They did not hike this day either. They went to Mr. Robinson's room, but he wasn't in, and they decided he must be off on other business. They left a note to have him call when he returned. Jim snickered, "Maybe he's hiding and too embarrassed after his tavern announcement about a breakthrough."

* * *

When Jim and Steffi were knocking on Mr. Robinson's door, he was alone and three quarters up a mountain on his second trek since the taverna dinner. He carried a marked-up 1:50,000 military map he had used to navigate before ever hiring Apostolos. He discovered he had drawn a red circle around the very slope Apostolos revealed to him the day of his hung-over climb. The cave entrance hid behind brambles and a wrinkle in the mountain. Without Apostolos he never would have seen it. The cave matched the location all the data from the Cairo messages suggested, and it fit logically with what he knew of partisan operations. "Feels right," he said aloud, studying the entrance, "If I had been Ian, I'd have found a cave just like this to hide men and material." He chuckled when Apostolos pointed it out to him, "Well, I'll be buggered." He slapped the shepherd on the back. "You are a clever chap."

On the day after the taverna party, all the pieces came together when it dawned on Apostolos where Mr. Robinson wanted to search. He grew animated, exposing the gaps in his teeth like a Halloween jack-o-lantern. Efforts to describe the area with the use of a map were hopeless. To Apostolos, a 1:50,000 map was nothing more than a sheet of paper with brown curving lines and blotches of green and blue. When Mr. Robinson made a model of sorts out of soil, showed him the slope where he hoped a cave might be, and pointed off in the direction of the group of mountains, a light had switched on in Apostolos.

Apostolos all but wagged his tail when Robinson patted him on the shoulder. Apostolos made hand gestures and sound effects close enough to nature to convey that he had first entered it during a thunderstorm. While Mr. Robinson couldn't understand Apostolos's explanation for why he knew about the cave in the first place, Mr. Robinson discovered just how reluctant Apostolos was to go back in when he invited him to enter with him. He vehemently waved his arms and aspirated the English word "No!" Apostolos gestured that he would wait, and recognizing something about the cave unsettled him, Mr. Robinson entered alone. When he did, Apsotolos sat down to guard the entrance with the same determination he used to protect his flock.

The tight squeeze through the entrance required Mr. Robinson to remove his pack and pull it behind him. Once he worked his way through, he was surprised to discover a vast chamber at least 50 feet across with a 30-foot-high ceiling of irregularly shaped rock that looked as though it had been chiseled by human hands. Rather than the dampness he expected, he found the atmosphere dry. The light of Mr. Robinson's lantern couldn't penetrate the darkness of a passage leading off from the back of the chamber. From the discoloration on the overhead rock, he determined the cave had been occupied before. Smoke had no doubt gathered above and then perhaps worked its way through gaps to the outside. Whether that was the result of cooking and heating fires during World War II or during other times over the thousands of years of human history on Crete, he could only guess.

Unlike so many of the caves, this one held a treasure trove of artifacts piled along one of the side walls: a half-decomposed ammunition crate, some buckles and nylon line that may very well have been attached to a parachute, some discarded fragments of cans. Close examination of one revealed manufacture in the USA, which he was only able to read by tilting the can at an angle in his electric torch light. Another can he suspected had been a container of rifle-cleaning solvent. He said quietly, "Looks like the very same kind of tin from my Army of the Rhine days." Some large rocks had been purposely arranged in a circle. For a moment he sat down to appreciate it all. "This all fits."

He used his walking stick to poke around the site a bit more. He discovered charred remains of what must have been a place for cooking and warming fires. From the crusty cave floor, he pried loose the heel of a British military boot. Along another side of the chamber he poked around and unearthed .303 rounds he knew belonged to British Lee-Enfield rifles, and in another spot, the bristly end of a rifle cleaning rod.

Suddenly Apostolos's voice broke into the cave and startled him with its volume and echo. "Okay?"

In Greek, he replied, "Quite all right, Apostolos. Not to worry, I shall be a while." His voice echoed back at him.

"Okay," the voice thundered back.

For a few minutes he stood quietly in the middle of the chamber. He switched off his torch, and the utter darkness of the cave enveloped him. In the darkness before him, he heard what he could only describe as sighing coming from what he figured was the direction of the passage. It was as if something living deep within the cave's recesses breathed. He shuddered slightly in response, quickly switching on his light, letting the beam sweep the wall of stone around him.

Reassured no mortal creature crouched near him, Mr. Robinson scolded himself, whispering out loud, "Afraid of the dark at your age, nonsense." But he couldn't deny that the sighing sounded alive. "Flight or fight reaction," he whispered. "No wonder primitives believed in monsters." He listened again and still heard the regular sighing. "Certainly tangible enough to create my own myth about it—a monster sleeping—a damn bloody big one at that!" At that moment the whole long history of the labyrinth on Crete flooded back with its Minotaur, the half-man, half-bull of Minoan mythology dwelling in it.

Careful of his footing over the irregular floor of the chamber, Mr. Robinson used his light to lead the way in the direction of the passage and the sighing. "I say, let's debunk this myth." The darkness gave the appearance of a black velvet curtain that limited how far his torch could penetrate. He remembered Daedalus's message to Ariadne which she delivered to Theseus: "To escape the labyrinth, use the silken thread I give you and let it lead you. Go down, always choose going down—never left or right. That was the way out: straight and down."

"Well, I don't have any silken thread, but I damn well have a reel of sturdy twine in my kit." Mr. Robinson had always been the consummate planner, ready for any emergency. He carried, as a matter of course, spare batteries, a small inflatable bladder to gather water, water purification tabs, hard candy, a signaling mirror, field shovel, two pocketknives with all manner of tools, some shock cords, a whistle, fire starter, compact first aid kit, and of course, his reel of sturdy twine. Before he explored farther, he dug his hands into the pack, the same one he had used for more than 30 years on his various hikes through Scotland, the Bavarian Alps, and the Italian Brenta Group, and pulled out the twine. Using his vast knowledge of knots, he lashed it securely to one of the rocks from the circle, and then began to unreel the line in the direction of the passage going straight and down.

Steadily, he explored ever deeper into the cave. The tubular shape of the passage looked almost man-made, like an underground aqueduct he had seen on the Greek island of Samos. The sighing grew more pronounced. "What the bloody hell is that?" he remarked in his normal speaking voice. For several more minutes he followed Daedalus's guidance and traced the passage down, never left or right. Caverns and other passages spun off in a myriad of directions. He thought, whether this is the famous labyrinth or not, it is an amazing maze. After ten minutes or more, he looked at his reel of line and determined only a handful of yards remained. But he resolved to push on, first securing the line to another rock. After another couple of hundred yards, he realized that the endless passages might very well swallow him up like the light of his torch, so he decided to turn around for the present, having neither reached an exit nor found the cause of the sighing.

Before he turned around, he paused to listen once more to the sighing, trying to puzzle out its probable cause. Just as he believed the roof of the first chamber contained cracks or holes that allowed smoke to rise, surely there were openings or shafts that perhaps acted as a whistle of sorts. From where he was, he felt reasonably certain the sound came from farther down, and might, when the wind blew, thinking of another alternative, cause a bellows effect, creating echoes through the endless passages. "Humpf, monster indeed, but damned if it doesn't sound alive." Mr. Robinson made his way back to the main chamber by first rediscovering the end of the twine after a few anxious missteps, and then following it the entire way back.

When he arrived in the chamber, he regretted his diversion, feeling he had wasted precious time. He felt it in his bones—a connection to Ian existed right here. Once again, he allowed his torch to play along the edge of the stone face. As the light swept back toward the area where he had found the discarded ammunition box and decayed cans, his eye caught an anomaly along the wall, but when he focused the beam of light on the area that had snatched his attention, nothing noteworthy popped out. He reasoned that perhaps the light had caught the dash of a rodent or a small lizard. Not entirely satisfied, he let the beam play over the area much in the way he had the first time. Again, the spot attracted his attention.

He edged a few tentative steps closer to the spot and redirected his light on it. This time he noticed what appeared to be freshly fallen spoilage of dirt and rock scattered along the base of the wall. He reasoned that such collapses must be a common event in the cave. He ran the beam up toward the top of the chamber to see if it had fallen from there. *Should really wear a helmet*, he thought. He could see, however, that the spoilage had come from near the bottom. He moved a few steps closer, enabling him to finally uncover the real cause of his attraction. There, jutting out of the wall, were angles that didn't belong to the rest of the soil and rock face, even though the colors of the angles matched the wall perfectly. "Right bloody angles!"

He reached down and touched the angles, still not entirely convinced that what he perceived actually existed. As soon as he did, he understood that his hand was on the corner of a metal box of some sort, half buried in the wall. Apparently, the looser material that had covered it had fallen away. He kicked around the edges and tugged at the corners. More debris tumbled around his boots. He pulled out his folding field shovel and dug around the box. After removing a few shovels of debris, he wiggled the box from side to side and with one final tug, managed to pull it free. Mr. Robinson brushed off the top of what was a sturdy, albeit rusty, two-foot long by two-foot wide box that was about a foot deep. With the assistance of the screwdriver tool on one of his knives, his shaking hands pried the lid open. When he trained the light on its contents, he gasped. Inside were a couple of oil cloth canvas pouches stuffed with papers, and resting on top of them was a Webley service revolver—one of the old dependable .455 varieties from the first World War that the British sent by the crateload to partisan movements around the world.

Just as he lifted one of the pouch flaps, a faint flickering light entered the cave. Mr. Robinson saw the vague outline of Apostolos hesitatingly entering the cave. He held what appeared to be a paraffin candle. Candles were as much part of the shepherd's kit as batteries and a flashlight were in Mr. Robinson's. Apostolos's quivering voice called out in English, "Okay mister?"

"Okay, okay," he replied, his voice echoing in confirmation, and then in Greek, "No problem Apostolos." For the present, Mr. Robinson wished to hide his discovery, and he wondered if Apostolos had seen anything. As Apostolos tentatively shuffled farther into the cave, Mr. Robinson reacted, "It's okay. Wait outside, I'll come in a jiffy," and then he offered a similar sentence in Greek. "No need to come inside. I know how it bothers you."

Apostolos's face materialized in the flickering and spectral candlelight. "We must be going now. Becoming late."

"Yes, of course. I'll come directly." Without another word, Apostolos slowly retreated through the fold in the rock, giving the illusion of passing ghostlike through it.

Mr. Robinson hurriedly restored the box to its original hiding place and covered it as best he could with the debris. He determined that he would return alone to study what he had found before he alerted anyone else. Brushing off his hands, Mr. Robinson picked up his light and rucksack and followed Apostolos through the narrow opening.

* * *

The day after the rain, Mr. Robinson set off at first light on his second trek up the mountain to explore his discovery. He had given instructions to Mrs. Phindrikalis to let Apostolos know he wouldn't be needed. Though guilt gnawed at him for keeping details of his find hidden, he rationalized needing to explore on his own to confirm whether he was or wasn't going down another rabbit hole. He prepared emotionally for another failure, yet his intuition argued otherwise, tugging at him with the tantalizing possibility that the mystery was about to be solved, and truth about his brother and perhaps others from a long time ago was to be unearthed. Robinson's lifelong experience was that discoveries and truth could as easily unsettle and disappoint as answer and soothe. He worried about what disturbing news or the absence of it might mean to Steffi, or, for that matter, Maria Phindrikalis.

* * *

After knocking, Jim and Steffi heard nothing stirring inside. For a moment, concerned for his health, they wondered if they should have Mrs. Phindrikalis open the room, but her Fiat wasn't parked behind the hotel, so they shrugged and concluded, "Harold must be off on other business." They knew he was to meet an old army buddy in Chania at some point, but they couldn't recall precisely when. "That must be it." They decided if they hadn't heard from him by the evening, they would seek out Mrs. Phindrikalis. Just then a bell tolling from the village below reached them. It was the first day of school.

Steffi cocked her head. "It isn't a somber bell, is it?"

The high-pitched bell clanged rapidly. "No, I agree, it's not."

"Then why does it make me feel somber?"

Jim gripped her by the shoulders. "One rainy day! Buck up. The rainy season is still weeks if not months off."

"The bell leaves me feeling I'm late, or like I missed being someplace important, or maybe that I'll never get something back."

"Let's debunk that spirit. It's a sparkling day. The kids are all in school; the August tourist rush is over; let's go to the beach." But in his gut, Jim shared something akin to what Steffi expressed. A season had changed, and the days were growing shorter. The bell marked how the sands of time had slipped through their fingers.

In her teasing tone, Steffi said, "You have so many great ideas, darling. No wonder I love you." They returned to their cottage, hurriedly gathered their things, and hopped into the car for the short ride to the beach. As they descended the hill, the intense blue of the water and sky was alluring. The return of dry, warm temperatures instantly restored their spirits. When they arrived, Jim was amazed to find all of the parking spots vacant. As they clambered out and hoisted their paraphernalia over their shoulders, they looked around, assuring each other that everything was in its normal place. The grocery store and bakery behind that section of beach had customers inside. One or two of the tourist shops were shuttered, but other-wise, all else seemed normal.

"Kind of weird. I can't believe the end of the main tourist season can cause such a dramatic change."

They strolled onto the sand and Steffi commented, "Well, the children are all back in school after all."

"Maybe. Kind of creepy though." They set up their umbrella in a choice spot, arranged their bags about them, and sat down with their arms wrapped around their legs, watching the sparkling water and the benign rollers washing the shoreline. "I forgot how peaceful it is down here. We've been hiking and gardening so much. I'm feeling perkier already."

"A perfect day that belongs to us, and a pox on bad feelings. And writing and painting can wait."

At that moment they noticed an older man approaching them on the sand without paraphernalia. He wore a short-sleeved white shirt and long, dark trousers. Jim snickered, "Okay, what's he going to try to sell us?"

"I bet those overpriced big doughnuts they hawk on all the beaches."

"That come with free sand attached, but he hasn't the usual pole to hang them on."

Finally, the man reached them, slipping and sliding in the gravelly sand. He addressed them in English with a quiet voice. "I'm sorry to be reporting, you apparently not have heard the news?"

"What news?" Jim asked, still sitting with his arms wrapped around his legs.

"I've come over from the shop over there." The man pointed to a distant store. "I understood immediately that you did not knowing."

"Knowing?" Steffi asked, hoping the man would fill in the information.

"Yes. Yesterday we had a great tragedy on this beach. A man and his son succumbed." He added, "Drownded."

"Oh, dear merciful God," Steffi exclaimed with her face anguished.

The man's lips twisted, "The father, he tried to saving the boy, and he succumbed both." He paused, "We have closed the beach out of respect for those to who are drownded."

"Of course, of course," Jim repeated, "Thank you for telling us. We will of course leave immediately. We didn't know." Steffi was already gathering their things.

"Yes. This is what I said to my wife. They don't know."

For a while they sat in the car saying nothing. They were both too pained and too embarrassed. Steffi spoke first. "This poor family. I wonder where they were from? We showed such disrespect."

"Steffi, we didn't know. It wasn't intentional."

"Jim, let's just go. The spirit here has changed."

"Now come on. The earth still spins on its axis even if we are tilting toward autumn."

Oddly, a memory of the globe the family kept in their home came back. His sister and he would compete to see who could spin it fastest.

Jim drove away and, once out of town, pulled the car over. He wiped a tear off Steffi's cheek. She felt the coolness as the dampness evaporate. "What should we do? I suppose we could drive to a different beach."

"Oh Jim, how could you? Really!"

"Right." After a few minutes of silence Jim offered, "We could drive to Gortyn. We said we wanted to visit it. It was the Roman capital, and it's where Saint Paul was, where he met Titus, I think."

"I don't want to visit any ruins." So they retreated behind their cottage walls.

The ringing bell, the season changing, the drowned boy and his father dissolved the eternal and inviolable fortress they believed their love had created. Against their will and permission, the cottage dissolved into a toxic cloud that hung around their bed. That evening, after making love, neither of them spoke, hoping orgasms would make things better.

"Do we still love each other, Jim?"

"Of course, don't we?"

"I thought our love would protect us, but the darkness is strong."

Suddenly, Steffi looked different to Jim—truly naked. A new scrutinizing eye studied the asymmetry between her left and right breasts. A birthmark on her right shoulder that had been invisible to him appeared from nowhere. The bunion on her left little toe was larger—redder—grotesque. She yawned, and he noticed how the filling in her right molar seemed to occupy half her mouth. It frightened him to think what Steffi was seeing in him. At that moment he wanted to run from the cottage as if it were ablaze.

Steffi grabbed Jim tightly. "Are we okay, darling?"

He forced a half-hearted smile to camouflage the sense of foreboding, "Sure."

"Really?"

"Absolutely. The tragedy on the beach has us on edge is all."

"It was awful. I will pray for those poor souls. But at least we have each other. It doesn't make things so bleak," she said in a cheery voice.

"Most definitely." But he wondered, what she was really thinking or hiding?

CHAPTER NINETEEN

This time Mr. Robinson brought a lantern and LED light as well as his headlamp and an additional flashlight. Even on the second visit he was amazed by how the darkness of the far passage blotted out light. The chamber was now sufficiently lit to allow him to appreciate it more fully. The artifacts he'd discovered when he visited the day before, as well as additional fragments he uncovered with better light, provided convincing evidence of its use during the war. Mr. Robinson's single-minded intention was less a careful survey of the chamber than a near frantic rush to remove the box from its hiding place and examine it. He pawed at the loose earth with his bare hands, and then tugged the box once again, pulling it free.

Weighing ten pounds or so, the box was light enough for Mr. Robinson to carry to a more convenient spot for closer examination. He sat on one of the rocks that he'd noticed in his earlier visit which had apparently been arranged in a circle and used, he guessed, for partisan meetings or perhaps meals and chatter during what must have been some long periods of idleness. He set the metal box in front of him and pried open the lid. He pulled out the sturdy Webley, and with some pressure was able to break the ancient revolver open to confirm it was unloaded. The extractor still functioned. Then he checked the action and the cylinder, both of which worked surprisingly well after sitting idle for more than 60 years. He suspected it had been generously oiled, which had slowed decay. Mr. Robinson unfolded a poncho next to him and carefully set the weapon on it. In a notebook he pulled from his rucksack, he catalogued his find. *"1. Webley model MKVI. Good condition."*

Next, he removed one of the oiled canvas map cases containing several drawings of what he assumed were German positions around various villages. Much of the writing was obscured, and without a reference to a more detailed map, he was uncertain about what area the sketches covered. On one he identified Souda Bay and Chania's environs. He gasped as he pulled out a sketch that he instantly recognized as drawn in Ian's hand, experiencing for a moment what a prospector must feel upon uncovering a seam of precious metal. Fragile and decayed as the sketch was, it unmistakably revealed Ian's sure, even pen strokes, which brought back memories of the remarkable pen-and-ink drawings Ian had been praised for in his youth. For several seconds he clutched the sketch to his chest.

A memory of sitting behind and to the left of his big brother returned. He had watched Ian's pen flow over the paper, sketching a jay perched on the branch of a pear tree behind their country home. Not one line was wasted as the bird's likeness was transformed onto the page. He ran into the house, came back with paper and pencil, but the jay was startled and flew off, perching on a distant oak limb. Ian laughed and said, "No bother. Do it from memory." So he made a sketch that was clumsy, out of proportion, and barely recognizable as a bird. Ian held it and smiled, "Capital job! You've got some talent, I'll say."

Mr. Robinson was now certain Ian at least knew of this place, even if someone else had delivered his sketch here. No, he convinced himself, Ian must have been here, and that thought steadied him. Mr. Robinson returned the old maps with their old purposes to the decaying case, their exact meanings now too obscure to decipher for the moment, and he set it next to the Webley. A second canvas pouch with similar contents was catalogued and set aside.

Next, he removed what appeared to be a locally made and oiled leather courier bag jammed with paper. As he uncased them, some flimsy sheets, apparently carbon copies of messages stuck together, crumbling like dried leaves as he separated them. There were longer reports, too, which he glanced through. Time had faded the ink, and many of the handwritten portions were apparently in the local dialect and penmanship style of the time, making them for the moment, undecipherable. He thought to himself that they might as well be written in Linear A, and he carefully stacked them on the poncho.

Finally, his searching was rewarded when he came upon a few pages clearly written in Ian's steady, cursive style. His arthritic hands trembled as he picked up the fragile yellowed sheets. Mr. Robinson pushed his wire-rimmed glasses farther back on his nose and stroked his moustache. Before he read a single one, however, he spied a notebook with a faded, self-portrait on the cover. The prominent nose and strong jaw—"Ian captured himself perfectly!" A broad grin covered Robinson's face. "Good show, Ian. I see you didn't let the war diminish your artistic talent." He thought how Ian would have gotten along famously with Steffi.

He placed the notebook on the poncho and pulled his signaling mirror from his rucksack. In the faint light of the chamber, he studied his own aging face. "Venerable." Then he picked up the notebook and steadied the self-portrait next to the mirror, willing the image to uncover a resemblance between them. *Maybe in the nose, but all of us old goats have prominent noses; the hairline—yes, it is the same.* "I still have my hair Ian, and some old crones fancy the color."

Returning the mirror to his rucksack, he opened the partially disintegrated notebook cover to discover the flavescent pages filled with Ian's writing, tightly compressed in order to fill the pages with as much text as possible. He decided that he would set aside the notebook and read it last to savor it. For the present, seeing Ian's script sparked jitters, so he reasoned changing tactics and doing a methodical cataloging would, after all, serve to calm himself, to prepare for what the notebook might reveal. He set the notebook down as if it were fragile porcelain and started on the stack of official papers crammed in the leather pouch. Mr. Robinson began to read and did not stop for nearly two hours.

The first few sheets were radio transcripts of exchanges between Cairo and Crete concerning resupply drops. The incoming messages had been decrypted on lined paper by someone other than Ian. They matter-of-factly detailed times and dates of parachute drops according to some system of coded drop zones. Lists of what was dropped were also catalogued. Copies of replies detailed what, if anything, was recovered, and listed requirements for the next mission. Mr. Robinson was appalled by how much was lost or destroyed. Most often the parachutes drifted over German-held areas. Food, ammunition, boots, radios, batteries, and medical supplies topped the lists. Mr. Robinson counted five separate attempts to deliver a radio. Four of five were either captured by the Germans or had their innards smashed in the drop.

Mr. Robinson scolded Ian out loud. "Tsk tsk, Ian—poor ops security, old boy—keeping these messages with Jerry roaming about." Why would he have done that? The messages would have been quite a find for Jerry. Another mystery to be solved—*you weren't there, were you, Major Robinson? Ian had his reasons, of that I'm sure. What the devil though? I would have brought you up straight for that one.* It was a strange feeling. For the first time in his life Mr. Robinson felt a bit superior to Ian. He smiled and then joked, "I got you there, didn't I, old boy."

The next couple of reports provided some bare bones accounting of money paid to partisans, and the recounting of the seesaw struggle for dominance on the island. One sobering report detailed two weeks' worth of German reprisals for partisan activity. The text listed number of houses burned, mature fruit and olive trees chopped down, and young men dragged off into custody.

The next sheet stirred such a physical reaction that Mr. Robinson gripped the rock below him, fearful of fainting. For a minute, he felt as though he were swimming in dark water. Something like vertigo enveloped him in the chamber's half-light. From the side pocket of his rucksack, he pulled out a small flask of Metaxa and carefully swigged what he believed was an appropriate dose. A few minutes passed before his head cleared so that his mind could accept as fact the text in the message before him. With a racing pulse, he read:

Coordinates to follow separate message. 1430 local 18 August: Ambush triggered. Two German lorries stopped and destroyed – seven rpt seven Germans killed, one German officer injured and abandoned, apparently presumed dead – captured and in custody – one Major Gerhard Rossbach. Approximately ten Wehrmacht soldiers escaped. Rossbach being treated for lower right abdominal gunshot wound. While round appears to have passed cleanly, I have been unable to control bleeding. Local physician reports prognosis uncertain. Will continue efforts to stabilize condition. If successful, will interrogate as appropriate and transfer if feasible to Cairo. End message.

If the previous messages caused vertigo, subsequent communications in the stack caused tectonic plates beneath Robinson to tremble.

1900 local 20 August: German Major Rossbach's condition improved but serious. No apparent sign of infection. (Break) Local reports indicate Rossbach's unit was returning from reprisal raid on Agia Maria when our forces triggered the ambush. Reprisal raid destroyed several houses. One child of partisan unit commander (read The Lion) died when Germans torched the chapel where civilians had sought shelter. Lion's Mother and wife were badly burned when roof collapsed. Local situation hostile. Partisans inclined to execute Rossbach. Have emphasized value of prisoners. Request Cairo reinforce importance of prisoner in effort to ameliorate local rage. End message.

"My God, Maria's family." Mr. Robinson ran his hand through his white hair.

Cairo replied: *Good show regarding ambush. Well done to all. Request transfer of Rossbach to Cairo on immediate basis next submarine rendezvous. Wish to emphasize importance of Rossbach to GHQ effort to obtain intelligence of German in theatre activity. Wish to thank in advance local unit cooperation in transfer of Rossbach to Cairo.*

One day later, *1500 local 21 August: Returned recce learned Rossbach allegedly succumbed to wounds. Physician circumspect about details surrounding death. Behavior of partisans, suspect. Have been told to discuss concerns with The Lion, but he has refused to address questions claiming the issue was "not a British concern." This incident has caused a fissure between partisans and British cadre. Further investigation of Rossbach's possible murder not recommended in order to repair tense liaison relationship in this period of intense operational activity. Barring GHQ contrary orders, intend to avoid further friction over the incident and get on with the mission. End message.*

Cairo replied, *1900 Cairo 21 August: Concur with suspension of investigation for reasons cited. Carry on.*

Robinson held his head in his hands for several minutes. The overwhelming rush of information morphed into a helpless feeling of being a pawn in a cruel game beyond his control. It was as if the ancient Greek gods had come alive in post-modernist Europe to toy with them. What he read defied all probability, but the facts were undeniable. All of them—Steffi, Mrs. Phindrikalis, James, and he—were entwined in a labyrinth in which they were fumbling toward some unknown climax. "One grandfather, one father, and a brother all living out chapters in their lives here, on this spot! All connected to the future. And James, unwitting in his role, brings us all together in a tangled Gordian knot." Here in darkness, what Mr. Robinson had sought for so many years, he found, and yet, his discovery left him more lost than before. In the background he heard the sighing from deep within the cave, and it caused him to shudder. A primitive primordial fear took hold as he sensed that somehow deep within this labyrinth of passages, far off stage, a Minotaur had a grip on them all.

Some time passed before Mr. Robinson was able to gather his wits; but he recalled the orders from Cairo to Ian and he thought, By Jove, if Ian could carry on, so can I. Bravely, he took the notebook in hand and opened the cover once more. The binding broke free, but he held it together as best he could. The first page was titled *Volume 3 – Begun 10 August.* The first couple of pages disintegrated in his hand. Several subsequent entries were mundane reports of the weather, available food, and random activity. In one entry Ian recorded his longing to "tuck into" a real meal. Finally, on the 18th, the entries fill in details of their ambush.

18 Aug: We've had a tough go of it. Supplies are scarce. If we don't get a better radio soon will be in some difficulty. Today started with what we all thought was a bit of luck. We set a bloody good ambush and caught a Jerry lorry column by surprise. We recovered some weapons and ammunition, both sorely needed. We shot several of the bastards but likely an equal number made off. A wounded Jerry officer, Major Gerhard Rossbach, had been left behind and presumed dead by his comrades, though I don't sense they were interested in loitering about to check. He's taken a round in his lower right abdomen. There has been significant bleeding, but the round cut through cleanly. From my amateur observation I should say the impact seems to have cut primarily through his oblique muscle. Believe it missed his pelvic bone, but I can't dismiss some internal damage as well. He's quite a find, and Cairo will no doubt be pleased to have a field grade prisoner, assuming we can stabilize him and ready him for the trek to GHQ.

By late afternoon we learned from couriers that our good luck was overwhelmed by tragedy, which is so often the case here. It seems the lorries were returning from a reprisal raid on the village of Agia Maria. They destroyed several homes and the chapel. What the bastards didn't know or perhaps did, since The Lion is now certainly well known to the Nazis thanks to informers, was that his wife, mother, and child were sheltering in the chapel, hidden there by locals, knowing the Germans would take them hostage if found. Perhaps an informer told them – it's all unclear, but they burned the chapel and a roof beam fell and killed one of the children no more than a toddler. The Lion's wife is burned badly and will no doubt be disfigured. More than one member of this partisan unit is from that village, and they are out for blood.

Robinson turned a page and squinted in order to put the time-faded script in focus. He pulled the lantern closer for more light.

19 Aug 0400: I find my leadership called into question by The Lion. Several of the others are moody and grumbling. Our usual laughing repartee has been replaced by quiet chatting among the partisans. I feel quite alone. I do wish Thompson would show up. He was due at this position last evening. The grumbling heightened when I demanded the physician treat Rossbach in our primitive surgery. The wound was sown and otherwise treated with a prophylactic for infection, but the doctor is skeptical about recovery. He believes that there was some internal organ damage and internal bleeding. One can't dismiss the damage a .303 round can do to the human body. The patient's blood pressure is stable but low. Earlier fever has dissipated which is encouraging.

19 Aug 0930: Thompson arrived with transcripts of radio messages. Most everyone else is out on patrol. Small force of sentries remains. Rumors are circulating that informers may have identified another of our mountain lairs if not this one. Scouts are deployed to see what intelligence we can gather. I've decided to cache this notebook and relevant messages should things boil up here over Rossbach. I'll make sure Thompson knows of the location so that if a post-mortem needs to be done some evidence can be unearthed. I try to identify with their feelings. These Germans are so bloody cruel. How would I feel if my house were burned to the ground and my sweet, dear brother Harry left to die inside?

The last sentence froze Robinson's attention. Slowly, one word by one word, he reread the sentence several times. Seeing his name in this war diary that had been buried in a foreign land for two generations seemed absurdly out of place, like discovering a hand-written personal letter in the pages of a neglected cookbook. Nevertheless, to see his name, to realize Ian not only remembered him but valued him, even in the midst of the overwhelming stress and emotions surging through him at that time, stirred Robinson to his core. Several minutes passed before he mustered the courage read on.

I try to explain that if they truly want revenge then a proper interrogation and the gathering of intelligence is the way to go. They shake their heads in agreement and then someone spits on Rossbach as he passes him. Their loyalty to The Lion is such that honor demands action. I will write Cairo in hopes of garnering support.

19 Aug 1445: Rossbach has rallied. I have discovered that he speaks clear and precise English, certainly better than my rusty schoolboy German. He's clearly afraid of the partisans and has every right to be. He doesn't understand a word of Greek, but it takes no language skill to decipher their feelings. They pass by one by one and gesture with their fingers the slashing of his throat, or make a noose and then bring it over to show him. I admit I've allowed some of this to let the lads blow off steam and create a better atmosphere for my own questioning of Rossbach. No doubt about it, they'd slit his throat in a minute if I weren't here. The Lion has shown me no support on this one. His moral authority as a priest and unit leader goes unquestioned. I appeal to the Christian in him, but his son was murdered, and no doubt Rossbach either ordered it or was complicit. What I see in *The Lion's* eyes make me tremble. I fed the prisoner some soup and he seemed grateful.

20 Aug 0800: I have the lads out on patrol again. Am feeling a bit dodgy about the situation. Reports of greater German activity in our sector have me concerned. No doubt they are aware of Rossbach's capture and are looking for him. But there is an aggressiveness to it, which also suggests some intention of possible attack. Jerry is predictable in his method. Thank God for that. It keeps me a chess move ahead. I believe I have made some progress in convincing the lads of the value of removing Rossbach to Cairo. Cairo has confirmed a submarine pick-up on Green beach four days hence. I'll be relieved to have him off my hands.

Last night I was alone for a couple of hours with Rossbach. He remains weak but improving steadily. He lifted his head to take soup. We chatted it up a bit. Seems he's from the Steirmark, and since I've done some skiing there and know the area somewhat, I was able to glean a fair amount of personal information. He brightens to talk about the mountains and, like all of us, longs to eat the food he knows. Lying there he seems obsessed with seeing snow again and drinking a Silcher, which he says is a special regional wine. It does bring back personal memories of the family in that wonderful Gasthaus several years back. Harry was barely walking. We did some sledding. Father and Mother were so happy. Every day we couldn't get enough food. We ate and ate. I recall most that wood-fired rye bread and the sharp sausage. Little did we know what was coming a few years hence.

Apparently Rossbach's wife is from Dresden and comes from a family of academics and medical doctors. He is an engineer and worked before the war in the Steyr truck works. That brought him to Leipzig and Dresden presumably for something connected, but Rossbach does drift off into delirium now and then. From what I understand, he was living in Leipzig until he joined the mountain division not long after the 1938 Anschluss.

21 Aug 0830: It was a difficult night. We had a para drop which brought much needed supplies. The Lion has a new pair of boots, which has improved his normal bad temper. Unfortunately, a young courier was

captured. The bloody Germans will sweat information from him. We can count on that. Plans are to displace from this position in the next couple of days. Regret abandoning hearth and home. Radio reception has been excellent here.

Before sunrise, I had another session with Rossbach. We spoke frankly of the reprisal raid on Agia Maria. It weighs heavily on him. But something I will never understand in that mentality. He said, "I had my orders," as if he had no other choice. Bloody hell! You had no choice but to order your unit to burn down a chapel with a woman and child? He claims he didn't know they were inside. I sincerely hope he doesn't think I buy that rubbish. We're in the same business after all. But he damn well understands the partisans would like nothing more than to butcher him. At one point he grabbed my wrist and pleaded that I express in Greek his deep sorrow and regret over the raid. "I'm an engineer," he pleads, "not a murderer." If the fire was an accident, then I don't know what one calls the sixteen-year-old his assault patrol hung from a tree limb. The boy tried to run is Rossbach's excuse. Running apparently earned a summary execution. This boy was the cousin of another from the unit. Rossbach insists, "It's a different war." Then he pleads again, "You must believe me. I'm not a murderer."

But alas that is what he is, and damn it all, so are the rest of us—The Lion can package it in glory and God's wishes, but he is, too—maybe even more so because he does seem to enjoy it. How can he celebrate Mass and hang German ears around his neck? And I go along with it, which makes me his collaborator. Maybe it is that Rossbach has managed to delude himself into believing he had no choice. Delusion seems to be the common currency among combatants here. The irony is—pious Padre Lion and dear Major Rossbach turn out to be related. They are true bothers in arms and married to delusion.

For me, I am long past such theatre, but certainly not past feeling responsible for what I've become. The truth is, it's ice water that runs in my veins now when I have a Jerry center mass in my Enfield sights. Bloody sick of the whole show—God and country—it's all just rot. Well, Rossbach, too late; we've all crossed to the other side, old man, and you can't undo what you've become. My regiment will play the pipes and will praise my courage, and your ranks will sing that damn song, "Erika," to cover the sin. I wager he enjoyed his uniform and the brass bands and all that. Seems I recall from some ancient memory, was it but a couple of years ago, being stirred similarly.

21 August 0500: I'll be off soon on patrol. I warned them. The sub was coming, and we needed R (illegible). I couldn't sleep a wink. So troubled. So righteous when the Jerries started the war. Oh, I want them smashed, make no doubt about that. Rid the world of the bastards. But it will never be the same for me. And I see in Rossbach's eyes the truth of what doing the unthinkable, the unspeakable, has done to him.

21 Aug 1830: Came back from patrol and saw clearly what we are facing. No doubt Jerry's effort is focused our way. We shall move tonight if we can. I heard a report of gunfire not long ago. Will investigate. Assuming Jerry's about to make his move, I shall hide this journal and relevant messages.

2000: Very little time. Hesitated to write this but duty dictates, returned to organize our withdrawal and found Rossbach dead! When I confronted the doctor, he shrugged. "He died. Internal injuries. I'm not Jesus." It's all he would say. No one will look me straight in the eye. The whole mess stinks. The Lion is haughty about the whole thing. He's strutting about, saying "God has judged, and the Major is now to enjoy his time in hell with the rest of the Nazis who would invade my sacred land." This from a priest, well, so goes the Gospels. Half of me would like to wring The Lion's throat, and the other half says good riddance. Rossbach would have only slowed our escape. But part of me wants to laugh in The Lion's face. In the end, I'll bury this with all the rest. What choice do I have? In the end am I really Rossbach's doppelgänger? I have my orders. It's a total war, after all, murder be damned and get on with it. I'm sure Cairo would concur. Someone can recover the box and judge for themselves. So I've made my choice. I'll defend this site with a couple of the others and let The Lion and his band of merry makers get away to frolic another day. HQ expects nothing less.

There were no further entries. Mr. Robinson slid the journal back into the pouch. He tipped the box and heard some metal roll about. When he looked inside, he saw a handful of .455 rounds for the Webley, and a handful of gold sovereigns. A tightly bound stack of Nazi Reichmarks clung to the metal. Mr. Robinson laughed out loud. "If ever there was fool's gold." Then his eye caught what were apparently letters which time had partly decomposed. The bottom ones were glued together into a pulpy mass, and the surviving ones were barely legible. He carefully separated the top one. *Oh Ian, whose only war when I knew him was a rugby test. Those athletic injuries he healed with a pint of bitter at the local pub, but these... poor lad.*

Thankfully Anne isn't here for this melancholy chapter of my search. She endured so much and with such patience. He shook his head as if he was trying to shake his sadness away. His reward for his long search was to discover how profoundly sad and crushed by war his brother was, and so alone.

As he carefully thumbed through the stack, he found a personal letter, and to his amazement, saw it was addressed to him. Recognizing his name brightened him. He separated it from the other sheets that decay had turned tissue-thin. He held the fragile sheet to his cheek. The paper felt like the skin of an old man. Tears blurred his vision.

Dear Sport: I had better hear from Mum you're keeping fit. If you desire to be a rugger and replace me at number 8 then do those drills I showed you. I miss you, Sport. We'll tuck into a good meal when I arrive back, just the two of us. What do you say? The Jerries are on the run and paying every day for the nonsense they started. I'm fit as a fiddle and living quite a life here. Plenty of sunshine and fresh air. Never felt better. My Greek is coming along. Wouldn't do to keep on with the ancient Greek I learned at Baliol. Doctor Smythe would cringe, but we're not translating The Iliad out here. By the way Sport, I could do with some proper British beef, but never mind that. There's work to be done, and there'll be time for roast beef later. Send my best to Uncle Bob and tell him how I'm thinking of him in the Great War... Just tell him I'm doing my bit.

A few fragments of an attached page were decipherable. The tone was a patina that Ian was on a high adventure. Other sentences suggested a palliative for parental worry. Another line caused Mr. Robinson to bow his head. "Stiff upper lip for the folks back home. There'll be bluebirds over the cliffs of Dover and all that. No, Ian, you weren't translating *The Iliad*, you were living it." With that, Mr. Robinson carefully folded the letter, placed it in a plastic bag, and gently slid it into his field shirt breast pocket.

When he stood, tiredness dragged at him. For the first time, he resolved to do what he believed was among the most unthinkable crimes committed by the Nazis and Soviets. He was going to revise history and rewrite the truth. "I dare say James would strongly disagree, but I can't possibly share all this with the daughter of The Lion and the granddaughter of Major Gerhard Rossbach. I will take this to the grave. Anne, I know you'll understand if you are watching. Some things are too toxic to be told."

He sorted out the messages that flattered The Lion and all the matter-of-fact references to Rossbach. He saved Rossbach's chats about home and food. And then he took the remaining paper over to where there had been fires in the past, and he burned it all, a funeral pyre, and watched the smoke rise, the gaseous, disintegrated remains of truth. He watched it gather at the roof of the chamber and slowly work its way through the rock, the way smoke surely had countless times before. For a moment, Robinson stood quietly figuring out his next move, that he compared to a premeditated murder. He returned the surviving messages to the box, repacked the Webley, and re-buried the metal box. He wanted to show Steffi and Jim precisely how he had come across it. "This is a Greek tragedy, but I shan't permit the climax. And be damned for playing God."

As the embers died away, he mumbled, "Well, the deed is done. Goebbels would be proud of my propaganda." He stepped on one last spark to extinguish the fire. "What choice did I have?" It dawned on him that they all said that—the Goebbels and Felix Dzerzhinskys of the world. The adage that truth was the first thing to be sacrificed came to him. But it was too late to bring the messages back. The smoke from the sacrifice of truth had already ascended to Olympus. He fought back, "I could have never told Steffi." He gathered his battery-powered lights, and, dragging his rucksack behind him, exited the cave.

CHAPTER TWENTY

Yanni was a contradiction sitting next to his cousin Apostolos in the high meadows where Apostolos spent his life. Yanni's pointed, narrow mahogany wingtips, the white dress shirt with the sleeves rolled to the elbows, and his shiny black slacks were artifacts of his life in Athens, hawking tourist busts of Athena and cajoling strollers into restaurants. On the other hand, Apostolos was an artifact of Kaftor. His archetype was largely unchanged since Minoan times. The winter nights were as cold, the sheep just as stupid, and glimpses of the sea just as breathtaking. His clothes matched the rocks and plants. The soil of the island had been ground or blown permanently into the fibers. The sun had creased the skin around his eyes well ahead of his 23 years. He smelled of sheep. Sinewy and rock-hard, Apostolos accepted rain and wind with the stoicism of the flock he tended. Lightning frightened him. A hot soup, cool mountain water, and sweet grapes were appreciated so much more than by those who only knew plenty.

Yanni's world existed in ephemeral dreams. He told relatives on Crete that he had been a partner in a swank Athens restaurant. His empty pockets upon his return from Athens were explained by a tortuously complex story of being swindled out of his share. When others asked relatives about Yanni's story, what they received in return was a shrug and break in eye contact. Prison was written out of the public story. The official story was enough for natives of small villages. No sense dwelling on stories of jail time or rumors of the national police asking questions. Nothing was gained by humiliation. Families kept secrets as they always had.

Yanni was Yanni, incubator of a thousand grand ideas that made him the genius for figuring out what no one else was able. Everyone knew it actually required a boot in the ass for him to do the minimum. "At least," his sister was fond of saying, "he's not, thank God," crossing herself, "a drunk; he just looks like he's been drinking." Yanni thought the two days of unshaven beard presented a rakish and debonair look. To others he appeared to be coming off a bender. His rheumy eyes suggested crapulence. When he did drink, he mostly carried on about himself: the women he had "fucked," his strong forearms, and how he had the answers to Greece's economic woes. Yanni's ambitions were tied to a victim's sense of entitlement in which he waited impatiently for his rightful share of riches, fame, and respect and maybe a Cadillac imported from America. But above all else, he craved recognition from the "Society:" their power, their violence, their disdain of authority.

Apostolos listened to Yanni when few others would. Apostolos dreamed too, but his dreams were about soaring over the island, or having a wife cooking a hot meal for him. Like his shepherd dog, Argos, Apostolos stared unspeaking with small bursts of rapt attention. Over time, like the reinforcement needed to train a hunting dog, Yanni's ideas found a home with the shepherd. For the first time in his life, Apostolos began to ask why it was he had been condemned to such misery. Apostolos was thirteen years younger than Yanni, so he had an inbred respect for Yanni's age. He finally believed Yanni's argument that they were both victims. Together, Apostolos and Yanni declared themselves victims of selfish rich people, cheating politicians, greedy foreign tourists, and a family that had never cared for them.

Mrs. Phindrikalis had warned her sister of Yanni's influence after he had returned from Athens, but her sister could only reply, "So what am I supposed to do? If I say, don't talk to Yanni, he'll do it more. Sometimes I swear I have better luck talking to a rock than Apostolos."

"I've even seen this in my man. Sometimes he comes back from these foreign lands all full of himself. Maybe Elias can sit Apostolos down when he comes home?"

"Thank you, sister." But then her sister passed away and Elias hadn't come home. Maria Phindrikalis laughed to herself thinking of Apostolos, Yanni, and Elias. "Thick-skulled, stubborn, distracted." Maybe it was better, she thought, that her husband was a sailor and home only a few months a year, pretending for a moment that he wasn't late by several months. A steady diet of these men could break a woman's back. At least when her man was home, he was a nice man. There were the presents, and he did little things for her. She had the hotel; her man's money had bought it. Nice people stayed there like Steffi, Jim, and Mr. Robinson. Guests like that became friends. Life could be worse. Being the daughter of a priest hadn't provided much material comfort, even when the priest was The Lion of Crete. When he passed on, all his personal effects fit into a single footlocker. At least Maria Phindrikalis owned the comfort of knowing that poems and songs about her father still excited the imaginations of schoolchildren.

In all fairness to Apostolos, living the life of a shepherd didn't provide a lot of human interaction, especially compared to Yanni's frenetic temperament. In Athens, Yanni developed a nose for human vulnerability, and for all his pathetic weaknesses in prison, it taught him street skills and a facility for taking a beating. He learned to take someone for a fiver as much as for five hundred. The only fleecing Apostolos understood was of a sheep. Apostolos liked Mr. Robinson because he showed interest in him and paid him, so he was glad to lead him to the many caves he had found as he herded the flock, even if he didn't understand why a rich man would want to spend time in caves. Apostolos knew Mr. Robinson was British, and Britain had helped Crete in the war. But he couldn't pick Britain out on a map, or explain why the British had been on Crete in the first place. He didn't understand Mr. Robinson's strange speech, and though his aunt told him that he was looking for where his brother lived in the war, Apostolos was confused about why anyone would choose to live in a cave with all that bat shit.

Changing Apostolos's mind about Mr. Robinson was a tough sell for Yanni, but he only needed his mind changed for a little while. Yanni provided details about Mr. Robinson that amazed Apostolos. How did Yanni learn these things? Yanni spoke Robinson's tongue, which sounded to Apostolos like someone with a hot potato in his mouth. Yanni told him the British had buried gold all over the island, and that the real reason Mr. Robinson was there was to find gold. Apostolos became convinced he too liked and wanted gold. Everybody liked and wanted gold; he wasn't stupid. If there was gold on Crete, like Yanni said, shouldn't it go to Cretans?

Apostolos sat on a rock next to Yanni. The sheep grazed nearby. Yanni whined, "Watch me, will you? That way I know you're paying attention."

But Apostolos's eyes kept returning to his flock by force of habit. His big sheepdog Argos was on his feet; something had distracted him. He took a few tentative trotting steps closer to the flock but then calmed down, circled around, and returned to lying in the grass, a safe distance from Yanni. He didn't seem to like Yanni. "I'm listening, Yanni."

"Tell me again what the Britisher said."

"I've told you over and over. He said something like, 'This is the place I've been looking for.'"

"That's not exactly what you said before."

"Uh, it was something like that. He don't speak the Greek right."

"Don't get cross with me, cousin. 'Something like that' is not good enough. Don't you know I have an important man in Iraklion waiting for me to send the word? I've told you about Stephanos. Something like that isn't good enough. He'll walk out on the deal if I can't do better. Don't forget we're doing something important here. We are returning Crete's dignity. All these people think they can take from Crete. It's been going on forever."

"Like the Turks."

"That's right. Just like the fucking Turks."

"Cousin, you have asked me so many times I don't even remember."

"But he said that he didn't need you to guide him to the place the next day, right?"

Apostolos exhaled deeply, "Yes. That is what he said. Said he'd go on his own. Aunt Maria told me. Said he could find it again. When I saw him this morning, he gave me an extra tip even though I didn't have to work, and said I was a big help in that funny voice of his when he speaks our language."

Yanni stood up. Argos stood too, warily eyeing Yanni. Yanni rubbed his strong hands together. "A tip! Imagine that. He's going to be rich, and he gives you an extra tip. This cheater!" Yanni eyed his cousin's reaction.

"But it was a generous tip."

"What, five Euros?"

"Ten." It was five, but Apostolos didn't want to admit Yanni was right.

"Okay ten, and he will be taking tens of thousands away to England, never to return."

Apostolos could only look down at his feet after he glanced at the flock. To think Mr. Robinson would do such a thing. He felt betrayed by him. He had seemed so nice. "He would do that?"

"What do you think? Do you have cement in your head? He'll take it and never look back. He gets richer and you get poorer. Think of what you could do with all that gold. Wouldn't you like to improve your mother's house?" Apostolos shrugged. The house seemed fine to him. "Listen, cousin, here's what we're going to do. You are going to lead me up there, and we're going to take what is ours."

"Well…"

What's wrong now? You're not afraid, are you? Stand up tall! You're a Cretan man who has braved the cold of winter and the heat of summer."

"I'm not afraid."

"Then what's the problem?"

Argos eyed Yanni warily; he didn't like his tone of voice. Apostolos poked at the bare ground with his shepherd's staff, all the while staring at something Yanni couldn't determine. The only things within the range of Apostolos's vision were some blades of dry grass and small pellets of sheep and goat manure that littered every square meter of the meadow. Finally, he said, "See, he found some old junk in the cave I took him to last time." He looked up and turned to Yanni. "It looked like the same kind of junk we find all over the island: ancient junk, new junk. You know, it's everywhere, a plastic bottle here, a box there. Or they find old stones they like, and the next thing, they start digging and putting tapes around it. You've seen it. What these crazy strangers do with it, I don't know. The junk I saw in that cave didn't look like gold to me."

"Did you actually go in?" Yanni knew his cousin didn't like to go in the caves. He had been lost in a cave once looking for a lamb.

"I, I hung around the entrance mostly, but I went in too." When Yanni's expression suggested doubt, Apostolos protested, "I saw good, Yanni. I'm pretty sure the Britisher said in Greek, 'Congratulations Apostolos, you've found it for me. It's the treasure we've been looking for,'" but Apostolos largely made up the quotation to please Yanni. "The old man was wiping lots of dirt off his hands. And I think he took some pictures because he turned on bright lights in there."

"Did he take anything out?"

"I didn't see nothing. He only said, 'I want Steefee and Geem to see this,' then he said, 'Let's go.'"

"How long was he in the cave?"

"A long time."

"What does that mean?"

"It means I was getting tired of standing, so I sat down outside the cave, so it was a long time."

Yanni could barely keep from screaming, but the sight of Argos held him back. "Then I don't see the problem."

"Well…"

Yanni cut him off. "Look. Enough. Here's what we're going to do to be safe."

"What do you mean safe? I didn't see nothing that was dangerous, Yanni. I could tell he was going through all kinds of stuff. I could hear a little bit."

"Like what did you hear?"

"Papers and scraping. And I heard him digging a little bit. He has that tiny shovel he carries."

"Do you think he buried the gold?"

"How should I know? I tell you what I hear and see, but that's never enough for you. Sometimes you are the hardest relative to get along with."

Hoping he was gullible enough, Yanni chanced, "Maybe these crazy foreigners will try to kill us when we take our gold back?"

"Do you really think so, cousin?"

"You never know." Yanni had to turn away to not betray the smile of success. He continued with a change in tone that caught Argos's attention. "And he's going back up there tomorrow?"

"With the other two. I'm sure."

"So, my colleague, you, and me are going to be up there ahead of them. There's really only one trail up from the hotel they can use, right?"

"Right. One trail, but if you drive way around to the other side of the mountain, there's a winding road, more of a goat path, that goes a lot of the way to the top. Used to be animal pens up there."

"Good. We'll use Stephanos's car and use the road and go the rest of the way on foot. We just need to be sure we're up there hiding before they arrive or at least after they've gone in the cave. When will they leave to climb up?"

Apostolos shrugged, "Early. A little after when I start work."

"Is the sun up?"

"Yes."

Yanni shook his head and took a deep breath, "Okay, then. We'll start before dawn. Fuck me. I hate doing things that early. If the old man did bury it, we have to get to him when he's in the cave and sweat it out of him if we have to. Use a little persuasion if they suddenly get amnesia."

"Listen, can't we just do this, you and me? I really don't know this Stephanos."

"Are you nuts? If we do it, the foreigners will be able to identify us if something goes wrong. There's more going on here than you know, Apostolos. A whole society will be watching this. Let Stephanos and I take care of the foreigners."

"Well as long as it's done fair. The gold belongs to us Cretans, right?"

"You got it. It's for all the poor people who lost their lives fighting the Germans. The brothers and sisters and cousins. The ones who lost their homes. It's for Aunty and her father, The Lion. Good people."

"When you say it like that, it's our duty."

"Of course it is, Apostolos. And don't worry, I have everything figured out. And don't forget to bring that old shotgun."

"The single-barrel one?"

"Right, that one. I remember uncle hunting with it."

"Okay, I'll bring it. But not to use?"

"Just to scare the foreigners more than your father did the birds."

Apostolos chuckled. He felt much more relaxed.

* * *

Steffi and Jim were outside when the school bell rang with its sharp, perky cadence. Today was the second day in a row of summer weather. They sat in the warming sunlight and washed each other's hair in front of the cottage, rinsing shampoo suds away with buckets of cold water. Steffi sat upright on a stool, stripped to the waist as Jim worked his hands through her hair. Between the thick suds and her tangled, dense hair, Jim had to apply muscle to knead and work his hands down to her scalp. Steffi appeared in a trance, her head flopping back and forth with no apparent resistance.

Jim lifted a red plastic pail, "Stand by, Steffi. Here comes the water." Steffi tensed but said nothing. Water and suds cascaded down her back and breasts, raising goose bumps on the delicate skin. Jim refilled the bucket and poured again. The cleansing water ran down the small of her back and spilled into the gap between her jeans and buttocks. Her jeans were dark with water.

Steffi arched her back. "Ayyyy!"

"I had to give you the full immersion treatment. There's so much soap." Steffi bent her head back to let the water drain behind the chair instead of down her jeans. Sunlight painted her breasts.

With two further buckets, Jim selectively poured water over spots of suds. Finally, he declared, "Done." He picked up Steffi's large comb and carefully worked the tangles out. More water dripped into the well of her collarbones, and she shivered. Jim squeezed her damp hair with a towel, then took a wide-bristled brush and stroked it through her hair. The warm sun began drying her hair immediately. He noticed how the sun had turned the tips of her long hair auburn, and there were streaks of auburn among the chestnut and darker strands. He found a single strand of silver hair but said nothing. Jim thought, *she'll never understand why I find it beautiful.* Her head swayed with each stroke. The faintest breeze arose and all but anesthetized them.

"You know, your hair's beautiful," he said, his voice languid and thick.

She struggled to utter words because Jim's hands in her hair, the sunlight, and the fresh scent of the soap had served as a narcotic. Finally, Steffi drawled, "Really, darling? I've always thought it ordinary." For a moment he wondered whether she really believed that, or was it all part of flirting? Still, the reply didn't surprise him. Beauty for Steffi wasn't a physical attribute, but something reflected by the heart.

Steffi's voice remained dreamy. "Will you work on your book today, or do you think we'll hike with Mr. Robinson?"

"Hike. I forgot to tell you Mr. Robinson called. Said he was anxious to show us something special and to be prepared to hit the trail. Said he would stop by mid-morning. Apparently the climb begins close by."

"Super. I mean I want you to finish your book, but I'm on 'pins and needles'—is this the right idiom?—about what he's found. About the search."

"The book's in fine shape. I want to know what he's found too."

She turned her head up to make eye contact. Squinting into the sun, "You do think he was serious, don't you?"

"Mr. Robinson is 'old school.' His word means something. If he says he's on to something, then he truly believes he is." Jim ran the brush through her hair a few more times.

"Thank you, Jim. You could probably do that for a decade, and I wouldn't complain, but it's enough." She swiveled on the stool and took his hands. "I wanted to tell you about the email from Katarina and the letter from Mother."

"Okay. I saw the letter on the table and was curious. Let me put the brush and things inside. I'll be back."

"In two shakes of a lamb's tail?"

"So you've learned that one too?"

"Yes. I'm crazy about it."

Jim returned and settled onto the bench along the stone wall across from her. "So, fill me in."

Steffi's smile spread across her face. "Well, Katarina gave me a heads up the letter was coming. Heads up, right?"

"Right as rain."

She ignored the idiom. "So I was prepared for a shock when I read the letter. Then, good shock. Mother wants to see me, said she should have trusted me more and was happy I was happy. How about that!"

"Wow. Good news."

"And she said she hopes to see me soon and wants to meet you."

Jim rubbed his neck. "Kinda makes me feel like a teenager. But it's good I guess."

"See, sometimes life does work out." Then Steffi's smile bent into a frown. "I've been thinking."

"Uh-oh. Déjà vu all over again." Jim leaned his back against the wall of the cottage and raised one foot onto the bench. His eyes drifted over the distant horizon, and in the far-off sea, he imagined a fleet of black, sleek-hulled triremes making way. For a moment he closed his eyes and let the morning sun warm his bronzed face. "I'm listening. Truly I am. Just enjoying the sun. My mind's a blank slate." But of course it wasn't. It escaped into historical fantasy, as it often did. His mind was filled with images of the Bronze Age. He imagined wearing a bronze breastplate polished so that it reflected the sun. He smelled the leather straps that bound it to him. He felt the bindings of the greaves covering his calves, and his hand rested on a fearsome bronze helmet with its cheek plates.

Steffi swept her hair over her right shoulder. "It's been a while since we talked about the Liliana thing. It's the, uh…"

With his eyes still closed, he said, "Five-hundred-pound gorilla in the room?"

"Silly idiom. Is this thing still lurking out there? Is it going to come back and—"

"Snakebite us."

"Stop it. I'm serious. I mean we talk about it and reassure each other, but… but sometimes I feel it out there."

"It's not a bogeyman, Baba Yaga or something."

"Of course, but I worry that some things, they can change things beyond repair, beyond redemption."

In a scolding tone, he said, "Steffi Galabova, I'm taken aback. You are the one who has lectured me about love and how love is about redemption."

"But how can you forget the whole thing?"

"I can't. But that's not the point. It's part of our stories that's woven together. It's not about forgetting. It's about forgiving and understanding. That I've learned from you. Any more *ist nicht die Rede Wert.*"

"But I needed to mention it."

Jim stroked her cheek. "So okay. We all have our Baba Yagas. Some days they are right behind us or in our bedroom closets. On good days they aren't." At that moment, he imagined her father comforting her because she was afraid Baba Yaga was hiding among the rafters. He felt the force of her father's love, and it filled him with inexpressible compassion because he also was no stranger to the same fears as a child and as an adult. "Steffi," Jim felt as if his own voice had been hijacked by something greater. "We wander into a labyrinth. Down some ways are horrible mistakes, born of selfishness. Other passages are dark and unknown. In some we discover things that are miserable, but we learn from them; and at other times, there's joy. But the main thing is we fumble through it. It's all right, Steffi. We have wandered into each other in the same damn labyrinth, and now we're walking through it together. All my grief and anger are gone." He paused a moment. "My God, I'm beginning to sound like you."

"But sometimes it seems too good to be true, so I keep checking. I like the image you used, 'in a labyrinth.' Sometimes it's so dark we're blind, but there's always the way out."

"Maybe because we're on Kaftor we feel the ancient myths of the place with Daedelus, the Minotaur, and all that."

Steffi abruptly stood up and smiled. For moment she appeared as though she was about to walk away but instead bent down and kissed him deeply and hard until his lips hurt. "Thought I'd give you a sample of the here and now, professor." Jim opened his eyes after the kiss. The bright sun haloed around her head.

Steffi walked away, saying over her shoulder, "I'm going to change out of these wet clothes." Jim said nothing and followed her back inside.

CHAPTER TWENTY-ONE

The chill of early morning lingered as Mr. Robinson, Steffi, and Jim struggled up the steep trail and topped the first ridgeline. Mr. Robinson commented that the fall rains weren't far behind. "I can feel it in me bones. And at the altitude where we're ascending, snow's not far behind." They knew, but didn't say, that the rains and cold would end the campaign season. Until Mr. Robinson's latest discovery, his voice had adopted a tone of doubt about ever being able to do another season searching for Ian. The village gossiped about him. "Crazy, this Britisher and his wandering," they said to Maria. "He should go back home." Steffi and Jim had heard fragments of this chatter, and they too worried about him; but seeing Mr. Robinson tackling this climb so vigorously and optimistically encouraged them. Robinson's tale of a breakthrough steeled them.

Chill or not, beads of perspiration trickled down Jim's neck. He walked "tail end Charlie," as they called the last spot in a Marine tactical column. Steffi was in between. Mr. Robinson kept his steady metronomic pace no matter how steep the ascent. Jim studied Mr. Robinson's energy-conserving, compact strides. "Obviously," he said to himself, "this isn't his first rodeo." He grinned thinking of how he would use this idiom with Steffi. Watching Mr. Robinson, his faint smile somehow communicating a belief in a God-given right to the trail, reminded Jim of the British adventurer and Cretan resistance fighter Sir Patrick Leigh Fermor. Jim suspected Harold Robinson fancied himself a reflection of Fermor's dash and derring-do? Jim had discussed Fermor and his place in the tradition of British adventurers with Robinson, who frequently paraphrased lines from Fermor's travel books. It was Fermor's exploits on Crete, particularly engineering the daring abduction of German General Kneip, that cemented Mr. Robinson's veneration of him.

As often happens on a trail, Jim's mind wandered. He thought of Mr. Robinson speaking about how Achilles's sea-goddess mother, Thetis, foretold his future with two stark choices for her son: Stay out of the Trojan War and live a prosperous life with a peaceful death in old age; or die a hero's death in war and have generations after tell of his exploits. Mr. Robinson recalled how their mother had prophesied similarly when Ian announced his decision to take a commission.

Steffi periodically twisted her head back to glance at Jim. It was as if she couldn't bear not seeing her love. For him, her eyes seduced his soul. After another fifteen minutes passed, Mr. Robinson called a brief halt. He stripped off the light anorak he'd been wearing, and Jim took the opportunity to yank off his favorite hiking pullover.

Mr. Robinson reached down into his pack. "Shall we have a spot of tea?" A sage green, liter-sized thermos emerged.

"How thoughtful." Steffi's cheeks were flushed from exertion.

Mr. Robinson pulled plastic folding cups out of his pack and asked Steffi to hold them open while he poured the steaming and sweetened milk tea. Steffi carefully passed a warm plastic cup to Jim. They sipped their tea quietly. Steffi sat cross-legged on the ground with her eyes locked on Jim's.

Mr. Robinson rummaged some more in his kit and declared, "Hallo, what have we here?" He offered them an open plastic bag of Mrs. Phindrikalis's favorite keks.

For several minutes all three were lost in their own musings. Jim thought about a frosty morning in Charlottesville while researching his thesis. Mr. Robinson recalled hiking in the Brenta Group near Madonna de Campiglio with Anne while on their honeymoon. Steffi recalled nature walks with her father in the Rodope Mountains.

Finally, Mr. Robinson declared, "Well folks, last call, drink up. We have a long climb ahead of us." Jim and Steffi slugged the last of their tea. "Keep the cups for the next pause."

Their pace quickened with the trail switching back and forth as they climbed farther out of a valley. At one point Jim sensed someone or something watching them. When he raised his head from the trail to the rock-strewn mountain face, he discovered dozens of goats among the rocks, silently observing them, camouflaged among the boulders. "Tonight, we roast a goat!" he shouted at them, but the goats only returned impassive stares.

Mr. Robinson chuckled, "Doesn't bother them, Jim boy."

Suddenly Steffi turned around, and as Jim closed the gap between them, she hugged him around the middle and whispered, "I love you."

"I love you, too." And with that, Jim hoisted her over his shoulder in a fireman's carry. "We can't fall behind Mr. Robinson."

Steffi yelped, and Mr. Robinson, a few paces ahead, kinked his stiff neck around to see what had happened.

With her head pointed back down the trail she caught a glimpse of someone behind them. "Who's that? Is someone following us?"

Mr. Robinson chimed in. "I saw him too. No need to worry. It's surely Apostolos. He's done it before. A simple but good lad. He worries I'll lose my way or injure myself, so Mrs. Phindrikalis says. He doesn't want to insult me or make me think I owe him money, so he keeps out of sight for the most part. Probably left Argos to tend the flock. When I told him I didn't require his services today, he seemed a bit perturbed. Feelings of duty, I suppose. Being a shepherd will do that, I should think." He removed his straw hat and wiped his brow with a linen handkerchief. "The truth of the matter is, I desired that we should experience this, just the three of us. I haven't been entirely forthcoming." With that Jim set Steffi down.

Robinson continued in a serious and carefully modulated voice. A wind began to howl, but his voice overcame it. "I know I told you I uncovered something, but I didn't explain the details, so I suppose this is the right time to own up. I've been doing a good deal of exploring on my own. I was hiking when you thought I was up to other things. You see, I needed to be sure, and the last thing I wanted was to disappoint, but this time, after years of effort, I have come upon something important." He looked directly at Steffi, his tone grave, "In fact, I found specific mention of your grandfather." He saw Steffi beginning to speak. "We'll be there shortly. Better to see it all than to talk in generalities here. Surely, you have questions, but let's trudge on. And let's not embarrass poor Apostolos by exposing his silliness."

Steffi beamed, "Why are we wasting time? Let's go."

"Right you are! Let's get on with it." With that, Mr. Robinson resumed his pace as if there had not been a second's pause.

For Steffi, everything about her life seemed to coalesce at that moment: love, health, art, family, spirit. Jim couldn't quite believe what he heard. It was as if his brain wanted to see a footnote with a proper citation before he could accept Robinson's comment.

They leaned into the trail; time clicked away. Their thighs ached and their breaths shortened. Finally, the space around them opened up with a broader vista in all points on the compass. The wind freshened, and the vegetation grew sparse. Jim assumed they were cresting the peak. As the thought came to mind, Mr. Robinson stopped several meters ahead and faced them. He raised his voice to be heard over the wind. "The cave is on the downward slope, just below the military crest. Shan't be long now."

Jim thought, "military crest," a term he hadn't heard for a while—the spot below the peak where a man standing wouldn't be silhouetted. They scrambled down among boulders along a less distinct goat trail, evidenced by their pea-shaped droppings. For ten minutes they traced the peak in parallel, finally moving into an area more protected from the wind and exposed to the southern sun. They crossed a fold in the mountain, and in the fold ran a narrow, gushing stream of icy water which Jim assumed would have been a good source of drinking water for the partisans.

Now that they were on the reverse slope, Jim saw a narrow, unpaved, and obviously little-used road switching back and forth about halfway up the mountain miles in the opposite direction from Plakias. Though clearly engineered by human hands, it was hardly wide enough for the Suzuki. Tracing it into its distant vanishing point put into perspective how far they had climbed.

Mr. Robinson stair-stepped farther down the slope. The vegetation grew thicker as yet another fold of the mountain bulged to the south. There, tucked far into the crease of the fold, Jim saw what he suspected might be a cave opening. Mr. Robinson hesitated, then headed directly for it.

* * *

Yanni and Stephanos had driven up the road Jim had observed and climbed the rest of the way on foot. They had stashed Stephanos's car behind an outcropping of rock, making it unobservable from farther up the slope. While the road offered an alternative approach to the cave and a quicker means of escape, there were no defined trails from the road. The climb, much steeper than the trail Mr. Robinson climbed, made it a rugged three-hour grind, much of it in darkness and faint early morning light. More than once, one or the other tripped or tumbled, often ending up barking a knee or scratching an arm. Neither possessed the cardiovascular fitness needed, and the effort left them spent. Yanni had no other shoes than his mahogany wingtips which he cussed both because the effort had rewarded him with blisters and because his beloved shoes had been shredded by rocks and brush. The climb inflamed their already dyspeptic constitutions, and then they added a few shared slugs from Stephanos's flask, injecting an accelerant to the fire of their prison-honed lust for violence. They lay beneath a ledge of rock commiserating about their wounds and wanting to punish someone as much as they wanted the gold.

Apostolos had guided them part of the way. Without his help it was doubtful they would have ever found their hiding spot near the cave entrance. When Apostolos split away so that he could be in a position to shadow Jim, Steffi, and Harold Robinson, his primitive, almost animal instincts sensed something wrong. These men communicated threat, and Apostolos noticed earlier how Argos had detected it in Yanni. He had always trusted Argos before. Shouldn't he now?

These men didn't know the mountains and high meadows. The mountains' grandeur was something on the horizon to be used as part of their hustle to get a German or Frenchman talking, but Apostolos was conflicted because what Yanni had told him also made sense. The money did belong to Crete and its people, but why did he need to bring a shotgun? Eventually, up against the wall of his own emotional and intellectual limitations, Apostolos chose pack loyalty over Mr. Robinson's complex story as told to him by Aunt Maria. His provincial suspicions of foreigners only added ammunition, so he followed cousin Yanni's instructions with the loyalty of Argos.

The wind whistled, almost muffling Stephanos's gruff shout. "That cousin is a fucking goat. Fucker never gets worn out. Good thing we arrived when we did because I was going to kill the son of a bitch before he killed me."

Yanni shrugged, "That's what he does. He climbs these hills and mountains every day. That's why we need him."

"Only until this is done." Stephanos drank water from the goat skin Apostolos had left with them. "And I'll tell yuh another thing, he's a dumb son of a bitch. So where the fuck is he going?"

Yanni ignored the vitriol. "He's going to intercept them some fucking place," he imitated Stephanos's inflections, "then shadow them. I want to make sure the old man doesn't have a trick up his sleeve and really has another place in mind."

"You said this job would be easy. This is bullshit. Why not stick them up when they come down off of the mountain?"

Yanni gave Stephanos a bored expression, "Because there's no chance of anybody else getting in the way up here."

"That's for fucking sure." Stephanos's lips were dried and cracked from the climb, and he moistened them with his lip. "My fucking knees hurt. These foreign bastards give us any shit, and I'll kill 'em first thing."

"Please, after we get the gold." Yanni looked down at his feet. "First thing I do when we get the gold is buy another pair of shoes."

Stephanos laughed for the first time and shot back, "Is that all you can think of, shoes? I got other plans for my gold. There's this Serb bitch I met."

Yanni cracked, "Serb women—they all have a moustache by forty."

"Shut the fuck up!"

Yanni turned serious and held up his hand. Over the wind, he heard them approaching. "They're coming!"

"Yeah, yeah," and Stephanos took another long pull on his flask. "You start giving me orders general, I'll shoot your face off."

He'd watched Stephanos in action and knew with the right impulse, he'd do it, not caring in the moment about the gold, the consequences, or anything else. He'd seen him beat a man to death for inadvertently brushing up against him, then calling him a "fag" as the man breathed his last. Yanni needed the likes of Stephanos and accepted the risks. It was at that moment they heard them approach. Yanni cautioned, "Let them get inside. Give them some time. The old man may have hidden the gold. Besides, we need to wait for my cousin to catch up."

* * *

Mr. Robinson disappeared through the cave entrance first, the jagged fissure in the fold of the mountain that marked the opening barely wide enough for him to slip through sideways, seemed to swallow him as if passing from one dimension to another. Steffi followed. For her, the image in her mind was of drawing a black velvet curtain aside at the back of a theater set. Jim was keyed up by the promise of historical mysteries to be solved.

Once inside, Mr. Robinson switched on a large battery-powered LED lantern. Then he passed headlamps to Jim and Steffi and demonstrated how to turn them on with a twist of the bezel ring. "I have a couple of electric torches as well, but I don't think we'll require them." Then he quipped, "A bit of a trip *Through the Looking Glass*, isn't it?"

Steffi had read the Lewis Carroll novel in Bulgarian as a youngster, and in English as an adult. "Will we meet Tweedledee and Tweedledum?"

"No doubt my dear, no doubt."

CHAPTER TWENTY-TWO

Both Steffi and Jim, like Mr. Robinson, were struck by the cave's dryness. Steffi expected dampness like other caves they had explored. She imagined this one with ancient pictographs and stalactites. Instead, the walls had a chiseled, smooth appearance. Turning around, Jim noticed how only the narrowest shaft of light defined the entrance. "A great hideout." As he trained his flashlight on the chamber walls, "It's as if the whole thing was hacked out by humans."

Mr. Robinson tilted his head Jim's way. "That thought occurred to me as well. Probably all due to water and ice, but as one works through the tunnels and chambers, the impression of the cave being made by men and not nature seems only stronger. You know, there are those who claim the labyrinth was at Knossos and others insist it was in a cave."

"Uh oh, that brings up the possibilities of Minotaurs. Wouldn't that be a find, if you had actually discovered that ancient labyrinth?" But Jim wished he could have taken back his words. They sounded facetious in light of the possibility that Harold Robinson had uncovered evidence concerning both Ian and Steffi's grandfather.

"Just for moment let's turn off all our lights and listen quietly." Neither Jim nor Steffi had ever experienced such absence of light. Except for a sliver of silver light at the entrance, nothing was visible, not the vaguest form. Then they heard it—the baleful sighing. It was as regular as a sleeping animal's breathing. A primitive impulse urged them to flee toward the few rays of light behind them, but they held their ground. After a minute or two, Mr. Robinson switched on the lantern and the powerful blue-white light illuminated the area around them, dissipating as it shone deeper into the cave. "Amazing, isn't it?"

"The more you listen, the more the breathing seems to draw closer." Steffi took Jim's hand. Jim added, "I could see how the Minoans might believe the sum of all their fears lived in here."

Robinson added, "Maybe it is that the breathing draws us to it." Turning to the more practical, he said, "With this lantern switched on, we shouldn't require our headlamps. Might as well save the batteries."

"Did they live in here?" Steffi's eyes wandered along the walls. "I mean partisans, not Minotaurs."

Mr. Robinson cleared his throat, and the sound rumbled through the cave. "Yes. From time to time they moved to new places. Inevitably some collaborator compromised them, so they were often on the run; but yes, essentially the whole campaign was often run from such places. And yes, I have found convincing evidence the partisans were here." Adjusting his glasses and looking Steffi square in the eyes, "And if you will be patient with me, I will show you that Ian and your grandfather were here."

Out of a sense of profound disorientation, Steffi only managed to weakly reply, "Sure. Yes, fine."

Jim felt energized, "How can we respond to that? Startling, is all I can say, and that word seems inadequate." He paused a moment, his eyes wandering about the chamber. "This does bring it all together for me. Though were I here in the war, my big anxiety would have been feeling trapped—one way in and no escape. If you get cornered in here, you're doomed."

"Quite logical, Jim, but I dare say this particular cave is a bit different. Not to belabor the point, but apart from the sculpted walls, it made me wonder if it is, indeed, another candidate for the 'Lost Labyrinth' of Minoan King Minos's day. I did a bit of exploring when I was here previously, and to my amazement, there's a labyrinth of passages beyond this room that may very well lead to liberation." Mr. Robinson pointed to a dark, foreboding opening ahead, "I followed Daedalus's advice to Theseus. Took a ball of twine because I didn't have the recommended silken thread, and I did bring a sturdy flashlight with extra batteries. And then I did as Daedalus instructed, kept going straight and down, never left or right, and I assure you there are numerous opportunities to make a turn. I couldn't prove a way out, but I trust old Daedalus. By the amount of water running farther on and the fresh air I felt, I suspect I wasn't too far from another exit. But I'll say this, if you don't know the way, well then good luck. You could spend a lifetime in there. The bloody Jerries could follow you in and never find their way out."

"All with one ball of twine?" Steffi asked.

Mr. Robinson's laugh echoed, "Well, you see, I ran out of twine, but kept going nonetheless, gave it the old go, feeling quite intrepid, and as you can see I made it back. I'll show you where I tied the twine to a rock farther on."

"Good show!" Jim teased, using the British idiom. "Seriously, though, this could be of significant interest. I can imagine archaeologists and cultural historians debating this for years to come. Has the labyrinth actually been discovered, and did Daedalus actually exist?"

Chortling, "That would be a jolly show to read about... In any event, I left my faux silken thread in place. They can all damn well follow it if they choose." With that, Robinson turned his flashlight on to the spot where he had secured the twine. Mr. Robinson brought them over to a spot a few meters deeper in the cave. "In the meantime, I wish to show you this," pointing to the charred area nearby. "There were fires here for warmth and light no doubt."

Steffi bent down to inspect more closely. "The smoke must have been terrible."

"It drifted up through some natural vents in the ceiling is my theory, Steffi." Mr. Robinson switched his flashlight on again. "I believe this torch is strong enough to be seen in contrast even with the lantern on. See the twists and turns to the rock." He maneuvered the flashlight like a pointer over the features several meters over their heads. "Some of the smoke no doubt gathered up there like a cloud. If you look carefully, you can see some discoloring. I suspect the whole place is a lot more porous than it appears and perhaps making it quite fragile."

Jim's hands rested on his hips as he followed the beam of light. "Fascinating. I wouldn't be surprised if they figured out a way to work their antenna up through one of the ventilation holes. Excellent way to hide the thing."

"I hadn't thought of that, but certainly, it makes sense."

Jim picked at the burnt fragments with the toe of his hiking boot. "Some of this ash looks fresh." He bent down, "Like paper."

Mr. Robinson's face burned from having been so foolish to leave evidence behind. He rushed the conversation along, not wanting Jim to examine the ash more closely. "As you can see, it is immediately evident that this cave has been used, but it could have been local scoundrels of one sort or another. The cave can't be a secret. After all, it was Apostolos who led me to it. The question I considered was, could I discover artifacts or other evidence to support the proposition that I was indeed in one of the caves used by the partisans and by Ian in particular? I know Ian was working in this part of the island. Given the responsibilities of your grandfather's mountain unit, I deduced this sector may well have been where he was active and then ultimately captured." He glanced over at Steffi, "The staggering odds of that, the fate of it all. My poor logical brain wanted to reject the evidence before my eyes. I'm accustomed to humbuggery and deceptions you see." Mr. Robinson picked up the lantern. "Let's move a bit deeper in the cave, and I'll show what I discovered." Mr. Robinson pointed back to his pack. "Be a good lad and bring my pack along."

Steffi's glance darted in Jim's direction with a twisted smile.

Mr. Robinson led them to a spot several meters on where he had sat before to study the papers. He pointed to the jumble of rock segmenting the space with stone barriers and natural ledges to rest things on. There among the rocks and on the rock ledges were the partially rotted wooden boxes and rusted tins of various sizes. Jim, as had Mr. Robinson, instantly recognized some as ammunition crates. Even though the smaller metal boxes had been almost entirely eaten by rust, Jim reasoned they had been tins of food. "This is rather convincing, Mr. Robinson."

"My heart leapt when I glimpsed all of this."

Had the supplies, Jim wondered, been dropped to them by parachute or carried in from the beaches, shuttled from submarines on rubber boats? "Haunting seeing all this here, just the way it was when they left."

"Yes, the dross is strewn about everywhere. I've even found some .303 Enfield rounds."

Steffi picked up a can, bent and half eaten away from corrosion. On one intact spot she was able to read the faded words, "Hormel."

"Wonder what it was?"

"Hormel? That would make it a can of Spam. My God, I can't believe the stuff made it to Crete. I know we sent a lot of it to the Russians in the war. It's a prepared meat."

Mr. Robinson chuckled. "But come along. Let me show you the buried treasure."

* * *

Apostolos crept up to the hiding spot with a stealth that surprised the other two and resulted in fiery responses. "What the fuck's the matter with you, you moron?" said Stephanos. "I could have shot you."

"I didn't want to be seen."

"You can be a pain, cousin."

Apostolos's eyes bulged, and his voice stammered. "But did you see them? Did you see them go in?"

"Of course."

Apostolos cut in, "I was thinking, maybe we could talk to them. They'll understand about the gold belonging to Cretans."

Yanni and Stephanos studied Apostolos with basilisk eyes. "Look, you dumb goat," Stephanos hissed, "We're here to take the gold, not negotiate. And once we've got it, you're going to help film us taking care of them, so no foreign bastards ever think of trying a stunt like this again. You'll be the most famous cameraman in the whole world when we post this on the net, if you even knew what the fuck the net was."

Apostolos resented this man. He knew nothing. Goats weren't dumb; they were clever.

For the first time that day, Yanni worried about his plan. Filming? What if somebody could identify him on the film? He heard on TV about some voice recognition robot some genius had created, and he had seen something like it track a terrorist in a Hollywood blockbuster. Suddenly, he saw himself back in prison for the rest of his life. But if the Society knew it was him, well then, he'd be a hero. Besides the gold, that's what he wanted, wasn't it? Yanni spoke up, "Dear cousin. Don't worry. You're doing the right thing. We're family; trust me," and Apostolos did, trusting Yanni much in the way Argos trusted Apostolos.

Yanni turned to Stephanos. "Don't worry about him. He got us here, didn't he? Take another swig, and let's get ready." It was the first thing that day that Stephanos agreed to, so Yanni pushed his luck and attempted to assert his leadership. "Stephanos, time to put on our masks and get ready to go in. Apostolos, can stand guard out here, so if anyone comes, he can shout a warning."

"Fuck that. We need your idiot cousin in there to film the whole thing, beginning to end."

"That's not the plan. Get the gold first. I can film it once we got the gold."

"That's your plan, Yanni, and I'm changing it. You're the big shot who wanted to be noticed by the Society, and I know how to make that happen. If you don't like it, I'll do the job myself and take care of you two right now."

Yanni looked over at Apostolos's shotgun. He could probably reach it with one stretch of his arm, but one of the two automatics Stephanos carried was already racked and ready to go. He could jump Stephanos, but he had seen him fight in prison. "Hey, don't get upset. What you said makes sense. Let's do it your way. This won't be hard. They're not going to put up a fuss. It's an old man, a girl, and one man."

"And if they resist, I'll bash in their fucking heads instead of shooting them later." Stephanos said after taking another pull on his flask. "In fact, that'd look even better in the film."

This was making Yanni uneasy, and he had been so positive. He was sick and tired of other people messing up his dreams. You can't count on anybody. He wondered how much booze Stephanos had drunk. But they were so close; it was like their winnings were sitting there stacked up on a table in front of them. He had put up with a lot of shit in his life. A little more wouldn't hurt him to get the kind of life he wanted.

For his part, Apostolos was terrified, and his stomach rumbled. He spoke up, "I, I, I can't go in caves." He turned to Yanni, "Cousin, can we talk?" Stephanos frightened him. He was like the rustlers he and Argos protected the flock against.

Stephanos sneered, "This can't be. Tell me he ain't serious, Yanni?"

"It's true. I didn't want to say nothing when you changed the plan because you were so pissed. Him going in the cave was never part of my plan. He got lost a while back in a cave. It's a long story. The point is, if he goes in, we'll be figuring out how to keep him calm, and we'll forget everything else. Plus, having a guard in case somebody comes—he can give us a warning. We have to cover all the possibilities, right?"

Stephanos shrugged. Maybe somebody might come along. What difference if this idiot stood outside. In that moment, he knew he'd kill Apostolos the second his usefulness was over. And if Yanni put up a stink, he'd take care of him too. "Okay, Yanni, have it your way."

Yanni tried to retake control. "Now, let's quit arguing and get this plan going." But they kept bickering.

* * *

"Look at the wall over here." Mr. Robinson pointed his flashlight in the direction he wanted. "What do you see?"

Jim shrugged, "Immediate impression? Nothing other than cave wall."

"Precisely. Then, more by accident than anything else, I noticed an anomaly during my spelunking adventure. See here." The light played off of a dirty right angle. "Besides crystals, one doesn't see too many right angles in nature."

"I see what you mean." Jim walked closer with Steffi behind.

"I've restored it just the way I found it. You see, this is what drew me—this angle. I came closer and brushed away some of the grit." Mr. Robinson did as he had the first time, and it became apparent the angle was from a box of some sort. "Perhaps erosion, or from whatever cause, the corner of the box became exposed. I suspect these walls and overhead rock may often crumble. We should wear helmets to be safe. Given the uncertain light of torches and the like, it could have remained undiscovered until the next civilization comes to Crete."

Mr. Robinson demonstrated how he dug with his foot and picked his way carefully around the box as a paleontologist uncovering a fossil. He pulled out his folding field shovel and lifted a few shovels of earth and rock free. In short order the entire box was unearthed once again. "So there you have it! And in here, dear Steffi and Jim, I found the most marvelous things." *Yes,* he told himself, *keep the narrative positive. You studied Soviet propaganda. Say a lie long enough, it becomes the truth, and then eventually the true history, just as Yank politicians used it to justify their foolishness.* With that he yanked the box free of the loosened soil and hefted it over to the area of arranged stones.

Jim quipped, "Like I'm in a pirate movie."

"It is a treasure chest to be sure," but even as he said this, the gall rose in Mr. Robinson's throat. *Revolting that I employ Soviet propaganda techniques for this charade.* He knew lies paved roads to nowhere.

The three huddled around the box as Mr. Robinson pried open the lid. Jim noticed how Steffi spun the blue stone ring on her finger, the survivor of the Dresden firestorm and the last tangible vestige of her grandparents. Jim's shadow shrouded the box, and he moved aside to allow in more light. On the top, wrapped in an oiled cloth, was the rusty Webley revolver. Mr. Robinson unfolded the cloth as if it contained a precious religious relic. "Serviceable, but barely. I pulled the hammer back when I handled it before. It can be done, mind you, but the ammunition, I wouldn't trust it. It's the old .455 model. Still had a lot of them in stock when the second show was underway."

"Is it...?"

"Ian's? I suspect so, Steffi." Mr. Robinson handed the hefty revolver to Jim, who probed the side of it, looking for a release so he could inspect the cylinder and be sure it wasn't loaded. "It breaks open, Jim. Like this," and he demonstrated how to do it with his hands. "It's the Mark VI. We carried them in Flanders, but we used them in the Second World War as well. Most of the lads carried Enfield 38s by then."

Jim finally managed to break it open. He turned the cylinder, but it balked from age. ".455. Wow, that packs a wallop." With some effort Jim was able to pull back the hammer, then he released it slowly to keep from damaging the firing pin. "You say the ammo is no good?"

"My guess. There are some loose cartridges, but after a half-century, hard to imagine they're reliable. Of course, there's unexploded ordnance still going off from the First World War and that's nearly a century old."

Jim set the pistol down on the oilcloth near the box. Next, Mr. Robinson emptied the box out onto one of the flat rocks in front of them, but left the few gold sovereigns and some Reichsmarks on the bottom. "This Nazi currency could be forgeries. I know we tried to put counterfeits into circulation. Interesting for historical purposes. Don't know what the sovereigns would fetch. I suppose one always hopes gold will buy loyalty. We'll turn them over to the authorities of course." That's when Mr. Robinson lifted up a roughly 300x200-millimeter ragged oiled portfolio. He took a deep breath, feeling guilty for his subterfuge and yet committed to going through with it.

Mr. Robinson lectured himself the night before that there was no reason after all these years to slash open wounds with the blade of unvarnished truth. There was Steffi's fragile state of mind about her granddad, after all. What value was there to handing her the devastating truth that her grandfather executed orders implicating him as a war criminal at minimum, and certainly making him guilty of a moral outrage. That he was at least partly responsible for the death of Maria's brother, whom she had never had the chance to know, as well as burns suffered by her mother. What was the point? And what would be the purpose of divulging evidence that pointed to Maria's father either ordering or committing Steffi's grandfather's execution because of his hysterical nationalism, his moral outrage? Will that truth set anyone free? "I simply cannot do it. So let God judge me," he had declared to the mirror in his room.

"Here's the real gold."

"Finally, something tangible," Steffi said. At that moment, above all else, she prayed that she could finally learn about her grandfather—understand the man—learn who he really was. What she hadn't yet revealed to Jim or anyone else was that a friend in a Bulgarian ministry had acquired the damaging essay her grandfather had written which had been used to shun her mother and drive the final nail into the coffin of her father's career. It was hateful Nazi writing and condemned Bulgarians, but she'd convinced herself that the Communists had hidden the truth and had fabricated the essay to make their case. It was impossible for her to reconcile that hateful text with the picture of the smiling man in the mountain photo.

"Sit down somewhere, this is all quite remarkable." He untied the frayed string that bound the portfolio and turned back a fold of cloth. The inside bulged with papers, some typewritten and others handwritten. Mr. Robinson carefully set them on top of his rucksack. All the while his hands trembled as he remembered how the stack had been more than twice as thick.

A strained, emotion-laden whisper emanated from Robinson. "Please, give me a few moments. This is all so overwhelming. I thought the second time through would be easier, but it's not." Years of searching and anticipating—he had foreseen a different ending to the script.

Steffi placed her hand on the shoulder of the venerable Harold Robinson. He removed his wire-rimmed glasses and wiped his eyes. Tears welled in Steffi's eyes as well. Mr. Robinson sat on one of the stones nearby and invited Jim and Steffi to gather closer. Steffi's hand remained on his shoulder, and Jim sat across on a flat stone. Jim distracted himself by focusing on the twine which Mr. Robinson had tied around a meter-wide rock and which trailed into the darkened depths of the cave.

"So sorry. Don't mean to carry on so." With a deep breath, Mr. Robinson's shoulders rose and fell. He pointed down at a handful of written papers done in a neat, elegant script, written during an age when cursive writing was the mode of long-distance correspondence. "These are letters to family and friends that Ian had composed but never sent." He paused and gathered his strength. "I presume he was waiting to send them on the next submarine or ship. They so perfectly express the young man I so admired—no, that's wrong— worshipped as a young lad. See here." He pulled a letter from the stack. "This one's written to me, late in 1943. Let's see. I was a little sprout, eight I suppose." He cleared his throat. "He's very concerned about Mother's roses." He cleared his throat but was unable to carry on even in light of his deception and having read the material before. Though the letters were palliatives for the folks back home, that knowledge hardly diminished their emotional impact.

Steffi rubbed Mr. Robinson's shoulder. "No need to read us the letters now. He seemed like a wonderful young man. Someone bigger than himself, and," she paused, "someone fond of his younger brother."

Mr. Robinson shook his head then said softly, "But then, Steffi, I came across this." He pulled out the text of what must have been a wireless message by the structure of it. It had a date and time stamp on the top and read: *In custody one Major Gerhard Rossbach, a Gebergsjaeger. Captured 03 September 1943 during skirmish with resistance sector 09. Wounded: clean lower left abdominal gunshot wound. Treated this location. Suspect internal bleeding. Will transfer by sea when stabilized. Interrogation inconclusive.*

Steffi stared at the message. Jim and Mr. Robinson let her be with it for a while. No one in her family had been aware of what happened to Grandfather, or that he had been a prisoner, sharing this cave with a captor who was the brother of a friend. Finally, Mr. Robinson whispered, "And there's more."

Steffi handed the radio message to Jim. Mr. Robinson held a letter out to Steffi. She glanced at it and saw that it was in German. For a while she stared at the script, then on impulse handed it to Jim, saying, "Could you please try to read it? Right now my mind is in such shock, I can't translate."

Jim studied it. In his research he had experienced German cursive writing from this period and struggled with it. Fortunately, despite yellowing paper the ink remained clear, and Rossbach's penmanship was sharp and neat, even with its gothic flourishes. Mr. Robinson had chosen not to burn this letter though he was unable to decipher it, confident a letter home by a professional officer would never report operational details.

"Well let's see, it says 'Liebling' or rather, 'Dearest,' of course it's addressed to Sommer." Looking to Steffi, "She was his wife, your grandma, right?"

"Yes," she said solemnly.

I am uncertain about whether this letter will reach you or when it shall. Jim's voice was halting as he unscrambled the syntax and challenging cursive. *Perhaps to be sure but this "brief,"* I mean letter, *is most difficult. It is aber necessary. It is not my absicht, rather intention, to frighten you but rather to inform you of my current circumstances and the random thoughts streaming through my mind. You see Liebling at this very moment I am a prisoner of the British, or should I say Cretan partisans. Be patient and read on. Try not to be frightened by this news. A most generous Captain by the name of Ian (He refuses to tell me his family name) has provided me with paper and pen. I fear you will worry unduly, but I have to say because the truth is so very important in such times, Aber ja, because of so many emotions but also because I am injured, struck by a bullet. Ian has treated the wound as well as a local doctor, probably a consideration I don't deserve, and at some point, if I recover sufficiently they shall move me to safe territory for them. How tired we all are of this madness. I feared this would be the result when this all began. But be assured, I am feeling better every day and soon we shall climb mountains in the Steirmark again, so do not despair. You are my love. I will wait...*

Jim cleared his throat. "Could you move the light a little closer?" Mr. Robinson did so mechanically. Jim studied the letter and continued his translation. *...for you as long as necessary. Give my love to the children. To see them would be a joy. I had to be shot, courtesy of our enemy, to gain wisdom. Paradox! I can hear you say it. So much dear, as I lie here with this wound, is a paradox for me. I feel peace and yet I am in pain and terrible guilt for being in this war. I have told this Ian that I forgive him and his men for having shot me. He was apologetic. And don't be frightened, Liebling, thinking such sweetness from this old cranky Austrian is a sign of my demise. But I see the care and concern when he inspects my wound, and though he strives to hide it, his friendly expression gives me hope. In the evening, because I have been unable to sleep I have spoken at length with Ian. We have bared our souls and shared the commonality of our experiences. No, such is the power of this wound to convert me that just days ago we were willing to kill each other. I wonder how many times this story has taken place on this island? I am asking you, should I not return...*

"The letter ends there." Jim looked up. "My God, so they knew each other!"

Mr. Robinson turned to Steffi, "So my dear, it seems the circle has been closed. The beginning and the end knotted together—the alpha and the omega so to speak—these mysteries of our families. We have ended up connected more than I could have imagined, a miracle surely."

Steffi appeared composed in the lantern's light, her voice controlled and hauntingly absent of emotion. Jim suspected shock as the cause. What Jim didn't grasp in her countenance was the depth of relief Steffi felt. Filtered through her emotions, the letter exonerated her grandfather. The voice in the letter matched the Grossvatti she knew in the mountain photo. Her thoughts cried out, *This frightened, injured man—how could he really have been such a threat to Todor Shivkov and his sycophants that decades after his death, they should use*

Grossvatti to bludgeon father and mother? Yet, at the same time, she had seen enough of life to know there was no limit to the paranoia of such men and their personality cults. Everything is a threat to men who had already been castrated by the lies that buoyed their lives.

Suddenly, Steffi was back in the present and thought to ask, "But what of Ian? What happened?"

"Ian transmits yet another message. Succinct, military-like. Your grandfather succumbed to wounds. I suspect it was drafted in a hurry. Something was developing." Mr. Robinson pulled a sheet from the stack. *German officer Rossbach succumbed to wounds. Will inter this location. Transport request rescinded. Will...*

"The draft cuts off there. Another message details plans to abandon the cave and displace to a new location, a different sector, overland at night. Apparently, they had been betrayed. That, I assume, is when Ian or a colleague buried the metal box. They didn't make it out of the immediate area. Must have been under duress to leave so much behind. Outside, I found what I believe are some graves, shallow ones. Perhaps one is Ian's. With permission of the authorities, I will bring back bone fragments to see if I can do a DNA analysis. Perhaps in one of the other graves rests your grandfather. I suspect the casualty registration that Jim uncovered with the misspelling is one and the same as your grandfather—missing and not recovered."

"My mother," she whispered, "If she had known this before... did she know and not say?"

"Oh, don't go there," Jim implored.

The remaining entries from Ian's journal, now fine ash, still burned in Harold Robinson's mind: *Some days now I hardly know where I am. It's all jumbled and confused. I'm truly worried I might tag along with the Germans if I'm not careful, out of sheer befuddlement. I can't tell the difference anymore. We ambushed a German patrol the other day. I fired my Enfield like I was a machine. It was without feeling—neither for the poor sod Germans I slaughtered nor the Greek boy, shot through the heart by the Germans. Was he a brave lad? Or a fool? I don't know. My dear brother is not much younger; yet, I didn't care that this lad had been shot. Not one bloody bit to be perfectly honest. Some of these Cretans, like The*

Lion, are so savage. Perhaps were we fighting in Shropshire or Kent and not Crete I too...

In another passage he had written: *The headaches have become worse. I blame it on the altitude and the cold and the bloody miserable diet and lack of a decent night's sleep. But it's due to none of that. I've asked to go back, and the fools in Cairo have agreed that I should escort the German prisoner back. They say I should have a proper rest. Been in theatre too long, they say. Did someone draft his reply over a sherry, or a gin and tonic? Well none of them will be out here to replace me, they who dispatch the submarines.*

Somehow, I seem to be an encouragement to the Jerry Major. What I hide from him is the fact that I'm most worried that he'll die, and if he dies, the reason for my trip to dear old Cairo will be canceled. It's my own arse I'm worried about. I've been at this dreadful business long enough to recognize that he's already done for. He clings to me. We are comrades, he has said. He's afraid to die alone, so now he believes he has found a mate. And the war-weary truth of me is I don't care.

The German died. Done in by my allies, I am sure. He had last been speaking about his wife in Dresden. And wouldn't you know it, I feel guilty for not caring. For being angry because it will surely muck up my boat ride to Cairo, and for being the one who wounded the bastard in the first place. I feel guilty for not having admitted that. I feel cold as marble. I don't know about his soul, but mine has left my body. That I'm sure of. At the last engagement I found myself walking back to the cave with a grenade still in my hand with the bloody pin pulled. One of the Cretans noticed. He handled the situation gently enough. He eased it from my hand, keeping the spoon depressed. Let it fly down the mountainside. Gratefully, none of them spoke about it. Not to my face, anyway. But they're a sight more cautious around me. I don't blame them.

Mr. Robinson still saw the smoke from the smoldering journal rising to the top of the chamber like incense from a censer in an Orthodox church or in an ancient temple to Apollo.

"Are you all right, Mr. Robinson?" Jim's insistence finally penetrated. His hand was also on his shoulder.

"Right as can be, fit as a fiddle."

Jim caught Steffi staring off into the distance. Scooting between the two like a triage nurse at a disaster site, he asked, "And you, Steffi?"

"This is the room—no, the burial chamber where Grossvatti died, and maybe Ian too. Surely, I'm the only one in the family to know this. Poor man. Alone he died without family or friends, just the kind attention of his captor, Ian. If he is buried in an unmarked grave outside, he should be brought home, don't you think? He was a good man. I knew that from his picture I carried all these years. He was my mother's father, Jim." Jim pulled her to him, and Mr. Robinson walked over to the lantern and fiddled with the switch.

* * *

They stood outside the cave entrance. "Okay, cousin, give me the scatter gun. When I count three, then we go in."

"You first, Yanni."

Yanni yanked the balaklava over his head. "So when do you start earning your share?"

Stephanos asked as he adjusted his balaklava, "Yanni, you sure there's light in there?"

"What do you think, they're standing around in the pitch black picking their noses? What would be the point of that?"

"Don't know. Just trying to think of all the angles because I'm thinking you didn't."

Yanni shook his head in disgust. "I've been listening to that old man brag for months. He thinks nobody overhears him. This didn't come to me in a dream. I did my homework and put this together piece by piece. We're moving now because it's time to move."

Stephanos's eyes glowed through the sockets of the balaklava, seemingly possessed by a greater power. "You better be right, 'cause if you're wrong and fuck this up for me, I'll gut you."

Yanni's mouth was dry and his voice labored, but he managed, "This isn't like curing the cancer bug. It's straightforward. We go in. Surprise them. Take the gold then make our statement in the name of the Society." Even Apostolos figured out what "make a statement" meant. Yanni looked around. "After we get the gold and take care of everything, we scoot down the mountain to the car and scram." He cocked his head in the direction of Apostolos. "After a few hours, Apostolos gets concerned and visits his aunt. Asks why the old man isn't back. He comes up and finds them and reports it, and he's free and clear. And we, we post the whole show on the internet."

Stephanos smiled, "Good plan, Yanni," knowing then that he had to take care of both of them. Stephanos knew how to fix up a crime scene. Apostolos would never shut up and take the fall. Besides, anybody would see through Apostolos with their eyes closed. When they started in on that moron, he'd rat on his cousin for sure. No, they had to die. Neither of them could be trusted. Then it occurred to Stephanos, almost triggering laughter with the thought, *Yanni will get part of what he wants. He'll make Yanni the martyr for the Society, and they'll praise him for it. What's gold and a prosperous life next to being a hero people will talk about?*

Yanni checked his cell phone to be sure he could switch on the camera, took a deep breath, and plunged into the dark cave, the shotgun in one hand, the cell phone in the other. Stephanos followed with his Glock drawn.

As soon as they disappeared through the narrow crack, Apostolos knew what he had to do. He didn't reflect or weigh options. It was all wrong. He reacted to the signals his twitching muscles communicated. Acting like a sheep with lightning striking the meadow, he ran. He clambered down the mountain as sure-footed as any goat. Never once did he look back. His goal, were he able to articulate it, was to run to the safety of Aunt Maria.

CHAPTER
TWENTY-THREE

Steffi saw them first, and the sound of her scream rippled through the cave. "What the fuck!" burst from Jim. Mr. Robinson uttered something unintelligible.

Yanni disguised his voice, croaking in accented English, "We shoot you in the face if you move!" The two menacingly pointed guns at the trio, Apostolos's single-barreled shotgun among them.

In his most authoritarian major's voice, Mr. Robinson demanded, "What the devil do you think you're doing?"

Yanni croaked on, "Please to be giving us the gold that belongs to the people of Crete."

"Gold, you say?"

"Yes, gold! The treasure."

"What the bloody hell gave you that idea? What, do you think this is a mining operation?"

Jim chose a soothing tone, "Take it easy, Mr. Robinson. They'll soon see there's nothing to it." In Greek he added, "We have some coins. We aren't here for money. Just memories."

Jim saw the two men glance at each other behind their balaclavas. Their weapons were leveled at the chests of Robinson and Jim. One of them seemed wobbly on his feet; the other shifted impatiently from one foot to the other. Jim's racing mind tied itself in knots as he struggled to figure out why they targeted them and what they really wanted. For an instant, Jim considered taking action, but the odds were vastly against him. He glanced down at the Webley, but who knew if it would work even if he could load it in time?

It was then that Yanni in his croaking, disguised voice uttered words that at once clarified the situation for Jim and terrified him as well. "In the name of the Sect of the Revolutionaries, give us the gold, or I will begin by shooting the kneecap off the lady."

Robinson looked to Jim, "What is the Sect of the Revolutionaries?"

Jim sighed, "Thugs, criminals, secular terrorists. Mostly wrapped up by the police I had heard. I guess these two didn't get the word."

Stephanos sneered, "Big funny man. Okay. Stop playing. Give us the money and gold now!"

Steffi studied Jim and Mr. Robinson, hoping to detect a clue that they knew what to do. Her mind was blank. She held her arms tightly folded in front of her to help control her shaking. These kinds of men were like *mutri* in Bulgaria—stupid, dangerous, fumbling. She didn't need to see their faces to recognize how the situation could end in an explosion.

Mr. Robinson said jovially, "Alright Jim lad, seems Tweedledee and Tweedledum have decided to come through the looking glass after all. Let's give them the money, but I want to see the face of the barkeep tonight when they try to exchange counterfeit Nazi Reichmarks." Then he chuckled in the faces of his assailants.

Yanni croaked again, "You big funny man too?"

"This is utter foolishness. Money. I should say. You should have your ears boxed. Threatening this young woman with a pistol! You should all be shot."

Jim cautioned with his palms turned out. "Okay, okay. Mr. Robinson, what's the point? They can have it all. It means nothing to us." Looking at the men, "I have to bend down though, okay? To get the money that's in here," pointing down at the metal box.

Yanni waved his hand toward the box and croaked in his disguised voice, "Hurry."

Stephanos asked in Greek, "Why is he not doing it?"

Yanni shrugged, "Maybe he needs encouragement."

With that Stephanos pulled his second automatic from his waistband, a Russian 9mm Makarov, and pointed it directly at Jim's head.

Jim involuntarily twitched when the barrel reached eye-level less than two feet from his head.

"Jim, *Aufpassen*," from Steffi. She ran up to Jim, and he wrapped his arm around her. Stephanos's finger had been within a pound of trigger pull from shooting Steffi when she ran. His vision blurred as his eyes caught up to the action.

"You move again like that missy, you dead," he said, slurring his words.

"It's okay," but Jim was horrified to see the man had trained his Makarov on Steffi. He made eye contact with Stephanos's glowing eyes, "Okay. I'm getting it, but no need to keep your finger on the trigger. You're the boss."

"The hell he is, lad," from Mr. Robinson.

"Mr. Robinson, please. Let's give them what they want." While calm on the exterior, inside, Jim was desperately grappling with figuring out options and assessing chances about how this scene might unfold. These two had, after all, blundered already. They didn't have what these men had expected. Was the threat of violence a bluff? No, it was serious. He knew guns well enough to know these weren't fake. The smell of alcohol introduced another volatile ingredient. Their hair-trigger edginess was a palpable aura around them. Violence, he concluded, was all but certain, with or without gold to hand over.

"Okay, lad, but be careful. Very unstable that one," Robinson said, no doubt referring to the wobbling Stephanos.

He turned to Steffi's ear just before he bent down, and spoke just loudly enough for Mr. Robinson to hear. "See the string, we'll follow that." Steffi was truly frightened then. She kept her eyes downcast, but she caught a glimpse of the twine tied around a rock. What good did the string do them? These men had guns, and we can't outrun bullets. Jim noticed the men had no flashlights. How stupid. A small thing, but maybe…

"Hurry! Last time I ask, or we shoot you in the face." The men signaled again with the barrels of their pistols.

Jim bent down and pulled up a wad of paper Reichmarks from the box, "Here. Here's your treasure. See?" He waved it at them. "Just worthless paper."

Stephanos barked in Greek, "What's this? This is not gold."

Mr. Robinson understood the Greek and answered back in Greek. "It's German money from the war. False money. Worthless except to collectors."

"Well no one is asking you, old man."

Mr. Robinson, without even a trace of anxiety, and perhaps with a note of scorn added, "Jim, show these brigands the coins. Perhaps that can be the end of this ludicrous and absurd show."

With his other hand Jim reached down and grabbed a couple of the Sovereigns, and then stood up holding them out for the bandits to examine.

"Ah, see, that's better." Yanni reached out and grabbed the coins. He pressed them in his hand and relished the feel of them.

"Now the rest!" Stephanos shouted in Greek, and fired his Makarov deafeningly in the air. The bullet whizzed and ricocheted around the chamber. Chips of rock cascaded down from the ceiling.

Steffi tightened her grip on Jim. She was too terrified to look up; her ears rang from the blast. With her downcast eyes, she noticed the shoes of one of the men in front of her—mahogany wing tips. Impulsively she shouted out, "My God. It's Yanni!" Sensing an opportunity, Jim threw the Nazi cash in the air, creating instant chaos.

The two men looked around frantically, screaming something incomprehensible in the Cretan dialect. Mr. Robinson used the distraction to reach down and grab the Webley with his left hand. "Hands up!" No doubt hoping a bluff with an empty revolver might alter the trajectory of events.

But Yanni was surprisingly quick to react, smashing Mr. Robinson's hand with the butt of his shotgun, sending the revolver skittering across the cave floor. In the corner of his eye Jim detected the other man leveling his automatics at Mr. Robinson, convincing Jim he intended to pull the triggers. Jim did the only thing he could in the hope of upsetting his aim. He booted the lantern, and the light extinguished instantly. A double flash of the discharging Glock and Makarov lit up the chamber in a surrealistic explosion of light. One round was close enough to Jim that he felt the ballistic pulse of the projectile pass his ear. With Steffi still holding on, Jim yanked her to the floor, as a torrent of shots rang out. The muzzle-flashes illuminated the scene in fractions of a second but long enough for Jim to fix in his mind the horrible visage of Harold Robinson's head disfigured and bloodied by a gunshot. He swept his hand along the rock floor and with some luck found the twine leading deeper into the cave. With his free hand he pulled Steffi. The muzzle-flashes still sparkled as after-images in the darkness. Jim struggled to overcome dizzying disorientation, but the need to survive drove him on.

Even as Jim tugged Steffi away along the length of twine, Stephanos dove where he last saw her and wildly grabbed at her legs at them, sinking his fingers in her calves in an effort to ensnare her. She kicked with all the force she could muster, loosening his nightmarish grip long enough to crawl free. In the darkness Jim couldn't comprehend why Steffi seemed to be resisting his tugs and wondered if she too had been shot, but then felt her closer.

For his part, Yanni, short of rational thought in the best of times, acted out in desperation, the only thought in his mind was that these foreigners knew who he was. He raised the shotgun to his waist and squeezed the trigger of the single-barrel twelve-bore. The thunderous blast and muzzle-flash not only made everyone's eyes and ears useless in the darkness, but the trauma shook loose more rock from overhead and along the chamber walls. In the muzzle-flash, Stephanos caught a glimpse of his prey and dove at Steffi's legs, but just as she felt him grab her again, scaling from the roof hit Stephanos's back, sounding like a broom thwacking a hung carpet. Stephanos grunted and let go.

It was a midnight escape nightmare, everything unfolded in slow motion with vampires and monsters drawing closer. Jim and Steffi felt as though they were wading through waist-high wet cement as they made their crouching escape, working their way along the length of twine, its rough texture a fragile lifeline. They wanted to run, but the ground was uneven, the cave pitch-black, and loose stone from the partial roof collapse tripped them up. They dared not risk turning on their headlamps.

From behind, they heard confused screams in Greek. Yanni's voice rang out. "They know it's me. I'm not going back to prison."

"Shut up you sodomizing ass!" They collided in the dark and cursed.

"Don't shoot blindly! Find the lantern," Yanni's recognizable voice terrified Steffi. She grabbed Jim's shirt, "But Mr. Robinson?"

"He's gone, Steffi, shot by these fools." The grip on his shirt twisted. "And if we don't escape, they'll kill us."

"We have to get him!"

"When this is over," he said, half dragging Steffi away. She resisted. "Steffi, do you want to have a life with me?"

"Yes."

"Then come along and be absolutely quiet, or I can guarantee it will never happen." He dragged her on. "Yanni and his friend aim to kill us. Please, for our love." And that worked. Without further complaint, they stumbled along, but all the while, Steffi experienced terrible vertigo with no idea whether she was going up, down, left or right. Finally, the string bent them to the right. Jim resisted the temptation to tug at the string which might alter its direction, so he played it through two circled fingers much like fishing line through a rod's guiding rings. Behind them specks of light flickered, perhaps from butane lighters. The acoustics of the cave made the angry screams behind them seem barely a meter or two back.

As they slogged on, the commotion behind grew more frenzied. Jim recognized the Greek verb "found."

Then, "Not that way, you idiot. Give it to me!"

They shuffled along farther downward. Jim thought, if they've found the lantern... For a moment Jim chanced turning on his headlamp on to better negotiate their way. Even with adrenalin rushing through his veins and overwhelming him with a single-minded goal of escape, the shock of seeing their friend, Harold

Robinson, horribly disfigured by a bullet, repeatedly flashed in front of him in bursts from gunfire.

From behind they heard, "There! Did you see it? Over there I tell you!"

Yanni panicked. His plan had crumbled. If he didn't stop them, he'd be in prison for sure. The old man was already dead, so that was a murder charge on top of everything else. The police would put two and two together and nail him for the mess he left behind in Athens. He'd never see the light of day.

Jim took a chance and switched his headlamp on and off for no more than a second. The image of the way ahead was made clear in his mind, so even with the lamp off, progress was steadier and faster. The two behind had not reacted, so the flash of light must have been hidden by a bend in the cave wall. In fact, the passage bore to the right. From the left, a fresh breeze of cool air brushed their cheeks. Jim reasoned it came from an intersecting passage. The air moaned as it rushed at them. Was it the Minotaur exhaling? He almost wished it were. Better to deal with the mythical half-man half-bull than the fools to their rear.

From behind him Steffi whispered urgently, "Jim, they'll trap us back here."

"We have no choice but to press forward through this labyrinth." Steadily they advanced, trusting in the guidance of a 3,000-year-old myth and Harold Robinson's encouragement.

Now they saw flashlight beams dancing off the walls, probing deeper into the cave and drawing closer by the second. Apparently, the two men had found flashlights left behind by Steffi and Jim. Fortunately, Jim and Steffi had advanced far enough and dropped down several levels, so for the present they were out of sight. Jim attempted a joke to ease the tension. "No doubt even Tweedledee and Tweedledum will figure out the meaning of the twine." They risked turning on their headlamps and picked up the pace. Two opportunities to turn left or right emerged from the darkness, but they kept on until finally the twine ended, secured firmly to a rock.

Three distinct directions confronted them. "Straight on, straight on, lad," Jim heard Harold Robinson say in his mind. Jim disconnected the twine and pitched it aside, hoping their pursuers might be confused at this junction. From behind he heard, "I see light." For a minute or more they were able to jog ahead gingerly. Once again they came to a turn with a choice of passages, but they kept on, straight and down.

From behind, "Go, go. Look, light!" Another shot rang out and more scaling rained down. The roof in this section of the passage was a mere two feet over their heads. Jim ripped the headlamp off Steffi's head and whipped it into a side passage, its light twirling into the darkness, hoping their pursuers would waste time or even become lost searching down that passage.

Yanni's voice rang out. "Faster, Stephanos!"

Another two blind shots rang out. Again, the rounds ricocheted. Jim remembered an old Marine colleague who had fought in the 1979 Mayaguez rescue. "Total chaos," he said as he related the story. Marines were being hit left and right while he tried to regain equilibrium to do his job. He told Jim he resisted a strange longing to simply lie down and curl up in the fetal position. Jim understood now. The same urge came over him, but he wasn't going to permit that any more than his colleague had. He damn well would save Steffi. He wrestled his emotions under control. What took over was primal—save the woman at all costs; try to kill these attackers. He grabbed Steffi's arm to urge her on.

Carefully, they threaded their way down a very narrow shaft, picking their way among loosely strewn rocks the size of bowling balls as well as other sharper pieces of scaling. The passageway seemed to slip a few degrees downward where they found it damper. At this depth in the cave, the walls and ceiling seemed less stable, with still more stones from scaling and fractures littering the passageway floor.

Footsteps chased them, scraping hollowly just behind. Jim assumed they heard their steps as well, but to move more stealthily meant slower. Panic sent their hearts thumping. Jim forced reason into his actions and stopped to search frantically for some means of defense. Other than his wits, nothing material besides a rock offered defense against their handguns. A piece of good fortune struck at that moment. Yanni and Stephanos were apparently fooled by the headlamp Jim had thrown down the side passage, and he heard their voices fading away. With this gift of extra seconds, he and Steffi pressed on, navigating by the narrow beam of his headlamp.

Perhaps ten meters down the false side passage the pursuers halted. Yanni urged, "I don't hear them anymore, but they could be hiding. You try farther down here and kill them if you find them. I'll go back the other way. We can't chance passing them by." Stephanos, desperately struggling to catch his breath, agreed. Yanni spun off back down the passage and Stephanos took a minute or so to recover, resting one arm on the stone wall. The whole stinking, blundering mess left him boiling in a psychotic rage.

Not more than a couple of minutes passed before Jim and Steffi once again heard what they agreed was a single pursuer. Despite their efforts, Jim judged the pursuer was closing the distance. At the same time, and not lost on either of them, was a sense that they were near the source of what had earlier sounded like sighing or an animal's sleeping respiration. Now the sound, louder and more distinct, seemed like a cornered predator. It was then they discovered the warm, moist breath of it vented from a pit off to the left of the passage.

When Jim peered into the pit, he wondered if was it the lair of the Minotaur. If so, it offered a slim chance at salvation. With no other alternative, and at least one pursuer determined to murder them over a nonsensical and nonexistent pot of gold, he decided to risk it all at this spot. On the opposite side of the passage from the pit was a curved indentation. Jim surmised it was caused by centuries, if not millennia, of water geysering and spinning from the pit, perhaps when a swollen underwater river pushed upward like an overwhelmed storm drain.

Without time to explain, he shoved Steffi into the indentation and signaled silence with his index finger. Next, he joined her, crouching within the indentation, hopeful that he was hidden from someone approaching down the narrow passage. Jim twisted the bezel ring on his headlamp, and a shroud of blackness enveloped them. He pressed the headlamp into Steffi's hand. In spite of the risk of taking on a man with a loaded weapon, the plan was simple. With a stroke of luck, he would uncoil with full force from the indentation and drive into the legs of his pursuer, sending him down the pit, accepting all the while the reasonable probability of his momentum carrying him over the edge too. The utter darkness was his one ally. The pit or shaft itself was all but invisible in the darkness until a light was trained on it.

Yanni moved cautiously ahead, sensing his quarry nearby. He probed both sides of the two-meter-wide passage with his flashlight but detected nothing. His finger was on the trigger. He wanted them both dead, but maybe, just maybe, after he killed the man, he'd fuck the bitch before he did her. Then he'd go back and find the rest of the gold. From ahead, he felt pulses of damp air. Ahead, his flashlight beam lost itself in a void, and Yanni guessed yet another passage turned to the left in what he declared out loud "a fucking maze." Could they be down this passage, he thought. For a moment he considered waiting for Stephanos. If he searched the passage without Stephanos guarding this spot, they might escape behind him.

Finally, he chanced a few tentative steps, kicking aside pieces of scaling. He shined his flashlight on the darkness to his left, which revealed not a passage but a dark, endless hole. As he bent down to examine it, damp air like a warm fetid breath blew against his face. At that very moment, as the fleeting thought crossed his mind that the hole surely led to perdition, his thighs just above his knees buckled from a strike of tremendous force. His flashlight cartwheeled in the dark as Yanni grabbed at air, and his body uncontrollably tumbled over the edge. The surprise was so total, the shock so consuming that he didn't even scream as his body, along with his white shirt and mahogany wingtips, careened like a pinball off the hard rock walls of the chasm, battering and breaking him on the way down until he finally slammed on top of a boulder that peeked from an underground stream.

When Yanni disappeared over the edge, Jim sensed, in the dizzying darkness, his own body's momentum delivering him into the Minotaur's lair as well. His right arm drove hard against the floor, scraping over rock and stripping flesh, but serving to break his momentum even as his head and then neck and shoulders slid over the abyss. While hanging partway over the shaft, he was treated to the sound of Yanni's body thumping along the rock walls in its final journey. He heard a scream from behind, saw a cone of light, and felt Steffi's hands pulling him back.

For a moment or two, he gathered himself on all fours as Steffi grabbed him around the waist and held tight. With another attacker out there, even a second's rest assumed a costly risk. Jim tapped Steffi's hands in a signal to let go as he stood up. Steffi collapsed back to the side of the passage, sitting with her back to the wall with the beam of her headlamp spotlighting Jim. The light was enough for Jim to spy Yanni's flashlight on the cave floor, and he picked it up. Just as he was about to lift Steffi by her hands, the bright blue light of Mr. Robinson's lantern emerged from around the bend of the passage with Stephanos holding it in one hand and an automatic in the other. Their eyes met, and Stephanos's finger reached for the trigger. As his finger squeezed, Steffi sprang forward with no other plan than to shield Jim. The shot exploded, and with it, Steffi spun against Jim.

The shot's report caused the already fragile roof to give way, showering rock and debris on top of them all. An enormous triangular stone a meter wide struck Stephanos squarely in the center of his skull. The rock gouged his head with a wound every bit as nasty as the one Stephanos had inflicted on Harold Robinson. A rock dropped painfully on Jim's foot and another scraped along his back and shoulder. Jim's body deflected at least some of the debris from striking Steffi.

Before he turned on his light, he knew Steffi had been hit by a bullet from Stephanos's 9mm. The momentum with which she spun back against him could have been caused by nothing else. She collapsed at his feet, uttering only a weak moan. Somehow his headlamp remained askew but around his head. He readjusted it and switched it on, but the light was insufficient to properly triage Steffi, who lay unconscious and pale, obviously in shock. Jim scrambled over the fallen rock to recover the more powerful lantern but found it smashed and useless.

A glimpse at Stephanos in the light of his headlamp released a shudder through Jim's spent body. Stephanos's eyes stared blankly but still possessed an evil, immortal glow. Jim kicked at the lifeless body to be certain of his death, but to Jim's horror, the body reacted to the stimulus, squirming, grabbing at Jim, and groaning. Seeing this lump of tissue brought the image of it remorselessly aiming automatics at Mr. Robinson, robbing life from a man whose energy, kindness, and intellect had earned Jim's respect and deepening friendship. For the first time in Jim's life, he experienced a freeing and selfless love, and now this woman, the object of this love, lay curled behind him, shot by this squirming maggot. The veneer of civility shattered and fell from him like scaling from the cave walls. Jim drooled and wailed as he hoisted the closest rock, and in a savage few seconds, beat Stephanos's skull to pulp.

Wiping his bloody and shaking hands on his hiking trousers and the spittle from his cheeks with his forearm, Jim wrestled panic as he rushed back to Steffi. He screamed in grief when the weak light of his headlamp fell on her gunshot wound. Even in that desperate, confused moment, the irony of the wound struck Jim. A bullet had cut along her right side above her hip. It was a near match for where Gerhard Rossbach, her grandfather, had been hit. In this case, the round fortunately came from the Makarov's weaker 9mm instead of the monster wallop of a .303 Enfield. He checked and found no exit wound. Steffi needed a modern hospital.

The 9mm bullet had taken its toll, and Steffi bled profusely. He removed his blue bandana, regretting he had no means of cleansing the wound, and squeezed the gash closed with the cloth and then pressed it firmly against the wound, hoping to stem the bleeding. Jim's hands and arms were scraped numb and burning from the struggle with Yanni and the roof collapse, so deadening his sense of touch that detecting her pulse was hopeless. As he returned the heel of his hand to the bandana, he lowered his ear to her nostrils and mouth and convinced himself he detected shallow respiration. With his soiled fingers, he pried open her eyelids to check her pupils, but the dusty atmosphere clouded his effort. Next, he removed his web belt and used it to wrap around her waist and tighten the pressure against the wound. He tapped her cheeks lightly. At first she was unresponsive, but then suddenly, she vomited. Grateful for the sign of life, Jim turned Steffi on her side and worked his fingers around her mouth to make sure her airway was clear.

With Steffi's bleeding slowed but not stopped, he left her side to determine whether the way was clear to journey back to the cave entrance, assuming he could find the way back. At minimum, he knew Mr. Robinson carried a first aid kit which might also contain a means for sewing Steffi's wound. Farther back, he cursed when he discovered that the collapse had been near total. Even in parts where there was a gap, it would be impossible to safely carry Steffi through it. Trying to clear the way, with his arm and back stiffening and foot numbed, could chew up precious hours. Steffi required immediate care. The only hope was to keep faith with Daedalus and pray his guidance had value beyond Bronze-Age campfire entertainment.

"Steffi," he whispered hoarsely when he returned to her, but she was limp and unresponsive. He began to think she had hit her head when she had spun into him and collapsed. Perhaps a rock had struck her too. He examined her head and discovered a large knot on the base of her skull. Thirsty, disoriented, tired, and in pain, Jim picked Steffi up as carefully as possible. Conscious that picking her up might worsen her head injury, yet also reasoning there was no alternative, he staggered, unsteady and limping, still deeper into the cave with Steffi in his arms. The sticky, blood-soaked bandana packed against her side frightened him, for he knew he did not have the situation under control. He stopped to cinch his belt tighter around the wound, hoping the added pressure would better stem the bleeding.

The darkness possessed its own gravitational force, bearing down and wrapping around him like a python. His headlamp only illuminated the power of the dark. Steffi's body hung limply without stirring or uttering a sound. Though he pushed back against the thought, the chance Steffi might die slashed at him.

As he staggered along, the whole experience played back in slow motion with his mind struggling to make sense of what made no sense. The whole event was absurd beyond any fantasy he had ever imagined. On Crete? On vacation? "Only the unpredictable is predictable in history," a professor had pontificated. Yanni, the disagreeable and irksome waiter, lecherous Yanni, that Yanni, he hatched this? Could he have been capable? The eyes of the other one came back as if they burned with fire ahead of Jim in the dark. "Well, I killed both the sons of bitches, Steffi."

How could they be together at a taverna one night and running for their lives the next day in a labyrinth of a cave that threatened more to entomb them than save them? And Mr. Robinson? Dead at the hands of these fools. Gold! What gold? A few sovereigns and counterfeit money? Absurd as it was, he knew it was reality and no nightmare. Everything that had been controllable in life was now uncontrollable. For the first time, he grasped the insanity civilians caught in the butchery and crossfire of war felt. Only one thing mattered now—delivering Steffi to safety.

Again, the labyrinth offered choices, but he dutifully obeyed and marched straight ahead and down. His thighs grew heavier. Adrenalin had fueled him, but that supply was depleted. The passages to his left moaned. One to his right seemed to inhale air from the left. The farther along the passage they stumbled, the damper the world became, like he was in the dark recesses of some giant lung. At one point, he looked up at the rock overhead and croaked desperately in hopes God would hear from this underworld. "Okay, that's it. I give up. I submit. I'm not fighting you anymore. I'm yours. Whether you're pulling strings or not pulling strings, I don't give a shit, just deliver this woman from here! Save her!" Only silence called back.

Cold drops of water splashed right between his eyes. He set Steffi down for a moment and wiped his face. He took the opportunity to check her bandage. Once again he attempted to check her pulse, but his sweaty hands and his own rapidly beating heart made this effort no more successful than before. He rotated his numb shoulder in hopes of bringing life back into it, but the effort brought on nothing but a pulsing ache. The flesh on his right forearm screamed with burning pain. At this juncture, he wasn't sure if it was night or day. Jim lifted Steffi, but his legs buckled, and his upper body balked, and as he wobbled forward, Jim nearly dropped her. At that moment he was a swimmer stroking against a powerful current with the shore looking farther away with each stroke.

The cave bifurcated again. He questioned the way, and wondered if they were lost forever. He did not understand, even for a moment, as he limped on, why he made the decisions to follow the twists and turns he had. The past and future were both fogged. He only knew in the present that he and the woman he carried were entwined, wrapped in uncertain consequences.

He fantasized the impossible hope of seeing more of Mr. Robinson's twine. He longed for guidance. He longed to feel God walking with him. "But I gave in to you! Please don't abandon her!" Twice more Jim dropped down through openings. Human reason told him all was hopeless. The labyrinth had swallowed them whole. Now water dripped steadily from overhanging mineral deposits. The air grew so humid and chilly that Jim saw his breath. How long had he been going—ten minutes, or ten hours? His chest heaved, and his throat burned from exertion, the way it had crossing the finish line of high school cross-country races. The chamber floor was uneven and slick from water. It turned ever so slightly to the left and continued downward, perhaps as much as five degrees.

It felt as though he had been fumbling in the cave through the length of Crete's recorded history—the Minoans, the Dorians, the Romans, the Byzantines, the Venetians, the Turks, the Germans—all of the occupiers who had inhabited this place seemed compressed in his aching thighs in the dark enveloping cave where only the next few steps were visible. In the damp chill and darkness, he swore he detected the putrefaction of it all. All the while, Steffi's lifeless body, the body of the first woman he could truthfully say he loved, and the person who had led him to a wisdom he had never known before, now seemed nothing more than a partner of this darkness. The past was fused with his present, and the future became nothing more than his present.

His headlamp beam grew paler as the battery weakened. He tried to form words of comfort, thinking Steffi might hear, but his dry mouth permitted no intelligible sound. But then the twists and turns of the cave, its walls and dripping ceiling, began to appear more as chambers in an elaborate palace. It was if they had come to Knossos in the time of King Minos. There were dolphins painted on the wall and depictions of the Minoan bull rituals. Just ahead there was even a painting of the Minotaur itself. Its human head transfigured into that of Yanni with his sly smile.

With that, somehow desperation gave way to calm, because all time came together then, not as something fearful but as an answer to their hopes when they first met at Athens airport. When linear time folds back on itself, it becomes infinity. Going forward and back are the same things.

Jim arrived on a spot where crystalline water purled from the stone wall. A spring buried in the mountain splashed into a pool and then apparently emptied somewhere beneath him. With his left hand shaking from exertion, he scooped the icy water and drank the reviving elixir. He wiped Steffi's forehead with the water, then he took the blood-soaked bandanna and rinsed it in the purifying liquid and once again applied it to the wound which appeared partially clotted. As he applied more water to Steffi's face and lips, he removed the stains of the struggle she carried on her countenance. He was struck how the water seemed no colder than her skin.

It was then he noticed a ribbon of light piercing the darkness ahead. At first he questioned whether it was a hallucination, but as he neared it, there was no doubt. A long line of intense light, like a door cracked open, was just ahead. For a moment he believed he had found the doorway from the labyrinth just as Daedalus had promised; yet when he, with Steffi in his arms, reached the light, he realized it was not a passage to the outside. The light came from above, beyond their reach, no doubt through a fissure, high above them. It poured through the opening with an intensity which seemed beyond any power to extinguish. The sun must have been directly over it. The light beams shone in the dusky air as if they were solid. Jim had no way to know that the fissure was a mere twenty feet above and to the side of the opening in the cave they had first entered. They had returned to the beginning.

Jim set Steffi down. Her face and part of her chest were illuminated in the warming light. He bent over her and touched her cheek and understood then that the coldness of her skin was not due to the cave's chilly air. His filthy hands embraced hers, and he felt the blue stone of her ring in his palm. Strangely, Jim felt no anger or grief. It was as if the shaft of light raised them above the fray. The physical pain either no longer existed or didn't matter. He had called out, and he had been answered. A time to rest had come, and he had Steffi with him. He lay next to her and wrapped his arms around her, content that all they had come to Crete to find had been delivered to them.

CHAPTER
TWENTY-FOUR

The tourist season was long past. There was but one guest at the hotel. The rooms Steffi and Jim had occupied were empty, looking as though no one had ever sat at the ancient table with its traces of blue paint. The plane tree was largely bare. To the eye, it was impossible to determine if it had grown in the last season. The cottage was bolted shut.

Maria Phindrikalis sat alone indoors. The heaviness she had lived with since Apostolos had banged on her door that afternoon had been partially lifted by good news. Elias had called. His ship had docked at Piraeus. He did not offer a reason for his months of silence, and Maria did not ask for an explanation. That he was back was enough. She had never needed him more.

The authorities had found Harold Robinson and Stephanos, but they had not found Yanni or Jim and Steffi. The energy for further searching waned as the colder weather crept in. For next spring the Robinson family sought permission to exhume the shallow graves outside the cave and gather DNA samples. They hoped Ian and

ıst be brought together in death. In spring the
ınue for the others as well. Cleaning out the cottage
ȷart for Maria. Some things, like the documents, were
ɔthers ended up in the trash. Maria saved a poem for
ıily that she found copied in Steffi's hand on the table in
ge. It rested now in front of her, next to one of her delicately
d porcelain demitasse cups.

I shall love
As long as there is breath in me
And care
I say I have been a strong lover
Hurt
Bitter
and know this
no matter
I shall love

Sappho

Outside, Crete's ancient hills off to the west were fringed in
orange as the sun settled lower in the sky. The ruins of Phaestos were
already in darkness. Were someone sitting on the bench along the
shallow stone wall that bordered the hotel's parking area, he or she
would have witnessed dark night drawing over the earth. Some high
cirrus clouds floated above, fringed in lavender and gold. The coming
evening turned the sea gray. No waves were visible either coming or
going. The stars were not out. Two ships rode the horizon. A green
starboard navigation light on one and a red port light on the other
were visible. They didn't seem to steam from their positions at all.

ACKNOWLEDGMENTS

I wish to thank Susan O'Leary and D.M. DiSantis for the many hours they spent assisting with the preparation of this novel.

Nemec grew up around Chicago. While Philip has poetry and fiction his entire life, he also served as a .e Corps infantry officer, owner of a small Wisconsin farm Wisconsin, and completed a 26-year overseas career with .e federal government. A father of two grown children, Philip resides with his wife, Harumi, in the Washington, D.C. area.